Praise for *Fool M*

"A hilariously sharp-tongued romance with an unforgettable, unapologetic heroine. *Fool Me Once* is a breath of fresh air!"

—RACHEL LYNN SOLOMON, bestselling author of *The Ex Talk*

"A love story for every truly hot mess… A romance with bite, wit, and heart."

—*Kirkus Reviews*, starred review

"A simmering slow burn bursting with banter, *Fool Me Once* has all the raunch, humor, and charm of a Judd Apatow movie but with the kind of flawed, dynamic heroine rom-com fans have been waiting for. This is a romance for anyone who's ever felt too messy to be loved."

—ROSIE DANAN, author of *The Roommate*

"I absolutely love a messy heroine; throw in political schemes and off-the-charts chemistry, and *Fool Me Once* delivers a wild, sexy ride from start to finish!"

—TRISH DOLLER, author of *Float Plan*

"Fresh, funny, and chaotically wonderful, *Fool Me Once* had me hooked from the very first page! Winstead weaves an undeniably sexy tale of will-they/won't-they that is sure to be a phenomenal addition to every rom-com lover's library."

—KATE BROMLEY, author of *Talk Bookish to Me*

"Sparks fly and laughs abound as Winstead rides the line between enemies-to-lovers and second-chance romance tropes. Readers will want to snap this up."

—*Publishers Weekly*

Also by Ashley Winstead

Fool Me Once

In My Dreams I Hold a Knife

For more information about Ashley Winstead, visit her website www.ashleywinstead.com.

Fool Me Once

ASHLEY WINSTEAD

GRAYDON HOUSE

GRAYDON HOUSE®

ISBN-13: 978-1-525-89974-4

Fool Me Once

Graydon House
22 Adelaide St. West, 41st Floor
Toronto, Ontario M5H 4E3, Canada
www.GraydonHouseBooks.com
www.BookClubbish.com

Printed in U.S.A.

For Melissa and Mallory, the ultimate heroines,
the reason I know what true love feels like.

Fool Me Once

1

A Minor Hiccup

Look, normally after a hookup, I am all about the graceful exit. Poll my friends, and four out of four will tell you that when it comes to guys, *graceful* is practically my defining characteristic—and if not that, definitely *exit*. What happened this morning I lay at the feet of the patriarchy. The moment I shut the hotel room door and tried to creep away, lest I wake the sleeping groomsman inside—thoughtful of me, yes, and nothing to do with the fact that I'd promised him my phone number when he woke—the frilly, *traitorous* sash on my yellow ball gown caught in the doorjamb and yanked me backward like a rubber band.

As I sailed butt-first toward the door I'd only just escaped from, I pictured my obituary: *Lee Stone died as she lived, embodying the height of glamour and respectability—not wicked hungover, thoroughly dicked and dressed head to toe as the fifth-best Disney princess, how dare you besmirch her memory.* Obviously, it would have to be written by a fellow PR professional, an expert in the art of spin.

The obituary image was quickly followed by the same thought that had haunted me over the course of the past eight months: Why, oh *why*, had I agreed to be a bridesmaid in a Disney-themed, Disney-located wedding? And for a college friend I was barely close to, no less. Did my shameless pursuit of open bars and men in tuxedos know no bounds?

Luckily, the layers of crinoline puffing up my ball gown finally proved valuable, muffling the sound of my body colliding with the door. I bent over, rubbed my stinging elbows and wrestled the sash away, cursing it for ruining my James Bond–worthy escape.

For the millionth time, I wondered what self-respecting woman actually got married at Disney World—and worse, forced her bridesmaids to dress up as Disney characters, knowing full well the odds were high we'd end up knocking boots with the groomsmen, themselves tragically outfitted as Cinderella's footmen. What special brand of saccharine-flavored sadism convinced a person *that* walk of shame was worth risking?

I mean, I knew the answers to those questions, obviously. Because here I was, staggering away from said footman's hotel room the morning after Daisy Taylor's wedding—excuse me, Daisy *David*'s wedding, since there was no way in hell that girl wasn't taking her husband's last name. Dangerously late for the airport, and seeing double thanks to the buckets of wedding champagne I'd consumed. Despite my fervent hope last night, it turned out there was no such thing as magical, hangover-free alcohol—even if you were drinking it overlooking a life-size Cinderella's castle. Duly and sadly noted.

I crept down the lush, brocade-curtained hallway of the royal-themed Disney resort—nothing but the best for the groomsmen—and scratched as quietly as I could on the next door down. Instantly, the door cracked open and a woman dressed as a giant white teapot squeezed through, wheezing. I yanked Mac clear a little too hard, suffering PTSD from my own escape, and we caught ourselves just before tipping backward, stiletto heels wobbling. Whoever said high heels were invented to make it harder for women to run away was clearly right on the money, and I was adding Disney costumes to the list.

"You okay?" I grunted.

Mac waved me off and shut the door whisper-quiet. "Don't want to wake…um, what's his face…" She gave me a guilty look for not remembering her groomsman's name. Mac, unlike me, cared about such things.

"Come on," I whispered back. "Our flight leaves in ninety minutes and we still have to sprint the entire length of the castle to our rooms, pack our shit and Uber to the airport."

"Crap," Mac said, scooping her giant teapot costume into her arms for better aerodynamics. "And we have to say goodbye to Daisy, too."

She took off, and I scurried after her, hiding my eye roll so Mac couldn't see. Screw Daisy. When she'd asked me to be a bridesmaid, I'd been shocked and instantly filled with guilt over the fact that I'd clearly meant more to her than she'd meant to me. I'd written her such a gushing email: Wow, Daisy, of course I accept! A thousand times, yes. Now, teetering across the hotel lobby while people turned to stare, I began to suspect I'd actually done something grievously wrong to Daisy in college, and she'd waited seven long years to exact her revenge.

A long con. I could almost admire it.

We burst out of the hotel's ornate double doors into the appallingly bright Florida sunshine and froze, cowed by the sight before us. There were people everywhere. Worse than people—*families*. Of course there were. Because we were smack-dab in the middle of the Magic Kingdom on a perfectly clear Sunday morning in September, and it had been so long since I'd been thoroughly and publicly humiliated. So where else would they be?

As Mac and I stood there, dozens of small heads swung in our direction. A high voice yelled, "Mommy! It's Beauty and the Beast!"

"Oh, Christ," I muttered, shielding my face. As if it was that, and not the yellow ball gown, giving me away.

"This way!" Mac pointed in the direction of Cinderella Castle, a vast expanse of white stone and blue spires. Once again, I cursed Daisy, whose dedication to fairy-tale romance meant she'd insisted on getting married right in front of the damn thing.

I didn't have time to list the reasons her obsession with fairy tales and true love was ridiculous, foolhardy and 100 percent going to lead to her eventual heartbreak. At the moment, the only thing I cared about was that Daisy's absurd old-fashionedness meant the groomsmen and bridesmaids had been booked in separate hotels, divided by the longest gauntlet of child-filled castle grounds I'd ever witnessed in my admittedly castle- and child-lite life.

"Mommy, I want to hug Mrs. Potts," came another child's voice, disconcertingly close.

"Of course, honey," someone answered pleasantly. "Let's go ask her very nicely."

Mac and I turned to find a mom tugging her tiny son toward us. The mom looked up, catching our eyes. I can only imagine the full picture of what she saw, since I'd been unable to examine myself in a mirror before sneaking out of the footman's room.

But Mac—oh, God, Mac's mascara had shifted downward to make little raccoon-rings around her eyes, her pink lipstick smeared from what I hoped was hours of high-quality making out. Her teapot costume, now that I really looked, was on ass-backward, Mrs. Potts's face grinning creepily from her back.

I searched my own body with mounting dread. No, no, my dress was on the right way, at least. But I could feel my hair hanging in messy strands out of my elaborate Belle-bun, and I was sure, from what I remembered doing with the footman last night, that my face looked at least as bad as Mac's.

"Oh, honey, actually, that's not—that's not the *real* Mrs. Potts," said the mother quickly. She shook her head at us and covered her son's eyes.

"We're so sorry. We were forced to wear these costumes. I begged not to." Mac wrung her hands with regret. Unfortunately, her confession reeked of some sort of Disney-themed S&M plot, and only made the mom twist her son around and hurry him away.

Mac deflated inside her bulky teapot. Now that innocent children were involved, she'd clearly reached her limit for personal debasement. Which, as someone who'd witnessed her dating life since college, was saying a lot.

Using precious seconds, I surveyed the scene. Even though the mom and her son had run away from us, their reaction didn't seem to be stopping the rest of the families from believing Mac and I were Disney World employees, here to entertain them as Mrs. Potts and Belle. They were crowding in on us from every direction, drawing closer like a tightening noose.

I may live according to my own moral code—what traditionalists might refer to as *morally gray* or perhaps *no code at all*—but even I had to draw the line at scarring this many children in one fell swoop. I made a decision: since there was no way around, we'd have to go through.

"Run!" I hissed, smacking Mac on the bottom to motivate her, as one would a horse or a high school quarterback. Then I sprinted for all I was worth.

We scythed through the crowd, stunning families—me in front, Mac in back, shouting, "Sorry, *so* sorry!" over her shoulder. Incredibly, some of the families started jogging after us, as if this was a game, and they had only to catch us to win a Disney-themed prize.

But I had our home plate in front of me, the hotel I could see just over the turrets of the castle. I narrowed my eyes and ran faster, glad my own dating life since college had prepared me for making quick escapes in compromising clothing.

"Mac, move faster! I can't have anyone recognize me walk-of-shaming."

"Oh, get *off* it," Mac huffed. "It's not like you're even remotely famous."

"It's the age of social media. That means anyone could take a picture of me, upload it to Twitter, and then everyone back home would see. My work is high-profile."

"Honestly, the ego on you. It's because she made you Belle, isn't it?"

Thankfully, we were drawing near. The wind against my face billowed my loose hair behind me like a victory flag. We were going to make it, just had to sprint around this giant fountain, with its gushing geyser of crystal-blue water.

My phone rang, triggering an instant Pavlovian response. I dug into my purse and pulled it out, checking the caller. *Wendy Kornbluth.* Oh, no. Wendy was the chief of staff at the company I worked for—correction, the company I *lived* for—and on the very short list of people I had to drop everything to talk to.

I halted so fast I swayed on my feet. Mac ran into me and bounced off, her teapot costume saving us both a lot of pain.

"Wendy?" I answered.

"What are you doing?" Mac cried, looking and sounding like an extra in *The Walking Dead. "They're going to get us!"*

"Lee?" Wendy sounded concerned. "Are you okay?"

I plugged my other ear and shot Mac a look. "Sorry, it's just a horror movie playing in the background." I took a deep breath and used my work voice—calm, collected and cool as ice. I was Lee Stone, director of communications for Lise Motors, the first female-led electric vehicle company in the world, and all-around boss. "What's up?"

Beside me, Mac watched the encroaching families with terror.

"Game-changing news," Wendy said. "You know how we've been waiting for the governor to fill his policy director spot?"

The governor in question was Grover Mane, the first moderate Republican governor Texas had elected in decades, and quite possibly—if all went according to my very ambitious plan—the first governor in the country to pass a bill embracing electric vehicles for government transportation statewide. We'd been in talks about the possibility for more than a year. It would be revolutionary if it happened—a climate game changer, an undeniable political victory, and a huge leap forward for Lise and our CEO, Dakota Young. Not to mention a giant boost for my career.

The governor had promised he'd get serious about marshaling the votes needed to pass the legislation once he'd filled his policy director position. We'd been waiting with bated breath for a long time as Governor Mane apparently searched for a human unicorn.

"Oh my God," I breathed, ignoring Mac tugging on my arm. "He got someone?"

"Not just someone—someone from *Silicon Valley*," Wendy said, voice dripping with satisfaction. "You know what that means."

"They'll want to go green." The odds were sky-high someone from Silicon Valley would agree electric vehicles were the future. Even the reddest Republicans in California registered lilac in Texas.

My heart raced even harder. It was happening. My dream.

"His name is Ben Laderman," Wendy continued. "He was

senior legal counsel and policy adviser at Google. Apparently, he helped the governor land a new Google center in Houston and that's how they got to know each other—"

But the rest of what Wendy said was drowned in the buzzing white noise that filled my ears. "Did you say…Ben… *Laderman*?"

It couldn't be. The world wasn't that small, or that cruel. There was no way.

"Yes, Laderman." Wendy's tone made it clear I'd interrupted her and she wasn't pleased about it. "Hometown Austin guy, actually, went to law school at UT."

Impossible. There was no way the Ben Laderman from my past, who'd kindly gotten the fuck out of Texas years ago, was not only back in Austin, but wedged between me and the thing I'd worked for my entire professional life.

Wendy stopped talking, trying to interpret my silence. "What, you know him or something? And are those children I hear in the background? I thought you said you were watching a horror movie."

Sure enough, even through the white noise, I could hear high-pitched voices squealing about princesses and singing teapots. Mac had dropped my arm and was backing away slowly.

"No, I don't know him," I lied, the words coming out before I had a chance to think them through. In fact, I couldn't think straight at all, with the kids and the costume and the dizzying amount of champagne still in my system. And, worst of all, with the conjured spirit of Ben Laderman circling overhead.

"I have to go," I said, feeling ill.

"Okay." Wendy was clearly confused. "He starts in the governor's office Thursday, so prepare yourself to fill him in and win him over. We meet with him nine a.m. sharp his first day."

"Yep," I said dazedly, ending the call.

When I looked up, Mac was staring at me. "Did I just hear you say the name Ben Laderman? As in *the* Ben Laderman?"

"I'm fucked." Why hadn't I noticed how unbearably hot the Florida sun was? Beads of sweat rolled down my back, dampening my ball gown.

"Use your explaining words," Mac said.

"You know that big plan Dakota and I have been working on for years to switch all the cop cars and buses and ambulances in Texas to electric vehicles?"

She blinked. "You mean your dream of dreams? Your professional Everest? What you've called your 'gift to the future' with a straight face?"

"Governor Manc finally hired the person who's supposed to help me make it a reality. Help me push the bill through the House and Senate, with all the political maneuvering."

Mac's eyes widened. *"Ben?"*

"Ben." I was in shock. That had to be what this strange faraway feeling was, like I was a little ghost, floating outside my body, looking down from a distance.

"The ex-boyfriend you drove out of the state?"

I glared. "You mean the one who tore out my heart and ran it over with a semitruck?"

"The one you tortured with every bad behavior you're capable of, which, by the way, we both know is a long and sordid list?"

This was the problem with having friends who really knew you. "I mean, yes, but—"

"The one you said, and I quote, 'I can't believe what I did to my grad school boyfriend Ben, I literally lit his life on fire, I really need to evaluate my drinking habits and my deep-seated need to destroy people's lives when they hurt me'?"

Yet another reason why it was inconvenient to have one of your best friends around when you received terrible news.

"Yes, okay, that one. The last person in the world I want standing between me and the biggest environmental victory in American history, and not to mention, between me and my promotion. Ben *hates* me."

I clutched my hair to ward off the memory of his face the last time I saw him, the way he'd looked at me, as if I was the Very Worst Person in the World. Which, to be fair, I might have deserved, after mistakenly assuming he was cheating on me and then cheating on him in revenge. In a truly flamboyant fashion. In front of everyone he knew.

Panic mounted. "Forget helping me pass the bill. He's going to tell everyone at work I'm a horrible person. Do you know how hard I've worked to keep my personal life and my work life separate? What if he tries to kill the bill or get me fired out of revenge?"

"Belle!" yelled an excited little girl with long, dark hair, flinging herself toward us on stout legs.

I froze in front of the fountain. "Oh my God, I *am* Belle. But instead of a book-filled mansion, I'm going to be trapped in the Texas State Capitol with something worse than the Beast. An ex-boyfriend. A very wronged, very crafty ex-boyfriend. I know for a *fact* he's read Machiavelli. I was there." I bent over to catch my breath and slow my heart, which was beating like a bass drum in an EDM song.

"There, there," Mac said, going full mother teapot, stroking my shoulder soothingly. "You're having a tiny baby panic attack. I'll call Claire and Annie. We'll figure it out, I promise. It's going to be okay. But first, I'm going to need you to take a deep breath and— Ah, crap."

Out of the corner of my eye, I saw the little girl with dark hair throw caution to the wind and careen toward us. She latched on to my legs. I looked up, desperate to find whom she belonged to—at the exact moment her father, grinning and giving me a thumbs-up, started snapping pictures.

Pop! Pop! The light from the professional-grade camera went off like fireworks, blinding me. I took a staggering step back, tripping the little girl, who lost her balance and tipped over, still clutching my ball gown, and I in turn clutched Mac.

I could hear Mac's *"Ohhhhhhh, nooooooo,"* in slow motion, as if it was coming from the end of a long tunnel. And then all three of us were falling, falling, falling, and it dawned on me where we would land the second before we toppled backward into the ice-cold fountain. For a moment, the world was all flailing limbs and water that smelled suspiciously like pennies.

I surged for air, sitting up in the fountain, and immediately grabbed for the little girl. To my surprise, she was already up, laughing and clapping like we'd orchestrated all of this for her amusement. I tugged her wet little body up to the fountain ledge and then, child secured, fell backward with a splash. Next to me, Mac floated on her back. Her teapot costume was acting like a flotation device, buoying her on little eddies of water.

"I think we're going to miss our flight," she rasped.

I simply stared. A grown-ass woman dressed like a sopping wet Disney princess, sitting in the middle of a fountain as a crowd of tourists gathered and the little girl's father continued snapping pictures. With my luck, we'd go viral.

But none of that mattered, because my life had hit rock bottom even before my ass had landed in this fountain.

The past I'd thought I closed was coming back to haunt me. Ben Laderman, my greatest mistake—the one person in the world who'd seen me at my worst, who'd seen the *real* me, whom I'd thought I'd really, truly loved—was coming back.

To ruin everything.

2

Wise Counsel

An artist would paint them as a tribunal of witches—four powerful women, coolly fingering the threads of my fate. Claire, Annie, Zoey and Mac were draped across the silken furniture on the back deck of my bungalow, their faces glowing in the candlelight, wineglasses held aloft.

The night was unseasonably cool for Austin in September. Despite the chill, I sat straight-backed, warmed by the force of their undivided attention.

Claire tipped back her wine, ruining the dramatic stillness that had fallen after I'd dropped the bomb about Ben. When she was done sipping, she arched an eyebrow. "Simple solution. Off him. I'll represent you at the trial."

Mac pulled her fleecy blanket higher over her shoulders. "Please. Criminal law is a world apart from corporate law. You're not the master of everything."

"And you learned that in *one* semester of law school?" Claire turned to her. "Astounding."

"Hey!" I snapped. "Constructive advice only." If I didn't stop a Mac-Claire repartee session, we could be here all night. Mac felt it was her holy duty to remind Claire that she was not an all-powerful, all-knowing being, despite the fact that Claire played one convincingly. Claire, for her part, liked to suggest Mac was a dilettante, simply because she'd attended one semester each of law school, business school and even cooking school, before landing her job in finance. Or banking. Or...something to do with money.

Honestly, none of us knew exactly what Mac did. It was a mystery that Claire, Annie and I were still trying to unravel. Sometimes we asked her pointed questions, hoping to get clues without tipping her off, but so far, her answers had been more confusing than illuminating.

But tonight, there was no time for an episode of *What Does Mac Do?* There were more important matters at hand. Exhibit A: my impending doom.

I sank lower in my chair and looked up at the night sky, where the stars shone weakly against the light pollution from the city. "I need *explicit* instructions for tomorrow. What do I wear? What do I say? Do I open with a joke? 'Hello, Ben, fancy seeing you back in the city where I ruined your life. Now that you have a shot at ruining mine, I'd love to hear you expound upon that New Age radical forgiveness I hear California's famous for.'"

"First," Claire said, "tell us again about how you ran for your lives from a horde of children at Disney World. I want to picture it in detail. It's going to be my new happy place."

"I'm guessing from all the context clues that Ben Laderman isn't a person we like?" Zoey looked expectantly between Annie and me. She and Annie had been dating for over a year now, but in that time, I had absolutely *not* been moved to share the Ben Laderman story.

Annie leaned into Zoey; they were curled together on my big outdoor armchair. "Actually, it's the opposite." Even teasing, Annie's voice was soft and warm, which was her way. "Stoner liked Ben very, very much." She looked at me. "I can still remember when you came home gushing about him after that first night."

"We *all* heard about it," Claire said, her face lit with that special brand of glee she experienced only when recounting my embarrassments. "She hadn't been that crazy about a guy since Danny Erickson in high school."

I opened my mouth to hiss at Claire for even mentioning Danny, but Mac cut me off. "And you know full well Stoner is *not* a romantic. She's like the farthest thing from girlfriend material on the planet. Doesn't fall in love. Guys are good for one thing and one thing only, wham-bam-thank-you-ma'am. Love-'em-and-leave-'em-Lee, we call her—"

"All right," I said, throwing a pillow at Mac. Satisfyingly, it clipped her in the forehead. "Zoey gets it. And it's not like she doesn't know me by now."

I raised another pillow and eyed Claire threateningly, just in case she was thinking about bringing up Danny Erickson again. He was a relic from long ago, back when I was a different person. A girl who still thought love and romance were possible. I didn't like to be reminded of it.

"Watch the wine!" Mac clutched her glass protectively.

"Okay, so this Ben guy was able to get under Stoner's skin." Zoey looked impressed. "Then what happened?"

"Then Stoner was Stoner," Claire said. "You know why we call her that, right?"

I groaned. This story did my reputation no favors.

Zoey blinked. "Because her name's Lee Stone and it's funny?"

"Oh, *that's* just a coincidence. No, in college, back when Stoner actually dated people for a hot minute, she had this boyfriend who was obsessed with her. Like, we all thought he was going to propose senior year."

I rolled my eyes. "Nate wouldn't have *proposed*."

"He totally would have," Mac said. "His parents came to visit one weekend and he organized this fancy dinner to introduce them. Well, Stoner forgot all about it and threw a huge party. Then she proceeded to get high as a kite. In her defense, someone brought great weed."

It was true—I did get high as a kite. But I didn't forget about dinner.

"We had this kick-ass house with a pool senior year," Claire said. "It was perfect for parties." Her eyes turned dreamy. "I miss that pool."

"You have a pool at your house," Annie reminded her.

"A *kid* pool." Claire sighed. "Not a party pool."

"Anyway." Mac set down her wine and sat up straighter. "Nate comes to the house to pick her up with his parents in tow. And they find her on the roof."

Zoey's wide eyes swung to me.

"It was a thing we did." I shrugged. "We liked to smoke pot on the roof."

It was a strange compulsion: the desire to be surrounded by people and, at the same time, completely alone. The roof was nice for having it both ways.

"And then guess what Stoner does?" Mac shook her head. "Nate and his parents are standing there in the middle of this crazy party, Nate's pissed, his parents look terrified, and Stoner yells down that she'll be right there. And then *she jumps off the roof into the pool*."

Zoey gasped, her eyes searching my body, as if I still bore hints of some long-ago, pool-related injury.

"Just like in *Almost Famous*," Claire said. "Like that idiot rock star on acid."

"I thought they'd appreciate I was taking the shortest route to dinner," I said, which was both silly and a lie.

"So she climbs out of the pool soaking wet and walks right up to them and says, 'Can we get tacos? I'm really craving tacos.'"

Claire leaned back in her lounge chair, lifting her glass. "Henceforth, and forevermore, she was Stoner."

I shook my head at the memory. "Nate didn't even break up with me after that. I still had to do it at graduation."

I'd tried everything that year to see what it would take to get him to break up with me. I think I'd stopped being into Nate the minute I realized nothing would do it.

Zoey was shaking her head, looking at me like she was seeing me anew. I didn't understand: at twenty-six, Zoey was three years younger than the rest of us. She should be the one who appreciated my antics the most.

"I swear," Annie sighed, "the lengths you'll go just to avoid intimacy."

"Thanks, Dr. Park, but I was only having fun." Annie was a therapist. Since I refused to book an appointment with any of her colleagues, she was constantly trying to counsel me on the sly. She'd been doing it for years, ever since we'd met in grad school, when she was a first-year PhD student and I was in the first year of my master's.

"So what, you got stoned and did something bad to Ben?" Zoey asked. "Is that what caused the breakup?"

My stomach clenched. Nate, I had no regrets about. Ben was a different story.

"No, she just fucked things up in general." Mac got up and poured herself more wine.

"Yep, classic Stoner," Claire agreed. "Honestly, what haven't you pulled?"

Well, *this* required alcohol. I gestured and Mac padded over, refilling my wineglass.

"If you want the whole story," I said, swirling the glass, "then yes, I liked Ben."

More than liked. I could feel the ghost of the feeling tugging at me, even now.

"I met him my first year of grad school. He was in law school. Generally, I avoided law school students because they were preppy douches—no offense, Claire. But one night I found myself in a bar, in need of a whiskey but down to my last five dollars. Remember, I was a grad student. These were desperate times."

"Zero money," Annie confirmed. "We were broke as hell."

"In walks a gaggle of law school guys. And I think to myself, hey, why not let these country-club popped collars buy me a drink before they go off to play beer pong? Everything was fine until, out of nowhere, Ben showed up. And he was different."

Mac held up her phone to Zoey. "Different as in *hot*. See?"

I caught a glimpse of her screen. Sure enough, there was Ben's face, wearing that half smile he gave cameras, like he didn't quite trust them. At a glance, he looked a little older than I remembered. "Hold up. Mac, are you still *friends* with Ben on Facebook?"

Mac shrugged. "Was I supposed to unfriend him just because you broke up?"

"*Yes!* That's exactly what you were supposed to do."

Zoey studied Mac's screen. "You weren't lying about the hotness."

I tried my best to avoid looking at Mac's phone, even though I wanted to desperately. "What I *meant* was that he was smart. And sarcastic. Cutting. He could tear people to ribbons. It was amazing to watch."

Zoey looked concerned. "That's what you like in a person?"

"He used his powers for good."

Until he didn't.

"He was funny. He didn't grow up with anything, so he wasn't coddled like the rest of them. He was unexpected. Once you earned his trust, he was kind."

Until he wasn't.

"Long story short, he intrigued me, I was drunk, we connected, blah blah blah. I was dumb and dated him. For a while, things were good..."

The memory flashed back: one night during those first months when we couldn't stand to be apart; the first night it snowed, a rare freezing Austin winter. His body draped over me in bed, hands cradling my face. The way he'd pulled back from kissing me, eyes suddenly serious. And I'd known in that moment what he was going to say, could read it plain in his eyes before his mouth formed the words...

For a while, things had been more than good.

"Then what?" Zoey prompted. I'd paused for too long. Annie was giving me one of her knowing looks.

I cleared my throat. "Then all the normal things that happen in relationships started happening. We argued, I didn't trust him, he wanted more of my time than I was willing to give—"

"She started snooping through his phone," Claire snorted.

"I won't apologize for gathering evidence," I said hotly. "People keep secrets in relationships, and I've learned I'd rather know what those are up front instead of waiting for them to hit me out of nowhere like a ton of bricks."

I left out mentioning that in this particular case, the overly friendly texts from a classmate I'd found on Ben's phone—the ones that had inspired me to cheat on him in revenge—hadn't amounted to anything more scandalous than a study partnership. Oops.

Annie shook her head at me. I could practically see her diagnosing my trust issues. But so what. By the time my stupid heart had made the mistake of falling in love with Ben, I'd come by those issues earned and honest.

"Stoner thought Ben was cheating," Mac said. "Or, like, *thinking* about cheating. So she went out and cheated on *him* with his law school rival right before his final exam." Mac said this with a little too much relish. Apparently, dissecting my love life was a welcome change from her own.

Connor Holliday. I could still picture the moment I'd walked into that bar—the law students' regular haunt—and locked eyes with him from across the room. Kept his gaze as I downed a shot of tequila. He'd smirked, and there'd been a dash of triumph in his expression that had nothing to do with me. We'd both known what would happen next.

Because that's just who I am.

"Ouch." Zoey grimaced. "His rival? Harsh." She knocked Annie's knee. "Never ever."

Lee Stone: A Cautionary Tale.

"You know those days when you wake up knowing you're going to get into some trouble, and nothing will satisfy you until you've gone and done the worst possible thing you can think of?"

A deck full of blank stares.

I sighed. "I was just doing it to him before he could do it to me. Everyone cheats eventually. It's practically a scientific law."

I remembered being sick with the certainty of it, sick with the lack of control: knowing one day, and probably soon, Ben would find another girl he liked as much as me—maybe a girl he liked more. And that would be that. Those texts from his classmate seemed to prove it.

Even though I'd accepted the inevitability, it still hurt. And that was the problem with Ben. Even though I knew it would end the same as the others, it was painful to think about. Knowing was supposed to *shield* you from pain, but it didn't with Ben. Maybe because of the small, rebellious voice inside me that kept whispering, *With him, it could be different.*

Tiny baby idiot Lee.

Annie kissed the side of Zoey's head and smiled. "Not us."

"Oh, it's coming for you." I gave the two of them, sitting cozy under one blanket, a pitying look. So adorable and in love; so naive and trusting. "Just give it time."

"If Simon cheated on me, I'd divorce him, take half his money, move back into the city and force him to take full custody of the kids." Claire flopped back in her chair. "He knows a part of me would enjoy it. It keeps him in line."

Claire and I had been best friends since high school. When we went to the University of Texas for undergrad together, we added Mac. Since we were eighteen, the farthest away Claire, Mac and I had ever lived was when Mac and I stayed at UT—me for my MA in environmental policy and Mac for her MBA—and Claire moved to Virginia for law school at UVA. When Claire finally moved back, with a husband and kid in tow—Simon and Mikey, now an apple-cheeked four-year-old—they'd gone straight to the burbs, a place teenage Claire had sworn she'd never live. She was still adjusting.

"Hate to break it to you, but betrayal is inevitable, even for the Claires and Simons of the world." I settled into my chair and looked around the deck. We'd gathered here at least once a week, ever since I'd bought the house two years ago. I was very proud of it. My bungalow was *our* place, the epicenter of our friendship. A girlie nest filled with overstuffed pillows and candles and wine. Where the four of us watched movies, ate dinner, got ready for nights out, and escaped children (Claire), terrible first dates (Mac) and needy clients (Annie).

It, and they, were my constant. The center of my world. They were the only people I knew for certain wouldn't let me down.

"You can choose to deny it and live in ignorance," I continued, "or you can scare someone into not cheating, but that only works for a little while. *Or* you can do what I do, and avoid being in relationships in the first place. I learned that lesson from Ben, as a matter of fact."

Ben Laderman: the guy who helped me realize, once and for all, that it was easier, and cleaner, to keep things casual. He was the reason I hadn't had a boyfriend in five years.

"Ben was so distraught about Stoner cheating on him that he flunked his final exam," Claire said. "His first-place class rank went to his rival, and he lost his clerkship. It was kind of a scandal among the other law students." I stared at her. How did she *remember* these details? Especially since I'd confessed this to her five years ago, over the phone, while she was still living in Virginia. "He thought the clerkship would get his foot in the door for a career in politics. After he lost it, and everyone started whispering about him, he actually hightailed it out of the state."

Okay, *that* I felt bad about. "Yeah, well, eventually he landed at Google, so he ended up fine."

Zoey brightened. "And now he gets his chance at politics again in the governor's office! That's really nice. I'm kinda rooting for him."

I glared at her. "And, in the ultimate twist of fate, he now has the power to kill *my* political dreams."

In the candlelight, I could see Mac shake her head. "This is why you should get your tarot cards read with me. Then you could see this kind of karmic retribution coming."

"There's no way he'd hold a grudge after five years, right?" Zoey bit her lip, which was stained purple with wine. "That seems like a long time to hate someone."

Sweet, sheltered Zoey. I wondered if her ability to believe the best in people was a younger-millennial thing. I met Annie's eyes and she gave me a small smile.

Claire kicked her feet up, crossing her heels. "Hell, *I'd* hold a grudge. I'd be chomping at the bit for a shot at revenge."

I settled back in my chair and groaned. "Me, too. So, what do I do?"

"I would approach with caution." Annie was using her therapist voice. Ultrareasonable. Reasonable on steroids. "Figure out where he's at emotionally before you do anything rash. Zoey's right—there's a big chance that after five years, he doesn't resent you enough to go out of his way to hurt you. You're probably not his favorite person, I'll give you that, but it takes a lot of energy and passion to hate someone for five years. That sort of emotion tends to peter out over time."

I tried to picture walking into the meeting at the governor's office, all smiles and olive branches, but it was like toeing over the line into no-man's-land—my mind immediately threw up Turn Back Now signs. "Are you saying I should just…act normal?"

"If I were you, I'd get him alone first thing and tell him if he does anything to ruin your career, you'll have his balls in a vise." Claire nodded satisfactorily, as if she'd just given me the ultimate gift of wisdom.

"I don't know," Mac said. "I like Annie's idea. Play it safe."

If *Mac*, who'd recently gone on a blind date with a children's party clown, was telling me to play it safe, I should probably listen.

"Okay. I'll use tomorrow to test the waters." I'd wrestled with it in the days since Disney World: Ben had to have guessed I still lived in Austin, since I'd once told him I could never see myself living anywhere else, except maybe—just maybe—Washington, DC. *If* my career went the way I used to dream it would.

So, what else could he know? Was he aware of the Green Machine bill—Governor Mane's silly nickname for our electric vehicle legislation—and if so, did he know it involved Lise, the company where I worked?

What if he didn't know any of it, and tomorrow he keeled over at the sight of me? What if I gave him a heart attack and ruined his life not once, but twice? But if he *did* know about me, then the Lee-Stone-of-it-all hadn't stopped him from taking the job, which must mean he no longer harbored resentment, right? Or was it like Claire said, and he was doing all of this to exact some long-overdue revenge?

"Or, *or...*" Zoey's voice was hushed, almost awestruck. "What if, despite everything, Ben's been in love with Stoner all this time, and he's here to win her back?"

There was a moment of contemplative silence in which distant crickets chirped and Zoey blinked hopefully at us. Then, all at once, like a dam bursting, Claire, Mac, Annie and I broke into sidesplitting laughter.

"Oh, *God.*" Claire wiped tears from her eyes. "Thank you, Zoey. I really needed that."

When the house was empty and quiet, I flicked on my living room lamp, pulled the cork out of a new bottle of wine and flopped backward onto my couch. Immediately, Bill McKibben and Al Gore, my two gray cats, leaped onto the cushion and curled into my side, their small bodies warm and soft. I scratched Bill's ears, then Al's, and lifted the bottle straight to my mouth. It was too late for cups, and besides, there was no one here to impress. Bill and Al already knew I was feral.

I closed my eyes. Tonight, we'd basically taken a tour through the haunted house that was my love life.

Where did it all go wrong?

If I had to choose, the thing that really screwed me up was my parents, and how happy they were. Growing up, I never heard them fight, not once. Instead, they were always so romantic—touching hands when they passed in the hall, smiling at each other across the kitchen table, snuggling on the couch while we watched TV. They signed all of their notes and letters to each other with a phrase that, over time, became burned into my heart:

Forever and a day, Richard.

Forever and a day, Elise.

I grew up believing that was possible. An enduring love, never-ending, bigger than life itself. In my bones, I wanted a love like that for my own.

Tiny, baby, idiot Lee.

Luckily, my father showed me the truth beneath the veneer, in the first of what I now call Lee's Four Major Heartbreaks. The four heart-cracking, life-altering experiences that shaped me into the worldly, glamorous, not-at-all-bitter Miss Havisham I am today.

The First Major Heartbreak started innocently enough. I was sixteen, in my father's office, using his old dinosaur desktop to write an essay on *The Scarlet Letter* for class. (I know, I know—it took a few years, but even I eventually appreciated the irony.) My mother was at my dad's bookshelf, sorting through old books to find giveaways for the library. My father was out at a work dinner.

And I accidentally opened his email. I've often thought about the different turn my life would've taken if only I hadn't pulled up the internet browser to sneak a peek at SparkNotes—yes, I know there's a lesson in there—causing his Gmail account to spring, unbidden, to the screen. Normally, I wouldn't have looked. Dad email accounts were presumably 90 percent TurboTax reminders and 10 percent golf coupons. Except the subject line on the first email caught my eye: I miss you—come back.

It turned out to be a love letter from a woman named Michelle. And it was the first of many, I discovered, as I scrolled and scrolled. All of them were signed with a familiar sendoff: Forever and a day, Richard. Forever and a day, Michelle.

I do regret gasping. After that, I couldn't stop my mother from reading over my shoulder. Not that I was in any shape to hold her back, because the minute I read enough, I froze. Not just in body, but in time.

Or at least I tried to. In that instant, sitting at his desk, I rejected the idea that time would progress, that the world would keep turning. That I would continue to tick along according to the current script, in which the hero had just been revealed to be a villain. Everything inside me refused it. My body turned still as a statue.

Unfortunately, as I have learned over and over, there's too much in life you can't control. I could not stop time, or stop my mom from crumpling to the floor behind me. I could not hold off the moment of confrontation when my dad came home, or the days and weeks of screaming between them. Worse: the cold, bitter silence that followed. By the end of fall semester junior year, my parents had reached out to a lawyer. On my last day of school that spring, they signed divorce papers.

Dad moved in with Michelle from the emails. My mother, in contrast, was more alone than I'd ever realized a person could be. My sister, Alexis, was only twelve. So she was sad, of course, but not sad like me. Not too depressed to skip summer camp with all her friends.

The day my father officially moved out of our house, my parents forced me to help him. He insisted he would always be my dad, and he wanted to spend time with me. When everything was in the U-Haul, and there was nothing left to do, he'd turned to me and said, *I still love your mother, Lee. Sometimes these things happen, and there's nothing you can do.* And I'd thought, *Oh. Right.* My dad loved my mom, but he was still leaving her. Which meant love was not enough. It was a wake-up call.

My dad and I had always been close. He'd always existed on a different plane from other people. But at that moment, he fell like a shooting star, straight to Earth. Hearing him say those words, I realized I had nothing left to say. I didn't want to give him any more of my heart—any more ways to hurt me.

So from that day on, I didn't speak to him. Didn't say another word. He married Michelle, moved from Austin to San Antonio, hosted Christmases with her kids. I didn't answer his calls or texts, didn't come for holidays, threw away the care packages he sent. I cut my dad out of my life.

He was the first cheater to break my heart, but not the last. Apparently, it took getting punched in the chest a few more times to truly learn my lesson. Less than a year later, in my Second Major Heartbreak, Danny Erickson—my first serious boyfriend, the boy I lost my virginity to—not only cheated on me, but publicly humiliated me in the process.

And then there was Andy Elliot, college boyfriend and Third Major Heartbreak, who'd announced his infidelity via an STD that left me peeing fire. Last, there was grad school Ben, the Fourth and Final Major Heartbreak. The ironic thing about Ben was that *I* turned out to be the cheater. I guess you could say I was guilty of breaking my own heart in the end.

When Ben fled the state five years ago, I'd come to grips once and for all with the idea that there was no such thing as true love or happily-ever-after. Since then, I'd decided to treat love accordingly, with the lack of gravity it deserved.

I sighed and looked up at my living room ceiling, tipping

the wine to my mouth. On the couch next to me, Bill and Al were purring. If only I'd stopped dating people after Danny Erickson and never made it to Ben. If only I'd known then what I knew now, and had left that bar in grad school the minute Ben walked in, skipping the year and a half of soaring joy and sinking pain that was so much better and then so much worse than anything I'd felt with other boys.

Or, at the very least, if only I'd just *stuck to the rules*: kept things light and distant, staying in control, leaving before it got serious. With Ben, I'd lost my head, and now I was paying the price, even five years later.

I clanked the wine bottle on my coffee table and stood. My two cats stared up at me, blinking sleepily.

Or maybe I was thinking about this all wrong. Tomorrow, my story with Ben would resume, like someone had cracked our chapter back open and erased *The End* from the last page. Now they waited, pen in hand, to write a new ending.

This was a chance to right my wrong. I could play it friendly, professional, distant—in other words, in control. I could have a new ending, the one I wanted, where it was clear to all involved that I was cool and indifferent to Ben. No more reckless emotions, like the first time. No more cringeworthy bad behavior. I would stick to the rules, do a little fence-mending and then we'd go our separate ways. Not only would that approach mend wounds, but it would ensure Ben didn't feel tempted to harm the Green Machine bill out of a sense of revenge.

That was the answer. I'd pass my bill, make history *and* fix the glaring black mark on my conscience. Untie the knot of guilt and shame that had, if I was being honest, twisted up my heart for five long years.

No time to waste. I hurried off to bed.

3

Grace Under Fire

The Texas State Capitol has always reminded me of Daedalus's labyrinth, large and elaborate and winding. It could be because I was studying Greek myths the first time I toured it at the tender age of eight, and was also plagued by a truly unfortunate sense of direction. But in my defense, the capitol is made of red granite, an oddly exotic color for a government building—something you might be more likely to find on, say, the isle of Crete.

As I grew up, both a feminist and an environmentalist in the staunchly red state of Texas, the idea that the capitol building housed a flesh-eating man with a bull's head struck me less and less as fictional, and more and more as an apt metaphor.

But today, there was no doubt Ben Laderman—at this very moment, holed up somewhere inside—was my Minotaur. And for all my wine-induced bravado last night, my hands trembled as we walked up the steps to the capitol.

The truth was, I'd imagined running into Ben a hundred times since we broke up, picturing exactly how I'd react. There was this one time I'd been sitting with my mom and Alexis in an airport parking shuttle, when a man Ben's height and coloring lugged his suitcase up the steps. For one dizzying second, thinking it was him, my heart had tried to beat its way out of my chest. Even though the man quickly revealed himself to be a Ben imposter, the buzzing adrenaline hadn't washed out of my veins until hours later, near the end of our flight.

How surreal that I was minutes away from actually facing him.

"The idea for today is to introduce Ben to the bill, since he probably hasn't had time to review it yet, and secure his buy-in." Wendy was walking beside me—actually, she was strutting beside me like the steps were a runway. Dakota's chief of staff was long and lean; everywhere she walked, the world seemed to fold itself into a catwalk just for her. She wore an all-black suit, as sharp and quintessentially no-nonsense as she was.

"Remember, the most important thing we can walk away with is Ben's enthusiasm." She cut a glance at me. "I need charm from you. Is that feasible?"

"Psshh." I gave her an affronted look.

If only Wendy knew the truth about what we were walking into. But there was no way in hell I was going to tell her the project we'd been working on for years, the one with the potential to catapult the company to stardom, could go up in flames thanks to my messy dating life. Somehow, I'd managed to convince everyone at work that I was a talented communications professional, concealing any hint of the Lee Stone that existed outside the hours of nine to five. If Wendy—uptight stickler Wendy—knew what I was really like, I'd be fired before I could count to three.

Within the monochromatic white walls of Lise, I was Lee,

or Ms. Stone to junior employees: a take-no-prisoners messaging maven. Outside of Lise, I was Stoner. And never the twain should meet.

"Lee's a pro," said Dakota, winking from my other side. "She already won over the governor. Besides, this is a good bill. The only reason they wouldn't go for it is *politics*." Dakota said the last word with scorn, and I knew why: she'd been fighting politics her whole life.

Dakota Young was my hero. She was only ten years older than me, but she'd built Lise from the ground up, thanks to her genius inventor's brain and business savvy. When I first started as Lise's comms director, the newspapers had called Dakota "the female Elon Musk"—when they mentioned her at all. My first self-assigned task was to inform them that Dakota had designed and produced *her* electric vehicle five years before Tesla was a twinkle in Elon's eye, and the only reason the journalists didn't know was because our patriarchal society dismissed female inventors. *Especially* Mexican American female inventors.

The truth was, Dakota had beat Elon to it *and* designed a car battery pack with twice the capacity of Tesla's, meaning our vehicles could go as far as a gas car before needing to recharge. And they took less time to do that, too. There was no reason our cars shouldn't be the clear winner in the e-vehicle market, but we consistently underperformed. My hypothesis was that it came down to our small profile.

The disparity in attention between Dakota and Elon had inspired one of my best ideas: changing the name of the company from Unified Electric Vehicles—the yawn-worthy UEV for short—to Lise, pronounced "leez," in honor of Lise Meitner, a nuclear physicist who'd helped discover nuclear fission, only to be excluded from winning the Nobel Prize for it. The award had gone solely to Otto Hahn, her partner. Her *male* partner, if I even need to say it.

I'd gambled on my instincts, telling Dakota we shouldn't shy away from being known as a female-led tech and auto company, but rather call it out as a strength. She'd gambled on *me* and agreed; the rest was history. The name change had exploded like a bomb in the press. Dakota was featured in *Science* and the *New York Times*, and on *Good Morning America*—even on Fox News, though that might have been because she's not only a badass female inventor, but with her long, dark hair and hazel eyes, a gift of her Mexican heritage, she's a beautiful, badass female inventor.

Since our rebranding, the whole country had been taken with her, as well they should be. Dakota was the smartest person I'd ever met, managing to toe the line of being a total boss while exuding kindness. She was, to put it mildly, my idol. And also, the older sister I'd never had. My feelings for her were totally healthy.

I had a good track record at Lise, but passing this bill would seal the deal, establishing that I was a leader. If I was successful, I could ask for a promotion to the position I *really* wanted: vice president of public affairs.

Ever since reading *Silent Spring* at the age of ten, I'd grown up obsessed with the fact that we were poisoning our planet, and I'd dreamed of going into politics to do something about it. Being Lise's comms director was a good position at a great company—nothing a millennial could turn her nose up at—but being in charge of our policy work was what I was really interested in, the goal that got me out of bed each morning.

And now I was *so* close.

Assuming, of course, I didn't dissolve into a fine mist the minute I set eyes on Ben.

I turned left toward the meeting room we always used when

we came to talk to the governor. It was the biggest room, filled with highly questionable artifacts from Texas history. These artifacts were supposed to paint a picture of Texans as bold, valiant cowboys—framed letters from Mexican presidents pleading to end wars and old-timey weapons in glass cases from the years Texas was "settled" (translation: stolen from indigenous peoples). It was a room that showcased the state's history without any sense of self-awareness, and being there always put me on edge. Made me question whether we should be working with these people at all, even on something as potentially transformative as the Green Machine bill.

But Wendy shook her head, tugging my arm. "No Alamo room today. We're down the hall." She pointed to the right and I followed her, wondering at the change.

The three of us halted outside a closed door. Dakota smiled. "Remember, this is bigger than us. We've got the health and well-being of the planet on our shoulders. Let's do this for the people."

"No pressure," I muttered, as Wendy swung open the door.

And there he was, the very first thing I saw. Ben Laderman. Sitting at the right hand of the governor at the conference table.

Time seemed to freeze as the impact of seeing him in the flesh hit me like a punch to the chest. All the years we'd spent apart were obvious, because he looked different. He wasn't the Ben from my memories.

But he was still the easiest person in the world to describe, at least in terms of the basics: Ben Laderman looked exactly like Clark Kent from old comic books. Not Superman, with his perfect, blue-black hair, little forehead curl and confident, square jawline—Clark.

Don't get me wrong, Ben had the dark hair and strong jaw and ice-blue eyes, but when I'd known him, he'd kept his hair super short and worn thick-framed black glasses that mostly obscured his eyes. He was well over six feet, but he'd always hunched, like Clark slinking in late to the *Daily Planet*, trying to creep about unnoticed.

The Ben Laderman sitting at the table now was… Well, there was no way to describe it other than *California Ben*. He'd grown out his hair and wore it tucked and curling behind his ears. He'd exchanged the thick-framed black glasses for a pair of thin, transparent frames that left no question his eyes were vivid blue.

And the suit he was sitting ramrod straight in—no more hunch—wasn't a dark, boxy number like what he'd worn in law school for mock trial. This suit was the same blue as his eyes, a fashion risk that was both startlingly handsome and startlingly playful for someone starting work in the Texas governor's office.

He was *different*. Still knee-wobblingly beautiful, but different.

And he was staring at me.

I could only blink wordlessly. Luckily, Governor Mane stood up to greet us, offering a distraction. I stole a glance back at Ben, trying to read his reaction, but his eyes had already moved off me; he was smiling at Dakota and Wendy, reaching out his hand to introduce himself.

Seeing me walk through the door hadn't given him the slightest pause.

That could only mean one thing: he'd *known* I'd be here. Well. First mystery solved.

I pushed down my desire to keep staring at him, analyzing what this discovery meant, and instead concentrated on shaking Governor Mane's hand. Mane was a big man with shiny hair, a former linebacker for the Longhorns who'd spun his natural charm into a political career. That career had reached its peak in his stunning gubernatorial victory over a hard-line überconservative incumbent.

It made Grover Mane the closest Texas had come to a Democratic governor in decades. He supported big business, like any good Republican, but was socially liberal, which meant as soon as he'd taken office, he'd changed immigration laws, revitalized funding for women's clinics, and committed to a number of criminal justice and health care reforms. Over in the Lise office, once we'd started to catch wind that Governor Mane was actually walking the walk, we'd decided now was our moment to pitch the transportation bill.

"Nice to see you again, Lee." The governor swept a hand in Ben's direction, his Texas drawl thick as always. "Meet Benny boy." The governor winked. "I got you someone your own age to talk to."

It was zero hour. How to play it? Say we knew each other because we went to UT together? That was true, and uncomplicated—

Ben extended his hand, face expressionless, blue eyes giving away nothing. "Nice to meet you."

Oh my God. He was pretending he didn't know me.

"Lee Stone," I said automatically, pumping his hand once before dropping it like it was on fire. Great. Now I was complicit.

You owe him, I told myself. After what I'd done to him, if Ben wanted to pretend a little, surely I could go along with it.

The governor sat, so we all followed. Dakota took the seat directly across from Mane, and Wendy took the seat to her left. Which left an open seat at the end of the table, right across from Ben. If I didn't take it, it would look weird. So I sat, and tried to soak up all the details of his face—parse some hint of what he was thinking—without being obvious.

"All right, I've got to keep this brief because I have lunch with the chief justice. I wanted to introduce you to Ben and get a plan going for the Green Machine." Governor Mane turned to his right. "Ben's excited about this bill, told me right from the start. I know that surprises the hell out of everyone at this table—a Silicon Valley transplant who's turned on by clean energy."

He paused to give us a chance to chuckle, which we all did, right on cue. I watched Ben. He smiled good-naturedly at the governor, like he'd grown used to assuaging powerful people. The Ben I remembered would have rolled his eyes.

His teeth were blindingly white. He was like a polished magazine version of himself.

The governor clapped a hand on Ben's shoulder. "In fact, he's already read the bill and marked it up." He turned to me. "Ben here's going to give you a run for your money."

I tore my gaze from Ben's face. He'd done *what*? Added what notes? I'd consulted with no less than eight environmental and transportation policy experts to write the bill language.

Governor Mane's eyes flicked to Dakota, and his expression turned a little bashful, like a boy confronted with the valedictorian and prom queen rolled into one. She had that effect. "What I'd like to do now is agree on a plan forward."

Wendy raised her eyebrows. "Does this mean we have your full support? You're willing to use your capital to push the bill?"

The governor's bashful smile melted, and he was back to game face. "Thank Ben. He argued it should be one of my signature initiatives. I wasn't sure at first, but it was one of his conditions in taking the job."

It *was*? My eyes found Ben's face again, but he was looking at Dakota, his expression coolly neutral. "Clean energy on this scale is the right thing to do."

"We're grateful you feel that way," Dakota said. "You're

going to make history, Governor. Make the world a better place for our children."

"Fingers crossed," said the governor, sitting back and crossing his arms. "So, let's talk strategy. How do we win this thing?"

Dakota turned to me and nodded. I took a deep breath, blocked out Ben's distracting presence and put on my boss face.

I looked around the table, making sure I had everyone's attention. "The House is solid blue. We've been in conversations for a while now, and we have vote commitments from more than enough representatives to pass the bill. It's the Senate we're worried about. We need to start by gut-checking with the Natural Resources and Economic Development Committee, where the bill will get assigned for review. Find out where they're at."

"Done," Ben cut in, and *finally*, we locked eyes. There was a challenge simmering there that I remembered from Law School Ben, the guy who reveled in oral arguments, in taking down his classmates.

"Excuse me?"

He didn't look away, just adjusted his clear frames to more perfectly center his eyes. "I got a jump start on vetting once I knew I was taking the job."

The governor nodded approvingly. "Didn't I tell you? Run for your money."

My face grew hot. I'd come to this meeting ready to be nice to Ben, to make up for the past. At the very least, I'd been determined to be professional enough to sweep our history under the rug. But he was challenging me in front of my bosses. I could feel my guilt, and my desire to be conciliatory, evaporate. In their place, anger swelled.

Apparently, Ben was now in charge, because he addressed the table. "Here's where we stand. The bill needs to clear the committee with strong endorsements, and we have three major holdouts. Janus, Wayne and—"

"McBuck," I practically shouted, desperate to contribute. Lame, because it was the obvious guess. Senator Roy McBuck's district was home to Mendax Oil, a huge oil and gas company that employed a lot of McBuck's constituents *and* a lot of lobbyists.

Ben smiled at me like I was a five-year-old who'd spelled her name right. "Exactly. We need to focus on winning over those three and not pissing off anyone else while we're at it. We do that, and we win."

"Excellent." Governor Mane stood up, adjusting his bolo tie. "I want you and Lee to work together to figure out how to convince each of them, and then I want you to execute."

What in the— Campaign with *Ben*? No, absolutely not. This was just supposed to be one meeting—get Ben's blessing, then go off and do the work myself. A short, tidy epilogue wrapping up our story. Panic gripped me.

"I don't think that's a good idea," I blurted.

Every head around the table swiveled to me. Wendy shot me a death glare.

Governor Mane squinted. "Why not? I thought you wanted to get your hands dirty. With your subject matter expertise and Ben's political savvy, you'll make a dream team." He looked at Dakota. "It's a bit of a lift for one person, so if Lee can't do it, I guess we can wait until I find someone el—"

"Oh, Lee *will do it*," Wendy said, and I actually gulped.

I looked at Ben, whose expression was still coolly neutral, except for the hint of a smirk at the corners of his mouth.

Oh, *hell* no. He *wanted* me to refuse to work with him and embarrass myself in front of everyone. I was walking right into his trap.

"Of course I will," I revised quickly. "I was only concerned about Ben, actually. He reads very California, and I'm not sure how that will play with our senators."

Ben flushed. *Ha.*

"Good point," the governor said. "Ben, buy yourself some boots and a ten-gallon hat. And for the love of God, don't mention you're a Democrat."

Ben was still a Democrat? I hadn't thought about it consciously, but as soon as the governor said it, my shoulders sank with relief, unloading an anxiety I hadn't known I was carrying. I realized I'd assumed working for Governor Mane meant Ben had gone over to the dark side. But he hadn't.

"Please," Ben muttered. "I know that much."

Wendy raised an eyebrow. "Employing across party lines. How out of the box, Governor."

Governor Mane waved his hand and walked to the door, followed by his small entourage, who scurried from their seats. "Cowboy on the outside, stone-cold tactician on the inside. Anything to win." He pointed at Ben. "Get yourself a hat." And then he was off to his lunch.

My panic climbed as Dakota and Wendy rose to follow him out. Dakota squeezed my shoulders, giving Ben a bright smile. "We'll leave the two of you to talk details. We're so excited to have you on board, Ben."

Ben blinked, caught for a second by Dakota-dazzle, then smiled back. "And I'm excited to be here."

As Wendy and Dakota slipped out of the door, I resisted the urge to throw myself at them, begging them not to leave me alone in this conference room.

But they shut the door with a resounding thud. Taking my restraint with them.

I whipped around to face Ben. "Scratch that. We are *not* excited to have you on board. What the hell, Laderman? What are you doing here—actively trying to fuck up my life?"

He shook his head slowly, grinning like a goddamn movie villain circling the wounded hero. "Stoner, Stoner, Stoner. Just the height of professionalism. You still go by Stoner, right?"

I hissed. "Don't call me that here."

Ben put his hands on the conference table and leaned over it. "Given what I recall about your lifestyle, I'm surprised you even remember me."

"Not remember the guy who moved to California because we broke up?" I scoffed. "Yeah, right. That dramatic exit is burned into my memory."

"I didn't move because we broke up, you giant narcissist." Ben narrowed his eyes. "But I won't say knowing you were working on the Green Machine bill wasn't an incentive to move back."

There he was: the old, competitive Ben I remembered. The supercilious mask he'd worn for the governor had dropped away.

I rose and planted my own hands on the conference table, mirroring him. "So you *are* back to take revenge. Ha! Just like I suspected. You want to ruin my life just because I ruined yours."

"I couldn't care less about ruining your life. I'm back because I want to turn my home state blue, working from the inside."

I blinked. That's what *I* wanted to do.

"Governor Mane is the best shot in decades. I came back for a once-in-a-million job. The kind of job I went to law school for in the first place, no help from you."

I pointed at him. "You *do* resent me!"

Ben pulled off his glasses and stared at me with unfiltered blue eyes. "You cheated on me with Connor Holliday. And then Connor stole my ranking because I was stupid enough to be upset. *Of course* I resent you!"

Well, second mystery solved: Ben Laderman *did* hate me.

I spun on my heels and stalked around the table until I was close to him. "You won't undermine the bill. I won't let you."

Ben didn't back away from my invasion of his space; he leaned forward and flexed his fingers, like he wanted to grab me by the shoulders but knew he couldn't, thanks to #MeToo. "I'm not going to undermine it, Stoner. I'm going to get it passed so hard the governor will let me do the next bigger and better thing."

How dare he? There was no bigger and better thing than the Green Machine.

"I'm going to kick your ass so hard at passing this bill they'll name it the Ben Laderman bill. Next year, everyone will try to remember the name of my assistant—"

"Assistant?"

"—who helped me, but no one will be able to recall much about you. Lee Stone, nothing but a fading memory. Just like you were the moment I drove across the California state line."

And there it was. The final mystery solved. Ben's revenge wasn't to kill my bill. It was much colder. He was going to *steal* it. My bill, and my glory. And probably my promotion. If he thought I would roll over and let him do it, just because I felt bad about our past, he was *sorely* mistaken.

I leaned over the table and swatted his glasses so they slid down the smooth conference table like a puck down a shuffleboard. "Over my dead body."

He smirked. "You don't even have a strategy."

"Don't I?" The words flew out of me. "James Janus, youngest state senator in Texas and one of *Texas Monthly*'s twenty-five hottest people in politics—a list that depends solely on publicist submissions, by the way, so he's got an ego. Up for reelection, so he doesn't want to do anything too radical to spook his voters. Convince his constituents they want to go green and he's on lock. And he comes from a diverse district that skews young. Climate policies *and* female-run businesses poll well there. They like our brand. He's our easiest get."

Ben arched an eyebrow, grudgingly impressed. "Senator Wayne is an old cowboy, about as red as it gets. His district's all ranches and farms. Any brilliant thoughts there?"

"I'll think of something."

"And McBuck? How are you going to counter Mendax Oil?"

"I don't know. How are *you* going to counter Mendax Oil?"

"Convince McBuck's voters Mendax is evil or give them something they want even more."

I rolled my eyes. "Obviously."

"Luckily, I have an in with Mendax's lobbying firm. I can keep my ear to the ground, anticipate their moves."

My spine straightened. That connection was worth its weight in gold.

Ben leaned back from me and folded his arms over his chest. "Face it. You heard the governor—he wants us both on the campaign. No matter how much we hate it, we're doing this together."

"There's no way in hell."

"Have fun telling your bosses you quit."

I crossed my arms. That was obviously the last conversation I wanted to have with Dakota and Wendy. "I guess…pooling our resources could be mutually beneficial."

Ben smiled. "That's the spirit. Why don't we make it a competition—like the good old days?"

"I hate to break it to you, but getting a bill passed is a lot harder than winning legal debates and playing drinking games. Games you weren't even good at, from what I remember."

Ben ignored the dig. "We both give this thing our best shot, and see who's better. Three senators, starting with Janus. The one who collects the most yeses wins."

"And the loser?"

"Makes sense you'd want to know. The loser becomes the other one's assistant for the rest of the campaign. I really could do with one."

I snorted. What a thinly veiled excuse. Ben didn't care about passing the bill—he clearly only wanted the opportunity to embarrass *me* for a change. And maybe there was some parallel universe in which I'd let him have this win—a universe where I had less pride, less ambition and a longer fuse. But that was not this universe. In this universe, there was no way I was letting Ben have it, no matter what I'd done to him five years ago.

"Fine." I spun toward the door. "I take my coffee fair-trade, two sugars and piping hot. Might want to memorize it."

"Piping hot?" Ben called. I could hear the smirk in his voice. "How does your ice-cold heart handle it?"

I slammed the door behind me like the seasoned diplomat I was.

4

Self-Care

There was nowhere in the world more soothing than the center table at Olive & Izzie's on a Friday night, the string lights glowing in the palm trees, crowd thick and buzzing in the background, friends talking close around the table. One dirty martini down, the second sweating sexily in my hands, and the promise of more to come. It was enough to make you forget all your problems.

Well, it was enough to make *me* forget all my problems.

"They're *sharks*," Claire declared, banging her hands on the table and jostling our drinks. "Circling around, all cold-blooded. No, scratch that. They're meerkats, popping up out of their holes to look at other moms, but never invite them in for a drink. They're a cross between sharks and meerkats."

"Shark-kats," Zoey said, then stopped and smiled to herself. "That would be adorable."

Claire was in high dramatics. "I'm practically throwing

myself at them, and nothing. No invitations to their dumb parents' association meetings and not a single mention that I volunteered to chair the pre-K variety show. I'm a busy, successful lawyer, for God's sake. You'd think they'd want me in their mom crew. Are lawyers not cool anymore?"

"I'm sure they're simply busy with their own lives and aren't aware you want to be friends," said Annie reasonably, stirring the straw of her spiked lemonade. "It's been a while since you've had to put yourself out there. Maybe you're a little rusty when it comes to making your intentions known."

Claire frowned. "It has to be the lawyer thing. They all have these trendy, weird jobs. One of them is a child yoga instructor. Another's a cartoonist and calligrapher—you should see the birthday invitations Mikey gets, like he's the queen of England. Does calligrapher trump lawyer in Austin? I never should've moved back to this godforsaken hippie cesspool."

"You're just annoyed you finally found people who didn't cave immediately to your usual tactics—shock, awe and bulldozing," Mac said.

"I could read through contracts for them," Claire grumbled, downing the rest of her old-fashioned. "You'd think that'd be a selling point."

Mac eyed the guy sitting at the next table. "I'll see your cool-girl moms and raise you my single-lady problems. I've officially run out of guys on Tinder, which means I'm actually going to have to meet someone by introducing myself in person. Which I don't remember how to do. Either that, or I die alone. And poor Stoner here's battling her jilted ex."

I'd called this Friday-night Olive & Izzie's quorum to fill them in on the latest Ben Laderman developments. As I'd hoped, I had their full sympathies for Ben's assholery and their ardent assurances that I would, without a doubt, come out on top in our political death match. That, plus the martinis, was making me feel much more at ease with my predicament.

"There's no use creating a problem hierarchy," Annie said. "Everyone's problems are relative. No one's are more important than anyone else's."

I took Annie's face in my hands and kissed her smack in the forehead. If there *was* a problem hierarchy, Annie's would sit on top, lording over us all. When I'd met her in grad school, Annie was engaged to Rick Song, a student at Dell Medical School she'd been dating for a solid decade. Her parents and Rick's parents were *entwined*.

Rick was nice and all, don't get me wrong, but he was flat. And I always thought he left Annie flat, too—nothing too bad or too good ever happened between them. Annie was never angry at him, but she was also never particularly happy. I'd learned not to bring up my observations, because every time I did, Annie would wave me off, saying I just didn't understand what a long-term relationship looked like. (Classic avoidance and denial, I see now.)

But internally it must have been a different story, because two years ago, right before they were supposed to be married, Annie shocked the world—but most of all the Park and Song families—by dumping Rick and running off with a woman named Beatrice, who was a barista at our favorite coffee shop. It was a particularly cool exit because Beatrice rode a sick motorcycle.

To say that Annie's parents were furious was an understatement. For nearly a year they'd barely acknowledged her at family dinners and holidays, which must have been awkward as hell, even for the world's most kind and diplomatic person, a title Annie held without competition. Lately, the frost had been slowly melting—which was a godsend, because Annie loved her family.

And she super-loved Zoey. After Beatrice, Annie had dated a few other people, until she met Zoey at the farmers' market one Sunday morning and it was lights out, everyone else.

It was almost enough to make you believe in love. But then again, most love stories were adorable and romantic—until they weren't. Someone had to be a pragmatist about it. And with the way Annie and Zoey were looking at each other over their empty cocktails, better me than them.

"All right," I said, hopping to my feet. "If we're going to wing-woman Mac tonight, everyone needs another drink."

Mac pointed at me. "No made-up names, and *no* fake accents. It's not as funny as you think it is." She switched her finger to Claire. "And no making guys cry. I mean it this time."

I smiled and ducked away, calling back over my shoulder, "Das is a hard promise to make, *Fräulein*!"

Mac's loud groan—audible even over the crowd—was the perfect soundtrack to my entrance to the bar.

I sidled up to the counter, shivering in the late-September Austin air-conditioning, and nodded at Izzie, who was finishing someone's drinks.

"Let me guess," Izzie said, running a tattooed hand through her buzz cut. "Rye old-fashioned, dirty vodka martini, two spiked lemonades and a PBR."

She and I grimaced at the same time. Mac and her shitty boy-bait beers.

"You got it, dude." I leaned on the bar and watched Izzie work, sifting through bunches of herbs, peeling lemon rinds. I thought about ordering Kyle, my itinerant hookup, a drink, but odds were high he wouldn't show until the tail end of the night, just like I liked it. After the Ben debacle, I was itching to jump into bed and work off some pent-up frustrations.

"Lee Stone, standing alone at a bar. Just like the night we met."

That smug, husky voice. It could belong to none other than Ben Laderman.

I turned, and there he stood, all those many inches of him. He'd exchanged the cool blue suit for a simple white button-down and jeans, no glasses, his black hair no longer carefully brushed behind his ears but askew over his forehead. It looked for a second like bedhead, and in a sudden flash, I remembered I'd seen him a hundred mornings over, shirtless and sleepy and tangled in his sheets. I pictured his wolfish smile when he woke, how he'd pull me toward him across the mattress, burying his face in my neck, hands sliding down my chest, skimming my stomach, lower—

The unexpected intimacy shot through me like a white-hot bolt.

I swallowed to mask it. Ben was my ex—*and* my competition. "What are you doing at my spot? Crashing my workplace wasn't enough?"

He looked around. "There's this constitutional principle called the right to free association. Besides, I'm pretty sure this bar belongs to every hipster in Austin."

Izzie put my drinks down on the counter and raised an eyebrow. "He's cleaner than you normally like them, but truly, not bad."

I snatched the martini. "Ben's not a paramour. He's a pest. He's the Ghost of Relationships Past, back to haunt me."

"I see. And what would the ghost like to drink?"

Ben looked over his shoulder to the corner, where two guys in matching button-downs were playing darts. "Two Shiners and a basil gimlet, please."

I nearly spit out my drink. "Which one of your friends is the 1920s flapper?"

"California introduced me to herbs, Stoner. I didn't get

much green stuff growing up, and now I'm making up for it. The drink is delicious. And it's too cool for you."

Ben had always skirted the topic of growing up while we dated. Clear sensitive zone. The most I'd been able to gather was that his dad split when he was ten, and his mom struggled to raise him and his younger brother, Will. Ben used to glow with pride whenever he talked about Will, who'd been starting undergrad at Duke when Ben was in law school.

"How's your brother doing?" I decided to play nice—a change in tactics. Lure him in with honey and then pounce on his vulnerabilities. It had nothing to do with the fact that I was tossing my martini down a little too fast. At this rate, I'd have to order another before I went back to the table.

Ben's face transformed, just like it used to. "He's in med school at Duke, top of his class. Going to be a surgeon."

"Congratulations. You must be very proud."

Ben grinned. "I am. Hey, remember the first thing you said to me the night we met?"

Izzie handed Ben his gimlet and he took a deep, satisfying sip.

Of course I remembered. "Hey, law douche. Bet you the bar tab you can't take more shots than me." Vintage Stoner.

Ben leaned an elbow on the bar. "You were always so competitive."

"*You* were always so competitive. I was smart, broke and doing a tidy business fleecing your classmates."

Ben's eyes crinkled, and something inside me twinged. "Well, those douches deserved to be fleeced."

"Fleeced you, too, if memory serves." There I went, draining my martini.

"I let you win."

"You have let no one win, at anything, ever."

A slow smile spread across his face. "True." He leaned in,

and his voice grew deeper. Deliberately provocative. "Hey, policy douche. Bet you can't take more shots than me now."

The thrill of competition raced through me, raising goose bumps in its wake. This was good; this was my comfort zone. "I don't need help paying the bar tab anymore."

"Prize isn't the bar tab. It's whatever the winner decides. You still ballsy, Stoner?"

I smiled and turned to Izzie, who watched us from behind the bar. "Two shots of Patrón, please. And keep them coming."

I tossed my second shot and bit into the lime wedge, relishing the sour sting. What I relished even more was the screwed-up twist of Ben's mouth that told me he was already struggling. Me? I brushed my teeth with tequila.

"Another," I told Izzie, and she poured.

"How are you *like* this?" Ben groaned. "I remember thinking you were secretly a Terminator robot, but that was because you laughed when Anna threw herself under the train at the end of *Anna Karenina*. I guess it should've been a warning sign, in retrospect."

"Pssh. Anna. So melodramatic." I held out my newly refreshed shot. "Ready to admit defeat?"

Ben's eyes steeled. "To you? Never. Besides, I'm pretty sure my friends ditched me a long time ago."

A cute guy had swung by a while ago to pick up the drinks I'd ordered for my friends, so I'd assumed Operation Help Mac Meet Men IRL was going well without me. "Are they new friends, or old?"

"Old. Guys I went to high school with."

"I guess you'll have to apologize for spending all your time with me."

Ben shrugged. "Eh. I was trying to make it work, but it turns out we don't have a lot in common anymore."

"Now that you're so California?"

"Am not." He grinned, dimples flashing, and tucked his hair behind his ear. For a split second I imagined him as Clark Kent, but instead of flying through the air, he was riding a wave on a surfboard. *California Clark.* Ugh—tequila brain.

"I still get along plenty well with you," he added.

I waved a hand between us. "You call bickering and trying to outdo each other getting along?"

"Is that not a perfect description of our past relationship? If you can call it a relationship."

"Ha." I turned away to face the bar. For some stupid reason that probably had everything to do with alcohol, Ben trivializing us was making a weird lump form in my throat.

"Hey." He laid a warm hand on my shoulder. Surprised, I turned to find him dangling his shot glass with a grimace. "Watch this. You're going to love it." He downed the shot and clapped a hand over his mouth, eyes widening, as the tequila clearly tried to come back out the way it went in.

I couldn't help it. He was right. I laughed.

Ben waved a hand at me, signaling *Your turn, for the love of God.*

I downed my shot smoothly, cocking an eyebrow. "Another?"

It took him a long, drawn-out moment in which I assumed he weighed the humiliation of losing to me against the humiliation of vomiting all over Olive & Izzie's. And chose poorly.

He shook his head. "I fold."

"Throwing yourself on my mercy. Older but not wiser, I see."

He rolled up the sleeves of his button-down and rested his forearms on the bar, leaning in against my shoulder. I leaned back, mostly because at this point in the night, I required a source of balance. I'd forgotten how hard his biceps were. Ben had always been religious about lifting. In law school, it was a low-cost way to relieve stress.

From what I could feel through his shirt, he still had plenty of stress to work through.

The smile Ben was giving me was one I remembered from countless nights home alone together. He used to do this thing where he picked me up and threw me on his bed, caging me with his arms while I laughed and tried to squirm away. This was the smile he used to wear right before he leaned down to kiss me.

"You win, Stoner. Let's hear it. How are you going to torture me?"

I was about to answer when my phone rang. Which was strange because no one outside of work ever audio-called me, and it was late on a Friday night. I pulled the phone out of my pocket and saw the ID: Alexis Stone. My little sister. That meant nothing good.

Ben caught the ID, too, and frowned. "Is she ok—"

I held up a finger and answered. "Lex, what's wrong?"

I heard crying, barely audible over the din of the bar. My heart dropped.

"Hold on." I spun away from the counter and pushed through the crowd until I made it out the door, feeling Ben's presence shadow me. Unfortunately, the patio was nearly as loud as inside.

Ben's fingers gripped my elbow, tugging me into the only dark and quiet corner in the whole place.

"Lee," my sister sobbed.

"Are you okay?" My heart was going a mile a minute. "Are you safe? Is Mom okay?"

"I'm safe. It's just...*Chris*."

Her boyfriend. What had the fucker done?

Ben had moved away to give me space, but I could see him pacing out of the corner of my eye.

"What happened?"

"He..." Alexis hiccuped. She'd always been a messy crier. "He *cheated* on me."

Her serious boyfriend of four years—the one she thought was going to propose—had *cheated*. Of course he had.

"Shit. I'm sorry, Alexis. What an asshole."

"I don't know what to do. I can't go home. He's there. I can't see him."

"Of course you can't," I said soothingly. "Go to my place. You can stay as long as you want."

Alexis hiccuped again. "Thank you."

"I'll head home right now," I said. "Get in an Uber. I'll meet you there."

Just as I hung up with Alexis, I felt another hand at my elbow. I turned, expecting to find Ben, but it was Kyle Sumner.

Oh, shit. *Kyle*. The hot, dirty hippie I called whenever I wanted to go home with someone but extend zero effort. My acquaintance-with-benefits. I'd totally forgotten I'd made plans to meet him at the end of the night.

"Found you." Kyle tossed his blond hair out of his eyes. He was one of those trust-fund kids who looked like he hadn't brushed his hair in years, but actually spent considerable money getting it that way. "You want to grab a drink?"

Ben walked up, but he kept a cautious distance, eyes darting from Kyle to me. "Stoner? Is Lex okay?"

I met his eyes. "Her boyfriend—" My throat went dry. For the life of me, I couldn't bring myself to tell Ben that Alexis's boyfriend had cheated and devastated her. Just like I'd done to him. "He dumped her."

Ben's eyes went soft. "Shit."

Kyle looked between us. "Who's Lex?"

Ben turned to him. "Who are you?"

"Ben, this is Kyle, my, er...friend. Kyle, this is Ben, my... old friend."

Excellent. Handled with grace.

Kyle and Ben examined each other. Kyle was tall, but he kept lean enough to fit into ripped-up skinny jeans. Ben had a solid two inches and quite a bit of muscle on him.

"Hey." Kyle tossed the greeting like it was a two-dollar tip to a valet. He wrapped an arm around me.

"Nice to meet you." Ben's eyes found mine again, and I could see the questions brewing. He finally settled on one. "Does Lex need anything?"

"She's a wreck, so I'm going to meet her at my house. She'll stay with me for a while." I squeezed Kyle's arm. "Sorry about that. Rain check?"

"Yeah, no problem. I'll walk you to your Uber."

My hand was still on Kyle's arm. The message couldn't have been clearer. Ben surveyed Kyle again, who straightened almost imperceptibly. Ben swallowed, his Adam's apple moving in his throat. "Right. Okay. I guess I'll see where my friends went."

I felt a surprising flash of regret, then remembered Alexis, who was likely sobbing in a stranger's Honda Civic, on her way to my house. There was no time to keep messing around with tequila shots and memories that I was better off leaving for dead, anyway.

So I did something I'd done before. Something that should feel familiar to Ben by now. And I didn't even think about how it was a repeat of history—a re-slash of an old wound—until I woke abruptly at 5:00 a.m. alone in my bed, covered in sweat but also somehow shivering.

I took another man's hand and walked out of the bar, leaving Ben behind.

5

Mature Adults

I might as well retire, because I was standing outside the men's bathroom at the Antonio Camarillo Convention Center, staring at the best PR idea I would ever have in my life.

Ben glared at me with the heat of a thousand suns, a look that very clearly said, *I wish you nothing but pain and misery for all of your days.* I was riding a professional high, and the fact that he was sinking to what I assumed was a new professional low made it all the sweeter.

"I will never forgive you," he said, adjusting his long, red gloves. "This is somehow even worse than what I imagined when I pictured working with you."

I clucked my tongue. "This is why you shouldn't bet against me."

I'd gotten the idea from Daisy David, actually, so I should probably send her a thank-you note. I'd cashed in my tequila-contest-win blank check for the promise that Ben would attend the first event on our Green Machine campaign trail—the Comic-Con in Senator Janus's district—dressed as Captain Planet. Let's just say it was probably not the noble start to his Texas political career he'd imagined.

Ben looked down at himself despairingly. "This is practically pornographic. How is this a character from a children's cartoon?"

I had to admit I'd forgotten how scantily clad Captain Planet was. Other than a little red crop top, he was basically wearing granny panties and knee-high red boots. It was a look oddly reminiscent of certain bachelorette trends I'd noticed lately on Rainey Street. Granted, Ben's costume was a full-body foam one that gave him Captain Planet's blue skin and endless cartoon muscles, but the overall package was still mighty suggestive.

I think my favorite part was the teal mullet.

"I will not rest until I pay you back," Ben promised, lifting the heavy box of glossy pamphlets—a concise explainer on the bill I was very proud of writing—out of my hands.

"I don't see why you're complaining." I flipped through the blank pages of our petition. All that beautiful real estate, ready to be filled with signatures. "This is Comic-Con."

I started walking and gestured for Ben to follow. Which he did reluctantly, folding his arms over his midsection in a move that reminded me of junior high, when I'd suddenly filled out and had tried in vain to hide myself every time I had to perform in my dance uniform on the football field.

"Everyone here is wearing costumes," I said. "You'll fit right in."

We made it to the end of the hallway and turned the corner to face the main convention space. The sheer buzzing volume of thousands of people milling around, going from booth to booth, taking pictures and signing autographs, was dizzying.

Abilene's Comic-Con was a huge draw for the district, bringing in people from all over the state and lots of tourist dollars. Practically everyone in Abilene attended, too, making it the perfect place to start gathering signatures and spreading the word about the Green Machine bill.

As I'd promised, a solid 60 percent of attendees were dressed in some manner of science fiction or fantasy get-up. But from the look on Ben's face, solidarity did not dull the sting of indignity.

"Think of it this way—you dressed as Captain Planet is the single best advertisement we could ever have for the bill. No one wants to hear a bunch of suits drone on about Senate Bill 3 at a comic convention. They want to hear how they're going to help save the world with Captain Planet."

Ben shot me a bloodcurdling look. Facial expressions aside, he was being awfully quiet.

"You know it's true. You're just upset to discover I'm an evil genius."

We walked through the crowd, passing She-Ra and *Star Wars* booths. I spied Doctor Whos, Ewoks, Hulks, Captain Jack Sparrows, and what I assumed—*hoped*—was Severus Snape, and not someone with a truly unfortunate personal aesthetic.

I elbowed Captain Planet. "Go on. Get out there and sell our bill."

Ben narrowed his eyes at me, sucked in a breath and then spun to a group of young men. "Hey, Planeteers! Do you want to take on the evil scum of pollution and save the world, just through a little political action?"

Oh. Ben was using *the voice*. He was committing to his character 100 percent, like they teach you in improv.

I slapped a hand over my mouth to keep my hyena laugh inside.

"Cool." One of the guys, whose sporadic beard growth

marked him as likely early twenties, nodded vigorously. "*Captain Planet* was my favorite. Such a throwback."

Ben seized on it. "Well, let me tell you about an extraordinary bill we want your state senator—Senator Janus—to support." He handed out pamphlets to the group as well as some nearby people who'd stopped to listen, caught up in the spectacle. Ben was significantly taller than the average Comic-Con attendee, and bright blue from head to foot. With his deep, booming voice, he was certainly attracting attention.

"It's a bill that would replace all of Texas's public vehicles—city buses, cop cars, fire trucks—with electric versions. Do you know how much good that would do for the planet? It would make Texas a world leader in environmental policy, which I'm sure is a sentence you never thought you'd hear.

"And I know you can see that hefty price tag—" all of the people listening to Ben widened their eyes at the four-billion-dollar figure in the pamphlet "—but look at the next number. After some up-front costs to build infrastructure, the savings on gas and antipollution measures alone would more than make up for it. And who can put a price tag on the health of the planet?"

I was impressed. Ben actually sounded like he cared about the bill, and hadn't just glommed on to it as the ideal way to spite me.

"It's about time we did something like this," said a young man in the back, who was dressed as some sort of menacing cartoon octopus I didn't recognize. "But how do we get Janus to support it?"

"I'm glad you asked." Ben spun to me, his whole face lit with excitement that this was going well.

I stepped to his side, a cool, suave political operative in my sleek black suit. "We'd love your signatures on this petition urging Senator Janus to help pass the bill." I passed the clipboard and pen to the man who'd asked. "And on the back of your pamphlet, you'll find Senator Janus's social handles as well as his phone and email. Flooding his office with support is the single most important thing you can do."

My heart swelled as heads nodded and people passed the clipboard from hand to hand. Chewbacca passed to a Ninja Turtle, who passed to Spider-Man.

This was really happening. My bill—my *baby*—was coming to life.

Ben and I grinned at each other. And then, emboldened by his success, Ben called out, "With our powers combined, we *can* save the planet!"

There was a fragile line you had to walk when courting certain young men, which I'd learned during my phase dating drug dealers who were really into anime, and then again with jam-band fanatics. It was a careful balance between trying just hard enough and maintaining indifferent authenticity.

The crowd around us exchanged dubious looks, the petition-passing slowing to a halt.

Spider-Man squinted at the guy beside him. "That's, like, a misquote from the show, right?"

I caught the octopus cartoon guy's eyes and shook my head at Ben. "Someone loves the environment a little *too much*. Nerd, am I right?"

The guy nodded gravely, a tentacle flopping over his forehead.

Ben managed to blush red under the blue.

Sacrifice made and balance restored, the petition started moving again.

"There has to be thousands of signatures here," Ben said in amazement, riffling through the pages.

I clicked my phone dark and slid it into my bag under the table at the Green Machine booth. "Wendy says there's already a big uptick in traffic to the website, and Twitter posts tagging Janus. By all metrics, day one is a success."

All week Ben and I had plotted campaign strategy from our separate offices, arguing via increasingly unprofessional emails, then texts, then phone calls over how much in-person outreach we needed versus digital ad buys versus broadcast. He'd been in the camp of maximum face time, and I'd argued it was all about a good creative ad. Each of us had been so stubborn that we'd ended up with both—no compromise.

But now that we'd spent the day here, plugging the bill to actual people and hearing their responses, I had to admit there was a certain magic to in-person campaigning. It seemed to really drive engagement and you got a little bit of opinion research as an added bonus. I'd never admit it to him, but I would remember this for my next Ben-less campaign.

It wasn't bad to work with Ben in person, either, truth be told. But that was surely chalked up to the fun of torturing him while being able to see his face.

"A solid 80 percent of those signatures are from women with Captain Planet fetishes," I said. "I'm pretty sure we talked to every woman at this convention."

We'd wandered for a few hours, drawing a crowd of followers who wanted Ben to say lines from the TV show and pose for pictures—which we'd obviously and shamelessly traded for petition signatures. The ratio of men to women in our following had quickly skewed toward women. Even after we'd retired to our booth, Ben proved just as much of a draw sitting in a fold-up chair, groaning about his back, as when he'd been posing.

I patted his head. His hair was stiff with temporary dye. "I credit your blue washboard abs."

He scratched at a flake of paint on his face. "I've never been this itchy in my life. I think my balls are on fire."

"Ew, did you paint your *balls*?"

The lights flashed in the convention center, signaling it was time to wrap up and head out.

Ben raised a triumphant fist. "I made it." He stood and started tearing the skirt off the table. "So..."

"So, what?"

"I know we've been focused on the campaign this week, and it's fine if you don't want to talk about it, but...is Lex okay? I could hear her voice through the phone at the bar and she seemed pretty upset."

When I'd arrived home from Olive & Izzie's last weekend, I'd found Alexis sitting in the middle of my couch, red-faced and sobbing, wrapped in a thick comforter from my guest room, with a bottle of rosé, a tub of chocolate ice cream and a mountain of tissues strewn around her. The cats were clear across the room, watching her gravely from their hiding spots.

Lex had cried on my shoulder, unloading the whole sordid story: how they'd been watching a movie on the couch when out of the blue, in a fit of guilt, Chris confessed to sleeping with a fellow accountant at work. A woman Lex had always been nice to, on the few occasions they'd met at events. It had taken hours of talking before I managed to tuck her into the guest bed. She'd planted herself right back on the couch in her comforter with tissues and wine every day this week, watching old Meg Ryan rom-coms with my mom on FaceTime and hiccuping the whole way through.

"She's morphed into a sad little Jabba the Hutt on my couch. She just sits there in her blanket and I bring her chocolate and rosé and she pats my face. I'm honestly surprised my mom hasn't made an emergency visit."

Ben winced. "Poor Lex."

I'd forgotten how much they always got along. Right off the bat, too, like they'd been friends all their lives. Ben was a year older than me, and I was four years older than Lex, so she'd always looked at him like an older brother.

"It sounds like him dumping her came out of nowhere." He shook his head and folded up the table. "That's the thing I hate most. How even when you date someone for a long time, they can still turn out to be a stranger. I hope Lex finds someone she can trust completely."

My face flushed hot. It was important to *me* to keep parts of myself to myself with anyone I dated. I guess you could say that kept me a stranger to everyone. Figures the thing Ben hated most was my MO.

I cleared my throat. "Well, now, in addition to the campaign, I have a side project where I'm plotting to murder her ex-boyfriend."

A woman who'd been passing by the booth, eyeing Ben's very real biceps working under his costume ones, paused to give me a startled look.

I smiled. "Hi, there."

Ben ripped up the cardboard box that had once held the pamphlets and was now gloriously empty. "Is your friend Kyle helping you plot?"

I finished folding the table skirt and tucked it into the plastic container that held our campaign supplies. "Nope."

"Are you guys serious?"

I shot him an incredulous look. "Are you asking if Kyle's my boyfriend?"

"What? Am I not supposed to? Sorry, I didn't realize I'd stumbled onto your one and only boundary."

"Kyle isn't my boyfriend, Ben. He's my walking sex toy."

A mother tugging a small boy dressed as R2-D2 gasped and earmuffed him. I was on a solid child-corruption streak lately.

Ben raised both eyebrows.

"And before you say anything, Kyle would be elated to

know I called him that. He knows I don't do boyfriends. Or monogamy."

"Since when?"

Since you. All of a sudden, I needed to find something to look at that wasn't Ben. The R2-D2 kid was now screaming bloody murder over his mother's shoulder, so that was an option. The grime on the linoleum floor—anything would do.

I shrugged and kept my gaze on my tote bag. "A few years now. Why bother getting serious with someone when over half of marriages end in divorce and way more than half of relationships go down in flames? The definition of *insanity* is trying the same thing over and over and expecting different results."

"That's why you learn from the disasters and evolve. You try different things in the next relationship."

I couldn't resist; I looked up, catching his eyes. Which—even in the blue of his face, stood out. "Does that mean you're going to give it a shot with that hot Smurf who slipped you her number?"

Ben shook his head, bending to pick up the plastic supply container. "I'm very happy with my girlfriend."

Girlfriend? The record needle screeched to a halt. "Say *what*?"

Apparently, the filter that normally at least half-heartedly tried to keep my thoughts separated from my mouth had packed up and run off.

Ben kicked a red-booted leg in the direction of the folded-up table. "You got that?"

I bent and picked it up. "I repeat, say *what*?"

He started walking. I scrambled to keep up. "Like it's a state secret. Are you not on any social media? That's weird, you know, for a comms director."

I was going to *kill* Mac for not using her traitorous Facebook friendship with Ben to warn me.

"Sarah. We've been together for a year. She got offered a great job in Austin, so we decided to make the move."

It was like one of the Chewbaccas had kicked me in the chest. I honestly felt like the wind had been knocked out of me. "You *moved* here for her?"

"Well, I found my dream job in the governor's office, so I'd say I moved for that. But yeah, the fact that Sarah was leaving got me looking."

For some reason, the shock of it was just not ebbing. I felt... *betrayed*. Completely illogical, but true nonetheless.

Ben peered over the top of the plastic box as we walked. "What is that look on your face?"

What *was* that look on my face? What were these feelings tearing up my stomach and storming through my chest?

I shook my entire body, like I could physically rattle them out. "I'm just allergic to people who make major life decisions based on fleeting relationships."

And there it was. I suddenly knew why this was hurting like a thousand tiny punches to the chest from a small *Star Wars* robot: Ben had left his life behind and fled Texas to get away from me. He'd uprooted everything and moved *back* to stay close to Sarah.

Call me the Machiavellian Ice-Queen of Relationships, but I had my *pride*.

"Well, Sarah and I aren't fleeting." Ben pushed open the doors to the convention center and walked into the parking lot. "We're serious."

"Excuse me." I placed the fold-up table I was carrying on top of Ben's box and rooted around in my bag.

Ben dipped under the added weight. "Oh, thanks, yeah, I'll just carry your things like a big, blue bellhop."

I found what I was looking for and pulled out my flask, almost as dear to me as Bill McKibben and Al Gore. It was beautiful: soft pink, and painted with a dark skull and crossbones and flowers. I untwisted the cap and took a shot of whiskey.

"What are you *doing*? We're in a parking lot. And you're technically on the clock." Ben was twisting his head in every direction, looking around the parking lot like we were in tenth grade and someone was going to narc on us.

"First of all, I'm no longer working. The convention is over, so it's officially Stoner o'clock. Second, I'm sorry, but I'm not going to be able to survive this campaign with you if you're going to continue to spout sentimental shit like that."

"I'm not going to survive this campaign with *you* if you get us arrested for public intoxication, or…indecency, or…" Ben was clearly racking his brain, trying to recall his long-ago class on criminal law.

I took another shot from the flask.

"Fine," he said, tilting his box at me so the table slid off and I had no choice but to catch it. "I won't talk about Sarah if you don't talk about your walking sex toys."

I shrugged and managed to twist the cap securely on my flask, even with my arms full. "Easy."

We walked in tense silence all the way back to his car—a Prius I suspected he'd rented solely to demonstrate his moral superiority. Or to avoid the judgment in my eyes when I spotted his real car, which was surely a truck or an SUV or something. In law school, he'd once waxed poetic about making enough money to afford his dream car, a Land Rover.

He popped the trunk and shoved the plastic container in.

"So." I kicked the gravel. "What does your girlfriend do, anyway?"

He spun to me, his mouth dropping open. "I thought that topic was off-limits. You won't survive, remember?"

I tossed the table in and closed the trunk. "Call me terminally curious."

Ben opened the passenger door, still shaking his head, and I hopped in. He held on to the door, looking down at me. "What does *Kyle* do?"

Stalemate.

Ben's lips quirked. "Because he looks like he sells weed to high school students."

We looked at each for an endless moment. Then we burst out laughing at the same time.

"Joke's on you," I said, adjusting my suit so it wouldn't wrinkle. "Kyle's unemployed at the moment."

Ben rolled his eyes.

"What's that for?"

He slammed the door and stalked to the driver's side.

"So, what about Sarah?" I asked again, as he settled in and buckled up.

He shot me a guilty look. "She's a lobbyist. With McGraw & Klein."

McGraw & Klein was a big-time firm. They had their hands in practically every Texas politician's pockets. I whistled. "Political power couple."

But why did McGraw & Klein feel so familiar? I could have sworn I'd just been reading about them…

Ben hummed, his eyes on the rearview mirror as he pulled out of the spot. "Uh, you know that connection I told you about, to Mendax Oil's lobbying firm?"

Bingo. That was it. M & K shilled for Mendax.

My eyes widened. "You've got to be kidding me. *Sarah?*"

"Sarah."

Well. Fuck.

Guess I was going to be hearing a lot more about her, like it or not.

6

Nothing to See Here

It was a bright, sunny day, and as far as the eye could see, wenches slung frothy beers in pointy-roofed taverns, minstrels wandered the grass, blowing high-pitched harmonies on their flutes, and fire-breathers danced in the middle of cheering circles. The smell of roasted meat-on-a-stick wafting through the air was enough to make even my vegetarian principles waffle.

Which figured. I was only ever tempted by things like Taco Bell, Krystal sliders and now this. Portable meat of dubious quality. Which was also, coincidentally, my nickname for my vibrator.

Ben nodded encouragingly to the man at the front of the line, who was doing a terrible job lobbing horseshoes around a stick. Probably because he was wearing a full suit of armor with only a small visor pushed back to see. It must be hot as hell in his armor-clad nether regions.

"You've got it this time," Ben called, even though it was clear from the knight's previous attempts that he truly did not.

Ben leaned close to me and held up his arms, letting his bell-shaped sleeves flap in the breeze. "I regret making such a compelling case for in-person outreach. Who knew Janus's district was home to a quarter of the state's festivals?"

"He loves those sweet, sweet tourist dollars." I watched the knight whiff it and turn, shoulders slumped, to let the next person in line take her turn.

"Use your Twitter—uh, tweet-tweet messenger birds—to tell Senator Janus you support clean energy," I called to the knight's back.

I'd learned my lesson from having to set up and take down the booth at Comic-Con all by ourselves. This time around, I'd brought a Lise intern to do the dirty work. Kaitlyn, a UT undergrad communications major, adjusted the head on her dragon costume and dutifully gave the next customer her Green Machine stress ball and pamphlet.

I turned back to Ben. "Come on. It's a beautiful day, and the Texas Renaissance Festival is the biggest in the country. You have to admit this is kind of cool."

Even though modern politics was usually something the Texas Renaissance Festival liked to avoid for multiple reasons, I'd pulled some strings with an event planner friend who had an in with the festival planners, and scored this cool open-air hut in the middle of Little Medieval Germany. We'd gone with a "Return Texas to Ye Olde Ways of Yore" theme, with games connected to all kinds of green transportation: wagons, horses and dragons. Kaitlyn was our live dragon, which freed Ben and me up to be the lord and lady.

He glanced down at his tunic. "It is unexpectedly fun. Plus, this outfit sucks way less than the Comic-Con one. Hell, I'm pretty sure I saw Google executives wearing shirts like this to board meetings before I left California. I feel right at home."

I nodded toward Kaitlyn. "She looks like she's got it well in hand. Let's wander and spread the good word."

Kaitlyn gave me a panicked look as Ben and I slipped out of the hut with handfuls of pamphlets. "Uh, Ms. Stone, ma'am, please—"

"Doing great, Kaitlyn!" I gave her a thumbs-up.

"It's adorable how she calls you Ms. Stone," Ben said as we walked. "Like you're an actual adult."

"Frightening," I agreed, looking resolutely away from the sausage-on-a-stick vendor. "If only she knew the truth."

My phone buzzed with another text update from Wendy. "Between the direct outreach and the digital and broadcast ads, there's been a 50 percent spike in Senator Janus's Twitter mentions. They're being flooded with emails and phone calls, too. His office just called, and they want to talk."

"Excellent." Ben smiled at a crowd of passing elves. "Hello, honored friends. Please help us send Texas's carbon emissions back to medieval times." The elves looked intrigued, so he passed out pamphlets and stress balls. He was getting better at reading crowds.

"Use your famous elvish cunning to convince Senator Janus to vote for SB 3," I added, and they cheered.

"What?" I asked, at Ben's look. "It was a solid guess. Every mystical creature thinks it's the clever one."

He stopped in his tracks, eyes lighting up at something in the distance. The last time I'd seen him this excited was the day he'd discovered he was going up against Connor Holliday in their first-ever mock trial. Ben had beaten him handily that day, but as everyone knew, Connor had gotten him back in the end.

"No way," Ben breathed. *"Axe throwing."*

★ ★ ★

I didn't think Ben would ever recover from how bad he was at axe throwing. I mean, he was good at the throwing part—his throws actually grew more…powerful, let's say…as time went by and he parted with more and more of his money. What they didn't get was more accurate. Poor guy could barely get his axes to land in the target circle—even when the guy who ran the show moved him to a much bigger target I assumed was for axe-throwing babies.

"The trick is to hold it lightly." I demonstrated a gentle grip. "And you want to hold it by the pointy part. Always grab things by the sharp end."

Ben looked like he wanted to use *me* for axe-throwing practice. He glared at me, pushing his hair off his face and huffing a breath. "Why don't I use *you* for axe-throwing practice?"

Well. At least I'd been right about what was going through his head.

I smiled winningly at him and tossed my axe.

The look of utter shock that crossed his face had me spinning to the target. My axe hung, perfectly dead center, in the middle of the circle.

"We have a winner," called the man in charge, in a thick German accent. Everyone around us started clapping.

Oh my God. I *loved* winning. It felt like someone had injected pure adrenaline into my veins.

I swung back to Ben, unsure what to expect, but all six feet three inches of him were glowing, practically radiating excitement.

He tossed his axe on the grass and grabbed my elbows. "You *did it.*"

"I'm a medieval assassin." I jumped up and down, his warm hands securing me, until my flower crown slid over my eyes, blinding me with petals.

Ben tugged the crown back to my forehead, and I got a quick flash of his wide smile, laugh lines crinkling around his eyes, before he turned away. I tried to ignore the punch of his blue eyes.

"Here's your prize," said the man in charge, handing me a giant, overstuffed plush wolf that was a solid third my size. The wolf smiled with a massive set of pointy teeth and canny eyes.

"Oh, thank you," I said, hefting the stuffed animal. "He's terrifying."

Ben laughed.

The axe-man nodded at the wolf. "It's a Beerwolf."

Ben laughed even harder. "Your college alter ego, Stoner."

I cocked my head. *"Beerwolf?"*

The man searched his brain. "Werewolf, I think? From German myth."

"Ohhh." I looked at the stuffed animal. Its canny eyes made sense now. They followed me as I turned my head.

"Here, Ben." I shoved the stuffed animal at him. "I want you to have him."

The mocking laughter left Ben's face immediately. "Are you serious?" He gripped the wolf. "I can have him?"

What a thirty-year-old man was going to do with a giant, menacing stuffed animal was beyond me, but I nodded emphatically.

Ben looked at the axe-man, as if he would rule against this sudden regifting, but he only shrugged indifferently.

"Thank you," Ben said to me. "He's a creepy fucker. I'll name him Stoner."

We walked through the festival—Ben, Stoner the werewolf and me.

"Wait here a second," Ben said, shoving the werewolf into my arms.

I started to protest, but Ben was already gone.

Great. I would just stand here, then, scuffing my feet and clutching a stuffed animal like a lost child. I looked at the people milling around and caught the eye of a woman about my age, with fire-engine-red hair.

Oh—*shit.* I knew her. It had been years, but I would never, ever forget that face. It was burned into my memory.

Rachel. The other woman. Well, one of them.

In a blink, I was sixteen again. Existentially shaken by my father's infidelity, my mom had decided she, Alexis and I would try this thing called church, where the people were supposed to be nice and you could soothe your mortal pain with the ultimate opiate: the promise of an all-knowing deity and a pleasant afterlife. Plus, there were doughnuts.

The chapel was a pretty building, and the songs were kind of fun, but generally, it was boring as hell. Or it was, until one Sunday morning when I looked across the aisle and caught the eye of a boy with dark hair—rakishly long—and dark eyes. When we stood up to sing, I saw he was shorter than me, but it didn't matter. He smiled at the opening bars and my heart burst into flames.

Danny Erickson: the first boy I ever loved. He was a few years older, technically college-aged, but still lived with his parents on ritzy Lake Austin. His dad was a doctor and had lots of money. After that Sunday's service, Danny walked right up to me and asked for my phone number, which had never happened before in my life. He called every night and we talked for hours. When my mom forced us to say good-night, he'd call me again, secretly, and we'd talk for hours more under the sheets. On and on it went.

When it was time for junior prom, he took me to Chili's and then to the dance, and I felt like a walking, talking princess, hair curled into ringlets and a white rose on my wrist.

Afterward, in the early morning hours out on the dock by his house, we sat with our foreheads touching and he told me, in a hushed voice, that he loved me. Then we sneaked back to his room and had sex for the first time, on prom night, like a cliché. But it didn't matter. Danny was the one good thing I had in the midst of my parents' divorce.

I wrote him poetry. I listened to the radio and inserted his name, so every song was about him. I thought, *He's the most handsome boy in the world. He's my everything. We'll love each other forever, no matter the odds.*

Tiny, baby, idiot Lee.

We made plans for college. Well, *I* made plans for college. Danny—who wasn't ambitious about anything other than playing guitar—made plans to go with me. My mom hated the idea; we argued, I held fast.

Fast-forward to April of my senior year. I got the email saying I'd gotten into UT with a scholarship, and Claire was going, too. It was perfect. I didn't even have to move from Austin. I couldn't wait to tell Danny. During the drive to church that Sunday, I could feel the announcement building, big and hot in my chest. I knew he'd tell me he was really going to do it, come with me, and we'd make life plans together.

But Danny wasn't seated in the pews. Which was strange, because his parents were, and they always dragged him. I tamped down the disappointment and told myself I'd call him right after the service.

It dragged and dragged, innumerable songs, the pastor droning on and on. And then, in the middle of a lecture on humility, the great, towering statue of Jesus on a cross behind the pastor started rocking. Everyone—even the pastor—stopped to stare.

No, it wasn't rocking. It was thumping—a rhythmic pattern. Thump, thump, thump.

The pastor began to speak again, resuming his lecture, but all of a sudden, the thumping grew so loud and so hard that a door behind the statue of Jesus flew open and Jesus himself circled—once, twice—then surged forward, aiming straight for the pastor. The whole church gasped as he dived out of the way, missing death by inches in a holy miracle.

Two people toppled out of the open door and rolled onto the stage behind the fallen statue. Naked as the day they were born.

I knew that short body, that rakish head of hair, that freckle on the left butt cheek. It was Danny, tangled up with another girl.

The sight had me by the throat. Without thinking, I stood up and yelled, "How dare you!" But my words were drowned in someone else's words—a girl with fire-engine-red hair from two pews in front of me, who'd launched herself out of her seat, shouting, "I *trusted* you!"

She turned in shock. We stood, blinking at each other, as the eyes of every person in the church turned from the spectacle of the naked people to the spectacle of the two furious girls. And it hit me: I wasn't even the only girlfriend Danny Erickson was cheating on.

As Danny's mother launched out of her pew, red-faced and yelling, "*Daniel Michael Erickson*, not again, I told you last time was the final straw," I decided to hightail it out of the church.

Unfortunately, the red-haired girl had the same idea, so when Danny—wearing pants, at least, and hurriedly buttoning his shirt—came running out of the church, he caught both of us.

"Please! Lee. Rachel." He looked between us. "I'm sorry."

He'd said he *loved* me. But he'd wanted someone else—two

someone elses. He'd taken the precious thing between us and dashed it against the rocks.

"Why?" It was a miracle I could speak at all with my throat closing up.

Danny took a deep breath and tossed his hair. "Look, I have a problem. I didn't tell either of you before because I thought I had a handle on it, but I don't. My therapist says I'm addicted to sex."

Rachel snorted. "Go to hell, Danny. And lose my number." She clenched her fists and stormed off into the parking lot. For some reason, I stayed.

"But you're only twenty years old," I said. For some reason, it was hard to accept that someone so young could have an addiction like that. It was even harder to accept that out of all the boys I could've fallen for, I'd chosen the sex addict from church.

"Apparently, I'm going to struggle with it my whole life. But I'm getting counseling and going to SAA meetings."

"SAA?"

"Sex Addicts Anonymous."

I'd never heard of such a thing, but right then it didn't matter. My despair crashed like a wave. "I thought you loved me."

"I do," he promised, looking at me with incredible earnestness. "The last thing I want is to lose you. I just can't help myself."

It was just like my dad had said: *Sometimes these things happen, and there's nothing you can do.*

When I got home, I collapsed into a pile of limbs on the floor of my bedroom and cried like I'd never cried before, the kind of crying you can only do as a teenager. I had a bottomless well of sorrow to draw from—it just kept coming and coming. The depth of pain was astounding; just as bad, if not worse, than what I'd felt with my dad. And there was nothing I could do to stop it.

That, *there*—that was the worst part. The rawest nerve. I'd given Danny my heart, and it had made me powerless.

Eventually, the well of tears ran dry. I lay there on my bedroom floor, tile cool against my cheek, and closed my eyes, ignoring my mom's gentle knocks on the door. As I drifted off to sleep, I knew one thing for certain: I'd been betrayed twice now, and I never, *ever* wanted to feel this way again. If this was the way the world worked, the least I could do was never allow myself to be taken by surprise.

It hurt all the way until college. But once I was on campus, something shifted. Two weeks into the semester, Danny called me out of the blue to beg for me back and I realized I felt *absolutely nothing.* The well was finally fully tapped. Instead of feeling sad about it, I felt free. I told him no thanks, hung up the phone before he was done reacting and reveled in what would turn out to be the most addictive feeling in the world: *I* was in control. It felt infinitely better to be the one doing the hurting.

Unfortunately, it turned out I'd been staring at Rachel for a long time, adrift in memories. Which probably explained why she did an abrupt about-face and beelined in the opposite direction, nearly mowing down a couple of gauzy-winged fairies in the process.

Oh, well. I didn't blame her. I was a reminder of a humiliating experience—maybe the most humiliating experience of her life. I wished I could say the same.

"Here you go," came a voice, and I jumped, my first thought, *Danny? But how?*

But it was only Ben, holding two literal sheep's horns.

He gave me a quizzical look.

"Dozed off," I lied, accepting one of the horns. "What is this?"

"Peek inside," he said, and tipped the end of his horn to his mouth.

I looked inside—and found wine.

"But we're on the clock," I sputtered.

Ben waved a hand. "We collected a ridiculous number of signatures and gave out all our pamphlets. Janus's office already wants to talk. Kaitlyn's got the rest. It's Stoner o'clock."

He tugged me down onto a stone bench, the legs carved like bending leaves. The bench was shaded by a large oak tree, and the stone was cool on my thighs through the layers of my dress.

We sipped our wine in silence, watching people walk by. I made sure not to look anyone in the eyes so as not to trigger any more humiliating portals to the past.

Ben turned to me. There was a ring of red wine along the outline of his lips. He was close enough that I could feel the heat from his body as he shook his head. "I say this *extremely* grudgingly, but maybe I was wrong when I said having to hang out with you was worse than the worst thing I could imagine. It's not all bad." He nudged the Beerwolf. "There's swag."

The look in his eyes was the same look from the night we'd met. Hours after I'd crushed him in tequila shots, and he'd crushed me in darts, and we'd woven our way through the other law students, dismantling their drunk arguments one by one, grinning at each other while their cheeks flushed with indignation, two discursive outlaws. This was the look from the end of the night, when he'd gone home, and I'd stubbornly followed. He'd opened the door to his studio apartment, and I'd walked in—and suddenly, for the first time all night, I turned shy. I was overwhelmed by the feeling that I'd accidentally stumbled onto something important, *someone* important, and I was in over my head. Instead of moving to his bed, I sat on the concrete floor with my back against the wall.

He hadn't said anything, just dropped down beside me. And knocked his knee against mine. When I'd finally braved a look, this was what I'd seen. *This* face. Unfairly beautiful Ben Laderman studying me at close range, his eyes shining with amused challenge.

Heat spiked through me. I slipped my hand into his like I'd done that night long ago and laced our fingers.

Ben's hand tensed. I blinked and realized instantly what I'd done.

"Oh, *shit.*" I yanked my hand back. "I'm sorry. I wasn't thinking. I was working off muscle memory. I didn't mean it."

"It's okay." Ben put up placating palms. "No worries. I know you know I have a—Sarah."

"Sarah, yes, exactly." I seized on her name like it was a talisman that could ward off this crush of embarrassment.

"It's just, I don't think of you that way anymore," Ben said. "After the way things ended—or, really, the way they imploded—I told myself I'd never be with another girl like you. I figured you felt the same way, because you're the one who, you know, did what you did back then. But if this is weird for you, I'll recuse myself and hand the campaign to someone else."

"No," I practically shouted, causing heads to turn. "I mean, there's no need. I'm telling you, it was a dumb mistake. I wasn't even thinking. There are no feelings here. *Ugh,*" I gagged. "See? Even the idea is gross."

Ben studied me.

I waved at my chest. "I'm basically dead in there, anyway. You have nothing to worry about. Except for the fact that I will *literally* kill you if you resign from the campaign."

Finally, Ben smiled, though it was hesitant. "Okay. If you're sure."

Jesus Christ, me. What the hell had happened? The entire point of working with Ben on this campaign was to rewrite our ending, which meant proving I was no longer the emotional, irrational girl I'd been in grad school. Yet between the bar, Comic-Con and now this, being around Ben was getting under my skin. What was next—would I crack open my rib cage and yell, *I see you're back, dangerous man! Please, why don't you play with my most vital, unguarded organ?* This was possibly more humiliating than Danny and the church sex scandal.

Lee Stone: One Thousand and One Ways to Self-Destruct, A Memoir.

Well, I was not that girl anymore. I gritted my teeth and downed my wine-horn, wiping my mouth with the back of my hand. "Ben. Trust me. I couldn't care less about you, except for whether or not you're going to help me win."

Ben's fingers flexed, and his lips tightened. He looked down at his horn and tossed the contents in the grass. "Right. Good. As long as we're on the same page."

He crushed his horn in his hands. "Probably time to call it a day." Then he got up and walked away, leaving me alone on the bench.

7

The Height of Diplomacy

Saturday night I vowed I was going to get Alexis out of the house and into a goddamn restaurant to drink sexy wine and eat pasta like a functioning adult, even if I had to club her over the head and carry her in on my shoulder.

It had been ages since she'd left the couch and seen the light of day, so I figured the light of night was probably a good transition step. It had taken nearly an hour to convince her to brush her hair and put on non-pajama clothes, and I'd only succeeded when I promised she could wear my best black dress with the plunging neckline.

If Daisy David could have gotten her hands on Alexis, she definitely would have traded me in as Belle. Maybe given me Mrs. Potts's cracked-up son Chip instead, which honestly fit my energy better. My sister and I had the same thick brown hair and big brown eyes, like our mom, but Alexis's were framed by Disney-princess lashes and flecked with green. She was an elementary school librarian, so plenty bookish, and also a sentimental sap who always tried to see the best in people.

It was her greatest flaw. And the source of the tension that had kept us distant for years, even though we lived in the same city. I'd seen more of Alexis in the last few weeks than in the last two years combined. I was determined to make good use of our time.

Which is why hearing from the condescending host of Bitter Honey that there were absolutely no tables for us—even at the sexy-late hour of 9:00 p.m.—was so very jarring.

"Are you sure?" I pressed. "We'll take a crammed corner. Or sit in the kitchen." My face brightened. "Or definitely the bar."

"We're fully booked," said the host, without even looking at me. "Next time I recommend reservations."

"We can go somewhere else," Alexis said, folding her arms over her exposed chest like a nun who'd accidentally walked into a bordello.

I didn't want to go anywhere else. Bitter Honey was one of the hottest restaurants in Austin. It was dimly lit, with a beautiful wine list and giant wineglasses you had to hold with both hands. The music was dark and pulsing, and most important, it was filled to the brim with hot guys who worked in tech and politics. Guys I was determined Alexis would meet tonight.

I scanned the restaurant, trying to think of some way to steal a table—should I let it drop that I was an important food critic for *Bon Appétit*?—when I saw a tall figure in a dark sports coat and whipped back around.

"Yes, let's leave immediately." I took Alexis's arm and practically dragged her toward the door.

"Stoner? And is that *Lex*?"

I had no choice but to turn in the direction of the voice I knew so well, because Alexis and I were intertwined and she was spinning around a mile a minute, her face lighting with delight.

"Ben Laderman? Holy *shit.* It's been forever!"

Alexis dropped me like a sack of hot potatoes and ran to Ben, who folded her in a hug. I stood there, tapping my heel, absolutely not noticing how perfectly Ben's sports coat fit his shoulders.

Ben mussed Alexis's hair. "You're so grown-up!"

"When did you move back to Austin?" Alexis shot me a dirty look. "Lee didn't say a word."

I rolled my eyes. "Sorry I didn't mention Ben's stalking me."

He threw his hands up. "I swear, coming here wasn't my idea. It was—"

A beautiful blonde woman materialized by Ben's side. She wore an expensive red sheath dress and dripped with David Yurman, the exact set I could remember coveting in college. She *looked* like a lobbyist. In fact, I tried very, very hard not to think about the fact that she looked exactly like the kind of woman a GOP scientist might build in a laboratory.

"Hi," said the woman brightly, extending her arm. "I'm Sarah."

Of course she was. She had a blinding smile that matched Ben's.

"Alexis." Lex pumped Sarah's hand enthusiastically. She loved making new friends.

When Sarah held her hand out to me, I observed it was quite soft. Her nails were also the exact red shade of her dress, a form of girl magic that had always confounded me.

Ben nodded toward me. "That's Stoner. Lee Stone."

Sarah's eyes lit up. "The stuffed-animal girl!"

"Uh," I sputtered, "I wouldn't call me *that*—"

"We couldn't get a table, so we were just leaving," Alexis

interrupted. "Don't want to hold you up. It was so nice to run into you."

"Oh, but you have to stay!" Sarah insisted. She looked between Ben, Alexis and me. "Ben said the stuffed-animal girl was an old friend."

When the hell did I get so horribly rebranded?

"Our other friends had to cancel at the last minute. We have two empty seats at our table. Please." Sarah made little prayer hands. "Join us."

How could you say no to that display without looking like a terrible person? I suddenly understood why Sarah worked at a top lobbying firm.

Ben met my eyes, and I could see my own thoughts—*Please, God, no*—mirrored in them. He started to say, "I don't think—"

But Alexis had already jumped in, playing the world's worst wing-woman. "We'd love to. Lee was so sad to leave. Right, Lee?"

Curse my well-known love of fancy dinners. And my extremely believable performance of casual indifference after I'd broken up with Ben. I'd clearly convinced Alexis he meant nothing to me.

Which is also what I'd told Ben himself, just days ago at the Renaissance Festival. And it was obviously true. So I couldn't go around refusing a perfectly civil dinner invitation from his girlfriend, could I? That would mean I cared.

I pasted a smile on my face. "Yay. Look at us. A little foursome."

Christ.

I would be on my best behavior. I would be on my best behavior. My best, best, best…

I used two hands to upend the wine bottle and shake the last drips out, catching the waiter's eye and waving. "Hello, yes, can we please have another?"

Alexis widened her eyes but wisely did not comment on the fact that this was the table's third bottle of wine. I was going to sink a week's paycheck into this tab, but I had no regrets. This was survival.

"I'll actually have a Jameson, neat," Ben said. "Thank you very much." He'd been a waiter in undergrad, and now he always smiled a little too long and bright at restaurant staff to convey solidarity.

Sarah turned to us. Her lips and teeth were stained purple with wine, like a vampire's—but dammit, it was endearing. "He always switches to whiskey when he wants to make it a wild night. Of course, wild for us nowadays means a late dinner."

I was not going to say a single word about how many whiskey-soaked nights Ben and I had shared, wild from start to finish. Because I was on my best behavior.

Instead, I guzzled wine.

"Someone's single-handedly keeping Napa afloat," Alexis muttered. She clearly couldn't hold out for too long against her natural instinct to be an annoying little sister.

I tipped her wineglass at her. "*You're* the one who should be drinking. Come on. I want you to chug until everyone in this restaurant is attractive."

"Oh, are you single?" Sarah asked. "I know lots of nice guys at work."

Lobbyists are paid to be nice, which doesn't count, I definitely didn't say out loud.

Because that would have been mean, and here was the deal: Sarah was really, really fucking sweet. And smart. And funny. All through dinner, she'd asked interesting questions and said interesting things. Even if it was a side effect of her profession, I was sold. In another Ben-less life, we could've been friends.

"I just got out of a relationship. It was a really bad breakup." Alexis looked down into her wineglass for a beat and then chugged it like a champ. "My boyfriend cheated on me with a coworker."

Well. There it was, out in the open: the adultery of it all. Ben's face turned bright red, and he looked down at his plate.

"That's horrible," Sarah said, patting Alexis's hand. "My last boyfriend cheated on me, too. What about you, Stoner?"

She'd insisted on calling me by my nickname all night, even though we'd only just met. It was breeding a sense of familiarity that was both unearned and totally working on me.

"Anyone seen any good movies lately?" Ben asked, tugging at the collar of his shirt.

"What *about* me?" I asked.

"Have you ever had an ex who cheated?"

Alexis snorted into her wine.

"What about Halloween?" Ben folded his napkin. "That's coming up. Let's go around the table and everyone can say what they're going to be."

Cheating exes—*dangerous* territory. I carefully avoided Ben's eyes. "There's been…cheating. In the past. But I don't do relationships anymore, so it's not an issue."

"*Anymore* being the operative word." Alexis leaned in. "I can still remember the good old days when Lee literally kicked Andy Elliot down a flight of stairs after she caught him cheating."

"I didn't kick him."

She waved. "Kicked, pushed, spooked. Whatever. The point is, he fell."

Ah, Andrew Elliot. My college boyfriend and the Third Major Heartbreak. So kind of Alexis to bring him up.

I could see myself now: sophomore-year-of-college Stoner, newly transitioned out of my freshman-year goth phase—a fuck-you to the cold, cruel world that brought me my dad and Danny Erickson—and into my Tracy Flick stage. There were sweater vests, pleated skirts, polo shirts. There were a lot of hair flips. Most of all, there was my burning desire to climb to the top of the college political food chain. I was dying to conquer student government.

Enter Andy Elliot, the sitting treasurer. Even among the tens of thousands of undergrads at UT, Andy stood out. He was tall, blond and handsome, with a swimmer's lean body. I'd never met anyone more naturally inclined to politics than Andy. He was next-level friendly and could remember anyone's name after only meeting them once. He had a devoted fan club on campus. I'd melted under his star power, even as I took notes.

After a month of sitting next to him at student government meetings, making casual small talk and just *happening* to run into him at his frat parties on the weekends, I made my move.

"Andy?" I asked, after the meeting ended.

He turned that megawatt smile on me. "Lee. What's up?"

"You wouldn't be interested in running for president and VP with me, would you?"

His eyes lit up. "How did you know? I was actually looking for a girl to join my ticket. Shore up the sorority vote."

"Right," I said, trying to push down the butterflies as his eyes scanned me head to toe. "That settles it. We should campaign together."

Andy stuck out his hand. "Welcome aboard, VP."

Well. I had actually intended to run as president with Andy as my VP, but at that point, I'd already shaken his hand, so it felt like a binding deal. Andy was more popular, anyway. He seemed like a natural fit, so...it made sense.

From that point on, we started spending more and more time together, planning our platform, making posters, securing endorsements. The road wasn't always smooth—I wanted to campaign on issues like raising the minimum wage for UT staff and getting the administration to commit to using 80 percent green power. Andy argued we needed to run on issues like getting better bands for Forty Acres Fest, and we could do the boring stuff once we got elected. I usually ended up folding because I worried Andy was right; and each time I did, things between us became harmonious again. Eventually, one thing led to another, and then one night, Andy pushed the markers and flyers off his desk and sat me atop it, kissing me with such verve it was like we'd just found out we'd won.

And then we did win. We dated all of sophomore year, through the campaign and the next year, we were kind of famous around campus as the president and VP couple. It was glamorous. We were in love; in fact, compared to what I felt for larger-than-life, presidential Andy, Danny Erickson seemed like a stupid high school crush.

However. It was hard to ditch the lessons I'd learned from Danny and my father. Once the initial buzz wore off, I realized, with horror, that there was no better candidate for cheating than the überpopular Andy Elliot. Girls threw themselves at him constantly.

So I launched a campaign of my own—a stealth mission of phone checking, email monitoring and social media snooping. I made Andy call me multiple times whenever we spent the night apart. I became extremely uncomfortable with the idea of him going to all of his frat parties alone, so I tried to keep glued to his side.

I may have become obsessed with the idea that Andy would cheat. And the longer I went without evidence, the more convinced I became that I simply wasn't looking hard enough. So I doubled my efforts, waiting each night until Andy fell asleep to sneak to his laptop and comb through all his files and accounts.

But the proof didn't end up being digital. One day, I sat

down to pee and screamed bloody murder. It felt like the lower half of my body was on fire. I practically ran to the health center and demanded a urine test. The results came back, and sure enough, it was chlamydia.

Normal girls might have experienced embarrassment or even shame. But not me. I ended the call with the doctor and raised my fist high in the air. I'd been right all along. Andy was cheating. I was strangely relieved to find the world did, indeed, operate by the rules I'd learned, even if I didn't like them.

I vowed that from that moment on, I would always assume the worst, like I had with Andy. That way, I would see the heartbreak coming from a mile away. But first, a confrontation was in order. Andy was at his frat house that night, lording over another one of their silly theme parties.

Before I went, I needed liquid courage. I eyed the bottle of Popov vodka that Mac, Claire and I kept for occasional drinks, and decided: *Bottoms up.* It was awful. Truly, the most disgusting taste. But it had a wonderful numbing effect, turning the pain in my heart into something distant and more manageable.

So I took it with me. And when I strode into Andy's frat house, the very first thing I saw was Mr. President, locking tongues with another girl. In plain sight. Not only a betrayal, but an infuriating undermining of my public reputation.

"Andrew Elliot," I'd yelled, and startled him apart from the girl.

His face fell when he saw me; but, just as quickly, he moved to righteous indignation. "It's your fault!" he called, crossing his arms. "You're so possessive all the time. It's suffocating."

Well. That was too embarrassing a public statement to endure without a response. So I hefted the handle of vodka and chucked it at him.

It didn't hit him, is the important part. Legally speaking.

It smacked into the stair below Andy and startled the hell out of him, which is when he lost his cool and tripped down the long and bumpy frat staircase to land at my feet.

He was *fine*. His broken leg healed well before the year was out. Our political dynasty, however, never recovered.

But I'd learned several important lessons. One, cheating and romantic disappointment were truly, truly inevitable. Two, never let a man compromise your political ambitions. And three, alcohol was a problem solver.

"It was a badass move, is all I'm saying," Alexis continued. "I only regret my ex Chris and I live in a one-story house."

Sarah nodded. "This is why people can't be friends with their exes. Too much unresolved emotion."

Like an angel descending from heaven, our waiter dropped off Ben's Jameson and poured my wineglass up to the brim.

"That's true." Alexis gestured around the table. "Except for Lee and Ben, obviously."

"What?" Sarah was confused.

I slid my chair back. "I'm going to go—"

"They dated and now they're friends, otherwise we wouldn't be sitting here."

"—jump out a window," I finished.

Sarah looked between Ben and me. "You *dated*?"

Ben stared at her without blinking. "I definitely told you."

"You didn't." Sarah's voice notched higher, and Ben swallowed his words. He wasn't even going to argue his case. What the hell? This was not the Ben I was used to.

Sarah turned to me. "I'm sorry. I feel like an idiot."

"You shouldn't." I inched my chair back a little more. "But we can just go ahead and pay our part of the check—"

"Who broke up with whom?" Sarah asked, looking between Ben and me.

"He did," I said, at the same time Ben said, "She did."

I eyed him. "Uh, Mr. Revisionist History. You obviously dumped me when you fled to California."

Sarah's wide owl-eyes swooped to Ben. "*That's* why you moved to Palo Alto?"

"No, you dumped *me*." Ben ducked his head and lowered his voice. "When you cheated on me with Connor."

"What?" I squawked, volume definitely courtesy of the wine. "I did not. I assumed when you yelled at me in front of everyone at the graduation party that you were totally, 100 percent dumping me."

Ben's face flushed. "And *I* assumed when you walked out of the graduation party with Connor, leaving me all alone with everyone watching, you were definitely, no doubt about it, breaking up with *me*."

"Does this mean y'all are still technically dating?" Alexis asked.

"I certainly hope not," Sarah said.

The waiter circled the table and held out a small menu with a flourish. "May I tempt you with dessert?"

Sarah shoved back from the table, her face panicked. "Oh my God, it's McGraw. My boss."

We all turned to see what she was looking at. Sure enough, Kenneth McGraw, notorious Texas lobbyist and head of Sarah's firm, was walking in our direction.

"We have a lovely chocolate tart," said the oblivious waiter.

Sarah ducked. "I can't let him see me. He'll ask about the pipeline and I'm nowhere near where I should be on negotiations."

My head swiveled like that little girl in *The Exorcist*. "The *Lonestar* pipeline?"

She looked at me, alarmed, like I would grill her on her progress, too. "Yes. I'm helping Lonestar convince the House to approve it."

My blood temperature surged from 98.6 to boiling. "You're trying to get it *passed*? As in, yes, pipeline?"

"Lee," Ben warned.

I waved a hand. "Oh, *I'm sorry.* You're working to pass a major clean energy bill and your girlfriend just said she's trying to put in a pipeline. How's that not a conflict of interest?"

"Oh, shit," Alexis said. "It just clicked. Lee and Ben—you two are *working* together?"

"Ben, you actually support this pipeline?" I asked.

"Of course not," he said. "I'm totally against it. It's not Sarah's favorite thing, either, but it's her job. Two months ago, she was working on a bill to protect teachers' unions. That's how it works."

"Our most popular item is the passion-fruit crème brûlée," tried the waiter, looking at us a little desperately.

"The pipeline has bipartisan support," Sarah whispered, still trying to hide from McGraw. "We're giving the House funding for a statewide after-school program in exchange."

"Fuck *bipartisan support.*" I felt every liquid ounce of the wine I'd poured down my throat. "That's code for an empty, vacuous deal where each side claims to win. And the loser is always the people."

"Stoner, you're being extremely reductive." Ben gripped his glass. "You know politics literally doesn't work without compromise."

"There are some things you don't compromise on. And the *Lonestar pipeline* is one of them."

My high-octave "Lonestar pipeline" must've caught McGraw's attention, because his head turned in our direction.

"Oh, *no*," Sarah breathed.

McGraw lumbered over. His nickname was the Greaser, both for all the palm greasing he did and his unfortunate comb-over. "Ms. Sarah Drake, what a coincidence—"

"Oh—my—God," Alexis shrieked, standing straight up out

of her chair. She knocked over her glass of wine and almost clipped McGraw in the nose.

"What the hell, Alexis?"

She pointed out the restaurant window, white as a ghost. "It's Chris. And his new girlfriend."

We all looked where she was pointing, even the waiter and McGraw. Sure enough, strolling outside our window was Alexis's snake of an ex, Chris Tuttle, his arm around a petite, dark-haired woman. As we watched, he leaned over and kissed her forehead.

Alexis made a shuddering sound, her eyes welling with tears.

And that was *it*. Even though Chris was just doing what all people in relationships did—straying, messing up—and Alexis would be better off steeling her heart and giving up on the idea of happily-ever-after, that didn't matter right now. It was clear by the look on her face that she was devastated. Chris was hurting my little sister.

Not on my watch.

I launched out of my chair and darted from the table, dodging fast-moving waiters carrying plates from the kitchen. I was vaguely aware that Ben had stood up the instant he saw me moving, and now he was only a few steps behind; but my anger at Chris and what he'd done to Alexis's stupid, fragile heart was giving me tunnel vision.

I swung open the entrance to Bitter Honey and ran down the sidewalk, shouting, *"Chris Tuttle."*

Chris spun around. The woman beside him looked at me like I was about to mug them.

"Lee? Is that you?"

"How dare you?" I raged. Anger was welling inside me, fast and hot, much more than I'd expected. "It's been a few weeks and you're already out in public with the woman you cheated on Alexis with?"

The woman drew a sharp breath.

Chris blanched. "I didn't think—"

"What?" I interrupted. "That Alexis would catch you? Well, she's in that restaurant, trying to recover from the misery of you cheating on her, and who does she have to see? *You*, you lying, good-for-nothing asshole."

I waved at the window of Bitter Honey, but unfortunately, Alexis was no longer sitting at our table, staring, which would have made my point much stronger. Only McGraw was, and the waiter. And the rest of the dining room.

Ben rushed up to my side and put a hand on my elbow. "Lee, I know you're angry, but now's not the time."

"Then when is?"

Chris recovered from his shock and glared at me, crossing his arms over his chest. "I'm allowed to walk down the street with anyone I choose. Mind your own business, Lee. Actually, why don't you tend to your own business? If anyone needs a lecture about their love life, it's you."

The anger flared inside me. My chest heaved. "I have no idea why Alexis put up with you for four years, but good riddance." I glanced at the dark-haired woman. "You're in for a world of mediocre sex, from what I've heard. If I were you, I'd jump ship."

"Lee." It was my sister's voice, sharp and horrified.

I turned to Alexis, who was now standing a step from Ben, her Disney-princess lashes wet with tears. Sarah stood a few feet behind her, wide eyes glued to Ben.

"Did you put her up to this?" Chris looked at Alexis. "You don't talk to me for weeks and then you sic your crazy sister on me? If you have something to say, say it."

Alexis's mouth dropped open. She was at a loss for words, clearly not expecting Chris to turn his bite on her.

"Grow a spine," Chris said, and Alexis's face shuttered.

Nope. I balled my hand into a fist and punched Chris in his smug, snake face.

"Holy shit," everyone cried, even the people behind the window at Bitter Honey, though it was barely audible through the glass. Even me, because I was pretty sure I'd just broken my hand on Chris's cheekbone.

Chris took a staggering step back and clutched his face. "You hit me, you crazy bitch!"

"Lee, how could you?" Alexis's hands flew to her mouth. She spun and fled down the street.

Ben seized my shoulders and practically dragged me backward. "Come on. We need to leave before he has you arrested for assault."

"You're insane!" Chris shouted after me.

"You're insanely punchable," I yelled back, twisting in Ben's grip.

Ben pulled me past Sarah. "I beg you, please settle the bill and I will make sure Lee pays us back."

She nodded reflexively, still in shock. "Sorry about your boss," I called, but by then, Ben was pulling me around the street corner and I wasn't sure she heard.

As soon as we were out of sight, alone in the little alley next to Bitter Honey, Ben released me. I wasn't expecting it and fell back against the restaurant's brick wall.

"What's wrong with you?" Ben was only half facing me, and his voice was quiet, not loud like I would've thought. His black hair shone in the amber streetlight. "You've gone off the deep end."

I straightened and squared my shoulders. "Chris hurt Alexis. That's what's wrong."

He turned, and the look on his face was serious enough that my throat went dry. "No, it's not. I'm talking about the bigger thing. The thing underneath. There was always something going on with you that you wouldn't talk about when we dated. Now you're hauling off and punching people? Clearly, whatever it is, it's only gotten worse."

There was a flash of pain as I thought of my parents, the way my dad betrayed us and everything that had happened since. "There's nothing wrong with me," I gritted out.

"If you were just consistent, I could predict it. But one minute you're disavowing monogamy, and the next you're punching Chris in the face for cheating on your sister. You act like everything's a joke and nothing matters, then you criticize Sarah for doing the wrong thing. I don't understand you."

Even though Ben wasn't yelling, my heart was pounding in my chest. I needed the focus off me. I needed to pivot. "What about you? You used to have integrity. You never used to be a shill, and now you're working for a Republican."

He laughed in disbelief. "You work *with* us."

"Because there's no other choice."

"I told you, working for Grover is the best way to change Texas."

"What about the fact that you're dating someone who's doing something you don't believe in? You used to care about what was right. Remember mock trials? You never let anyone get away with anything."

"Mock trials were a game. All I cared about was winning, and proving myself to all those stuck-up, silver-spoon people."

"So that's it—you're indifferent? Where's your passion?"

"I have lots of passion. But I'm also a grown-up. I make compromises because I live in a world where people disagree and I want to get things done. I don't want to just tread water in an ocean of idealism. Even if it comes with a lovely sense of superiority to keep me afloat."

"You're a sellout."

"Grow up, Lee. And I say this as a friend—figure out your shit."

"My shit," I blurted, "is that all my life, I've been faced with a parade of men I've been expected to bend over backward for, chase and idolize. If I want something, I have to put on a show, or compromise, or trick them into it. Governor Mane, all the state senators, every guy I've ever dated. My dad. Whether it's a bill or a relationship, you're all the same. So forgive me if I'm sick of playing nice with assholes." My chest heaved. I didn't know where this was coming from.

Ben stepped closer, eyes searching my face. I could see his Adam's apple rise and fall in the column of his throat, and when he spoke, his voice was rough. "I don't want you to feel that way about me."

Well, he was right about one thing. I was all over the map. Because, like a flipped switch, my anger dissolved and suddenly all I wanted was to be held.

Wordlessly, Ben opened his arms and I stepped into them. He hugged me tight, one hand fitting into the space between my shoulder blades and the other cupping the back of my head.

"Just a pity hug," he murmured into my hair. "Don't get any ideas."

"Shut up." Hugging Ben was somehow better than I remembered. He held me close, like he really meant it.

I pressed my face into the crook of his neck. He smelled like a cologne that was new to me, and a little bit like whiskey. I stayed there until finally he drew back and looked down at me.

"Sarah's waiting, so I need to go. Are you and Lex okay to Uber home?"

I looked into his eyes for a heart-pounding moment before

I realized that wasn't a good idea. I lowered my eyes to the inches of collarbone that were visible under his shirt collar, then thought better of it and looked at the street. "Of course. If she hasn't left already."

He stepped away. Obviously, to go back to Sarah. Beautiful, grown-up Sarah, whom he lived with, who'd inspired him to move back to Texas. Who probably hadn't punched anybody in her life.

Maybe I couldn't exactly explain why I did the things I did. But as I watched Ben stride out of the alley, I knew I didn't regret them. Not any of it. Not ever.

Because if I let in one sliver of doubt, I would be forced to examine all the choices I'd made. And there was a very real chance that if I did that, my life would come tumbling down.

So, truly—regret was not an option.

8

Anyone Could Have Thought of That

The governor of Texas was irate. He sat next to Dakota at the sleek white conference table in Lise's largest conference room, frowning at us and tapping his fingers. For a frightening moment, I wondered if Kenneth McGraw had leaked what happened at Bitter Honey. The lobbyist surely had a direct line to the governor; maybe he'd called to report that two people campaigning in the governor's name had been involved in a very public street brawl. Grover certainly looked annoyed enough.

Though the governor had walked in with Dakota, he still seemed out of place inside Lise, with its angular, modern furniture, stark white coloring and subway-tiled walls. The aesthetic of the office was minimalist and futuristic, and Governor Mane, with his excessively broad linebacker shoulders and ever-present bolo tie, did not match.

Ben, on the other hand, looked right at home in his transparent glasses and another bold suit, this time olive green. He hadn't said anything to me beyond a simple hello when he walked in, and in the few tense minutes while we waited for Wendy to arrive, he'd avoided my eyes.

Fine. All business, then.

The governor cleared his throat. "Bad news. Janus isn't going to support the bill. He called to say it was too risky with his impending election."

"What?" My jaw dropped. "But we went to every festival in Abilene for weeks. Everything from Comic-Con to the Polish Festival to Shakespeare on the Green. We got thousands of signatures."

"And the ads have been performing great." Ben looked equally stunned. "Janus's Twitter is blowing up. I heard his phone's ringing three times the normal volume."

Governor Mane drew his hands together. "Well, it's not enough to convince him the bill's popular enough to take a swing. Man's so risk averse I'm starting to wonder if anything short of an endorsement from God would move him."

Ben's eyes lit up.

"Is there nothing you can do?" Dakota put a hand on the governor's shoulder. "I hate to say it, but is there any pressure you can put on him?"

"Trust me, I applied a thousand psi, but there's no talking sense to a politician when his election's on the line."

"Is there anything we can give him?" Wendy asked coolly. "A bill he wants that we can trade for? Anything that isn't too egregiously bad."

I remembered Sarah saying that she was working on negotiating with the House to trade the Lonestar pipeline for an after-school program, and felt a creeping sense of dirtiness. If this wheeling and dealing was real politics, maybe I didn't like it, after all.

"Hold that thought." Ben stood abruptly from the conference table. He looked excited. "Just—give me a few days. I have an idea." He heaved his shoulder bag and beelined for the door.

Ben had a brainstorm and he wasn't even going to *tell* me about it? Or even make eye contact, so I could try to discern the clues in his face?

Screw weeks of persuading fanboys, chucking axes and reciting *Much Ado About Nothing*, apparently. Maybe it was because of the fiasco at Bitter Honey, but the tentative comradery we'd forged over the first leg of the campaign seemed to be over. It looked like it was every woman for herself again.

The rest of us watched through the glass wall as Ben hustled down the hallway, moving urgently, like a schoolboy late for class. We tracked him all the way until he made it past the receptionist's desk and disappeared.

Dakota, Wendy and I turned to Governor Mane.

"Care to comment?" Wendy looked bemused.

He shrugged. "Benny boy has an idea. Can't be bad, right?"

Oh, yes, it could. But mostly just for me.

Dakota lifted her champagne glass, smile as buoyant as the tiny bubbles that fizzed and raced to the top. "Here's to Ben, whose brilliant plan won Senator Janus over and saved the day."

"Saved our *asses*," the governor corrected.

"Hear, hear," Wendy said. "One step closer to passing the bill."

Everyone raised their champagne glasses—even me, though I was prepared to fling myself out of my chair if anyone asked me to make a toast. I suspected it would literally kill me if I had to swallow the anger boiling inside to push some words out. We were sitting at a lovely patio table at Clementine's, a favorite lunch spot for Austin politicos, but the gentle October sunshine and breeze were wasted on me.

Obediently, I joined them in clinking my glass in the center of the table. Through the sparkling wine, I could see Ben sitting across from me, beaming like he'd just won the lottery.

I was officially losing our competition. Ben had catfished me with friendship, lulling me into a false sense of calm, only to sneak in and steal Janus's yes right from under my nose. I think it was safe to say I now hated him with a renewed vigor.

"I'm only glad Willie remembered me and is such a big supporter of the environment." Ben's tone was overly modest. I could see right through him.

Dakota tugged on his sleeve. "Show us the Instagram feed again. I love it."

Ben almost fumbled his phone into his soup, he grabbed it so fast. I rolled my eyes. He held up his phone so the whole table could see. The mural's Instagram account was already up on his screen, which probably meant he'd been checking it lovingly all morning. Gross.

It turned out my ex-boyfriend-turned-nemesis-turned-partner-turned-nemesis-again Ben Laderman had the gall to be in the possession of Willie Nelson's personal phone number, thanks to a deal Willie made with Google a few years back to use one of his songs in an ad campaign. According to Ben, he and Willie had hit it off during legal negotiations—which was obviously a lie, because who liked anything to do with *legal negotiations*?

Nevertheless, when Ben heard Governor Mane say that nothing short of an endorsement from God would sway Janus, he thought to himself, *I'll do us one better*, and picked up the phone to call Willie. And Willie actually answered.

Ben laid it all out for him—the Green Machine bill and how we needed to sway Janus—and Willie agreed to record a video praising Senator Janus for supporting clean energy. He even wrote and performed a song about it, which Ben swore was all Willie's idea.

The video went viral so fast that some enterprising street artist was inspired to paint a mural on the side of a building in downtown Abilene: Willie with his arm around Janus, a green, fertile Texas landscape in the background and the title of Willie's song "Heroes of the Future" in the foreground. The mural was an overnight hit with tourists, who lined up to have their pictures taken in front of it. Now the damn thing had its own Instagram account.

Janus had never been cooler in his life, and he was elated. He'd called the governor within an hour of the Instagram account going up and agreed to support the bill.

Ben kept all of this hidden from me until my news alerts for the Green Machine blew up and I called him, demanding to know what he was up to. By then, it was too late. The damage was done. The first yes of the campaign had gone to him.

To add insult to injury, Dakota had insisted on meeting for a celebratory lunch at the exact restaurant I'd imagined us gathering to celebrate *me* and my policy win and my eventual promotion.

"Look." Wendy pointed to Ben's screen. "Janus even got his picture taken at the mural. Painted Janus and real Janus, side by side."

Ben nodded, clicking his phone dark. "He made it his profile picture across all his social media channels."

"There's no backing out now," Mane said. "Not when all of Willie's Twitter fans will line up to roast him if he changes his mind."

Dakota winked at the governor, then turned to Ben. "You know, with all this talent, we just might have to steal you for

Lise. We have a VP of public affairs position I think you'd be perfect for."

No. She. Didn't. Dakota's words shot through my chest like a quiver full of arrows, piercing my heart. I pressed a hand to my chest, expecting to find it ravaged.

"Don't even joke about that," the governor said, resting one of his large, football-player hands over Dakota's slim wrist. "You can't have him."

I didn't have the bandwidth to wonder at Governor Mane's overly familiar gesture. Because I was having a hard time breathing. I couldn't sit here and watch Ben steal everything I wanted.

"Excuse me," I said, standing so fast my chair tipped back and almost fell over. My napkin floated off my lap to the ground. "I have an important call I can't be late for."

Wendy narrowed her eyes. "What call? The meeting with the Canada team isn't until four."

I bent and picked up the napkin, wringing it in my hands. "It's, uh, the *New York Times*. They're interested in a story on the Herschel motor. Surprise!"

Ah, shit. The Herschel motor was Dakota's latest invention, named after famed trailblazing astronomer Caroline Herschel. It increased our cars' mileage by a third and was going to revolutionize the market. Other than popping in for Green Machine updates, Dakota had been spending all her time perfecting it. Now I was going to have to pitch the *Times* real fucking fast.

"That's great," Dakota gushed.

Wendy nodded, grudgingly impressed.

"Tease the Green Machine while you're at it." Governor Mane steepled his fingers on the table. "Wouldn't be a bad idea to build some buzz for the bill with a national outlet."

"Oh, definitely." I could mention the Green Machine in my nonexistent phone interview with the *New York Times*, no problem. Easy. I tossed the napkin on the table and practically tripped getting away. "'Bye now."

The minute I made it out the front doors of Clementine's, I bent over and put my hands on my knees to catch my breath. What was wrong with me? I hated losing, sure, but normally I used setbacks like rocket fuel to double my efforts and do better. Right now, I couldn't squash the overwhelming feeling that I'd been betrayed and abandoned, and it was throwing me.

I was taking this too personally. Just because Ben had been nicer to me lately didn't mean our competition was null and void. He'd been consistent on his end. All the flip-flopping and assumptions had been in my head.

"Stoner, wait up."

I turned to find Ben jogging over, and my heart dropped.

I straightened and took off through the parking lot. "I'm not going to plug your Willie Nelson mural to the *New York Times*, so don't bother asking."

"You don't have a call with the *Times*."

I whipped around, almost falling into a row of motorized scooters. Which would have been disastrous, since they all would have tipped like dominoes.

"I don't, but I perfectly well could have, so I resent your assumption."

Ben grinned, showing off his dimples. "We've got to stop hanging out like this—me chasing you out of restaurants."

I crossed my arms. "Too soon, Ben. Read the room. Alexis only just started speaking to me again. It's been a chilly few days at home and I'd like to put the whole thing behind me."

I did not ask what Sarah had said to him after he finally returned to her from the alley, because I was not curious. Nope. Didn't care that she probably thought I was bananas. It's not like we were going to meet at the mall to shop for outfits to celebrate her future pipeline deal or anything. What would even fit the occasion—a power suit stitched together from clubbed baby seals?

"I thought you'd be stoked about the endorsement." Ben still wore that lottery-winning grin. "Janus said yes. *We got him!* The bill lives."

"Jesus, how many congratulations do you need? Would you like me to throw you a parade? Hire a skywriter?"

Ben's smile wobbled. "I got us Willie Nelson."

I took my chances and leaned against one of the scooters. "Yes, well, it's extremely annoying when a coworker you dislike is good at their job."

"Just because I said you're treading water in an ocean of idealism, you suddenly dislike me?"

"That wasn't great, but it was actually the part where I kind of thought we'd evolved beyond our bet into partners, then you hid your plans to make sure you got all the credit for winning with Janus. Unfair advantage, by the way. Do you know what I could have accomplished if *I* had Willie Nelson's number on speed dial? I probably would have cured global warming by now."

Ben nodded knowingly. "I see. You stopped playing to win and now you can't handle the heat. You're seeing your future, and it has *assistant* written all over it. I'm not going to apologize for being excellent."

"No one's asking you to. Let's just stop waffling back and forth between being rivals and friends. No more hanging out in bars or restaurants or on the campaign trail. No more reminiscing and no more banter."

"No more banter?" Ben clutched his heart. "Oh, what will I do?"

I ignored him. "I want to focus on kicking your ass."

Unfortunately, the power of my statement was undercut

by the scooter giving way under me, wheels spinning. It and I pitched toward the sidewalk—

—only to be rescued by Clark Kent. Ben's muscled arms seized me and set me upright, hands gripping my shoulders, keeping me steady. A single lock of dark hair fell over his forehead as he leaned closer with a look of wonder.

"You actually fell standing still."

I shook his hands off my shoulders. "Wrong again. I was just getting on the scooter to ride home."

Ben raised two skeptical brows sky-high. "You, ride a scooter? Two weeks ago, when we were leaving Shakespeare on the Green, you saw someone on a scooter almost get run over by a car and said, 'Darwin doesn't win every time.'"

The truth was, I'd ridden to lunch with Wendy and actually did need a way back to the office. I glanced at the instructions. Goddammit, I had to download an app to get this thing started.

"I don't know what you're talking about," I said. "They're very good for the environment."

"Okay." Ben leaned back and crossed his arms. "Let's see it."

"You're going to watch?"

"You bet your ass I'm going to watch. There's nothing in this world I want more than to see you eat it on a scooter."

I finished downloading the app and linked it to my Venmo, silently praising millennial entrepreneurs for making it frighteningly easy to give this motorized scooter access to my bank account. I might regret it later, during Skynet times, but for now I was one step closer to getting away from Ben.

"What are you doing this weekend, by the way?"

"Not seeing you," I said quickly.

"Obviously. I'm just making conversation. Otherwise we're standing here in silence."

"If you must know, Chris Tuttle changed his Facebook

status to *In a Relationship* with that woman we saw him with outside the restaurant. Alexis lost her shit. It's why she's talking to me again—I think she's secretly grateful I punched him now. I promised her we'd spend the weekend drinking wine and watching rom-coms."

Which reminded me that maybe it wouldn't be the worst thing if this scooter turned on and catapulted me into oncoming traffic.

Gathering my dignity, I mounted the scooter. It vibrated under me and I had a moment of blinding panic. But then I saw Ben's triumphant grin and steeled myself.

"Goodbye, Ben."

The scooter shot forward. *Oh, God.* That was precarious. I widened my stance and found equilibrium.

"You're welcome for Willie Nelson," he shouted at my slowly retreating back.

It would be classier to ignore him. So I did, straightening my spine and scooting away.

9

Easy Intimacy

"Don't get me wrong," I said to Alexis, hanging upside down off my couch so Al Gore could eat my hair. "I love this shit. Just say the words *Jennifer Lopez* and I'm salivating. But when do we get to watch a rom-com about a woman with actual character flaws?"

Alexis, who was slumped on the chaise part of my sectional, leaned forward to suck on the straw she'd shoved into a wine bottle, which she cradled against her chest. "What do you mean? They're all workaholics. And the Runaway Bride's a commitmentphobe."

Al happily chewed my split ends. "Those are not problems. I want the woman who stole money from her dead grandma, or did something unforgivable to her childhood best friend, or, like, screwed over everyone who trusted her to get a promotion at work. Serious emotional issues. I want to watch *those* women find love."

Alexis hit the end of her wine. Her straw made those air-sucking noises. "Well, you're the only one. No one wants to watch people they don't like fall in love."

I tugged my hair out of Al's mouth and sat upright on the couch, blaming the tiny flare of pain on the head rush. "Well, *I* do."

"Ugh," Alexis said, dropping her empty bottle onto the coffee table. "We're out of rosé."

"I've got something better." I opened the drawer on my side table and pulled out my blunt box. Then I crawled across the couch to Alexis and opened the lid so she could see the beautiful joints lined up inside. She reached a hand in and I snapped the lid at her.

"Eeee!" she squealed. "You *Pretty Woman*-ed me."

"You don't get one until you repeat after me—Chris Tuttle has a lackluster micropenis and I'm thrilled he showed his true colors before I spent all my savings on a bust wedding."

Alexis flopped back on the couch and pressed her face into a pillow. "I can't believe he did this to me. I thought we were perfect."

"Well, believe it, because it's Facebook official." I took out the biggest joint and stuck it in my mouth, lighting the tip with a Bic. I sucked in and blew out slowly, letting the warm, herbal smoke fill my lungs. "You're better off without him. Here's my advice. Stop trying to make a relationship happen. They're doomed. Date multiple men at all times and never get emotionally attached. Guard your heart."

Alexis held out her hand for the joint and I passed it to her. "That sounds terrible. And you're totally projecting."

"You're not allowed to hang out with Annie anymore."

She sucked in a deep breath and blew out a perfect O, like I'd taught her when we were teenagers. "Don't freak out when I say this, but…you know Dad was human, right? As in fallible? Just because Mom and Dad's relationship failed doesn't mean every relationship is doomed."

I would be lying if I said Alexis's words opened an old wound, because that wound was still fresh as hell. Our different opinion on the matter of Dad was the reason things hadn't been normal between us for years. The tension always sat in the back of my mind, even when I tried to make it go away.

I stole the joint back. "I don't want to get in an argument, so let's drop it."

Alexis sat up, resting her head in her hand. "We have to talk about it sometime. Annie thinks you've never really processed what happened and it's keeping you in arrested development. You and I were in different places with Dad. I'd understand if you had complicated feelings…if you feel regret…"

I heard Ben's voice: *What's wrong with you?… I'm talking about the thing underneath.*

I shook my head. "I told you once, and I'll tell you again, I don't regret anything that happened between me and Dad."

Regret was not an option.

Alexis sighed. I could feel her looking at me, studying my profile. I kept my eyes trained ahead, sucking on the joint, letting the haze creep into me and mellow things out. Onscreen, Kate Hudson snapped her fingers and a band of minions followed her.

Alexis scooted across the couch. She looked at me for a long time. And even though I meant to turn my head to meet her gaze, I didn't.

I thought there was a chance she'd put her head in my lap. And maybe I would get to stroke her hair. The image came to me in a rush: closeness between sisters. But she stopped an inch from me and rested her head on the couch cushion instead.

My hand rested near the crown of her head. I could run the

pads of my fingers over her temple, push back her hair, twist it into a loose braid, like when we were little.

But my hand was frozen. I couldn't move it.

This is why I avoided thinking about Dad. I'd spent sixteen years with Richard and Elise Stone, the King and Queen of Marriage. I'd believed in forever and a day, a love bigger than death. But then my father had gone and disproved the concept of unconditional love. Obviously, if he could kick my mother to the curb, he could do it to me. And if your own *father* could leave you, any man could.

Alexis was more forgiving. Or more gullible. Within months of our parents' divorce, she was speaking to Dad again, talking about his new wife, Michelle, like she was part of the family, going to their home in San Antonio for the holidays.

So that was how it was for eleven years. The new normal. Mom, me, Alexis, and a wide gulf of icy silence separating me from Dad.

Then, two years ago, everything changed. I woke one morning to Alexis screaming on the other end of the phone that Dad had been in a car accident and he was dead. He'd been on his way to the grocery store for a gallon of milk, and someone T-boned him at an intersection. Instant death. Over a stupid twenty-minute errand. He was lactose-intolerant, so the errand hadn't even been for him. It had been for Michelle. Slain in an act of thoughtfulness for his new wife.

It wasn't a thing I liked to talk about, even with my family. Even with my best friends.

Because what would I say? That my dad died thinking I hated him? If I said I regretted my years of punishing silence—if I admitted I'd made the wrong choice, not forgiving him like Alexis—then the following had to be logically true: my stubborn anger had cost me the last years of my father's life, and there was nothing I could ever do to get him back.

I'd had a *dad*—warm hugs when I was scared and two steady hands on my shoulders when the training wheels came off and tears of pride at graduation. And then I'd lost him. And now, for the rest of eternity, he and I would remain broken. There was no going back, no mending, no last shot at redemption. There never would be, and it was all my fault.

If I admitted that, I would never forgive myself.

Alexis shifted on the couch. A few strands of her hair brushed my knuckles.

Suddenly, I wanted to hug my sister. I had this memory of lying next to her in bed when we were young, reading bedtime stories, our small bodies curled together, shoulder to shoulder. I wanted that again. But I was scared, or nervous, or something I didn't have the words for. And that something kept my limbs still.

There was a chance something was wrong with me, like Ben said. Ben, who didn't know my dad had died since we'd last seen each other. Ben, the man for whom I'd taken on my father's role, the cheater, in a messed-up little twist.

It was better not to talk about any of this. There was nothing I could do, so better not to open it up. Better to take another deep inhale of this joint and wait for the feelings to melt away.

The doorbell rang, and I practically jumped out of my skin.

"Please tell me you ordered pizza," Alexis groaned. "I'm starving."

I hopped up, grateful for the interruption in my train of thought, and ran to the front door. Sitting on my doormat were two brown bags—the first full of pink rosé bottles that rattled when I moved it, and the second crammed with every kind of chocolate from the grocery store: Hershey's and Reese's and Snickers and M&M's.

There was a note on top of the chocolate bag. I unfolded it.

TO LEX: SOME SUPPLIES FOR YOUR WEEKEND. KEEP YOUR CHIN UP. NO GROWN MAN WORTH HIS SALT STILL UPDATES HIS RELATIONSHIP STATUS ON FACEBOOK.

TO THE OTHER STONE SISTER: I SUPPOSE I'M GLAD YOU DIDN'T DIE ON A SCOOTER. IT WOULD HAVE MEANT A LOT OF PAPERWORK.

The note was unsigned, but scrawled in Ben's slanted, all-caps handwriting. Unmistakable as a fingerprint.

What was he playing at, being thoughtful and generous? We'd *just* talked about not blurring the lines between friendship and rivalry, and here he was, blurring. Well, it wasn't like some principles over Ben's zigzag was going to stop me from eating this candy. I dragged both bags inside.

Alexis appeared beside me and peeked into the bags, then clutched her hands together like a rom-com heroine presented with a diamond ring. "For *me*?"

"Yep. From Ben, our gentle stalker."

Alexis tore into a Snickers and shoved it in her mouth, very ladylike. "Remind me why you two aren't dating?"

"Because I destroyed his life—and he is *very* uninterested in a repeat. And because he has a girlfriend. Remember Sarah?"

She waved. "Oh, her." That was a rather cavalier attitude for someone who'd recently been cheated on. A zealous look was creeping into Alexis's eyes. I could smell a breakup project.

Better nip it in the bud. "Because Ben used the last five years to become an actual adult, and I'm still me. We live on two different planets."

"Maybe that's your charm."

"Pssh."

Alexis chewed. "You know you're funny and smart and

beautiful, right? You're like a force of nature when you're after something. A total catch. And I'm not just saying that because I'm high."

I hefted the bag of rosé to my hip and walked to the refrigerator. "Trust me, I don't need the confidence boost. This is your weekend."

"I'm just saying, the way Ben looked at you at dinner was not the look of a man who was over it. You guys reminded me of two little magnets straining not to leap together."

I patted her head. "Sweet little Alexis. Now I *know* you're high."

"He left you presents on your doorstep."

"He left *you* presents on my doorstep."

Again, Alexis waved dismissively. "Everyone knows the way to your heart is through the people you love."

That stopped me short. "They do?"

When Alexis smiled next, her eyes softening with tenderness, it was almost as good as being hugged. "Yes. Inside you're still a romantic, like when you were young. You've just buried it, and redirected all those emotions onto other people. From the outside, it's easy to see."

I tossed and turned that night before falling into an uneasy sleep. Immediately, my mind cast me into some no-man's-land, halfway between a dream and a memory.

I was lying on my stomach in bed, back in my grad school apartment. I could tell, even though the details of my old bedroom were hazy around me. All my senses had dulled except for my sense of touch, which was vivid. I could feel the sheets bunched under my legs; the pressure of the cotton pillow creased into my cheek. I wore a spaghetti-strap top and cotton shorts. The air was cool, icing my exposed shoulder blades.

From behind, Ben slid over me. He braced his hands against

the bed, caging my shoulders, but his weight was a delicious pressure. I felt him hard between my legs and squeezed my knees together.

He leaned down until his chin was at the back of my neck, his mouth at my ear. I squeezed my eyes shut into the pillow.

"Everyone knows the way to your heart," he murmured, and slid his palms down the backs of my thighs, pulling my shorts down, spreading my legs apart. My world narrowed until it was nothing but anticipation. Slowly, he pushed inside me.

I gasped, breath hot against the pillow, and clutched at his arm, pulling him closer. He gripped my hip bones and drove into me deeper, until I bit the pillow and clenched it between my teeth. He found my hands and stretched them above my head, lacing our fingers, and I pushed back against him, feeling his rhythm quicken, until the muscles inside me clenched and started to pulse—

—and I woke, shuddering, covered in a sheen of sweat. I lay in my bed, trying to catch my breath and blank my mind. And then it came to me—the most improbable thing.

I knew how to reach Senator Wayne and steal a yes from under Ben's nose.

10

A Regular 4-H Queen

There were no two ways about it: Ben made a better cowboy than me. His tight jeans hugged his muscular thighs, and his pearl-snap shirt stretched across his chest, sleeves bunching around his biceps. As we walked through the dusty tent of the Corsicare County Rodeo, smack in the heart of Senator Wayne's district, I tried not to remember what Ben used to look like coming back from the gym or a run, his tank top and shorts plastered to his slick body, earbuds still in as he moved seamlessly through the apartment to wherever I was. Finding me and kissing me, sweaty and hot-skinned, despite my protests.

Seeing Ben in person, it was impossible not to recall the dream I'd had, the weight of his body pressed on top of mine. My skin retained the feeling like an imprint, a muscle memory, calling it up every time I glanced his way. It looked like he hadn't shaved for days—his square jaw was shadowed in stubble. I knew what that stubble felt like under my fingers, wet in the shower, or dry and soft when he just woke up. Knew what it felt like scraping down my stomach, against my thighs—

"It's this one," Ben said, stopping short and pointing to a large open pen with a crowd gathered around it.

I accidentally stepped into him, catching his chest with my own, and had to force myself to step back from his warm, hard body. It was criminal for anyone to smell as good as Ben smelled. I was going to have to find out what cologne he'd switched to and buy it, just to calm these demons. Maybe spritz it over my bedsheets…

"Uh, Lee?" Ben was staring at me like he was concerned I'd fallen off the deep end. Which I completely had. One sex dream and some tight jeans and now I could barely focus on work. I felt like a live wire, electric and dangerous, ready to connect if he so much as brushed me.

It was a very inconvenient way to feel about a work rival.

I shook myself, forcing my gaze from Ben to the task at hand. "Are you sure this is us? That's an awful lot of people."

Ben nodded at the sign on the pen: "Calf roping contest, sponsored by Lise Motors. Judges Henry Cricketty, Beau Simoneaux, and special guest judges Ben Laderman and Lee Stone." That was us, all right.

He swallowed as he surveyed the crowd. "Did you read the Wiki pages I sent you on calf roping?"

I made a dismissive noise and pulled a book out of my tote: *The A–Z History of Texas Rodeos*. "Please. I see your Wiki and raise you a book." I'd decided to read the book, it should be noted, mostly to get my mind off Ben these last few nights so I could actually get some sleep. But still. You took your moments for one-upmanship when they presented themselves.

Ben gestured toward the pen. "Then by all means, Stoner. You're the expert, you take the lead."

I pushed past him to the little table I figured served as the judges' quarters. Two men in their early sixties already sat there, looking like extras in an old Western: they were dressed in the full shebang of bolo ties, Wranglers, boots and cowboy hats. Their faces were wrinkled, likely from hours of squinting moodily into the sun.

Both men stood as I approached and offered their hands. "You must be Ms. Stone," said the first, with the deepest Texas twang I'd ever heard. "Henry Cricketty."

"Please, call me Lee." I shook the second man's hand, and he swung it straight to his lips and gave it a kiss, winking at me. "Beau Simoneaux. What a lovely lady."

"Charmed, she's sure," Ben said dryly. He made his own introductions, and then the four of us settled into our chairs at the table, facing the pen. Next to these two genuine cowboys, I felt like my jeans and boots were pure costume. Which, of course, they were.

Henry nodded at a young man on a horse who waited opposite us outside the pen. "Don't take offense, but have y'all ever seen calf roping before?"

"Of course," Ben scoffed, from his seat at the end of the table. "We were both born and raised in Texas."

I didn't know what he was playing at. I'd never stepped foot inside a rodeo.

"We'll follow your lead," I said quickly, shooting Ben a look. "We appreciate you letting us be part of the fun."

"Well, we appreciate you giving us your money," Beau said, with another wink. He waved a hand at the pen. "What do you think of the signage?"

There were Lise banners strung over nearly every square inch inside the pen, a wall-to-wall display of ads that would rival the Daytona 500. "Looks great," I said truthfully. Talk about bang for your buck.

Henry spoke with his hands, making little practiced gestures that told me we were not the first people he'd tried explaining calf roping to. "The gist of it is, the cowboy is trying to swing his lariat around the calf's neck. Once he does, he dismounts, runs to the calf and ties its feet. Doesn't hurt them," he added quickly, seeing the look on my face. "Best time wins, so judging's easy."

I nodded. "Got it."

"All right, then." Henry slid the microphone closer to his mouth, and his twangy voice boomed through the space. "Welcome, one and all, to the Corsicare Rodeo Calf Roping competition." He pronounced Corsicare like *Kor-see-care*, lingering on the "care" in that unhurried way some Texans had. "First up we have Matt Tanner, fastest roper out there at Corsicare High and a rising star on the circuit. Matt, take it away."

A country song blared from the loudspeakers as part of the pen swung open and a calf ran out, kicking up dirt. Another gate swung open and the young man who'd been waiting on his horse galloped out.

I clutched my hands together. "Run, calf, run," I whispered.

Beau gave me an inquisitive look. Apparently, my allegiance was with the wrong party.

As Matt Tanner rode in circles, swinging his rope over his head, I leaned closer to Ben and poked him with my elbow.

"Be nice," I hissed. "We're supposed to be gathering intel on how to persuade Wayne."

Ben darted a glance over my shoulder at Beau, who luckily wasn't paying attention, before whispering back. "He shouldn't feel entitled to kiss you and comment on your appearance just because you're a woman. No one's kissing *my* hand. It's gross."

I pushed away all thoughts of kissing Ben's hand or anywhere else. "Yes, it's definitely sexist. That tells us these guys are old-school, so let's use it to our advantage."

Ben looked at a loss for how to do that, his face frozen in

a frown. His eyes were so blue and long lashed. I wanted to brush my finger over his lips, trace the stubble on his jaw. Christ, he was even more beautiful now than he'd been five years ago.

Okaaaay. It had been far too long since I'd had Kyle over, I was now realizing.

The crowd burst into cheers. I whipped my gaze to the pen, where Matt Tanner was tying his calf.

"Two and a half minutes is the time to beat," Henry boomed into the mic. "Next up is Deshaun Travers, last year's reigning champ."

A new country song started over the speakers and another calf shot into the pen.

Henry leaned back in his chair, away from the mic, and crossed his arms. "So, Lee. Tell me about this fancy company you work for. When we talked on the phone about the sponsorship, you mentioned something about a bill?"

A thrill raced through me. Here was my shot. I reached down and pulled a heavy stack of pamphlets out of my bag, passing one to Henry and Beau. "I was hoping you'd ask. And I'm hoping you'll let me pass these out to the crowd when the competition is over."

Henry raised an eyebrow.

"Lise Motors makes electric vehicles that require only a small amount of dirty energy to build. Then they run on electricity—clean energy—for their entire lifetimes. They're four times more efficient than fossil-fuel-powered cars, and infinitely better for the environment."

Infinitely wasn't exactly the correct quantitative term, but rhetorically, it was strong.

"Like a Tesla?" Beau asked.

"Better than a Tesla," I said. "In fact—" I nodded at Ben "—we're working with the governor to try to pass a bill right now that would replace all the fossil-fuel vehicles the state uses—public safety vehicles, maintenance vehicles, you name it—with electric versions. That shift alone would make a huge difference in making Texas a healthier, more verdant place. Best of all, the government would build all the infrastructure private citizens need to feel like they can make the switch to electric without having to worry about whether there will be a charging station when they need it. Overall, that means a stronger, more efficient power grid. Remember the ice storm, how helpless we were? We're going to fix that."

"No offense," said Henry, steepling his fingers and giving me a shrewd look. "But isn't clean energy a lefty talking point? We don't have many lefties out here in Corsicare. We're a community of farmers and ranchers. Traditionalists. You might be barking up the wrong tree."

Out of the corner of my eye I could see Ben's mouth flatten.

"But that's exactly why everyone here in Corsicare should like this idea," I said, resting my hands on the table and leaning forward. "Who's closer to the land than you? Who depends on healthy rivers and clean air and soil more than you to raise your animals and all your amazing crops?" I jerked a thumb in the direction Ben and I had come from. "You think Mrs. Martha Mason will be able to produce those blue-ribbon tomatoes much longer if we keep feeding poison into the atmosphere and letting it rain back down on us?"

Henry gave me a thoughtful look, so I took my chance and leaned over Beau, placing one hand on his shoulder and the other on Henry's. They both gave me their full attention. From the other end of the table, Ben gave them a dark look.

"Think about it. Farmers and ranchers have always been the guardians of the American landscape. Defenders of the land."

Obviously, I was sidestepping the fact that farmers and ranchers only had plots of American land to defend because it had been stolen from indigenous peoples. But a potent combination of opinion research, voting history and instinct told me mentioning that fact would cause an immediate end to the conversation, so I continued without it.

"By going green, you'll not only be doing the right thing—you'll also protect your livelihoods. Really, no one should care more about passing this bill than you."

Henry rubbed his chin. "It's like Don't Mess with Texas, but on a grander scale."

"Exactly."

Beau slapped his hand on the stopwatch as the crowd erupted into cheers. "Three minutes, twelve seconds!" he shouted into the mic, and we all turned to see Deshaun tying off his calf.

"It's kind of interesting when you put it like that," Henry said, amid the cheers still sounding from the crowd. "Feel free to pass out your flyers. People might be willing to hear what you have to say."

Time to go for broke. Beau was announcing the next calf roping contestant, so I had Henry's undivided attention.

"What we really need is to convince Senator Wayne to support the bill. You served on his reelection campaign two years ago. Any chance you know how to get through to him?"

Ben drew infinitesimally closer to me—like he wanted to prop me up or shield me, I couldn't tell. But I appreciated it.

Henry raised both eyebrows. "You know, I like you two. You're a cute couple, working on this thing together. Reminds me a little of my wife and I, on the ranch."

"We're not—" I started, but Ben elbowed me.

"Senator Wayne keeps a close council of people he trusts, people he grew up with here in Corsicare. They advise him on big decisions. Back during the reelection campaign, if they said no to something, it was gone. If they liked something, you had a shot. If you convince his council, you'll win over Wayne."

"And who are they?" I asked, just as a Shania Twain song I actually recognized started playing from the speakers.

Henry scratched his ear, contemplating. Beau finished announcing and rejoined the conversation, shooting Henry a look I couldn't quite interpret. Henry shrugged in response, a kind of *well, why not*, and Beau turned to me.

"If you want to convince Wayne, there's really only one person you need to talk to. His name's Ely Gunther. Runs Gunther Ranch way out in the sticks. He and Wayne have been close since they were boys. Anything Ely says, goes."

"Thank you so much," I said. Henry and Beau had just handed us gold.

Beau nodded, looking at the pen, where a new man atop a horse swung his lariat. "The guardians of the American landscape. Now, I like that."

"There's no way you can carry all that back to the car." Ben made a "give me" gesture. "Hand it over before you topple."

After the calf roping competition was over and we'd passed out every single one of our Green Machine pamphlets to the crowd—who liked my line about guardians almost as much as Henry and Beau—I'd made Ben stop at the farmers' market on the way out. There, I'd proceeded to channel my triumph over the successful day into a produce shopping spree. Vegetarian nirvana: I now had veggies for days.

Ben pulled two heavy brown bags out of my arms and we started walking again. I stole a glance at him. The muscles in his arms flexed as he gripped a bag in each hand. This is what he used to look like when we went grocery shopping together: face serious, concentrating, balancing brown bags on his hips as he fished his keys out of his pocket to pop the trunk. A wave of nostalgic tenderness washed over me.

No—bad. I couldn't keep letting myself think of Ben from the past. That time was over. Now he was my work partner-slash-competition. A little lust was one thing, and could be solved by calling Kyle, but tenderness was a bridge too far.

Ben settled the bags of produce in the trunk of the Prius—which he was spending a fortune on renting, it must be noted, just to prove a point—and reached for mine. When all was tucked away, he slammed the trunk closed, then leaned against it. Without warning, he gripped the top of his shirt with both hands and yanked. The row of pearl snap buttons ascended to their highest form by doing what they were born to do: snapping open to reveal the elegant lines of Ben's collarbones, the hard planes of his chest and a smattering of dark hair.

Down, Stoner.

"It was so hot in that tent. Especially since you made me stand around forever, listening to you haggle with those farmers." Ben laced his fingers together over his stomach in repose.

"Three dollars a cucumber is highway robbery." I clutched at my own collar to let some air in. It was October, but it was also Texas, and today had been unusually warm. And, of course, there was Ben. He of the square jaw and broad, muscled body, newly unsnapped.

I really needed to get laid. I was moving it to the emergency column.

He squinted at me against the setting sun. "You were good in there. You managed to find people who really knew Senator Wayne, and then you had the right things to say to them. I'm grudgingly impressed."

Pride almost dizzied me. "Yeah, well. Everyone knows the best way to someone's heart is through the people they love."

Ben cocked his head and smiled quizzically. "I guess so."

I cleared my throat. "Now all we have to do is track down Ely Gunther and plead our case. Best to do it in person."

"I'll find him," Ben promised. "The might of the government, and all that."

I started to shift toward the passenger door, thinking we were done, but Ben reached out and gripped my arm.

"You never told me. How was the rom-com weekend?"

I smiled and stepped closer—but only a little, so Ben's hand wouldn't move off my arm. His hands were big, his fingers slightly rough from the gym or whatever he did in his spare time that I would not think about.

"Luckily, some anonymous hero dropped off provisions right when we ran out, so the weekend was saved." I shifted closer, and Ben's hand dropped, grazing my waist before he gripped the back of the car. "Thanks for that, by the way."

He smiled—and didn't move away, despite how close we were. He just kept looking at me, his mouth eventually softening into a smaller smile. It was knowing, tender, the way he was looking at me—there was no other way to describe it. It was exactly the way I was afraid to look at him.

"You're lucky to live close to your family," he said finally. "I wish I lived closer to Will."

"You *could* move to North Carolina and go work for their governor. Get all up in their business. Be a pain in someone else's ass. Just a thought."

He flashed a grin, then thought of something. "Hey," he said cautiously. "I've been curious. Have you and your dad started talking again? I get your reasons not to. But I used to hope you would one day."

It's strange how things hit you. One minute, I was standing in a rodeo parking lot, having a normal day, and the next, I was free-falling into a long, dark well. I jerked back.

"Oh, shit." Ben straightened. "What's wrong?"

"No." I forced the word out. "I never did."

There was a long, stretched-out moment of silence, in which I looked desperately at the inside of the Prius, where I wanted to be sitting, this conversation wiped away. I felt like a wounded animal. I wanted somewhere to hide.

"Lee?" Ben put a hand on my elbow like an anchor. "I'm sorry I asked. Do you want to go home?"

A stupid heat burned behind my eyes, and I looked away, blinking fiercely. There was no way on earth I was going to cry in front of Ben, so I gathered myself and looked back at him. And you know what? Fuck it. I felt an urge to be self-destructive all of a sudden. Maybe I'd shock him and Ben would fumble for his keys and drive me home in silence and regret ever trying to know me. I cleared my throat. "My dad died in a car accident two years ago."

"Jesus." To my surprise, Ben reached for me and pulled me firmly against his chest. "I'm so sorry, Lee."

I blinked against his shirt.

"Why didn't you tell me?" he asked.

"I never made up with him." I spoke the words into his chest, giving him my closely guarded confession. "He died thinking I hated him."

Ben drew me tighter. "No. He knew you loved him. Trust me, Lee. He called you every few months, remember? He knew. He was just waiting on you."

Suddenly, I didn't care that we were in the rodeo parking lot and anyone could see us. Ben was holding me, and it was like a dam had finally broken.

"I wanted to tell you right when it happened," I said. "Isn't that stupid? We hadn't talked for years and I knew you hated me and still I wanted to call you."

"I wish you had. And for the record, I've never hated you, exactly." Ben pressed his chin to my forehead, and I closed my eyes. In that moment, I had the strange feeling that this was what I'd been waiting for, ever since my dad died—waiting to tell Ben, who used to be my best friend, the man who loved and knew me. But that was a crazy thought because I'd had no clue I'd ever see Ben again until a little over a month ago. So how could this have been the thing I'd been waiting for?

I pushed the confusion away and reluctantly pulled back. "I don't normally like to talk about it. But you asked me at the restaurant what was wrong with me, and I think this is part of it."

Ben's eyes were so serious. "I'm glad you trust me enough to tell me. Really. I always felt this distance between us. I was kind of desperate to know you better." He smiled self-consciously, cheeks pinking. "I mean, I just feel like we're on the way to being friends now. Which is nice."

"Yeah, well, lucky you, now you have a friend with raging daddy issues. Every minute I'm not planning my lower-back tattoo is another minute I'm resisting my destiny."

Ben hiked a leg up on the Prius's bumper. "In that case, schedule mine, too. I have plenty of daddy issues."

We stared at each other.

"It doesn't work for me, does it?" Ben asked.

I shook my head. "Definitely not."

"What I mean is, I haven't seen my dad since he left for a work trip when I was in fifth grade. My mom couldn't even find him to pay child support. Will was five when he left, so he doesn't even remember him. But I had just enough time. I was so hurt. I felt like he'd abandoned *me*, specifically. I took turns being more furious that he left me, then Will, then my mom. It was like a little torture rotation over the years."

I knew the basics of the story, of course, but I'd never heard this much detail. I bumped his arm. "Your dad's the stupidest person in the world to miss out on you."

"It was hard for my mom to work and take care of us. So early on, I decided I was going to be a dad to Will, and a better dad than our real dad would've been. That way, Will wouldn't feel the loss."

Of course. That explained Ben's extreme pride in everything Will did. It was more than brotherly—it was paternal.

"I think that's why I had a chip on my shoulder for so long." Ben gave me a wry smile. "*Definitely* when I met you. I felt like I had something to prove to the world, and especially to my dad, wherever he was. Competing in law school—grades, mock trial, job interviews. Everything was to prove myself. I felt like my whole life was this ongoing conversation I was having with a ghost—making this argument to my dad about why I didn't deserve to be left."

"I liked you with a chip on your shoulder," I admitted. "I loved watching you take everyone down. You're one of the smartest people I've ever met. But your dad's an idiot."

"I say all this because I want you to know I'm kind of an expert at broken families. So trust me when I say it's obvious from everything I remember, and heard, that your dad loved you, and you loved him—fight notwithstanding. And you pretty much have to believe me because I just shared my sob story and it would be rude not to."

I rolled my eyes, but before I could say anything, Ben slung an arm over my shoulders and tugged me in the direction of the passenger door. "Will you look at us. *Two* sad saps with daddy issues."

I wrapped my arm around his waist. "Destined for a life of wet T-shirt contests, tramp stamps and getting boners for older men."

"It's a constant struggle." Ben squeezed me, then opened the passenger door so I could slide in. When he shut it, in the brief time it took him to jog around to the driver's seat, and it was just me in the car, I realized: I suddenly felt so much less alone.

11

A Commendable Act of Friendship

Macoween was, without a doubt, the single most important holiday of the calendar year. Since Halloween had the amazing good fortune of landing on Mackenzie Portney's birthday, we'd redubbed it Macoween in college, and it was a blessed day. Not ever for Mac herself, unfortunately; but for the rest of us, it had always been a day of extreme good fortune.

One Macoween past, Annie had won ten thousand dollars in a scratch-off. Another, Simon had proposed to Claire. And every year, without fail, I drank to my heart's content and woke up the next morning without a hangover. A true Macoween miracle.

This year, as we gathered outside a boxy, modern mansion—its squat, minimalist lines marking it as the likely home of a guy who'd made too much money too young in Austin's tech industry—it was clear that Mac was determined to finally carve out a little Macoween glory for herself.

"To be honest, I don't know this guy." Mac gestured at the mansion with the frank authority of a general addressing her troops. "So I don't know how fun this party will be. The host is Kelly's sister's boyfriend's cousin."

Blank stares around the group revealed no one knew who Kelly was. So...probably a work friend from Mac's mysterious job.

"Therefore, I brought these." Mac lifted her trays of orange and purple Jell-O shots high. "No matter how lame the party is, these will kick it up a notch."

Claire snorted. "What'd you put in there, ayahuasca?" Like every previous Macoween, Claire was dressed as Sharon Stone's character from *Basic Instinct*, in a super-sexy white turtleneck dress, white heels and white coat, her blond hair pulled back severely, just like in the interrogation scene. Claire's philosophy was, no need to mess with a good thing. Also, coming up with costumes was a lot of work.

Standing next to Claire, Simon—who always came out with us on Macoween, since it was the anniversary of his and Claire's engagement—wore what *he* always wore: Michael Douglas's blue shirt, brown tie and brown sports coat, with a police badge hanging at his hip. None of the details helped, though—it was a running joke every year that no one could ever tell who Simon was unless he was standing next to Claire (and they explained it). Guaranteed, at some point in the night, Simon would repeat his favorite line: he and Claire came as a pair, and he was nothing without her.

"No drugs," Mac clarified. "But I did put in twice the recommended dose of mescal." We all straightened to attention. "Listen," she continued. "I expect maximum fun out of all of you. Remember, this is my birthday, so give it your all. I'm meeting Ted for the first time, and I really want to make a good impression."

I winced. "Once again, I repeat, are you sure you want to go on a first date—a *blind* first date—on your birthday? Way high pressure, Mac."

Annie nodded in agreement, but Mac gave a curt shake of her head. "This is my *thirtieth* birthday." She paused to let the gravity wash over us, which it did. "I'm the first one into the breach. So if I want to use my birthday to go on a first date in the hopes that I won't enter the next decade alone, you *will* support me. You will dance. You will drink. You will make merry."

Zoey bowed. "Aye, aye, Captain." Which was kind of silly, since Zoey was dressed as a mermaid, not a pirate.

"Good." Mac adjusted her hot-pink sash, which screamed *Sweet Sixteen* in giant gold glitter letters. She'd leaned fully into her hybrid Halloween-birthday by dressing like one of those spoiled children from the *My Super Sweet 16* MTV show. Her hair was heat-damage-stick-straight, and she wore one of those body-con dresses, a tiara atop her head. In fact, with Zoey dressed like a children's cartoon and Mac dressed like an actual child, I was anxious to get them both off the streets before any Halloween pervs cruised by.

"And for what it's worth," Mac said, "I'm almost guaranteed to like Ted. He does amortization. I connected with him through work friends."

Ah. Mac's job. Tread carefully.

We glanced at each other.

"Does he work, you know, *internally*, and that's how you connected with him?" Annie wore a look of innocent curiosity. "Or is amortization more of an external thing for your company?"

Mac waved. "Oh, he works at MacArthur's with me. Just in a different department. You know how huge the place is."

"And how would you say *amortization* compares to your work?" Simon asked carefully. "Would you say it's the same, or opposite, or highly related…"

Smart of Simon to get context clues. *Amortization* was a word we could google later.

Mac rolled her eyes. "You guys are hilarious. Come on. Let's get this mescal in our bloodstream. I only have half an hour to reach the perfect level of tipsy before Ted shows."

She charged ahead, her Sweet Sixteen sash blowing in the wind, leaving the rest of us to shrug.

"We'll figure it out one day," Annie promised, her voice a tad muffled under her mustache. She and I were wearing matching mustaches we'd purchased together. She'd paired hers with a thin nightdress and carried a smoking pipe—a Freudian slip. I wore a white tank top and acid-wash jeans, with a studded belt and armband. Pure Freddie Mercury, ready to rock and roll.

"Good luck hooking up tonight," Claire said, with a pointed look at my mustache.

"Oh, please." I hooked my arm through Annie's and strode toward the house's glowing lights. "Sit back and watch me catch a dick."

"As for me," Alexis said, waddling after us in Mac's cast-off Mrs. Potts costume, "I'm trying to catch zero dicks tonight."

"We can tell," Zoey said kindly, patting her shoulder. "What with the costume barrier you've erected around yourself."

"Hey, Mac did extremely well in that thing at Daisy's wedding," I pointed out. "In fact, Lex, it's probably good you're not planning to meet anyone tonight. I think if that costume saw any more action, it would probably burst into flames."

Alexis looked down in horror at Mrs. Potts's smiling face.

"Watch the *chandelier*!" cried Zane, the owner of the boxy, modern mansion. He was a very short, very distraught guy who had indeed made his youthful fortune in virtual reality tech. "And *please* don't climb on the table!"

Luckily, thanks to Zoey, Beyoncé's iconic Coachella performance was blasting from the huge TV in the living room, and it was nearly impossible to hear. I could blame my disobedience on that.

I climbed onto the table and pulled Mac up beside me, shouting, "All hail the birthday queen!" to a round of thunderous applause that left Mac beaming. Disobedience aside, Zane really should be thanking us, because in just a few hours, we'd transformed his staid, boring Halloween party into a rocking affair no one would soon forget. We'd turned the volume up to eleven, fed everyone highly potent Jell-O shots, tripped partygoers into the pool until they'd started a pool party, and yelled motivationally at people until they started dancing. That last part was a specialty of Annie's—it required a careful mix of beratement and encouragement that was best left to a psychological professional.

"Pretty good birthday, yeah?" I shouted in Mac's ear.

She looked across the room to where Ted was standing, watching her with a goofy grin. He'd turned out to be pretty cute, in an extremely straitlaced, finance-guy way. Most important, he hadn't batted an eye at any of our shenanigans and had taken his shots like a champ.

"Best birthday ever!" Mac called back, with a look of anticipatory triumph on her face that told me she was definitely boning Ted tonight.

Zane made his way through the crowd. "Hello, can you please, *please* not dance on my dining table, I inherited it from my grandma—"

"What, it's your party and you want to get up here? Say no more." I grabbed Zane's arms and lifted him onto the table with Mac's help—luckily, he was rather small and easy to lift.

Mac and I danced around him. "Isn't this fun?" Mac called. "It's my birthday, you know."

"Here," I said, leaning dangerously far across the kitchen

counter to grab one of the last Jell-O shots, which I'd been hoarding. "Have this."

Zane's hips were moving in a half-hearted attempt to sway to Beyoncé. "Oh, I don't know."

I tipped the shot over his mouth and tapped the bottom so the Jell-O slid out in one delicious, gelatinous glob. "Bottoms up."

"Mmm, tasty," Mac prompted.

To our relief, Zane swallowed his mouthful of Jell-O and grinned, eyes wide with wonder. "It hurts going down, but then it's *good*."

"How many can that table hold?" Claire strode into the room, a line of women following her like ducklings. It never failed—whenever we went to a party, other women flocked to Claire, attracted to her big personality like moths to a flame. She was a woman-magnet. If she ever wanted, she could start a cult, no problem.

Huh. It occurred to me that might be why Claire was so bothered the pre-K moms didn't like her. She prided herself on being the sun around which every girl gang revolved.

"The more the merrier!" shouted Zane, who had apparently forgotten about his grandmother's legacy and was now throwing his arms and legs around wildly, in an act only the most generous would label dancing.

I was distracted from the imminent threat of getting clocked by the sight of Alexis rolling into the dining room with two forties taped to her hands.

"Lex!" I called, from high atop my table-throne. "What are you *doing*? You know I banned you from playing Edward Fortyhands when you were in high school."

She spun to me. "But it looked fun. All the cool kids were doing it. And you're not the boss of me."

Yikes. Through the time-traveling power of alcohol, Alexis

had clearly reverted back to the same age she'd been the last time she played Edward Fortyhands, when she'd come to one of my college parties and ended up sleeping in a bathtub. To get her home and past the eagle-eyed scrutiny of our mother the morning after, I'd had to *Weekend at Bernie's* her, waving her arms and nodding her head at questions until I could get her safely tucked into bed. To this day, it remained one of my most impressive ventriloquist performances.

"Come on," I said, lifting Alexis onto the table. "I need your teapot girth to form a shield between Mac and the party host."

Indeed, Zane was now gyrating his hips pointedly in Mac's direction.

Alexis hopped onto the table and swept her gaze over the crowd. "Oh, look!" She pointed. "It's Ben's girlfriend!"

I followed her finger to the corner of the living room, where a group of guys surrounded a beautiful blonde woman. Who was, sure enough, Sarah Drake. Sarah even wore another red dress, like it was her signature color: this one strapless and sequined, her hair in loose curls over her shoulder. She was Jessica Rabbit. Say what you wanted about Sarah, but you couldn't accuse her of not having a solid lock on her brand.

I scanned the party for any sign of Ben, trying to ignore the way my heart beat extra hard at the possibility I would suddenly spot his square jaw and blue eyes in the crowd.

But there was no Ben. I swung my gaze back to Sarah, who was laughing hard at something one of the guys was saying. As I watched, she leaned forward and gripped the guy's arm, using it for balance, laughing harder.

Excuse me?

All right, it wasn't strictly scandalous. In fact, it was no more contact than Ben and I had on a daily basis. But it set my alarm bells ringing. What was Sarah doing here without

Ben? Obviously, you didn't need to be glued to your boyfriend's side every moment of the day. In fact, it was perfectly reasonable for her to go to a party without him. But this was Ben we were talking about, so why would she want to? And what was up with all the guys?

The man whose arm Sarah gripped slung it over her shoulders and tugged her in the direction of the massive arch that led out of the living room. My eyebrows flew up. This was very intimate body language. I tracked the two of them as they sauntered through the arch, on their way to somewhere else. Who knew where? *Outside?* To a *bedroom*?

Oh, no.

I was so busy remembering the way Ben's face had shuttered the moment he realized I'd slept with Connor Holliday—the flashback like a punch to the chest—that I didn't hear Mac yelling it was time to ditch the table for keg stands until it was too late. The mass exodus of Mac and Zane and Claire and Claire's minions sent the table wobbling. And then, in a twist of fate probably no more punitive than I deserved, Alexis swung around and her teapot handle clipped me in the chest, sending me flying.

As the top of my Freddie Mercury coif lightly brushed the bottom of the chandelier, then followed gravity's arc swiftly downward, all I could think was *How in the world will I tell Ben?*

12

Cruel and Unusual

"If you don't pull over so I can buy breakfast tacos, I swear to God, I will roll myself out of this car. And when the cops find my body on the side of the road, they'll know it was your fault."

Ben shot me a skeptical look from the driver's seat, his hands flexing over the steering wheel. "How?"

"I've obviously planted letters around my house implicating you in my death. I wasn't going to embark on our competition without some insurance. This is not my first rodeo. That was actually last week."

Ben shook his head. "You're saying you're still hungover from *Halloween*? Three days ago?"

I groaned and rested my head against the window. "Don't remind me. Mac got all the luck this year, and now I'm stuck facing the side effects of my advanced age. There's a chance I can no longer party like I used to."

"You're twenty-nine, Stoner. Wait until you hit your thirties."

I waved a hand at him. "Ugh. Don't remind me of your elderliness."

"I'll get you breakfast tacos just to have a moment's peace while your mouth is occupied," Ben muttered.

It was true I'd been a bit annoying since we'd set out on our road trip to Ely Gunther's ranch, which was way out in the boonies in Senator Wayne's home district. In my defense, I was not only battling a three-day hangover, but jittery nerves. I knew I needed to broach the subject of Sarah, but I had no idea how. When in doubt, deflect.

"What were you doing Halloween night, anyway?" I peeked at Ben out of the corner of my eye. There wasn't much water-cooler gossip about Ely Gunther, who was apparently a pretty private guy, but we *had* heard he preferred things laid-back and casual. Ben was wearing a gray long-sleeve T-shirt pushed up to his elbows, and another pair of those fitted jeans. He still hadn't shaved, so his five-o'clock shadow had grown thicker. It highlighted the strong bones of his jaw, like an artist had traced the outline with charcoal.

The muscles in his thigh flexed as he shifted to brake, and I gulped, lifting my eyes to his tanned, muscled forearms, braced against the wheel.

Nope. That wasn't better.

"I stayed home and did some makeup work for Grover." Ben's eyes slid to mine. "There's a million things on my plate, and this campaign is kind of all-consuming. I use the weekends to catch up."

"Oh. Sorry."

He scanned the road, then glanced back at me and smiled. "I'm not complaining. Plus, I got to hand out candy to kids all night."

Ben's gaze was making my skin flush with heat. I closed my eyes. "What a nerd."

Inside, I thought, *A poor, sad nerd whose girlfriend is about to break your heart.*

"Ah, *here* we go." The Prius whipped off the road, and I flew across the car, smacking into Ben's side.

"Sorry," he said, throwing the car into Park and setting me upright. He pointed out the windshield. "Tacos."

Sure enough, we'd pulled up right in front of a little truck on the side of the road, with giant pictures of tacos emblazoned across the front, the visuals-to-text ratio a sure sign of quality. The fact that Ben saw the truck, too, meant it wasn't a mirage.

One expensive purchase later, Ben and I spread out on a nearby picnic table, legs stretched out to catch as much early November sunshine as possible. Ben had thrown on Wayfarers, so I couldn't read his eyes when he turned to me.

His mouth curled into a smile. "I wish I'd seen you as Freddie Mercury." He leaned over and tapped above my lip. "In a mustache."

"Sarah was there," I blurted, shoving my taco wrapper aside.

He blinked. "Where?"

"At the party. On Halloween. I saw her."

He shrugged. "She went out that night. Funny that you ended up at the same party."

I swallowed a mounting sense of dread. "She was with… a lot of guys."

Ben's lips tightened. "So?"

He was going to make me spell it out, just like he'd done years ago when I had to confess about Connor.

"She was really…touchy-feely." I hesitated, fighting the urge to cringe. "There was this one guy she was all over."

"What do you mean, 'all over'?"

Jesus, Ben the ice machine. He was rigid as a statue. "You

know, leaning into him, touching him. The guy put his arm around her and they went off together."

"And then?"

"Well, I didn't see her again. I kind of fell off a table at that point. I'm really sorry, Ben."

"Why are you sorry?"

I frowned. "Because she was stepping out on you. She was all over this guy while you were stuck at home." *You've been cheated on*, I wanted to say. *Yet again*. All the signs were there.

"Why are you telling me this?" he asked stiffly.

I blinked at him. "Because it's the right thing to do. And because I owe you."

"Ah." Abruptly, Ben stood and crumpled our taco wrappers. "There it is. You cheated on me, so Sarah must be cheating, too."

"I didn't say that. I'm just trying to help—"

"You know what, Lee? I *really* don't need your help. In fact, you're the last person in the world whose help I need."

My mouth dropped open as Ben shoved the trash into a nearby trash can and strode to his car, yanking open the driver's-side door. I'd expected him to be hurt and disappointed, of course, but I hadn't expected him to shoot the messenger.

I followed him. "I was just trying to protect you, which I realize now was a misguided instinct. My bad. It will never happen again."

Ben threw himself into the driver's seat and turned to me, cheeks flushed, eyes still hidden behind his sunglasses. "You're not trying to protect me. You're trying to undermine my relationship."

"I am *not*."

"What, are you on some mission to prove faithful relationships are impossible? Is this part of the patented Lee Stone shtick you've got going on? Everywhere you go, relationships turn to dust?"

The seeds of a deep hurt sprouted inside me.

"Or is it just me?" Ben turned and stared out the windshield. "Are you trying to prove I'm uniquely qualified to be cheated on? If it's not just you who did it, you're off the hook. Something like that?"

Anger filled me, masking the hurt underneath. "That's not at all why I'm telling you, and it's an asshole thing to say."

Ben jabbed the ignition button. "Funny how the sting of you calling me an asshole lessens every time." He jabbed the button again, but instead of firing up, the engine gave a pitiful whimper. Ben's jaw tightened. He tried again, but the car still didn't start.

"Shit." I crossed my arms. "Are you happy now?"

Ben pushed his Wayfarers to his forehead and turned a truly murderous set of eyes on me. Then he stomped out of the Prius and popped the hood. He stared down, arms crossed, biceps straining under his shirt.

"Well?" I prompted, feeling extremely uncharitable.

"I don't know how to fix it," he gritted out. "This is my first hybrid."

"Ha!" I said triumphantly. "I knew you were renting it."

"I'm not renting it, you birdbrain. I own it. I just haven't worked on it yet."

"Ely Gunther is waiting for us at his ranch," I pointed out. "Today's the only day he would agree to meet us. It's now or never. Today, or say goodbye to Senator Wayne's vote."

"I realize the urgency of the situation," he snapped. "If we hadn't stopped for your stupid tacos—"

I lowered my voice to an icy hiss. *"Do not blame the tacos."*

Ben slammed the hood, laughing in a way that sounded borderline desperate. "I *told* myself, Ben, you and Stoner can be friends, sure. But you are never, *ever* getting mixed up in her messy bullshit again. Remember what happened the last time."

"Messy?" I was going to murder him and leave *his* body on the side of the road. There was no way he'd thought to plant letters implicating me in his death, so I had a solid advantage.

"I *promised* myself I'd stay at arm's length. Yet here I am, stuck in the middle of nowhere with you, arguing about whether my girlfriend cheated on me and whether I own my own damn car. Which leads me to no other conclusion than I am truly an idiot who hasn't learned his lesson."

"At least we can agree on something."

He blew out a breath. "Okay. How's this, Stoner. You're the expert at getting out of situations when you're tired of them. So—now what?"

"We really, *really* appreciate this, Mr. Gunther," I said over Ben's shoulder. "Truly, it's above and beyond. So kind."

"Call me Ely." He nodded at the road stretched out in front of us, his thick silver mustache twitching. "And what's the point of owning a tow if I can't rescue two city folks from the mean wilderness of Corsicare?"

I could see Ben flinch at being called *city folk*, but seeing as he was scrunched between Ely Gunther and me in the truck cab, his shoulders pressed up against his ears, he didn't have much room to emote.

"Well, we really appreciate it," I said. Ben and I were practically in each other's laps, and the fact that we were back to hating each other yet again was doing nothing to calm my body's reaction to the feel of all his firm muscles pressed against my side. My body, it went without saying, was a traitor.

"I'll get you settled," Ely said, "then I'll take a look at the car. Can't make promises, though. I've never worked on one of those Priuses."

Probably introducing ourselves to Ely Gunther by way of broken-down hybrid was not the best way to make our case that he should endorse a move to electric vehicles, but still—I was here to shoot my best shot.

I smiled like nothing was wrong. "I'm sure it will be up and running in no time."

Ely leaned against the front door of his house and wiped a rag over his oil-stained hands. "I'm afraid I have no earthly idea how to fix that car."

He shifted so Ben could walk in the house behind him, wiping his sweaty forehead against his shirtsleeve. "I think we're going to need to tow it into town. Find a shop."

I looked out the windows of the living room at the darkening sky. "Will there be any shops open?"

"Not at this hour," Ely said, and that seemed to take Ben by surprise. Ely shrugged. "We don't work city schedules out here."

"Do you have...Uber?" I felt ridiculous asking, but the box had to be checked.

Ely snorted. "No. But don't worry. It's been ages since I've had guests over—other than John, of course. Fortunately, I think I remember how to do it."

John. He must mean Senator Wayne. They truly were close, then.

Ely clapped a hand on Ben's shoulder. "Why don't you take a shower in the guest bath down the hall? I can get you a change of clothes." He gestured at his shirt and Wranglers. "Hope you don't mind fashion a little different than you're used to."

"Not at all," Ben said. "I really appreciate it."

"When you're done, we'll start us a fire and make some dinner. How does that sound? I know you two came here to pitch me something, and there's nothing better than talking under the stars. You can stay the night, and we'll tow your car in the morning."

"You don't have to," I protested. "It's way too generous." Christ, we'd come here to win Ely Gunther over, and now he was clothing, feeding and sheltering us. What a great impression we were making.

Ely waved. "Nah. It's nice to have company. John doesn't come around nearly as much as I wish he would." With that, he turned and ambled into the kitchen.

As soon as he was gone, Ben padded pointedly past me in the direction of the bathroom. My eyes tracked him as he slid inside and twisted the shower knob to get the water going. He pulled his shirt over his head, exposing the broad, tan expanse of his back—his muscled shoulders and the long lines that tapered to his waist.

He turned to kick the door closed behind him, and I saw a flash of the abs I remembered from when we were dating, except now even more pronounced. Like he'd been spending more time in the gym than usual, working off extraordinary amounts of stress. What froze me was the sight of the black hair that trailed lightly from his chest to his stomach, and down into the waistband of his jeans…

The bathroom door slammed shut, and the sound made me jump.

"Lee?" Ely called from the kitchen. "Want to give me a hand?"

I spun, like a child caught red-handed. "Coming!"

Ely's ranch covered hundreds of acres of land, but the only building on the property was his modest house. In the absence of civilization and all its pollutants, the stars were dazzling, like fistfuls of diamonds tossed against black velvet.

I leaned back and gazed up at the sky. The only noise was

the fire, crackling and spitting. After a stressful day, it was nice to have this moment of peace.

"You sure you're full, Lee?" Ely's voice was worried. He'd looked at me with fatherly concern ever since I'd told him I was a vegetarian and wouldn't need the steaks he was planning to grill, just the vegetables. "You ate like a rabbit."

"I ate my body weight in carrots and potatoes."

"Exactly," Ely said, tilting his head like I was a puzzle. "Carrots and potatoes."

From across the fire, Ben grinned softly to himself. Then he caught me looking and wiped the smile off his face.

All right. Yet another instance in which Ben—full-fledged meat enthusiast and devourer of one and a half steaks, much to Ely's approval—was the favored nation. When I got home, I was going to have to take a hard look at my favorability metrics and possibly make some adjustments. Could I alter my laugh to be more inviting? We would see.

In the meantime, it was time to plead my case to Ely.

"So, Ely, the reason we came out here to talk to you—"

"Besides needing towing help," he interjected, settling back in his Adirondack.

"Besides that," I agreed. "The reason is that we have a very important piece of legislation we're working to get passed. A game changer for Texas."

Ely nodded. "Figured it was something like that." He put up a hand. "Give me a second." He rooted around next to him and pulled up an unmarked bottle. "Can't talk politics without something to take the edge off." He untwisted the cap and poured a healthy amount into a tin cup.

Forgetting our stalemate, Ben and I looked at each other over the fire. "What is that?" I asked.

"Moonshine." Ely handed me the cup. "My own recipe. This stuff'll put hair on your chest. Might be a little tough to handle on your rabbit diet."

"Ely, you have no idea." I drank heartily, and—*ouch.* That burned like gasoline. But I didn't bat an eye, which earned me a raised brow. Then Ely got busy pouring for Ben and himself.

"All right," he said, when he'd taken his first sip. "Continue."

I looked at Ben, and he made a "by all means" gesture. And even though I couldn't tell if it was because he thought I was the best at persuasion, or because he was torturing me with the largest burden of work, I forged ahead.

"I'm going to lay our cards on the table, Ely. We want to pass a bill to help combat climate change by switching all state vehicles to electric cars."

He whistled. "Expensive. Could you even run electric vehicles reliably out here? Don't they need charging stations every few miles?"

"The bill would make a massive investment in infrastructure to support the change," Ben piped in. "That might be the most important part, actually."

"We're hoping with the infrastructure in place, people will feel safer buying electric." I added something I hadn't told anyone else: "We're aiming for the majority of vehicles driven in Texas to be electric within the next seven years." Three to four years for infrastructure building, I estimated, three to four for culture change.

Ely took a long sip of his moonshine, and I followed suit. "You did say Texas, right? Not California?"

"Yes. Texas."

"They even doing this out in California?"

I shook my head. "Texas would be the leader."

"Well, that's something. The old statehouse boys will like that, at least. Even better if you can tell them the ACLU's against it." Ely squinted into the dark. "Hard to picture charging stations out here in Corsicare. Plugging in my truck like it's a children's toy."

"Not too hard," I countered. "Just picture a gas station, and replace the gas pumps with electric." *Honestly.*

That got a little smile out of Ely. "Where you going to get the money for all that building and buying?"

Oh, yeah—this guy knew politics. It was always about the money.

"We're raising taxes just a smidge on the wealthiest 10 percent and ending tax loopholes for corporations." I took another sip. "All those big companies that relocated to Texas after the recession can cough up to invest in the state's health."

Ely whistled. "Your funeral. Though it is nice to think of someone standing up to them for a change..." He swept a hand at the land around us. "Used to be I could make a good living, before all those conglomerate meatpacking firms moved in. Now it's hard to scrape by."

"Those companies should at the very least pay their share." Ben scooted closer to the fire. "And it's the same with the oil and gas companies—everyone bends over backward for them, without considering whether it's the best way. We think it's time Texas stepped into the future. A lot of the old ways worked—I'm not saying they didn't—but a lot of the new ways are better."

I frowned, studying Ben's face in the firelight. He was looking at Ely intently, his dark eyebrows drawn, the muscles in his jaw working. It sounded like Ben was talking about something bigger than electric vehicles and corporate taxes.

Ely smiled ruefully and held out his tin cup to clink against Ben's. "I suppose you're right."

Interesting: Ely harbored sympathy for the little guy and was open to change. I could use that.

"Do you want to hear more about what we're planning?"

I asked. "More about the bill? To be completely transparent, we're here because we know you're close to Senator Wayne and we're hoping you'll convince him to vote for our legislation."

Ely was quiet for a moment. Then he said, "Tell me about this future you want. What does it look like? Paint me a picture. More than cars—broad strokes."

I glanced at Ben again, wondering how far I should take it. Should I be honest, or say something I thought would appeal to Ely, who'd lived for the sixty-five years of his life in this small, conservative ranching district—and who, by all evidence, largely eschewed the company of people in favor of cows?

But Ben's eyes had a faraway look in them, like he was imagining his own future, so I couldn't read his reaction.

Left to my own devices, I took a deep breath and decided to go with my instincts. "Well, Ely, I want a future where we reverse the damage corporations have done to the earth, and everyone takes responsibility for caring for our planet, like you do here on your ranch. Where no people have to migrate because of water or resource shortages, and no animals go extinct or lose their homes. I want humans to be *good* for this planet."

"What else?" Ely asked. He wasn't looking at me.

"What do you mean?"

"Besides the environment. Anything else you care about?"

Yes, actually. There was a lot. But it wasn't good comms to go off message. And I would probably be a terrible political strategist if I showed more of my cards. I glanced at Ben—but he was still dreamy, still no help.

I considered the impression I'd gotten of Ely today: independent and hardworking, sure, with that tried-and-true Texas cowboy streak, but also kind at his core, a kind man, willing to go out of his way to help others. And lonely. I thought back to his comment that Senator Wayne didn't visit as much as he wished, and decided to go out on a limb.

"I want a future where everyone has the right to love whomever they want," I said carefully, watching his face, though it stayed unreadable. "Be whoever they are in their hearts, and feel safe and secure with the food and housing and education they need to thrive." Just like that, I fell into the familiar rhythm of the words I'd written in college, back when I used to imagine myself as a candidate in need of a platform—before Andy Elliot took the president slot, publicly humiliated me, and I stopped running for things. "I want a future where we've dismantled systemic sexism and racism and every other bias that keeps cis straight white men in charge of society and everyone else under their heels. I want innovation and competition *and* strong safety nets. I want to celebrate autonomy *and* recognize the fact that we're all hopelessly bound together, whether we like it or not."

I paused. There was plenty more, but I tried to read the proverbial room. In my experience, telling older white men you wanted to level out their power didn't often go over well. Neither did using the word *cis*.

Across the fire, Ben's eyes were shining. The sight stiffened my spine. I looked at Ely. He upended his cup and set it on the grass next to his chair, casting his eyes up to the stars. "That's an awful lot of political ambition for an electric vehicle employee."

"I guess—"

"But," he interrupted softly, "it sounds pretty nice to me."

When my eyes could barely stay open anymore, Ely poured water on the fire and we watched the wood-scented smoke curl skyward. Sleepily, we gathered our things and made our way back to his house. We stopped in the living room.

"I apologize, but I only have the one guest bedroom." Ely's mustache twitched as he stifled a yawn. "I do have this couch, though. Fairly comfortable." He looked between me and Ben. "I don't want to presume whether you're together. I could take a guess, of course, by your chilly demeanor and all those sidelong looks, like a couple after a fight, but—"

"The couch'll be fine," Ben said hurriedly.

"Just warning you, it gets cold out here. You'll want blankets." Ely headed for his bedroom.

"Ely?" I called.

He turned.

"I don't want to be presumptuous, because you've done more than enough for us. But is there any chance you'd consider talking to Senator Wayne about our bill?"

Ely gave me a weary smile. "I think it's time we let some young people with better ideas and possibly better hearts take their shot. I'm tired of letting the old ways dictate my life. Doing what other people tell me, just because someone made up the rules a long time ago. It's time to shake things up."

Again, I got the feeling Ely was talking about something bigger than electric cars and climate change.

"So I'll do you one better," he continued. "I'll talk to John and I'll write a piece for the *Statesman*. I've only done it a few times over the years, and it always gets his attention." He smiled ruefully. "I think it's about that time again."

My heart glowed, and I couldn't help it—I reached for Ely, pausing only to make sure it was okay.

"Bring it in," he said, lifting his arms.

I wrapped him in a hug. "Thank you, thank you, thank you."

13

A Curious Case of Insomnia

I tossed, and I turned; I pulled the blankets over my head so all I could see was cottony darkness. I counted to one hundred, counted sheep, hummed the only four bars I could ever remember to "Twinkle, Twinkle, Little Star."

And *still*. My eyes were drawn to the bedroom wall—on the other side of which Ben Laderman was stretched out on Ely's couch, sleeping. There was only a thin layer of drywall and plaster separating his body from my body.

What would happen if I crept out of the room, closed the door whisper-quiet behind me and sneaked into the living room to watch him? It would be a hate-watch, of course. I would invent curses and whisper them over his prone body.

He'd probably been out like a light the minute his head hit the pillow, and was halfway into some dream about winning our contest and lording it over me by now. I'd always marveled at Ben's ability to fall asleep as soon as he decided it was time.

Meanwhile, here I was, replaying our argument by the taco truck on a loop, and also the way Ben had looked, sweaty and covered in grease after car repairs, and then shirtless before his shower, and then dreamy as he gazed up at the stars from the other side of the fire. *The Many Faces of Ben Laderman: A Twelve-Month Calendar for Naughty Girls.*

I knew what was happening, and it was classic Stoner. Ben was off-limits—both because of his girlfriend and because, at best, he thought of me as a work frenemy he'd once regrettably dated. And now, consequently and causally, I was once again fascinated by him.

There was no better example of how my messed-up brain worked than the fact that I couldn't stop thinking about Ben *now*, after we'd gotten into a fight, right when it was clearest he could barely tolerate me. In the past, my need to prove myself had caused me to chase many a man who was verboten or simply didn't seem interested. Then, the instant I won him, the thrill was over and I dropped him like a hot potato. It always ended badly.

This was my self-destructive impulse hard at work. Well, not today, Satan. I would deny all my instincts when it came to Ben. Unlike five years ago, this time I wouldn't allow my feelings to guide me. They simply couldn't be trusted.

A knock sounded at the door.

I yanked the comforter off my head and sat up straight as a board, heart thumping. "Yes?" I squeaked.

The door swung open silently and Ben stepped inside. He still wore the flannel shirt Ely had lent him and his own jeans. He was barefoot, and it was a sign of how ridiculous my brain was that the sight of his bare feet made me shiver, the intimacy thrilling.

"Did I wake you?"

With his eyes on me, goose bumps flared to life. I drew the

comforter back up to my chin. "No." *I was lying awake remembering, inch by inch, how beautiful your face looked in the firelight.* I cleared my throat. "What's up?"

Ben crossed his arms, still standing in the doorway. "It's freezing in the living room. My teeth are actually chattering, which I didn't realize happened in real life. Ely mentioned there were blankets, but I couldn't find any. Do you have spares in here?"

"You're free to look," I said, settling back against the pillows.

Ben flashed me a quick, tight-lipped smile and crept inside, footsteps barely making a sound on the wood floors. No wonder I hadn't heard him coming. Laderman was a ninja.

I watched him by the moonlight coming in through the window. He opened the double doors to the wardrobe and rustled inside; then, coming away empty-handed, he moved to the dresser by the side of the bed. He wrestled open the top drawer, which clearly wasn't used to being opened.

I sat stiff in bed, unsure what to do with myself, and hyperconscious of Ben's body only a foot away.

Ben stuck his hand in the next drawer and peered into it as he rummaged. "Congrats on getting Ely to support the bill, by the way."

"Thanks," I said, suspicious about the nice words, given our argument. "Even better that he's going to write an op-ed."

"Hope it works on Wayne."

I leaned back more deeply into the pillows and crossed my arms. "*Do* you?"

Ben paused what he was doing and grinned at me. "Sure. You can have Wayne. There's still McBuck left to convince."

I snorted. "And you've got the in with Mendax Oil's lobbyist. Yeah, yeah. Don't get cocky."

Ben arched his eyebrows playfully, but turned back to the drawer. We fell quiet.

In the silence, I thought about how surreal it was that I'd been picturing Ben stretched out on the couch on the other side of the wall, wishing to collapse the distance between us, and now, if I reached out, I could slide my hand under his shirt and touch his waistband.

"No blankets," he said, pushing the last drawer closed with a thud. "Just a bunch of old clothes. There's an army dress uniform in there. Did you read anything about Ely being in the army?"

I shook my head. "Senator Wayne was, though. I remember from reading his bio, because I was thinking about ways I could work a military angle into our pitch. You know," I added, "neither of them ever married."

Ben and I looked at each other. His face softened. "Ely said he was tired of letting the old ways dictate his life."

"Yeah." I looked over his shoulder, head swimming with a mix of tenderness and frustration. "Stupid, backward Texas," I said finally.

Ben was quiet for a beat. Then I felt the side of the mattress dip and looked over to find him sitting gingerly on the edge of the bed, his back to me. He turned, and I could see his profile in the moonlight. "Sarah was hanging out with her brother Halloween night. The group of guys you saw her with were her brother and his friends, in town from Dallas for the weekend. That's why she went out in the first place, instead of staying in with me. She wanted to show them a good time."

Oh. My stomach dropped. I'd been so sure Sarah's actions were flirtatious…

Because they were what I did to *Ben* when we hung out. Oh, no. Ben was right: I'd been projecting.

I clapped a hand over my mouth. "I'm sorry."

He cocked an amused eyebrow at me over his shoulder. "What was that, now?"

Reluctantly, I removed my hand, finger by finger. "I said I'm sorry. I jumped to conclusions, and I was wrong."

He twisted around on the bed to face me, drawing one leg up, his other foot still resting on the floor. "Will you look at that. Hell has officially frozen over."

I rolled my eyes, but he kept going. "I didn't know you were physically capable of apologizing." He leaned over and rested a hand on my forehead. "You're not feverish?"

"Ha. Get it all out. I know I deserve it. Me and my *messy bullshit*."

Ben cracked a smile—then abruptly shivered, rubbing his arms.

"Oh, shit, you weren't lying about being cold." I'd felt kind of guilty taking the comfortable bed while Ben slept on the couch—which I suspected was barely long enough to fit his tall frame, anyway, on top of being cold. "Here." I lifted the comforter. "If you want to warm up."

Ben eyed the comforter, then eyed me. He didn't move.

"Oh, *please*. It's just for a minute. Then you can go back to your freezing wasteland in the living room. I promise to restrain myself from so much as *thinking* about touching you. I'll have to use all my willpower, but by God, I will keep my hands off your devastating body."

Ben rolled his eyes so hard I hoped for a moment they'd get stuck there. "Fine. Just for a minute." Then he climbed up the bed and slid under the comforter, drawing it up to his chest.

We lay there, side by side, staring up at the ceiling. I was deathly still, not wanting to move and accidentally brush him. I could feel the heat from his body even with the distance.

Ben sighed. "I hate to admit it, but this is so much better."

"Good." I was trying to get my breathing under control,

but my heart and my lungs were contracting way too fast, like my body thought we were in an entirely different kind of situation.

"Ben?"

He shifted in my direction. "Yes?"

"I'm not wearing any pants."

I could feel him stiffen beside me. "Oh?"

"I forgot to mention it before you got in. You know I don't like to sleep in pants. They're restricting."

Ben nodded, the movement slight. "Right. You catfished me. I should have seen that coming, so that's on me. Just… stay on your side of the bed."

"Ben?"

This time he turned so his whole body faced me, bending his elbow and resting his head in his hand. "What is this, Lee's confessional hour?"

"The reason I was worried about Sarah cheating on you was because I still feel guilty about how things ended between us. What I did to you."

He was quiet for a painfully long time, during which I blinked anxiously at the ceiling. Then, finally, he said, "That's actually nice to hear."

I twisted to face him, mirroring him with my elbow bent, head resting in my hand.

His face was serious, eyes cast down to the empty stretch of bed between us. "The night I found out you cheated, it was almost like we were competing to see who could piss the other off more. Win the breakup or something. There was a lot of yelling. I know I'm guilty of it—actually, the guiltiest—but still. We didn't leave a lot of room for apologies."

I nodded. That's exactly how it had been. Connor had run off and told Ben we'd slept together, and Ben had confronted me. I'd known it was going to happen, known the truth would eventually come out—hell, part of me was anticipating it. But still, when I was faced with the reality of having to confirm it, having to watch Ben transform, before my eyes, into the cutting, cruel version of himself, who was so good at punishing his enemies, my brain went into self-protective overdrive. Instead of trying to smooth things over, I'd responded to his acerbic anger with anger of my own. Which only escalated things.

Example ten thousand and one of my self-destructive nature. I was always doing the exact opposite of what would get me what I wanted. Doing the exact things that were going to cut me deepest in the end.

Ben drew a breath, and I realized his eyes were lingering on my face, watching my thoughts play out. "I guess I've always wondered if you were even sorry you did it. I kind of… assumed you weren't."

I looked Ben square in the eyes, even though my heart was pounding; even though the vivid blue of them, framed by his long lashes, was distracting. "I'm really, *really* sorry for sleeping with Connor. Especially right before your final. It was the ultimate dick move, and I've regretted it ever since."

To my surprise, Ben leaned forward and mussed my hair. "Thanks, Stoner. Really." He settled on his back and snuggled beneath the covers.

I blew the hair out of my face. "Really? That's it? I hand you this big, emotional apology and you rub my head like I'm a kid on your Little League team?"

Ben shrugged, closing his eyes. "You want me to make you grovel?"

I rolled on my other side, turning my back on him. "I don't know," I muttered. "*Something* to mark the milestone might be nice. Maybe a certificate that says 'Lee Stone is officially forgiven and off the hook. And no longer, by any definition, a practitioner of messy bullshit.'"

A noise from behind had me glancing furtively over my shoulder. Ben's eyes were still closed, but he was *laughing*.

The nerve.

"Good night, Stoner," he said, still laughing.

I stared evilly at the distant wall, listening to his breathing slow. After a few minutes, it became a steady, soothing sound. *In, and out. In, and out.* Ben at peace. I closed my eyes and started to drift.

Then it hit me, and I jerked awake.

Ben was only supposed to warm up under the covers for a minute. I turned—and sure enough, he was sleeping. In the same bed as me. Only inches away. Surely this violated every code in the Geneva convention.

I panicked and rolled to him. "Uh, Ben?" I placed a hand on his shoulder, shaking gently. "Benjamin?"

He mumbled something incoherent and tugged my arm.

"Ben, *wake up*," I insisted. But he was sleepy and persistent, and suddenly, like it was a routine gesture, his fingers slid under my shirt, skimming my stomach, and he tugged me flush against his chest. With his arm encircling me, I was trapped, unless I wanted to yell in his ear to wake him, then banish him back to the cold couch.

Our bodies fit like a lock and key. I could feel the blood pumping under his skin, a delicate warmth, his heartbeat against my chest a slow but steady rhythm. This close to the source, his smell suffused the air, and I breathed deep. Woodsmoke and salt and a clean note from Ely's soap. Underneath, the barest hint of Ben himself: his skin, and hair, and the musk from under his arms.

I went still, but it didn't stop what was unfolding inside me. My heart beat faster, pumping blood to the tender place between my legs, to the surface of my skin, so it flushed and tingled, suddenly achingly sensitive to every centimeter where Ben and I touched. I pressed my legs together, but still, the feeling scythed through me.

All right. It had come to this. I would admit it. I wanted to fuck Ben Laderman.

I wanted him so much I felt like I would burst into flames in the middle of this bed, my ashes a sorry relic for Ely to clean up. I wanted him so bad that every inch of my body pressed against his felt like it was crackling with electricity, all the nerve endings sparking, almost painfully alive with the potential of what I could do if I just leaned closer and woke him.

I wanted his large, rough hand on my stomach to slide down, cupping me between my legs. I wanted to turn around and rotate my hips against him until I could feel him push, hard, with a soft groan, against the small of my back. I wanted to kiss him awake, arch against him until he ran his hot mouth, his stubbled jaw, down my neck. I wanted to bite his shoulders, feel the muscles flex under my teeth as he picked me up and straddled me across his hips. I wanted him to lean in close and whisper, voice hoarse, *I tried but I couldn't keep my hands off you. I'm going to make you beg for it, make you come so hard you forget the last five years ever happened.*

I could do it. We were lying so close. The air was thick, charged with possibilities.

But—and this was the bucket of ice water to the face—I knew exactly why I wanted to do these things. It was because I wasn't supposed to. Because Ben was my ex-boyfriend, my competition, and he wanted nothing to do with me, romantically speaking. He was in every way forbidden.

I had to ignore these feelings and stick to my original plan of simply besting Ben at work, putting a nice and tidy bow on the story of us, and going on my merry way, unbothered by his presence in the world. I needed to extricate myself from his arms or, at the very least, remain utterly still for the next eight hours. Force my eyes closed until I fell asleep. Then say nothing tomorrow, act like it didn't happen, so as not to embarrass him.

I swallowed as Ben shifted and his thigh nudged my legs apart.

Come on, Stoner. *Character growth.*

14

A Rising Star

Governor Mane sat in his leather wingback chair and lifted Sunday's edition of the *Austin American-Statesman*, giving it a vigorous shake. "Fucking brilliant, Lee. Go to Wayne's best friend, the man he respects most, and get him to publicly call on the senator to endorse. It's the perfect tactic for those old cowboys. Activate their honor and loyalty and all that shit. No surprise, Wayne ate it up." The governor pointed at Ben. "We just came from a meeting. We've got his vote."

"Excellent." Dakota, seated on the governor's antique couch, beamed at me. "Lee's a political genius."

I was practically soaring. In fact, I was close to needing to tether myself to the armchair I was sitting in to make sure I didn't float right out the open window. It was surreal enough to be sitting in the Governor's Mansion—when I got the call from Wendy that the governor had invited us here, I'd asked her twenty times if she was sure—but to be here, celebrating my *win*? It was exactly like one of those daydreams I used to have in the middle of boring sales meetings.

Ely Gunther had been true to his word. He'd written a sparse but direct editorial urging his compatriots in Corsicare County to support a greener Texas, and then he'd directed a special plea to Senator Wayne, "the tireless champion of grand, old Texas," to embrace the new and vote yes on the bill. My heart had swelled upon reading it. I'd actually gone out and found a physical copy of the newspaper, cut out the piece and stuck it to my refrigerator like I was a five-year-old with an A on a spelling test.

And sure enough, just like Ely predicted, Senator Wayne had been swayed by the public plea. I'd gotten my yes. Ben and I were tied now, neck and neck. There was only one more vote to win.

I tried to meet Ben's eyes from across the room. He'd shown up in a conservative suit today, all boring navy with a red tie, Politics 101, with a depression beard and wan skin, dark circles under his eyes. As soon as he sensed me looking, he cast his gaze to the carpet. It was a swirling, paisley affair, one of those patterns only men think are attractive, so I figured it would occupy him for a while. I stifled a sigh.

The instant we'd woken up, tangled in Ely's guest bed, Ben had leaped out of it like it was on fire, apologizing profusely in between muttering, "Shit, shit, shit, you *idiot*," like a broken record.

I'd worked very hard in that moment to *not* feel offended that Ben was reacting to sleeping next to me the same way he might receive a herpes diagnosis. I reminded myself it hadn't been *my* idea for him to fall asleep or wrap his arm around me, and that, in fact, I had remained as rigid as one of those metallic-painted street performers out of sheer strength of character all night. Which honestly should earn me a pat on the back.

But Ben had barely spoken to me during the ride to town in Ely's tow truck, which was a feat, considering we'd been mashed up against one another. And then he'd continued the silent treatment as we waited for the Prius to get repaired, and then on the long ride back to Austin. The last time I'd endured that much quiet was when Mac got super into meditation and dragged us to a silent yoga retreat in the middle of Hill Country. Riding in Ben's passenger seat, staring morosely out the window, I got trauma flashbacks of the gruel they'd served us for breakfast—"millet and bulgur oatmeal," they'd called it—and the night I'd snorted what turned out to be dandelion root powder meant to be put in our smoothies, thinking Mac had come to her senses and was ready to ditch the yoga for a party.

Well, it had been a week since Ely's, and we now had a verified victory under our belt. But Ben was still being awkward. Great.

"I have to agree it was a stroke of genius." Wendy gave me a grudging nod of respect. "This campaign is coming along faster than I expected." She looked at Ben. "You two make a good team."

Ben straightened in his leather wingback chair, which matched the governor's. "This one was all Lee. She figured out the strategy and made it happen. Honestly, I was just along for the ride." His eyes flicked to mine with a quick smile. Then he looked away.

"Well." Governor Mane slapped his thighs. "You two really are the Dream Team."

"Problem is," Wendy said, crossing her legs, "we've saved the hardest one for last."

"Senator Roy McBuck." Dakota said the name like it tasted sour.

"The thing about persuading McBuck," said the governor, "is you're really doing battle with Mendax Oil."

Wendy shivered. "Samuel Slittery. Bane of our existence."

Samuel Slittery was the CEO of Mendax Oil, which was beginning to rival Exxon for output and profits. There was no low-down trick in the book Slittery wouldn't try to protect his power. He was a full-fledged climate change denier, and even refused to acknowledge that years of oil drilling had made any impact on the environment whatsoever. He was anti regulations, anti EPA and, most of all, anti electric vehicles.

We suspected he was secretly behind a number of social media groups that existed for the sole purpose of tearing down Lise Motors—and specifically, Dakota. Why they didn't go after Tesla with the same fervor didn't take much guesswork, since much of their hate centered around the fact that Dakota was a woman. Some of the things they said about her were downright disgusting. They'd even gone after Dakota's husband, George, who was a sweet stay-at-home dad, and her two elementary-aged kids.

All in all, Slittery and his goons were slime. Unfortunately, they were rich slime; slime whose manufacturing center was located in Hudson County, in McBuck's district. That meant a huge chunk of McBuck's constituents worked for Mendax Oil, and wouldn't want to support any bill that undermined Mendax's profits and threatened their jobs.

It was going to be an uphill battle. I honestly didn't know where to start.

"Slittery's a hard one," the governor agreed. "Hell, I accepted campaign donations from him when I was running for office." He must have seen the look on my face, because he tsked. "Now, now, Lee. I know you're a purist. But he was offering a lot of money." He gestured around the room. "And look at me now, pushing the Green Machine. It's not like his money determined my behavior."

"I'll give you that," I said grudgingly.

Wendy stood. "I hate to interrupt, but will you point me in the direction of the restroom?"

Dakota leaped up. "I'll show you. It's down the hall and tucked into this little corner near the butler's pantry. It's kind of hidden—took me forever to find it."

Ben and I lifted our eyebrows at each other, awkwardness temporarily forgotten. How did Dakota know how to find the bathroom in the governor's house? As far as I knew, this was the first time any of us had been to the Governor's Mansion, a historic, white-columned home just a stone's throw from the capitol. I suppose she could've come here for a social thing I'd somehow missed. But we'd done a deep dive on each of our political connections when we were planning the Green Machine campaign, and she'd never mentioned a friendship with the governor. I thought we'd all met him at the same time.

I added the strangely intimate gesture to my list of weird things about her. It's not like I tracked Dakota's whereabouts or obsessed over her daily moods or anything, but I'd noticed she'd been hard to read lately: largely absent, though that was probably because she was spending most of her days in the lab perfecting the Herschel motor before it went into mass production. When she was around, she seemed distracted and out of sorts. Today, her normal polish was gone, replaced by frizzy hair pulled back into a low bun and thick-framed blue-light glasses that didn't mask her tired, red-rimmed eyes.

Ben gave me a shrug to say he didn't get it, either.

The governor settled back in his chair, steepling his fingers. "Unfortunately, Benny boy, you're not McBuck's favorite person right now."

Ben nodded sheepishly. "I know."

"Why not?" I asked.

"He hates me for suggesting his constituents get paid a living wage," Ben said dryly.

Governor Mane waved a hand. "I've got Ben working on a bill to get the restaurant industry to raise minimum wages. What they pay people is criminal. Fast food's fighting us tooth and nail, of course. And McBuck's close friends with the CEO of Taco Muy Rico."

"Let me guess," I said, meeting Ben's gaze. "They have an army of powerful lobbyists."

The governor laughed. "They always do. Taco Muy Rico hired Kenneth McGraw's firm, that wily bastard."

At least Ben had the decency to grimace.

"What'd we miss?" Wendy asked, as she and Dakota stepped back into the room. I wondered if Wendy knew why Dakota was so familiar with the governor's house. I made a mental note to ask her the next time we were alone.

"Just explaining to Lee that we're already behind the curve with McBuck," said the governor.

Dakota sank into the couch and kicked off her shoes, curling her legs underneath her. I actually ran a finger over my jaw to make sure it hadn't fallen open. On the one hand, Dakota sat like that all the time in her office, where she felt at home, and it was kind of adorable. On the other, did that mean she felt at home here with the governor? We weren't that close, were we? What was I missing?

"I have full faith the Dream Team will find a way to win McBuck over," Dakota said. Even her vote of confidence wasn't sending me into waves of delirium like it normally would, because half my brain was still trying to puzzle her out.

"We've got it," Ben promised, standing and brushing off his slacks. "But you'll have to excuse me. I have a meeting in the capitol."

The governor jerked a thumb in his direction. "Kid's making me redecorate the Alamo room. Can you believe it? No appreciation for history."

"That room is racist," Wendy said, without batting a lash.

"What?" Governor Mane sputtered. "It's been unchanged since the capitol opened in 1888."

"Repeat that to yourself until you hear it," I advised. I watched Ben's back disappear through the front door. "In the meantime, please excuse me, too."

I got up and raced after him, shooting out the door and clambering down the first set of ornate white stairs that led to the street below. I looked down and groaned. Only twelve million more steps to go, and Ben was somehow at the end of them.

"Curse governors and their delusions of grandeur," I muttered. Then I yelled, *"Ben!"*

He froze and slowly turned. I can't say the expression on his face when he finally made it around was particularly welcoming.

"Wait up!" I jostled down the infinite stairs until I finally made it to him and bent over, trying to catch my breath.

"What's up, Lee?" From my vantage point, I could see Ben's foot tapping impatiently.

"*Lee?* Ouch. I thought we were back to being friends again."

The foot tapped faster. "And I thought you specifically asked me not to call you Stoner at work."

"A girl can change her mind." I blew out a breath. "Damn, I need to step up my cardio. A solid sex life does *not* count as much as you think it will."

Ben's feet spun in the direction of the street.

"Wait, wait." I pulled myself upright. "Only kidding."

His brow furrowed. "Was there something you wanted?"

"Are we cool?"

Ben was quiet for a second, during which I studied his face and determined the exact shade of the circles under his eyes: midnight blue, like a velvety sky over a campfire. Then he blurted: "I shouldn't have fallen asleep in the bed at Ely's house. First of all, it was unprofessional, and I'm sorry. I hope you know I value you as a talented professional, and didn't mean to cross boundaries."

"Yeah, it's a little too late for that. Which is *my* fault, mostly," I added, when I saw the look on his face. "Ben, you can toss your unwanted-advances-in-the-workplace apology script. It's fine. Who's to say I didn't cut the heating in Ely's house to lure you into bed and take advantage of *you*, anyway? Why do men always get to be the sexual deviants?"

Ben's eyes widened behind his clear-framed glasses.

"Kidding. Yeesh. Such delicate sensibilities. Listen, Ben. We're old friends who fell asleep next to each other on a work trip. Nothing happened. You can't make up what a nothing burger that is. Bor-*ing*. If I tried to call HR to report myself, I'd make it thirty seconds in before the rep fell asleep on the other end of the line."

"Forget what I said about valuing you as a professional. It's worrisome you're in charge of communications for an actual company."

I waved a hand. "I'm just saying, stop fretting. I'm not."

"I don't only regret it professionally," he said. "There's personally, too."

Right. There was Sarah, and Ben's promise to himself that he'd never get too close to me again. "You have nothing to regret," I said. "Trust me. Sleeping next to you was the definition of meaningless."

Ben's expression flipped to the same one he'd worn the day we met in the governor's office—coolly neutral. Then he turned his gaze away. "Glad we're on the same page."

"Hey," I said brightly. "The good news is, we've got two out of three yeses under our belt. That's huge. Only one more to go. Whoever wins McBuck's vote wins the competition."

He took a deep breath and nodded, seeming to center himself. "You're right. One more leg, and the campaign is over.

We'll keep it professional, pass the bill and go our separate ways. Back to normal."

He nodded at me, satisfied, and gave me a clipped goodbye, then jogged down the last few steps and out the governor's wrought iron gate.

One more yes, then some silly peacocking over *winner* and *assistant*, and then there would be no more reason to see Ben. I'd go back to life BBRI—*Before Ben Rudely Interrupted*. I'd either win and get the bill over the line, then make my case for vice president of public affairs, or I'd lose, and settle for communications. But—and this was an important but—either way, I'd get to walk away with the personal victory of knowing I'd kept my thoughts and feelings about Ben under control this time. I'd walk away as smoothly and professionally and indifferently as he would. I could revise that Fourth and Final Major Heartbreak from a Level 5 Catastrophic Life Event to a Level 2 Minor Blip with Eventual Resolution.

On the one hand, there would be no more bill to chase, so there'd be no more goal to give my life purpose. But on the other, without Ben, I could go back to being carefree Stoner, messaging maven by day, practitioner of the debauched arts by night. There'd be no one around to throw a wrench in my life by asking invasive questions like, *What's wrong with you?* or making me think about my flaws or grinning at me with a wide, sexy, smart-ass charm that made me want to chuck the meager amount of self-restraint I possessed.

I would go back to regular life, except with the added twist that Ben was no longer thousands of miles away in California, but right here in Austin, potentially around every corner. And yet, in every way that mattered, just as untouchable.

It was what I'd wanted from the beginning. So. Obviously, I could not wait.

15

No Comment

It was 8:00 p.m. on a Friday night, and—stop the presses—Ben Laderman was *drunk*. Not regular drunk—goofy, overblown facial expressions drunk. Too invested in unimportant things drunk. No filter drunk. And at a *work* event, no less. Credit where credit was due: it was all thanks to Mrs. Alice Graham, sexagenarian wife of Mendax Oil's VP of international sales. Avid lover of yoga, oysters, virile young men and long walks on the beach. That was, verbatim, the way she'd introduced herself to Ben, emphasis on *sex*agenarian.

Alice was the grand dame of the Hudson County Wine Festival, the premier wine-tasting event in Senator McBuck's district. As such, she had unlimited access to every single vintage on display tonight. All of which she'd poured, together with increasingly suggestive eyebrow arches and forearm strokes, into Ben's tasting glass.

For all of his defensiveness and whip-smart verbal acuity when it came to taking down snotty law students, Ben was rendered helpless when it came to certain demographics. Kids. Single parents. Anyone in need of financial, emotional or physical aid. And, apparently, lonely, thirsty older women. In the beginning, he'd tried to protest each new glass of wine Alice handed him, but—outmatched by her persistence—he'd finally given up, resigning himself to tasting each new glass with a murmured *Hmm, oaky* or *You're right, the tannins are quite voluptuous.*

From the moment Alice zeroed in on Ben and beelined to our table, right after we'd set up the Green Machine signage and fanned out the pamphlets, I had ceased to exist, allowed to simply stand back, watch Ben grow increasingly red-faced and awkward, and take scrupulous notes on Alice's highly advanced flirting techniques.

Needless to say, it was possibly the best night of my life.

"I don't think that was a full pour," I pointed out, helpfully tapping the high-water mark on Ben's glass. "He won't be able to really *taste* it unless he's got enough in there."

Alice blinked behind horn-rimmed glasses for a second, taking note of me for the first time in an hour. Her white hair was curled uniformly into a bob under her chin, and she wore a cotton-candy pink dress that hugged every curve of her body, screaming *look at me.* It was a look I was, in all honesty, extremely into. I would have asked her where she bought the dress, but something told me Alice Graham and I weren't in the same economic bracket. Maybe it was the rope of fist-sized diamonds around her neck.

While I was cataloging every article of her clothing, Alice, for her part, seemed surprised to find someone else was standing behind the Green Machine booth besides Ben. But, with practiced composure, she quickly hid her shock and nodded.

"Quite, quite. Not enough in the glass to taste." She tipped the bottle over Ben's glass and more red wine glugged out. "You know, New Zealand pinots are all the rage right now. Eugene—" here she slid Ben a sly look to see if he'd taken notice she'd referenced her husband "—bought me a case the moment the bottle prices started skyrocketing."

Unfortunately for Alice, Ben was too busy shooting me a look that said, *What the hell are you doing, you enabling fiend*—all sky-high eyebrows, panicked eyes and indignant twist of mouth—to be piqued into jealousy by the mention of her husband. Fortunately for me, he'd drunk enough wine that I was sure he'd forget my transgression in a minute or two.

"Al," I said, taking the liberty of giving Alice a nickname and a gentle pat on the arm. "Speaking of Eugene, I think I saw him looking for you."

Alice jerked away, scanning the grounds.

I pointed. "Over there, by the Barbaresco tables. He seemed worried, judging by the look on his face."

She straightened, clutched her bottle and glanced at her watch. "Oh, look at the time. I should probably get back to the gals."

"Thanks for the generous pours," I said, because even though she hadn't poured a single ounce of wine into my glass, I'd had fun drinking what Ben couldn't finish.

"You," Alice said, directing her full attention to Ben, who gulped. "You have the face of… It's so familiar…"

"James Dean?" he suggested, pulling his shoulders back and sticking his thumbs in his belt loops like he was posing in a leather jacket.

"Clark Kent," I supplied. Ben was wearing contacts tonight, which was why she was thrown.

Alice's eyes lit up. "*Clark Kent.* That's exactly it." She slipped a hand up her sleeve and, right in front of my eyes, turned out a business card. "This is me. Cell's on the back."

Whoa. I made a mental note: *learn magic card trick.*

"Uh, thanks," Ben said, holding Alice's card gingerly by a corner, as if she'd slipped it out of somewhere other than her sleeve.

"Call me the next time you're in town," she sang over her shoulder, blowing Ben a kiss.

The minute Alice was out of hearing distance, Ben spun to me. "How did you recognize Eugene?"

I patted the side of his smooth, freshly shaved face. "Oh, sweet summer child. I have no idea what that man looks like."

Ben's mouth twisted, and I resisted the urge to let my fingers drift to his lips. "Just because you saved me in the end doesn't mean I forgive you for the last hour. You're the worst campaign partner of all time, you know."

I grabbed his very full glass of wine and sipped it. "On the contrary. While you were making time with Alice, I gave out *every single one* of our pamphlets." I spread my fingers over the empty spot on the table where the pamphlets had been displayed. "Really, you're the slacker."

Ben looked up at the tent ceiling, seeming to call for strength from some divine source. "Fine. You're just the worst friend. How's that?"

This was much better. First, he'd called me a friend. Second, I liked mean, quippy Ben. It was silent, distant, morose Ben—the Ben he'd been for the last two weeks, ever since Ely's—that I couldn't handle. Seriously. Every time I'd seen him lately, he'd looked upset and disheveled, and wouldn't say more than two words to me. Tonight was a vast improvement. Thank you, wines of the world.

I put down the glass and gripped his hands. Ben cocked an eyebrow, but didn't pull away.

"Don't tell me you're actually sad you had to suffer through a night of free booze." I pressed his hands together. "The Ben

I remember would sit through three-hour law review meetings just to get the free pizza at the end. Old, *fun* Ben used to work the college lecture circuit just for the watered-down wine."

Amusement curved his mouth into a smile, then spread, glowing in his eyes. "Oh, yeah? Old, fun Ben?" He lifted my hands and spun me like we were dancing. I stopped with my back to him, our clasped hands crossed over my chest.

"You're remembering old, *broke* Ben," he said into my ear, and I shivered with my whole body. I hadn't realized he'd stepped so close. "And no, I'm not sad about the free wine. The only thing that hurts is the delight you take in feeding me to the wolves."

"Guilty," I said, resisting the urge to turn my head and close the inch of space between us. His arms around me were making my heart race. Oh, I was guilty, all right.

Because I, Lee Amelia Stone, had stacks and stacks of willpower when it came to fighting for Lise and Dakota and the environment. But when it was Lee vs. the forbidden? I was as wobbly as a Jenga tower missing half its blocks. No, scratch that. I was a Jenga tower missing half its blocks, who'd always wondered to itself how deliciously bad it would feel to just let it all go and topple. I needed to resist my natural instincts, before I did something that threw Ben and me back to square one.

Ben's breath was a tickle at my throat. "Every time I looked at you for help, you winked and smiled that wicked smile that means you're fully aware you're doing something bad and you're happy about it. Absolutely no empathy."

"As a lawyer, you should know I can't let you get away with slander. If I was to concede there was a little less intervention than there could have been, it's only because—" *When you turn red with embarrassment, my pulse races. When I watch you laugh, it reminds me of every time I've ever made you do it. Because I got to stand here and look at you, uninterrupted, for an hour.*

"—I knew it would put me at a competitive advantage." I brushed away the inconvenient thoughts and dropped his hands, stepping out of his arms and spinning to face him. "Who would have thought—Mr. Professionalism, getting drunk on the job. Now the work glory's all mine."

He smiled again. A lazy, sexy grin that was the best advertisement wine could ever hope for. "To quote a paragon of propriety, the festival's over." He hunched up his shoulders and started moonwalking backward. "It's officially Laderman o'clock."

I shook my head. "You are in *rare* form tonight. I've got an idea. Let's keep you drunk all the time. I like you like this."

Ben laughed. "I like *you* like this."

Just like that, the air between us lit with electricity. I froze, not wanting to make the wrong move. Ben had a girlfriend. And he'd tasted a lot of wine, so even if I wasn't imagining this charge between us, that explained it.

I cleared my throat. "So. Who'd you have to sleep with to get us into this festival, anyway?" I was embarrassed by how weak my voice sounded, but I was doing the right thing by changing the subject. That was what mattered. For once, I was standing on the moral high ground.

And I was also genuinely curious. Ben's idea to come here tonight was brilliant. The Hudson County Wine Festival was sponsored by Mendax Oil, and the event was full of Mendax employees. I'd seen enough interested, contemplative expressions when I'd passed out our Green Machine pamphlets—along with an on-brand glass of vinho verde, Portuguese green wine—to think maybe we had a fighting chance at winning over McBuck's constituents. The mystery was how Ben had heard about the event, *and* how he'd scored us a seat at the enemy's table. Or a booth, to be exact.

The charge in the air disappeared with my question. Ben

looked away, suddenly fascinated by a loose thread on his sweater, which was the exact cerulean of his eyes. "I may have overheard Sarah talking about it a while ago...and called the festival...pretending to be from McGraw & Klein," he mumbled.

I swallowed past the lump in my throat. "Ben, you dirty dog. Spying on your girlfriend for intel. Ice-cold. I approve."

You're doing the right thing for once, Stoner. This was good, really it was. Maybe I could explore this whole restraint thing—lean in to this upstanding-choices kink—like a new fetish.

Ben's face radiated intensity. "I didn't use anyone." A lock of his dark hair fell over his forehead. "And there's actually something I wanted to tell—"

"Benjamin?" called a high, familiar voice.

I ducked my head. "Incoming. Sexagenarian at twelve o'clock."

Alice swept back up to our booth, an alarmed expression flushing color high on her cheeks. She grasped both of Ben's hands from across the table and squeezed them like they were about to depart a sinking *Titanic*. "I just heard from Eugene that you're working against us, on something that would hurt Mendax Oil."

Ben stiffened. "It's a piece of legislation. But it wouldn't hurt Mendax. Maybe it would hurt the company's bottom line a little. But it's good for the planet, so it's good for everyone—"

"Hush," Alice said, putting a finger to Ben's lips. I died and ascended to heaven. "I want to help you. I hate Mendax, too. The men at the top are a bunch of liars and assholes. And they wouldn't know how to find a woman's G-spot if you drew them a map."

Ben's eyes widened in a vivid picture of alarm, but since he couldn't actually speak with Alice's finger buttoning his lips, I said, "First tell us how to win. Then draw Ben the map."

For the first time, Alice really *looked* at me, assessing, and I could tell she liked what she saw. Maybe it was the mercenary glint in my eyes. She nodded, voice terse. "Upper management's against you, but the key is the rank and file. They're undervalued. Convince the staff there's something in your bill for them and you'll win in a landslide."

Her eyes darted around. "They're on to you. You should leave before Eugene and Samuel Slittery find you. I was never here." She removed her finger and blew a kiss at an astonished Ben. "Goodbye, my darling. Think of me when you drink New Zealand pinot."

Ben and I both stood there as Alice flitted away. Then Ben burst out laughing.

I shook my head. "I can't believe your luck. The last time some old dude was aggressively into me, he just followed me around the grocery store asking if I wanted to eat spaghetti *Lady and the Tramp* style. Your stalker gave you solid work advice."

Ben's mouth quirked. "Tramp was a good guess—"

I punched his arm.

"—but he should have known you're more of a Cookie Monster."

He was undoubtedly referencing that time in grad school I'd been desperate to avoid studying for a final and had procrastinated by baking every kind of cookie in *The Environmentally Conscious Chef*, a blog run by this hard-core vegan who lived in a commune somewhere in Oregon. Ben had taken one bite of one cookie and declared veganism a flavorless sacrilege that had no business in his apartment. To prove him wrong, I'd eaten every last cookie over the course of forty-eight organic-sugar-crazed hours. Strangely, in the end, Ben still did not concede to me. He'd always been so stubborn.

We stood staring at each other, warm in the bubble of our shared joke, both a little too happy and blurry from the wine.

Then Ben's gaze swept past me and his face abruptly changed. "Oh, *shit*. I think that's actually Eugene."

On the opposite side of the wine festival, an irate silver-haired man in a sports coat stomped through the tasting booths, headed in our direction.

"That's our cue." I yanked the Green Machine banner off the booth, pulling at the Velcro seam, and shoved the crumpled heap into Ben's arms.

"No pamphlets to grab?"

"I told you, I gave them all away." I hustled to the mini-fridge that had come with the booth. "I just need to grab the rest of the vinho verde."

"Stoner, we don't have time."

I stacked wine bottles in my arms. "Shh, he doesn't mean it."

"Party crashers," Eugene yelled. "Stop right there."

Ben yanked me from the fridge. "Let's go, *now*."

"This doesn't mean I don't love you," I called, stumbling to keep up with Ben.

"Hoodwinkers!" Eugene yelled from behind us. "You are *not* from the lobbying firm!"

Ben glanced over his shoulder. "Shit. He's faster in those boat shoes than I expected." He turned to me and took my hand. "Run for it?"

"Are you serious? We're not teenage shoplifters."

"Tell me what you said to my wife!" Eugene demanded at the top of his lungs. "You uncouth gigolo!"

"And that's my limit," Ben said, tugging me faster. "I'm not getting murdered over this."

"Ahhh," I shrieked, as Ben and I sprinted through the massive white tent, passing a sea of astonished faces, my bottles of vinho verde clanking like angry maracas with each step. We streaked into the grassy parking lot and down the rows of cars.

Ben jerked left and I was forced to follow, since he still had a grip on my hand.

"What are you doing? We're parked in the opposite direction."

"Throwing him off our trail," Ben called.

I rolled my eyes, which was nowhere near as effective as I wanted it to be, since we were now in the farthest part of the parking lot, past the lights, and it was so dark Ben couldn't have seen. But I would admit—silently, to myself—there was something exhilarating about running like this. All your blood rushing, muscles alert and working. I could see why people did it.

Eventually, Ben looped us back in the direction of his Prius. When we finally reached it, I dropped to the grass and let the bottles roll away from me.

Ben crouched down. "Here," he said, gathering the wine. "I'll put this in the trunk."

"Thanks," I huffed, still catching my breath. "I'm going to need a minute. There's a possibility all that weed is less than ideal for my lung capacity."

His laugh came from the back of the car, followed by the thud of the trunk closing.

"Come on," he said, extending a hand. "Let's get you in the car."

I took his hand and he pulled me up with so much strength I rocked off my toes. Show-off.

"You know we can't drive home after all that wine."

Ben opened the passenger door. "I know. But it's cold out, and there are roaming Mendax employees with axes to grind. Best to get in."

I obliged, hopping in and rubbing my arms in the passenger seat, waiting for Ben to climb around to the driver's. He was right. In the festival there'd been patio heaters everywhere, but out here, once the flush of running wore off, the November chill was biting.

Ben jumped in and turned on the car. I pressed my hands against the heating vents, waiting for the air to warm.

His voice was deadpan, like he was narrating a movie trailer. "Two rogue political operatives, on the run from corporate villains."

I turned to face him, hands still on the vents, which were thankfully starting to heat up. "Running from Eugene was the highlight of your life, wasn't it? Don't lie to me, you nerd."

Ben leaned back in his seat. "I *do* rather feel like James Bond."

A beat of silence passed, and then Ben couldn't help himself, and turned to look at me. A self-satisfied smile spread over his face, growing wider and wider.

"Ben. Are you waiting for me to tell you you're *exactly* like James Bond?"

The smile became a grin, stretching ear to ear.

I settled back in my seat. "You are terminally goofy tonight."

He shot me a wry look. "I'm starting to think it's a side effect of hanging out with you. You should come with a doctor's warning."

I looked out the windshield, up at the dark night sky. "Universe, give me strength."

There was a moment of silence. Then Ben's voice, gone all quiet, filled it. "I broke up with Sarah."

My head snapped in his direction. "What?"

"After we got back from Ely's."

My mind reeled. He'd broken up with *Sarah*? The woman he'd moved back to Texas for? After Ely's—that meant weeks ago. Is this why he'd been so grumpy and distant, so out of sorts? "Why didn't you tell me?"

"I'm telling you now."

"Why did you break up with her? If you don't mind me asking." It was dangerous territory, but I would tread lightly.

Ben stretched out his hands and gripped the steering wheel. He wouldn't meet my eyes. "It just wasn't working out."

That was PR spin if I'd ever heard it. "It didn't have anything to do with…you and me, in bed…right?"

I'd lain beside Ben that night, imagining how I wanted him to touch me. What had I manifested?

He laughed, though it sounded a little desperate. There was a long, stretched-out span of silence. My heart beat so hard and so fast I was afraid he could hear it.

When he finally spoke, his voice was low, tension cracking each word. "What did you do to me? No matter how hard I try, I can't stop thinking about you. I can hardly breathe. Why am I like this?"

His voice sank under my skin, electrifying me, causing a charge to build, low in my body. He still wasn't looking at me, but I could read him: there was an urgency burning right under the surface. He was hanging on to control by a thread.

I couldn't do it anymore. I couldn't resist. I was officially a terrible person because even though I knew it was a bad idea, just looking at Ben—here, in his car, where I'd stolen a million glances at him, wanted him a million different ways—pushed me over my limit. Making bad decisions was who I was, after all. Why keep fighting it?

I stopped thinking, leaned over the console and kissed him.

I could feel Ben's surprise in his sudden intake of breath. But it was only for a second, and then he unleashed, kissing me back with such searing urgency I rocked back in my seat. He followed.

It was weak, but I'd wanted him so badly, and now I wouldn't hold back. I opened my lips against the warm, delicious pressure of Ben's mouth and tasted him, stroking his tongue with mine, every touch lighting the nerve endings between my legs, until I lost control.

Ben gripped each side of my face, twisting me to deepen the kiss. Desperately, I touched every part of him I hadn't been allowed to: his strong, square jaw, the soft place on the side of his mouth where his dimple flashed, his thick, arched eyebrows, the curls looping in his hair.

He groaned softly into my mouth, and an electric thrill shot through me. I kissed him harder, pulling him closer with two hands on his throat. Closer, closer, closer—he'd been too far away for too long. Ben made another sound of need and seized my waist, lifting me in one smooth show of strength over the console and into his lap.

I straddled him in the driver's seat, heart pounding, blood rushing to the surface of my skin, making every inch where Ben and I touched so sensitive I ached with pleasure.

The way I was sitting, flush against him, I could feel him hard as steel between my legs. He gripped my hips and rubbed me up and down, pushing me over him.

I broke from his mouth with a gasp, and he twisted one hand in my hair, keeping the other on my hip to guide me as I ground against him. He angled my head back, exposing my throat, and then his teeth scraped my neck, mouth hot as he closed his lips over my skin.

With my head canted back, eyes closed, I spoke my only thought. "I missed you."

"I missed you, too," he said, voice raw, kissing the words into my throat. "More than I—"

Suddenly, he stilled. And withdrew his mouth.

I looked down at him. Ben's dark hair was wild and messy,

lips raw and cheeks flushed from kissing, making him more handsome than ever. But the look on his face was something else entirely: he looked stunned. It froze me.

"What's wrong?" I could barely speak.

"What am I doing?" His voice was low, disbelieving. "I told myself I wouldn't."

Shit. *Shit.* I'd known this was a bad idea, and I'd done it anyway. I leaned back to put distance between us. "It was just a moment, Ben." I waved between us. "This doesn't have to mean anything."

"Exactly," he said. "It doesn't to you. You and I are different. And I swore to myself, never again. But here I am, right back where I started, kissing you in the middle of a parking lot like an addict. What's wrong with me?"

"Relax," I told him. "Stop making everything so serious. I told you, it doesn't—"

"If you say it doesn't mean anything one more time—" Suddenly, he switched to his calm voice, the quiet one that brooked no arguments. "Actually, just—please get off."

This was the voice he used when he'd made up his mind. I had a terrible flashback to the tail end of our breakup—to the part that had truly undone me, when he'd simply cut me off. No more calls, no more texts, and then one day, without warning, no more Ben. The memory unlocked a feeling of panic, of inevitability, like I knew where this was going.

"Wait a second," I said, desperate to derail.

"Lee, don't." Without waiting for me to move, Ben lifted me and placed me back in the passenger seat. His touch was gentle, but it did nothing to stop the stab of pain.

"I thought you said you forgave me for the past."

Ben had been in the process of unlocking his phone, but at my words, he froze. A tense silence fell over us.

"I do," he said finally. "I just can't do it again. I'm sorry,

Lee." With that, he went back to his phone. "I'm calling an Uber to take you home, okay?"

He couldn't stand to be around me. Now there were a million stabs of pain. "What about you?"

"I'll get my own ride."

The car had turned suffocating. I jerked open the door.

He dropped his phone. "What are you doing?"

I hopped out into the cold. "I'll call my own Uber." And slammed the door shut.

Ben rolled the window down. "You don't have to leave. The Uber's coming."

I ignored him, cutting through the chilly grass. I needed to be anywhere Ben wasn't. If that place happened to be on the side of the road in the middle of nowhere, Hudson County, well—better than here. Maybe I'd get picked up by a murderous truck driver. Or a truck driver with a heart of gold. Honestly, I was not in the mood to be picky.

Of course Ben had rejected me. He'd made his feelings clear from the beginning. And he wasn't even wrong. After everything we'd put each other through, kissing was a terrible idea. That didn't make this any less humiliating.

I couldn't believe how quickly I'd abandoned my principles and seized the chance to kiss him again. How on brand for Lee Stone, Queen of Bad Decisions. Guaranteed to do whatever would get me the opposite of what I wanted in the end.

Case in point: I was pretty sure I'd just ruined my relationship with Ben.

16

Stone-Cold Heart

I checked my phone for the millionth time, but still nothing from Ben. Over the last week I'd texted, emailed and even called him, but received nothing in response. Classic Ben, just like five years ago. I would hand it to him: if torture was what he was aiming for, his methods were very effective.

"Honey, are you working on Thanksgiving?" My mom peeked around the corner, holding her hands up like a surgeon about to go into the operating room. Both of her hands were covered in flour, like dusty white evening gloves.

"Nope, I swear." I closed out of my texts and tapped my internet browser, where I'd been hard at work on a wholly different project. "I'm just getting your Tinder set up."

Mom blinked in confusion. "My *what*?"

"Ew, why Tinder?" Alexis swept past Mom, tossing a dish towel over her shoulder. "That app's only for people who want to hook up. At least set her up on eHarmony or something."

I stretched out on the couch and rested my shoes on the cushions, exactly like I wasn't supposed to. Mom and Alexis rolled their eyes in perfect unison. *Whew*, the genetics were strong with those two. "Maybe Mom just wants to bone—have you thought of that? She deserves a little action."

Mom, who was a total dish with her sage-green cardigan, chunky pearls and shoulder-length brown hair, the same shade as Alexis's and mine, opened her mouth to speak, but no words came out.

Alexis lifted my feet off the couch and dropped them unceremoniously on the living room floor, then sat in their place. "What Mom *deserves* is an epic romance."

Now it was my turn to roll my eyes. "Those don't—"

Alexis held up a finger. "Don't you say those don't exist, you heartless troll."

I kicked her. "I was going to say they don't last for *long*, Princess Sunshine. As everyone in this room knows firsthand."

"Actually," my mom said, leaning against the wall. "I'm already seeing someone."

Both our heads snapped and turned to her, like meerkats springing from their hidey-holes. "You're *what*?" I screeched. "An adult man?"

"Details, now," Alexis demanded.

Mom wiggled her flour-covered fingers. "All I'll say before I go put the bread in the oven is that his name is Ethan, he's a widower, no children, and he's a successful tax attorney." A naughty smile spread over her face. "And an *excellent* lover."

"Eww," Alexis and I shrieked.

"I thought you just said I deserved to bone." Mom shook her head and turned back to the kitchen. "My children, ladies and gentlemen."

"Look what you manifested." Alexis kicked me from her side of the couch, and I kicked her back, and soon we were fighting like two little crabs who'd toppled over and had only their legs to work with.

"We're happy for you, Mom," I called into the kitchen, getting Alexis good in the side. Though the weird thing was, I wasn't sure I was telling the truth. I'd led the campaign to get Mom laid for years now, but I think I'd always been secretly happy when she said no. Now that she was seeing someone, did that mean she was over what Dad did? And if she'd gotten over it...well, without the vivid pain of a fresh wound keeping Dad alive, would he begin to fade away? I stopped kicking Alexis, feeling a sudden, terrible certainty in the pit of my stomach that he would.

Alexis kicked me hard in the crotch just as Mom came back into the living room with clean hands. I actually *woofed* out loud.

"Alexis Rosalie Stone," Mom scolded.

I pointed. "Get her."

Mom settled in her favorite armchair, the floral one by the window. She'd moved two hours away to Houston a few years after the divorce, to be closer to my grandparents and her sisters. The house was smaller than the one we'd grown up in, because Mom was down to only her income from her animal-welfare nonprofit. But the nice part was, everything inside the house was my mom's exact taste. It was all flowers and soft, muted colors. It was her nest, like I had mine. Our little spaces to ourselves, that no one could take away.

"Don't think I don't know you're the instigator," Mom said to me with a look. "Wherever there's trouble, you're behind it."

That reminded me uncomfortably of Ben, so I changed the subject. "Weren't we talking about Alexis and Chris before the great bread-making adventure?"

"Ugh," Alexis said, flinging her head back against the

couch. "Why can't I get over him? He's out there dating another woman and I swear I'm still in love. Is that pathetic?"

I nodded vigorously, but stopped at my mother's sharp look. "You're allowed to feel however you feel, hon. If you still love him, you still love him. We can't talk our hearts into feeling anything they're unprepared for." Mom swung her eagle eyes back to me. "Speaking of. Alexis says Ben moved back to Austin and the two of you are working together. How are you handling *that*?"

Alexis, the loudmouth. I shot her a treacherous look, and she had the good sense to sink into her corner of the couch.

"It's fine," I lied. "We broke up five whole years ago. He's just my campaign partner now."

Alexis snorted, the witch. "Yeah, right. Something happened last week that made you come home and listen to Frank Ocean for forty-eight hours straight in your room. The smell of the—" she glanced guiltily at our mom "—*sage* coming from your door was enough to get an herbal contact high."

"You're evicted," I said. "Effective immediately."

Mom crossed her legs. "You never told me how the two of you broke up in the first place. I mean, you told me dribbles, but I want the whole story, from the beginning."

I looked between her and Alexis. They both wore identical expressions of eager expectation. Two lifelong romantics, looking for a hit. This was the problem with my mom: unlike my little sister, whom I could manage, my mom had an uncanny ability to get me to open up whenever she sniffed deeper emotions. It was why I normally worked to keep my tone light and casual around her. This time, however, I'd stepped in it.

I sighed. All right, *fine*. If they wanted to hear about the Fourth and Final Major Heartbreak, aka the saga of Ben Laderman, aka the last tragedy before I gave up on love, I'd give it to them in all its glory. Hopefully they wouldn't judge me too harshly. Unlike the man in question.

"You know I met Ben a few months into grad school," I said to Mom, and she nodded. "At that point in my life, the last thing I wanted was a boyfriend. Then, of course, I met Ben and threw all caution to the wind."

"That's always how it goes," Alexis said dreamily.

"We had a good year together. Kind of a perfect year. I…" For some reason, I couldn't bring myself to say it.

"You loved him very much," Mom supplied, and I nodded, grateful.

"So much I started to freak out, I guess. I worried he'd find someone else or get bored with me. Leave me. All the inevitable things."

"That doesn't happen in *every* relationship," Alexis protested.

I waved a hand at the three of us. "The proof is sitting in this room."

"What'd you do when you started to have those feelings?" My mom held her chin in her hand, studying me the way I suspected Annie did to her clients in therapy sessions.

I squirmed. "I knew I couldn't fight inevitability. Relationships end, no matter how you feel about it. I prefer to cut to the chase."

Both Alexis and my mom gave me blank looks.

"I started looking at Ben's phone when he wasn't around, searching for proof he was cheating. Or at least thinking about it. One day, I found these messages from a girl named Clarissa. She was in law school with him, and I knew her—she was really pretty. The messages were so flirty, all about needing him to study and how important he was to her GPA. I figured the texts were proof."

My mom clucked. "Did you ask Ben about them?"

"No. In my defense, though, I'd never been wrong about

a guy cheating before. I thought if I at least initiated it myself, it wouldn't hurt as bad when our relationship ended. So I kind of went out and found someone—" *full truth, Stoner* "—his *rival*, and slept with him. Ben found out, and things blew up from there."

I'd been studying in Ben's apartment when he'd come home that night, and the instant I looked up from my books, I knew he knew. Ben sat stiffly next to me on the couch and asked me, point-blank, if I'd slept with Connor Holliday. The rumors were flying at the law library, started by students who'd been at the bar the night I'd left with Connor. Ben had dismissed the talk as jealous bullshit from classmates who were angry he was going to graduate at the top of their class, but then he'd run into Connor. And Connor had delighted in confirming the truth in front of everyone.

Instead of answering, I'd demanded to know the nature of his relationship with Clarissa. Ben was stunned and pulled up Clarissa's Facebook profile, which had recently changed to *Engaged*. So it turns out they really were nothing more than study buddies.

I'd confessed about Connor right then and there, and Ben made me painstakingly recount the night it happened, drawing out every detail like a punishment. He'd grown colder and colder as I spoke; I would never forget the shell-shocked, bombed-out way I'd felt, the mounting realization that I'd fucked up in the worst way possible. It had been a terrible decision I wanted to take back, and there was no way I could. I would never forget the way I could practically *see* Ben slipping through my fingers.

"Oh, Lee," said my mom, her hand covering her mouth.

"I didn't realize you cheated on him," Alexis said quietly, looking at her lap.

"Yep. I'm just like Dad and Chris. But that's not all."

Since all my survival instincts were apparently dead-ass backward, I took that desperation over Ben slipping away from me and transformed it into anger. Ben was good at figuring out the exact right things to say to hurt and punish me; after all, picking people apart was his specialty. To hit back, I told him all the reasons I was glad things were ending, how it was exactly what I wanted. Damn lies.

"We got into a huge fight. The next day, he was a wreck and forgot to bring all the notes he'd spent weeks preparing for his exam. I heard about it from some of the other students. He bombed his final and lost his ranking." It had meant so much to him, to graduate on top. Another win; another point made to his long-gone father. To Ben, graduating number one would have been proof he was worth staying for. "The guy I cheated with took first place, actually."

Alexis winced. Well. The way she was looking at me was no more than I deserved.

"Buckle up," I sighed. "We're not done. Then Ben did the worst possible thing you can do to another human being."

"Besides cheating?" Alexis asked, but I ignored her.

"He completely iced me out. It was like I didn't exist anymore. He wouldn't answer my phone calls or texts. He wouldn't answer the door when I showed up at his apartment, even though I could see his car in the parking lot. I was so mad—"

"You weren't mad," my mother corrected. "You were full of regret, and scared he was leaving you."

"Right," I accepted. "Scared, not mad. I was so scared that it felt like the only way to get his attention was to show up at the big law school graduation party as Connor's date. That was the guy I cheated with," I added for clarity.

Alexis straight-up gasped.

"Ben was furious, as you can imagine. There was alcohol

involved, and Connor was being a dick, and Ben and I ended up getting into a huge fight in front of everyone. Pretty embarrassing, in hindsight. Ben *really* wouldn't talk to me after the party. Then I found out from some of the other law students that because his final grades dipped, he got edged out by someone else for his clerkship. I went to his place to apologize, but his neighbor came outside and told me Ben had uprooted and moved to California. He didn't even say goodbye."

In that moment, standing outside his apartment, the world had tilted. I'd felt like falling to my knees.

"Makes sense," Alexis said. "You kind of blew up his life."

I supposed that was true, and Ben's actions were reasonable. I supposed when you laid out our relationship like this, it wasn't hard to see why he was so determined to not repeat the past.

My mother, gingerly sidestepping a verdict on my behavior, asked, "And then he just showed up back in Austin to work with you, out of the blue?"

"To work for the governor. Ben's helping me pass that bill I told you about, with the electric vehicles."

She arched a brow. "What an interesting test of your emotional growth over the last five years."

I threw my hands over my face. "Mom, if it was a test, I failed it."

"What happened?" Alexis breathed, apparently too drawn in by the drama to remember she was talking to the villain in the story.

"At first, Ben and I were competing at work. Then we became friends again." I curled into a ball on the couch, as if I could make myself small enough to disappear. "I should have left it at that. But I…sort of…found myself attracted to him again."

"Well, you're only human. And Ben was always a standout," my mom pointed out. "Even more so now, from what I can tell from his Facebook photos."

"Mom—Jesus, you're still friends with him, too?" Great. Add my mother to the list of my loved ones who'd refused to let Ben go after the breakup.

"He has a girlfriend," Alexis said. "We actually went to dinner with her one night." She sniffed in my direction, and I knew she was pointedly leaving out the rest—*the night Lee punched Chris in the face*—so as not to give my mother a heart attack.

"*Had* a girlfriend, actually."

Alexis sat up straighter.

"But it doesn't matter. Ben made it clear to me from the start that he wanted nothing to do with me romantically, ever again. Which, now that you know the whole story, you can see makes perfect sense. And I was only attracted to Ben again because he was off-limits. I told myself I was going to keep things friendly, and then..." Oh, this was embarrassing. "Then I kissed him."

Alexis gasped again. She really needed to lay off watching whatever was teaching her to react like a heroine in a telenovela. "You *kissed* him?"

"I really, *really* kissed him. And Ben got upset with himself, and it was terrible, and now he's not talking to me."

"Oh, no," Alexis whispered.

"That about sums it up. I'm an idiot."

My mom left her armchair and squeezed between me and Alexis on the couch. She brushed the hair off my forehead, and out of the corner of my eye, I could see she was doing the same to Alexis. Her fingers were cool and soft, the skin of her hands almost paper-thin. I closed my eyes and couldn't imagine anywhere I'd rather be.

"Neither of my daughters are idiots."

"Hey, no one said anything about me," Alexis protested.

Mom stroked my forehead. "Lee, why did you think you were only attracted to Ben because he was off-limits? Couldn't you have genuine feelings?"

"Psshh." I shook my head. "This isn't about *feelings*. Not for me and definitely not for Ben. Man," I laughed. "Can you imagine if I *was* dumb enough to have feelings for him again? That'd be like slapping a sign on my forehead that said Please Kick Me. I would deserve the universe shredding my heart. I'd be asking for it."

"Pain is a part of love," my mom said calmly. "When you open yourself up, pain is inevitable. But you do it anyway because love is worth it."

"Even when it doesn't last?" I stole a look at her out of the corner of my eye.

"Even when it hurts you so bad you don't think you'll survive?" Alexis added.

Mom patted us. "I'm not saying you should accept abusive relationships or stay with people who consistently hurt you. I'm just saying that when you give someone your heart, you have to accept they might break it. And if they do, it doesn't mean you weren't right to give it in the first place. Or that you shouldn't give it to someone else again."

"How can you believe that," I whispered, "after what happened with Dad?"

It had been a long time since the three of us had addressed Dad this openly. It honestly hurt to mention him. I clung to that hurt, the way it felt like he was suddenly in the room.

"Honey." Mom stopped brushing my forehead. I looked up at her. "I have absolutely no regrets about your father."

My jaw dropped. "How can that be true? He crushed you. He left you all alone. You're just now starting to date again."

"Of course, I wish it had ended differently between us.

And I wish he'd never been in that car that morning, on his way to the grocery store." Mom's face was gentle. "But even knowing what I know, I'd do it all again. Fall in love with him, marry him, have you two. And I won't let the possibility that Ethan could hurt me like your father did—or in new ways—stop me from giving him my all."

"You're very brave," Alexis said, snuggling into my mom's side.

I stared at the two of them. *Was* she brave, or was she foolish? Shouldn't she have learned from what happened, and made sure she was never in a position to be hurt like that again? That seemed like the reasonable answer. Not throwing herself out there again without armor. That was downright masochistic.

Mom shrugged. "I forgave your father." She squeezed my shoulders. "I'd like you to forgive him, too."

"Forgive him, and forget him?" I asked.

"No." Her hand was back on my forehead. "Forgive him, and remember what a good dad he was. Forgive him, and love him in his absence. Forgive him, and forgive yourself."

I wouldn't pretend I didn't know what she was talking about. So I simply closed my eyes and enjoyed the feeling of my mother's fingers skimming through my hair.

17

The Empire Strikes Back

I'd learned two important things tonight: first, Mendax Oil employees had a *lot* of grievances to air, and they were not shy; second, Ben had possibly *more* grievances to air, and yet he could go a full two hours with zero eye contact and only a few terse words.

As we sat side by side in uncomfortable folding chairs at the Mendax employee town hall, I found myself fantasizing that Ben would leap out of his chair, run to the microphone at the front of the room and say, just like the guy currently up there, "Well, since you *asked*, I *will* tell you what's on my mind." But instead of venting about bad vending machine snacks in employee break rooms, Ben would finally get everything he was thinking about me out in the open.

Getting on the Mendax Oil town hall agenda had been my idea, and I was amazed at how simple it was to pull off. I'd been scouring the Mendax Twitter feed for clues about what they were up to when I saw the post about the town hall. Turns out anyone could get on the agenda as long as they were an employee. I'd found the email address for a random engineer, begged him to add "A thrilling, mutually beneficial, history-making announcement from Lise Motors" to the agenda, and the sucker just agreed! There was either a solid mutiny brewing in the ranks at Mendax or an extremely small number of give-a-fucks—either way, a good sign.

Unfortunately, attending this town hall was not the reunion with Ben I'd imagined. For the first time in our campaign, we'd committed the environmental cardinal sin of driving two cars to the same location. I'd had no choice, since the only response I'd gotten out of Ben since the night of The Verboten Kiss was his reply to my email about the town hall, and it just said, See you there. Our saving grace was that he drove a Prius and I drove a sleek Lise Model XX, so between the two of us, our carbon footprint wasn't astronomically high.

Luckily, no one at Mendax Oil had slapped our faces on any posters: "Wine festival crashers, climate hippies and upstart lotharios, wanted dead or alive." Also lucky was the fact that Hudson County authorities hadn't caught me stumbling down the side of the road the night of the wine festival, crying messily into my phone to an Uber driver, three too many glasses of wine and one too many humiliating Ben encounters under my belt. Therefore, I had not been summarily captured and booted the moment I reentered county lines.

The Mendax employee relations manager—a supremely bored-looking man in a tweed suit and wire-rimmed glasses, with a shiny head—glanced down at his clipboard from the front of the room. "Thank you, Mr. Kasen, for that long diatribe against our vending machine snacks. HR will take your point that low-fat granola bars are a human rights violation under consideration. Next up, Ms. Lee Stone, to discuss—"

he squinted at the agenda "—'a thrilling, mutually beneficial, history-making announcement from Lise Motors'?" He blinked out into the audience. "Is this a prank?"

I didn't need to look at Ben, because I could *feel* his eye roll as I scrambled to my feet.

"Not a prank," I assured Mr. Manager. Instead of facing him, I swung the mic stand around to face the crowd of employees. Many of them straightened in their chairs at the unexpected move. I smiled my most winning smile.

"Good evening, y'all. The history-making part is that I'm here tonight to ask you to support an important piece of legislation that would dramatically increase Texas's use of electric vehicles."

Tittering among the crowd.

"Before you say, 'Lee, are you bananas? I'm an oil and gas employee—why would I support electric cars?' let me say that you *are* employed by Mendax, I know, but that's not really *who* you are. Who you are is moms and dads and uncles and daughters and sons. You're the people who raise money together every year for your local homeless shelter, to support people in your community who are down on their luck." Yes, I'd done my research about Mendax's yearly employee charity drive. "You're the people who paint your streets with beautiful rainbows every June to make your Pride parade more festive. You created a viral video last year reenacting *Hamilton* to ask the cast to stop by your local theater because a little girl with cancer wanted to meet them. You—"

"Excuse me, Ms. Stone!" Mr. Manager interrupted hotly. "This is highly inappropriate. Does corporate know you're here?"

"Let her speak!" someone called from the back, and it straightened my spine.

"No, corporate doesn't know I'm here. But I think the employees of Mendax Oil can be trusted to think for themselves—"

"Ms. Stone, I'm going to have to insist you leave this town hall immediately."

"Hey," a deep voice boomed, and my heart skipped a beat. Ben stood up in the middle of the crowd. "Are you in the habit of quelling free speech? And interrupting women when they're talking?"

"Booooo," yelled the crowd. *"Let her talk!"*

Mr. Manager gaped at the people flagrantly disregarding his authority. I saw my window.

"Thank you." I beamed, and the booing calmed. "As I was saying, you're a whole lot more than oil company employees. You're good people and great neighbors and concerned citizens who I imagine want the world to be healthy and safe and beautiful for everyone. That's why I'm asking you to consider writing Senator Roy McBuck to say you're a Mendax employee who supports the Green Machine bill."

"Will this bill kill our jobs?" a man yelled from the back.

I squinted, trying to find the man's face in the crowd so I could look him in the eyes. "If all state vehicles switch to electric, it could mean a loss of profits for Mendax in a few years. How that will translate into layoffs is up to Mendax, but I won't lie to you—it could."

The crowd broke into loud, unhappy murmurings. I could tell I was losing them.

"But think about the long-term gains. The oil industry will take a hit, yes, like the coal industry did when we moved to oil and gas. And even though I couldn't care less about the oil and gas CEOs—"

Definite head nodding and affirmative noises at that.

"I know we need to talk about finding new jobs for folks who get displaced. We will have that conversation, I promise you. But I hope I'm convincing you that, in the big picture, our bill would be good progress for society."

I took a deep breath and looked around. There were a lot of frowning, thoughtful faces. No downright sneering or jeering, so at least there was that. This was probably the best I was going to get for now.

"Thank you for hearing me out. There will be more information coming to you in the mail, and in the meantime, you can shoot me questions by email. I'm Lee at Lisemotors-dot-com." Awkwardly, I bowed in conclusion. Then, cursing myself, I walked away from the mic as quickly as I could, making a pit stop to collect my jacket—careful not to look at Ben—and continued down the aisle of the Hudson County community center to the exit.

I walked out the doors calmly—nay, gracefully—and then, as soon as they were shut, I scurried full speed into the parking lot, my breath leaving a trail of small clouds in the icy air.

That went well, right? I didn't often have to speak publicly—I was merely the pitch girl, so the task usually fell on Dakota's shoulders, all the interviews and announcements hers to make. But I thought I'd done well. I hadn't stumbled when things got hard, and I hadn't stammered on any words. There was that unfortunate bow at the end. Maybe it was like flexing a muscle—the more I did it, the better I'd get.

I felt a sudden rush of pride. And, given all the anxiety I'd been feeling lately, the positivity was like a balm.

"Lee, wait up."

Ah. And now the source of my anxiety was jogging toward me.

I glanced from Ben to my car, which was only a few feet away. I could probably make it inside and get the engine running before he reached me. I'd wanted Ben to talk to me for two weeks, yet now that it seemed imminent, I was getting cold feet.

Ben was back to wearing his dark, boring navy jacket and red tie, like that time after Ely's house when he'd been supremely grumpy. Wait a second—were Ben's sartorial choices the key to deciphering his moods? I wondered for a second if what he was wearing was a sign of his innermost feelings, then shook my head to clear my thoughts. Ben was voluntarily talking to me. This was a big step. *Focus, Stoner.*

"Thanks for sticking up for me in there," I said carefully, folding my arms over my chest. My puffy jacket was very thick. It felt like I was hugging a giant marshmallow.

A look of scorn twisted Ben's face. "What a *dick*, that guy. You were good, is what I came out here to say. Really good. I wouldn't be surprised if McBuck starts getting emails from Mendax employees. Or if you do." He dropped his eyes to his feet and tucked his hair behind his ears. "You used to want to be a politician, remember? Texas, then DC. The first person to ride a climate platform into the White House." He'd worn his glasses tonight, so when he looked up at me through them, his lashes brushed the lenses. "I just wanted to say… maybe you should revisit that idea. I think you could do it."

I smiled gently. "Ben, you and I both know I've done far too many drugs to ever hold office."

He grimaced. "I don't think that matters anymore."

"Well, the *sex tapes*," I started, then saw the way his eyes narrowed and quickly changed the subject. "Yeah. My old dream. I think working at Lise and doing things like this campaign might be the closest I get. But I do appreciate the vote of confidence."

Ben looked out over the parking lot. It was a dark, cold night, the kind most people preferred to spend at home. He shoved his hands deep in his pockets. "Okay, well. Guess I'll see you." He turned to leave.

"Ben?" My mouth moved before my brain caught up with it. He turned around, rubbing a hand over his mouth, and my heart pounded.

"I hate that what happened after the wine festival caused this rift between us."

He shook his head. "Me, too. Sorry. I just needed space to think. And I realized you were right. What happened was just a mistake. We don't have to let it get in the way of the campaign. We can forget it happened, stick to being friends."

"Perfect," I said, trying to push away the strange pain in my heart. "That's exactly what I want."

He turned the full force of his blue eyes on me. It was like he could see right through me, the look was so intense. His eyebrows lifted in surprise. "Stoner. You're lying."

I— *What?* I must've just had an inconveniently timed acid flashback from all my experimentation in college, and invented Ben's words. "No, I'm not—"

"Well, well, well," cut in a slimy, self-satisfied voice. "If it isn't the two climate crusaders."

My body went rigid. I knew that voice. I'd listened to it in countless news clips. Samuel Slittery's voice was as greasy as the oil he peddled.

Slittery slunk out of the dark. He wore his signature boxy, ill-fitting, ten-thousand-dollar suit and rattlesnake cowboy boots. Each footstep made an ominous crunch on the gravel.

"Quite a performance back there." He tipped an imaginary hat to me. "Don't think it's going to get you very far, though."

"I didn't know the CEO of Mendax Oil made appearances at employee town halls," I said. "From what we heard in there, it doesn't sound like employee needs and concerns are a priority."

Slittery smiled pleasantly. That was the thing about him. He looked like every other genial, white-haired grandpa in the world. When, in reality, he was pure evil. "All you ladies at Lise are so opinionated. You could use a lesson in decorum, I think. Learn when to shut up and smile pretty. Take that as a compliment, by the way—that smile's the best thing you've got going for you."

That line—*learn when to shut up and smile*—was what so many of those internet troll groups said about Dakota whenever she made the news for complaining about sexism in the tech industry. I narrowed my eyes.

"Hello, you tired, sexist dinosaur." Ben matched Slittery's deceptively pleasant tone. "What do you want?"

"Shame the governor brought in a radical leftist to ruin his administration. Remember this is Texas, boy. We don't do things like California, and we're damn proud of it."

Ben made a "get to the point" gesture with his hands.

"We'll do things better than California when we pass the country's most sweeping clean energy bill," I couldn't help saying.

Slittery's eyes glittered with triumph. "Sorry to burst your bubble, dear. You can hunt after my employees' support all you want, but it won't matter. They're powerless. While you've been touring the state handing out pamphlets, I've been making a series of very generous donations to Senators Janus, Wayne and McBuck. Coincidentally, the three outstanding votes I need to kill the Green Machine."

My stomach dropped into the gravel.

"And I've just learned I can count on their votes. Funny enough—" now a spiteful smile curved his lips "—a few House Democrats have seen the light, as well. Money has a strange way of talking over everyone else in the room, wouldn't you say? Greatest power there is."

"That's impossible," Ben insisted. "We secured Janus and Wayne weeks ago. And the House is solid."

It was sweet that Ben was in denial. I wasn't. Texas politics had let me down far too many times before. I understood immediately that it had happened again. The votes had fallen through. The most money had won. Of course.

The air pressure suddenly dialed up in the parking lot. There was a strange ringing in my ears.

"Ask them yourselves," Slittery said. "And can I be a fly on the wall for those calls? That would be fun." He sucked in a deep, satisfied breath and turned on one rattlesnake heel. "This was fun, too. I was going to break the news at the Governor's Ball next weekend, but I'm glad I didn't wait."

He pointed his finger at me like it was a gun, then blew the tip. "Rest in peace, Ms. Stone. Your bill's officially dead."

18

An Unexpected Guest

There should really be an award given to people who are able to shove aside the fact that their own lives are crumbling in order to focus on a friend—say, for example, the Selfless Human Award. Or maybe the Lee Stone Medal of Valor for Friendship under Extreme Duress, in honor of my heroic efforts tonight.

It was Annie's thirtieth birthday, and we were having a dinner party at Il Tempesto, one of Austin's most romantic Italian restaurants. I'd ignored the fact that my life was a dumpster fire in order to sling on my sluttiest party jumpsuit and plaster a smile on my face. I was borrowing Alexis's nicest pair of heels, too, which she'd offered to help cheer me up. It was a disconcerting reversal of our usual roles.

Il Tempesto was a lovely restaurant. We had the wine cellar all to ourselves. Candles made the dim room glow with warm light, wineglasses were wedged between big bowls of pasta, and the table was full of our friends. Mac and Ted the finance guy sat next to me, lost in their gag-inducing new-relationship bubble. Alexis sat across from me, her date obviously the Chianti bottle she was feeling up as she poured her next glass. Claire and Simon sat at one head of the table, and Annie and Zoey at the other. Annie looked especially gorgeous tonight. Her face radiated happiness.

The seat next to me was empty, so I'd kicked it away from the table, deciding not to read it as a mocking sign from the universe. I'd thought about inviting Kyle tonight, but had ultimately decided I didn't feel like hearing about whatever new start-up he was launching with his parents' money. His last idea had been an app that delivered molly and ecstasy upon demand, and so I'd had to break it to him gently about a little thing called criminal law that even applied to trust-fund children. The specifics of Kyle aside, the important thing was that I *could've* had a date if I'd wanted one.

I turned to Mac to share this insight with her, but she was too busy rubbing her nose against Ted's to pay me any attention. I sighed and stabbed at my napkin with my knife.

"Ben, it's been so long!" Annie called.

I jabbed my knife into my bread and whipped my head in Annie's direction. There was no way, it couldn't be—

It was. Ben walked toward the table, holding a gorgeous bouquet of pink peonies. Hard to get in winter, and Annie's favorite flower, though I had no idea how he'd remembered. He looked ridiculously beautiful in jeans, a herringbone gray button-up and a dark gray blazer, a peacoat slung over his arm. In that moment, it was like I was seeing him for the first time. It struck me anew how tall he was, how deliciously his blazer fit over his broad shoulders, how perfectly the candlelight lit his elegant cheekbones and long lashes.

But—and this was the important part—what the fuck was

he doing here? Unbidden, his recent accusation floated back: *Stoner. You're lying.*

I did *not* want to resume that conversation.

I swept dagger-eyes to Alexis on the other side of the table. She had the stones to give me a double thumbs-up. Annie stood, opening her arms to receive Ben's hug, but before she did, she looked at me and winked.

I almost gasped out loud. *Saboteurs.*

"Happy birthday, Annie." Ben squeezed her. "Thank you for inviting me. I'm honored."

"You're very welcome. These are gorgeous." Annie accepted the peonies from Ben and placed them in her present pile. Embarrassingly, she put them right next to my gift, a bong with the words *My Favorite Therapist* painted across it. Ben eyed it and stifled a laugh, but he didn't look at me, so I couldn't explain it was only a gag gift and I would obviously give Annie her real present shortly. As soon as I bought it.

"This is my girlfriend, Zoey," Annie said, and Ben shook Zoey's hand with a wide smile.

Zoey blinked up at him. "Wow. You're even more handsome in person than on Facebook."

Christ, Zoey, way to have *zero chill.*

Ben grinned, full dimples, rolling with it. "Thank you. It's great to meet you."

"You remember Mac, of course," Annie said, gesturing around the table. "And Claire and Simon from when they visited in grad school."

"Great to see you again." Ben was smiling so hard he looked like one of those contestants waiting to audition for *American Idol*. What was his angle?

Claire nodded coolly. "Benjamin. Nice to see you."

"And that handsome gentleman there is Ted, Mac's boyfriend. You can sit next to Stoner." Annie pointed to the empty chair I'd discarded, and I suddenly realized I'd been trapped in Annie and Alexis's twisted game from the beginning and just hadn't caught on.

My body went very straight and still as Ben pulled up his chair and leaned in close to me. "Hello, Stoner. Fancy seeing you here."

"Annie's my best friend," I whispered, ignoring the fact that I could feel Alexis watching us from across the table. "What are *you* doing here?"

"Attending a birthday party for an old friend," he said smoothly.

I leaned in closer, deciding to get it over with and clear the air. "You accused me of lying about being glad we're back to being friends. I'm not lying. I am glad we're friends."

He gave me an amused look. "Trying to get me uninvited from a party is an interesting way of showing it."

At the head of the table, Annie clinked her knife against her glass.

"Ben, I—"

He shot me a look, and I fell quiet with the rest of the table.

Dammit. One Medal of Valor, presented to Lee Stone for her remarkable patience and restraint, coming right up.

Annie beamed at us. "Thank you, dear friends, for celebrating my birthday with me. I want you all to know that I love you very much and think of you as my chosen family."

"Except for Ted and Ben," Claire said reasonably. She gave them an encouraging look. "But maybe one day, if you stick around."

Ben nodded. "Too true. Thank you."

"*All* of you are family," Annie insisted, giving me another wink. She was in quite a saucy mood tonight. As well she should be, on her birthday. I blew her a kiss.

"That's why I wanted you to be here when I did something

brave and hopeful." Annie slid her hand behind her into her jacket pocket and pulled out an unmistakable, velvety ring box.

Gasps circled the table. My heart pounded with surprise. Alexis looked like she might faint from pure, unadulterated happiness.

Zoey pressed her hands to her mouth, but Annie gently pulled them away and gripped them with her own. "Zoey. You are the love of my life. You make me happier than I ever realized a person could be, and I work on making people happy for a living."

She opened the ring box, revealing a beautiful emerald solitaire. My first reaction was *Damn, son, look at those carats,* and then the more appropriate *Oh, good, not a blood diamond.*

Zoey started crying. Annie held up the ring, taking Zoey's other hand.

"There's nothing I want more than to spend my life with you. Thick and thin, young and old, rich and poor. You're going to make beautiful art for the rest of your life, and I'm going to be by your side, in awe and supporting you." Annie gripped Zoey's hand and my heart swelled. "Will you marry me?"

"Yes," Zoey sobbed immediately, grabbing Annie's face and kissing her before Annie could even give her the ring.

We cheered so loud the wine bottles lining the walls shook. "Holy shit, you're getting *married,*" I shouted, still in shock. Ben put his fingers in his mouth and whistled his celebration whistle, which he'd once told me his dad taught him to do every time a baseball player hit a homer, at the one and only baseball game they'd gone to before he took off. I looked around the table and found I was the only person with dry eyes. Poor Alexis and Mac looked like they were competing to see who could drown themselves first in human tears.

Zoey and Annie broke apart with a laugh, and Annie slipped the ring on Zoey's finger, where it sparkled.

"I'm going to be a wife," Zoey squealed, and all of us burst into even louder cheers. Ted darted away and came back with a waiter and champagne, and from that point on, the night dissolved into bubbles and teary laughter.

It wasn't until much later, when I glanced away from a story Simon was telling Ben to look at Annie and Zoey, that it hit me. They were entangled, arms around each other, heads resting side by side. And the thought popped into my head: maybe there was such a thing as lasting love.

The idea immediately had my stomach clenching, my brain hurrying to deny it. No, no, that wasn't true. It couldn't be. Who had it ever been true for?

But Annie and Zoey were glowing, and they so obviously loved each other, and when Annie proposed, and Zoey said yes, I had *believed* in that moment they'd be together forever.

A cold fist squeezed my heart, and suddenly I felt like I was going to have a panic attack, right then and there, in the middle of the lovely, happy wine cellar.

"Excuse me," I said quietly, and when no one objected, I scooted away from the table with my jacket in hand and practically ran out, making my way into the garden patio in the back of the restaurant. It was empty, thanks to the fact that it was December. I tugged on my coat and leaned against the brick wall in the corner, trying to steady my breathing.

In, and out. In, and out. Who in their right mind had a panic attack when one of their best friends got engaged? What was I so afraid of? That Annie and Zoey would prove I'd gotten it wrong about love—that real, lasting love was possible, and there was actually no excuse for my dad and Danny and Andy and me to cheat? That maybe I'd made a series of terrible decisions in my life, pushing people away because I'd believed a lie, and now I was doomed to a life without Annie and Zoey's particular kind of happiness?

No. Nope. That couldn't be it.

I thrust my hands in my pockets and concentrated on the twinkle lights strung through the garden trees, like dainty necklaces with small, shining jewels.

"Lee?" The voice coming from the door was cautious. "You all right?"

I knew who it was; I didn't need to look. The brick wall was cold through my jacket as I shrugged. "Just getting some air."

Ben slid on his peacoat and buttoned it to his neck, then leaned against the wall beside me, crossing his arms over his chest. "This place opened a few months before I left. You and I went here once on a date, remember? I always liked it."

I'd taken my friends here after Ben left for California because it held happy memories, and that's how it had become one of our favorite spots. But I wouldn't tell him that.

I could sense him glancing at me by the way his body shifted in my direction. "You know, I'm acutely aware I keep following you wherever you go." He scrubbed a hand through his hair. "I don't seem to be able to help it."

"What are you doing here?" I asked him.

After a beat of silence, he cleared his throat and changed the subject, looking down at me through his lashes. "You still wear that perfume I like. With the roses."

I splayed my fingers over the cold bricks. "Yeah, well, you changed yours." Strange how it sounded like I was accusing him of something. "But the new one's not bad."

"Stoner, are you upset Annie got engaged?"

"Not at all," I said quickly. "I just don't believe in love, so these things fall a little flat for me."

Ben didn't say anything for an excruciatingly long time,

until I couldn't stand it anymore and wrenched my eyes from the twinkle lights to stare at his face. It was guarded.

"I was under the impression you loved me," he said finally, voice quiet. "Back when we dated."

It was hard to admit, since I'd taken such pains to convince Ben of my indifference at the end of our relationship. But I did it anyway, because of the way he'd turned his gaze carefully out into the garden, as if he was steeling himself against my next words.

"I did love you, back then."

"And then you stopped?"

"I just knew it wouldn't end well. Love doesn't last, Ben. Not for me or my parents or my sister. Not for Annie and Zoey, no matter how perfect they seem right now. Love builds you up, then it tears you down, exacting the most pain it can. But only if you let it."

"I see." He leaned closer. "And you're determined not to. That's why you don't do relationships anymore. That's why kissing someone doesn't mean anything."

"Right." I watched him warily.

He glanced at me, and I was surprised to see he looked almost angry. "Why didn't you tell me this when we were dating? You never let me see how hurt you were. I would have *killed* to have known this about you. I was always trying to figure you out."

"It's not about hurt, Ben. It's about pragmatism. A clear-eyed understanding of how the world works. Besides, I never would have had a conversation like this back when we were dating."

It was true. As fast as I'd fallen for Ben, as strongly as I'd felt, there was something different about our relationship now—the long hours spent together on the campaign, working toward our shared goal, the months of friendship without the possibility of anything more. It made it feel safe to say these things.

I changed the subject. "Your dad abandoned your mom, too. We have the same history. I don't understand why you aren't as worried as I am that the person you love most in the world will crush you one day."

Ben's entire face changed. His eyes flashed with incredulous anger, and he flung himself off the wall. "The person I love most *did* crush me, Stoner. Or do you not remember what happened five years ago?"

He stormed into the garden, leaving me alone against the wall. Oh, that was *not* fair. I stormed after him.

"That's obviously not true," I said, raising my voice. "You know I was talking about your future wife. Someone like that."

He spun on his heel, anger radiating. "Are you kidding? Do you not understand what you meant to me?"

The words hit me like bricks to the chest, and I froze. Ben had told me he loved me when we dated, but I'd never let myself think it was the serious kind. At least, not on his side. In fact, my certainty that our feelings were mismatched was one of the reasons I'd been so convinced he would one day cheat like all the others.

"No," I said thickly. "I don't."

Ben's voice was anguished. "Goddammit. You broke my *heart*, Lee."

The words hung between us, alive and electric, charging the air. I couldn't look away from him, standing there like a vision pulled from one of my dreams during the years we'd spent apart—his eyes burning, face half-shadowed by the string lights. I'd spent so much time burying myself under layers of armor that it was startling to see a person expose themself like this; a jolt to recognize this was the real Ben, straight through. He'd cracked open his chest to show me his heart.

And so I laughed, in panic—this time *I* was the desperate one. "Yeah, well, I broke my own heart, too, okay? I'll admit it. I ruined everything. Happy?"

Ben's eyes pinned me. "When I woke up next to you at Ely's, I wanted you so bad I couldn't think straight. For a minute, I lay there and imagined kissing you, touching you. *Being* with you."

He'd done exactly what I had.

"And you know what? I'll confess, too." He clenched his jaw. "It wasn't the first time I'd imagined it. But then I thought about what it would be like to really be with you—to try again—and all I could picture was a repeat of history. I don't want to get hurt again, Stoner."

"And I don't want to hurt you," I said. "So let's call it. I'll stop chasing you, and you stop chasing me. Do the sensible thing and leave. You've done it before." I could feel the old pain rise, sharp as ever.

"The problem is—" Ben's eyes dipped to my lips, then back up to my eyes "—I don't think I can."

"Fine," I said, bolder than I felt. "Then try it my way. Just be with me, no feelings. No expectations."

I could see it in his face: Ben was at war with himself. He was going to reject me, just like he'd done at the wine festival. Of course he was—our history was too much.

I turned to go, blinking quickly, but he grabbed my arm.

"God help me," he said roughly, then slipped a hand into my hair and crushed me to him.

The kiss was greedy and possessive. Ben held me against his chest and took his time, kissing me slowly, torturously, dragging his teeth against my lips until I gripped his biceps, needing more, stifling an uncharacteristic urge to beg. The feel of his tongue slipping inside my mouth lit something deep down, turning my bones to liquid.

I pulled back, and he made a noise of protest deep in his throat, eyes still closed.

"Ben—"

"All right, Stoner. You win. No feelings."

When he opened his eyes, they were burning.

He wasn't being sensible. He was breaking his rules, choosing me even though it was wrong and he might pay for it later. But I didn't care about right or wrong—I didn't care about anything other than the fact that I could have him. The look in his eyes lit five years' worth of longing like dry kindle and my body went up in flames.

I seized him, kissing him with urgency, drunk on the taste and touch of Ben Laderman, and he met me with the same need, walking me backward so fast he was practically lifting me. My shoulders hit the brick wall of the restaurant and he tugged at my jacket, yanking it down my shoulders. I couldn't unbutton his coat fast enough. I needed him now, no more waiting—the world could burn around us, for all I cared.

Ben tipped my head back, kissing me at an angle, deeper, gripping my waist and grinding against me—

"Ahh, shoot, I'm sorry—oh, stupid Ted."

Ben jumped back from me, and cold air rushed inside my open jacket. I pressed a hand to my chest, trying to catch my breath. Ted stood only a few feet away, frozen outside the door to the restaurant, face stricken and tomato red, staring.

"Mac sent me to look for you." The words tumbled out. "I swear, I barely saw you kiss at all, and the picking up and the wall thing—"

"It's okay, Ted." My whole body was on fire. Nothing would be okay until I was touching Ben again.

"They're all waiting for you inside," Ted said apologetically.

"The restaurant's closing. I promise, I won't say a word. I can make up some excuse—"

His words cut through my fogged mind. Alexis and all my friends were right inside. I couldn't explain this to them. I clutched my jacket tighter and dared a look at Ben, who was breathing hard, pupils blown, lips full and swollen.

He kept his eyes on the ground like he didn't trust himself to look at me. "Tomorrow," he said roughly. The promise in his voice almost bent me at the knees.

"Tomorrow," I said, and followed Ted back inside.

19

Just Like a Fairy Tale

"Don't look now." Ben's eyes were dark as he adjusted his bow tie. We were alone for the first time all night, in the corner of the room, and I was in danger of getting distracted by the way his eyes cut to the side, giving someone his patented scathing look, 100 percent heat. He leaned in close to whisper in my ear. "Slittery spotting, twelve o'clock."

I ignored his instruction not to look and slid my eyes discreetly across the room. Sure enough, the CEO of Mendax Oil held court near the bar, surrounded by a circle of minions, laughing heartily at some story Senator Roy McBuck was telling with overly dramatic hand gestures. Slittery's rattlesnake boots had been polished until they shone tonight, and he wore a turquoise bolo tie, every inch the gussied-up Texas oilman. I was surprised, frankly, that he'd never thought to grow a mustache for the purpose of twirling it evilly.

"He's kissing McBuck's ass," Ben gritted out. "Rubbing it in our faces."

We'd known Slittery would be here tonight, along with the who's who of Texas politics. The Governor's Ball, thrown each year in early December, was the political event of the season—and after years of longing for an invite, tonight was my debut. It was as magical as I'd imagined. People like the heads of the Texas ACLU and Texas Organizing Project were walking around the Governor's Mansion in black-tie finery—just out in the open, where anyone could see! I was feeling as starstruck as a thirteen-year-old girl backstage at a K-pop concert.

Naturally, I'd decided my debut dress should make a scene because you only got one chance to make a first impression. I'd chosen a plunging, chiffony, fir-green number that allowed me to sweep through rooms like a sexy, billowing Christmas tree. The way Ben's eyes kept drifting to me in the middle of important conversations was enough to justify the astronomical price tag, or so I would continue telling myself.

Although we'd known crossing paths with Slittery was unavoidable, Ben and I were determined to use the night to undo his damage. After all, it was December, and the legislative session didn't start until January. We still had a few weeks to change people's opinions before the vote. If we couldn't sway Janus, Wayne or McBuck with money or direct outreach to their constituents, we just had to find a way to make the Green Machine bill so damn popular they couldn't imagine voting against it. It was a much harder task than our targeted approach, but something had me feeling optimistic lately.

I glanced over and drank in the sight of Ben in his tuxedo, blue with black lapels. It was a standout in the sea of boring black tuxes, but really, its greatest function was showcasing Ben himself. Tonight, he was *Hollywood Ben*. His dark hair—longer than ever—curled rakishly over his forehead, but his stubble was perfectly groomed to showcase the strong angle of his jaw. And his suit was only a few shades darker than his eyes, which made it difficult to look at him and remember we were at a work event—especially after what happened at the restaurant last night. Possibly the breathless feeling I got when he smiled had something to do with my newfound optimism. Or maybe it was the whispered reminder running on loop in my brain: *Ben Laderman wants me.*

"What'd the governor say when you told him about Slittery?" I asked, wrenching my eyes from Ben's face so I could focus. After our run-in with Slittery at the town hall, we'd both immediately informed our bosses the oilman was gunning for us.

"He told me it was unsurprising, that Slittery is slippery, and that we'd better find a way to outmaneuver him." He ran a frustrated hand through his hair. "Or something like that. He's been really distracted lately. I can barely get him to focus on work."

"Same with Dakota," I said. "Except she's launching the Herschel motor, so at least she has an excuse. Damn. Now is not the time for them to lose track. We've got to bear down or we'll lose."

"Trust me, I know. But I think whether this bill lives or dies is on our shoulders now. I just wish I could figure out some way to get around Slittery."

We'd spent a whirlwind night talking to everyone we could—state reps, comptrollers and chiefs of staff, but also analysts, aides and even a few interns. We would leave no stone unturned in the mission to rescue the Green Machine.

Ben and I had tried to make the million small-talk conversations fun for ourselves by seeing who could most creatively segue into mentioning the bill. After our last conversation dragged on for too long without an opening, I'd desperately seized on the next conversational turn—a bit of gossip from the attorney general's spokeswoman about a rogue state's attorney who'd been caught red-handed visiting a prostitute. In a few short moves, I made some frankly stunning verbal leaps from the need to legalize sex work to other forward-thinking bills I'd love to see pass in the legislature, including this upcoming bill called the Green Machine—had they heard of it?

I could actually see Ben's panic unfolding in real time as I jumped dizzyingly from topic to topic. But hey, I'd managed to memorably work in the bill *and* cut the boring conversation short, so win-win.

I knew Ben was right about the bill's fate resting on us now. We'd arrived at the Governor's Mansion in a big group tonight, but they'd promptly abandoned us. There was Wendy and her husband, Cody, a big bear of a mechanic with tattoo sleeves and a heart of gold. Exacting, perfect Wendy and laid-back, easygoing Cody were an extreme opposites-attract situation that not-so-secretly delighted me—much to Wendy's annoyance, as she did not approve of anyone getting overly familiar with, or attached to, their colleagues. Wendy had a lineup of people she said she needed to introduce herself to ahead of the Herschel launch. She'd gone so far as to print a tightly paced networking schedule to keep herself on track; and, needless to say, it did not have Ben's and my names on it.

In the category of people who were as soft as Wendy was sharp, Dakota had brought her husband, George, who absolutely beamed on her arm. He always loved an excuse to dress up and take the night off from watching the kids, and tonight was no exception—he seemed almost as excited about the Governor's Ball as I was. Seeing his tanned face and blinding white smile made me realize just how long it had been since I'd seen him. Before the campaign, Dakota used to bring her husband to work events all the time.

George had squeezed me in a hug and asked me what was

new in Lee-land—he loved to sigh wistfully as I described going out to restaurants at 9:00 p.m. and lounging all day in pajamas, things he couldn't do with two young kids—when Dakota yanked him in the direction of Governor Mane. I'd spotted them with the governor's coterie of friends—who, judging by the size of their shoulders, I suspected were mostly former Longhorn players and not the political operatives it would have been more useful for Dakota to hobnob with. Worse than that, poor George was relegated to the edge of the circle, looking left out and supremely bored. I'd have to check in on him later.

Lastly, there was Alexis, whom I'd brought as my date. She'd finally opened up to the idea of a new boyfriend, and I'd thought, what better than to give her access to the sizzling buffet of eligible, well-connected men at the Governor's Ball? She and I shared the same genetics, so I knew she was biologically predisposed to finding an open bar and men in tuxedos irresistible.

However, Alexis heard Ben's and my plans to spend the night networking, took one glance at the crowd of young aides by the bar and promptly left us for greener pastures.

All in all, that left Ben and me to do the schmoozing on the Green Machine. But it was fine. The bill was my baby, and this was obviously a test for my future job as vice president of public affairs.

I scanned the crowd, searching for Alexis, when my eyes caught on a blonde woman in a scarlet gown cutting through Slittery's circle. As I watched, Slittery greeted her with a familiar kiss on the cheek.

My veins turned to ice. *Sarah.*

"Uh," I said eloquently, turning to warn Ben. But he'd already spotted her.

He shrugged. "It was bound to happen. We run in the same circles."

"That's very nonchalant of you." I lowered my voice. "Does she know…?"

He grinned rather wickedly. "Know what?"

I leaned in and felt Ben's hand come to rest on the small of my back, where my dress gathered in a low V, his fingers warm against my bare skin.

"About…us." Well done, Stoner. Leave it vague.

Ben's thumb absently stroked my spine. "No. I figured that was my business."

I looked back to where Sarah stood smiling, not realizing she was being watched. Sure, she was a mercenary lobbyist, willing to hitch her wagon to whatever project got her paid, *including* the Lonestar pipeline, and I did not respect that. But the truth was, I'd thought about Ben over and over while they were dating. Which meant I'd committed grievous thought-crimes against her. And even though thought-crimes were less serious than many of the other crimes I'd committed, I felt strangely, inconveniently guilty.

Abruptly, Sarah's eyes flicked to Ben. And then to me. Oh. Right. Because we were physically connected. Ben yanked his hand off my back, but not before Sarah's eyes darkened.

"What're you two talking about?" Wendy asked, popping up out of nowhere, Cody on her arm, George trailing them.

Ben and I jumped a solid foot apart. Our first work outing as two-people-who-were-physically-attracted-to-each-other-but-harbored-no-feelings, and we were practically giving ourselves away left and right. Wendy, it went without saying, would *murder us* if she suspected there was even the tiniest hint of impropriety that could cast a shadow over the campaign.

"Just, uh, talking about how much we despise Old Moneybags over there." I nodded in the direction of the bar.

"Ah, yes." Wendy's eyes narrowed, and she elbowed her husband. "That man at the bar is the one trying to kill our bill. He's an oil tycoon who knows his time's up, so he's getting in bed with every politician who will take his money. Kicking and screaming just to hold off the inevitable." Her voice darkened. *"Samuel Slittery."*

"More like Samuel *Slag*-ery, if you ask me," Cody said, and I mentally added supportive quips to my list of reasons to stan.

"That's the man Dakota thinks pays people to harass her online." George's chest puffed out. "I should have words with him."

Unfortunately, like a demon from hell, we'd spoken Slittery's name out loud the required number of times to summon him. His gaze jerked right over to us. A predatory smile curved his mouth. He grabbed Senator McBuck and Sarah and strode over.

"Uh-oh," said Cody, who also had a gift for understatement.

"If it isn't my vanquished foes." Malicious humor oozed in Slittery's voice. He turned to his companions. "Sarah, Senator, do you know Ben Laderman, from the governor's office? And these women are from a cute little outfit in town called Lise Motors."

"They're not a cute little outfit," George said hotly. "You listen here—"

But Senator McBuck cut him off, narrowing his eyes at Ben. "Oh, I'm quite familiar with Mr. Laderman." Like Slittery, McBuck was an old man who, if only he'd kept his mouth shut, could've been mistaken for someone's kindly grandpa. He actually looked a lot like Santa Claus, which caused a lot of confusion for me internally, as I battled my natural instincts to smile like a good girl and maybe even rub his belly. "He gave the restaurants in my district quite a headache with his dangerous minimum wage proposal."

"Just think how much your other, less advantaged constituents will appreciate you," Ben said smoothly. "You're a champion for the working class."

"Ben Laderman—slick as usual," Sarah interjected, taking quick notice of the foot of space between Ben and me. "Some might say you're pretty good at blowing smoke up people's asses, telling them what they want to hear, just so you can get what you want."

Holy subtext, Batman. My finely honed ability to read between the lines was telling me Sarah might have caught Ben's hand stroking my back.

"I was under the impression blowing smoke up people's asses to get what you wanted was the lobbyist's manifesto," Wendy said coolly. And thank God, because the strange, inconvenient guilt I felt toward Sarah rendered me defenseless against her, and I could see Ben squirming, too.

"Well, who cares what the working class thinks?" said McBuck, adjusting his little Santa Claus wire-rimmed spectacles. "The working class doesn't vote. Fast-food tycoons, on the other hand, write big checks."

"Not everything in politics is about the money," I said, finally finding my voice. Except my contribution made everyone stop for a second, then collectively shake their heads and move on.

"The reason I came over," Slittery said, "is to see whether you're going to accept my proposal, Ben."

I shot Ben a look. What the hell was he talking about?

"I'm sure we can talk about it later," Ben said.

"No, hear me out. I'm sure the good governor has an idea up his sleeve. Something he could offer." Slittery gestured at McBuck. "To both of us, of course." He patted Sarah on the shoulder. "My adviser suggests it could be beneficial to parley."

Ben froze. Dread filled me as the implications sank in.

Slittery smiled at Wendy and me with paternal beneficence. "Best to leave the tough negotiations to the men, right? That way, we can get down to brass tacks. Talk straight without having to worry about ruffling anyone's feathers." He chuckled, cuffing Ben's shoulder. "Have your people set up the meeting with my secretary. Just you and me, like I said."

Just you and me.

"And tell your boss the party's nice this year," Slittery added, and then he and McBuck walked away. But Sarah lingered, fists clenched, ignoring the radioactive silence that had fallen over our group.

"Tell me the truth," she said to Ben. There was a daring quality to her voice. "Did you really end things because we aren't right together?" She glanced at me. "Or is it because you're still into your ex?"

Oh, Sarah, now was *not the time.* I spun to Wendy, Cody and George, who were, as I'd feared, tracking Sarah's every word. But Wendy wasn't lunging to throttle me—in fact, she was watching Sarah and Ben's exchange like it was a real-life soap opera, starring interesting but ultimately tangential colleagues… Oh, right, because she *didn't know* I was the ex in question. Ben and I had lied about not knowing each other from the very start, and that lie was now saving me from getting outed. Whoever said two wrongs didn't make a right was a fool, obviously, but that wasn't the pressing issue at the moment.

The pressing issue was, Ben needed to assure Sarah their breakup had nothing to do with me. Then Sarah would disappear so *I* could confront him and find out if the terrible thing I suspected he'd done was true. I could barely contain myself; the question was burning in me.

But Ben took a different tack. He locked eyes with Sarah, his gaze softening. When he spoke, his voice was gentle. "It was for both reasons."

Cody, who'd clearly become too invested, gave a small gasp.

Sarah's eyes glittered in the dim lights, and she blinked quickly. But she wasn't down for long—the next moment, her spine straightened and she lifted her chin. "I see. Well, I hope you know this means I'm going after you and your bill now. No more advising Slittery to parley. No more protections." She turned to me and, to my surprise, drew close, her voice a whisper in my ear. "Two years together, and he left me just like that. There's a part of him you'll never touch, you know. In the end, he may love you, but he'll always put himself first." She flicked me a final look of warning and walked away.

I stood in the aftermath of Sarah's words—words that zeroed in on my greatest fear—and let them seep under my skin. I shouldn't care if Ben could never fully be mine, because I wasn't asking for that. We weren't in a relationship. What we had was physical—no feelings.

But that didn't mean he couldn't still betray me. I gathered myself, taking a deep breath, and turned to Ben, forcing my voice to come out low and measured. I would not cause a scene at my first Governor's Ball. "Slittery tried to set up a secret meeting with you. When?"

"Not secret. I only didn't tell you because—"

"Answer the question." Out of the corner of my eye, I could see even Wendy's spine straighten at the ice in my voice.

"Fine," Ben said, and I could tell from the zipped-up quality of his expression that he was trying as hard as I was to stay calm. "He tried to set up a meeting a week ago. I guess Sarah talked him into it."

"A week ago? You were going to cut me out?"

"No. I was just thinking, maybe—"

"Say no more," I said. "I get it. Of course you wanted the win." There was Sarah's whispered warning, already echoing back: *There's a part of him you'll never touch, you know. In the end, he may love you, but he'll always put himself first.* It was true, wasn't it? It was always Ben vs. the world: Ben against his father. Ben against his law school classmates. Ben against me, when we nearly killed each other breaking up; when he pressed the nuclear button and drove off to California. Clearly, Ben was still out for himself. And why shouldn't he be, if the thing between us was only physical? Why would I assume kissing him had changed anything? I'd certainly worked hard over the years to make sure no kissing had ever changed *me.* I'd made myself a safe life where no matter how men might touch me, they could never really *touch* me. Why had my unconscious automatically rewritten the rules for Ben?

This was the problem with Ben five years ago, and it was the problem with him now: something about him kept slipping past my defenses, like a thief in the night. I kept waking up to find him already in the heart of my kingdom, kneeling over me, sword at my throat.

I turned to leave. My anger was boiling over too fast to remain in public.

"Lee, hold on a minute."

"No, really," I assured him, gathering my dress in my hands. "I'm only mad I didn't think of it first. How silly of me, getting distracted with—" I glanced at Wendy "—*everything else.* How will I ever make it in politics without your killer instinct?" I turned to Wendy, Cody and George, who were all eyeing Ben like he was Benedict Arnold. "Please excuse me." Then I shouldered my way out of the governor's living room.

I needed to get out of this mansion. I could hear Ben calling after me, but I ignored him, walking swiftly down the hallway, flashing the people I passed tight-lipped smiles. This house was a maze, and I was running through it like some sort of demented princess in my ball gown. "Cinderella and the Glass Knife in Her Back." "Betrayed Beauty and the Ben-Beast." "Snow Whipped."

I turned left, then right, trying to remember the little I'd seen of the floor plan from our meeting with the governor weeks ago. Through this door and down the hall, that had to be right, then one more turn and there'd be nothing but a gauntlet of stairs standing between me and my freedom.

I twisted the knob and yanked open the door, only to be confronted by a sight so surreal it honestly took my brain a few seconds to process. I'd thought the door led to a hallway, but it was actually a roomy coat closet. Someone shrieked, and finally, my brain caught up and registered what I was seeing.

Alexis was on the floor, scrambling to pull up the top half of her canary yellow ball gown, lipstick smudged over her face like a drunk clown had painted it on. Her legs were still entangled with none other than Senator James Janus, dashing young friend of Willie Nelson and bullshit turncoat.

"Lee!" Alexis shouted, then slapped a hand over her mouth. "You scared the shit out of me. I thought you were… I thought you were *Mom* for a second."

"Alexis Rosalie Stone, what are you *doing* in here?"

She shot a panicked look at Janus, who was in the middle of zipping his pants back up. He froze, midzip, and she gulped. "Getting to know each other?"

Senator Janus got busy with his shirt, fingers slipping over the buttons. "We were, uh, talking, and maybe we had a few too many cocktails, and then—"

"No," I said simply, shaking my head. "My sister did not hook up with the senator of District 27, one of three crucial votes for my bill."

"Oh, shit." Alexis's face crumpled. "I had no idea. Wait." She turned to Janus. "Senator? You're not *married*, are you?"

He burst out laughing. "*Christ*, no. Can you imagine?"

He gestured at his half-unbuttoned chest. "All of this, locked down?"

"Oh, right," Alexis said. "This is why you talk first."

I closed my eyes and took a deep breath, trying to center myself. If only I'd paid better attention at Mac's yoga meditation retreat, instead of spending all my time trying to trick the employees into giving me my cell phone back. "I am rewinding the video tape in my brain so as to unsee this and therefore remove all emotional scarring."

"Lee, there you are." Ben ran up, his eyes intense, hair standing on end, like he'd run his hands through it a thousand times in quick succession. "Listen, I'm sorry about the one-two punch of Sarah and Slittery—" He stopped cold, seeming to realize we had an audience, then peered into the closet. "Is that…Senator Janus?" He squinted. "And *Lex*?"

The appearance of Ben was one straw too many. I spun on my heel and took off in the opposite direction. All my instincts were clearly wrong. Trying to head toward the exit in this maze of a mansion had only brought fresh horrors down upon me, like accidentally turning the page in some sort of sadistic pop-up book. So I would go deeper inside the house instead. I spotted a grand, gleaming staircase. Even better: I would go up.

That's right. I pounded the stairs, two at a time. Nothing worse than what I'd just seen could confront me up here.

20

As Nature Intended

I flung open the door at the end of the second-floor hallway, only to be confronted with a guest bedroom that looked like someone's grandma had designed it in the throes of an acid trip. There was an astonishing number of florals. Chintzy, magnolia-patterned wallpaper, rose-patterned bedding on the four-poster, illustrated flowers in silver picture frames. Ceramic angels peered down from crowded shelves. I stumbled inside and bumped into a side table, cursing as I tugged on a lamp, and— *Ah!* Jesus Christ, that was a doll. A very human-looking doll with haunted eyes that I was going to place face-down now, so she couldn't watch me.

I was certain some governor from the 1800s had possessed a madwoman in need of locking away, and this had been her room. All the governors since, including Grover Mane, had clearly been too lazy to bother with redecorating. Or maybe they'd had women, too.

Nevertheless, it would do.

I'd no sooner sat on the bed than the door flung open to reveal Ben. I could tell he was gearing up to say something grand and sweeping, but then he registered the room. And gave a little start. "Jesus, Stoner. Next time you lure a man somewhere to murder him, take it down a notch with the decor. You're tipping your hand."

"No one asked you to follow me."

Ben strode in and kicked the door shut with one foot. "I was considering the meeting because I thought I could make things better with Slittery."

I leaped to my feet. "Oh, right. In that case, can't have me around. Not if you're actually trying to *fix* the situation. What, you think I'm not good enough at my job? Unprofessional?"

I'd been stupid to trust him. Professionally and personally. He'd betrayed me so quickly!

Ben shook his head and laughed, yanking at his bow tie to loosen it. "Slittery's a misogynist, which I know isn't news to you, but, Stoner—he loathes the idea that a woman like Dakota is going to end his industry. He hates you by association. Yes, it's shitty, but he won't even come to the table if you're there. I thought if I met with him alone, and got him to see reason—maybe find something else he wanted—I could save the bill. It was a Hail Mary."

I stepped closer so we were only an inch apart. I wanted him to see the look in my eyes, see how much I meant what I was saying. "I don't care if your intentions were good. You were playing on Slittery's terms, which meant I was going to get cut out of a professional situation I deserved to be part of."

Ben's jaw clenched. His blue eyes burned. "You're right," he admitted, voice thick. "I'm sorry. Never again."

"Well, we're neck and neck for the win, right? And the nice thing about doing things my way is that kissing each other doesn't change anything else between us. So you do you, and I'll do me. I don't need your pity inclusion. I'll win this fair and square."

"Fuck the competition," Ben said. "We've been a team for a long time, and you know it."

"You can't make a fool of me." The words tumbled out, daggers aimed at his heart. "I know how much you care about winning, how at the end of the day, it's you against the world. I know you don't trust me. You've said it a million times. So why would I believe you?"

Ben wanting to meet with Slittery out of naked self-interest, I could understand. Like Sarah said, a case of *Ben Laderman vs. everyone else*. But Ben following me around the Governor's Mansion apologizing and telling me we're a team, after going to great lengths to clarify he didn't trust me enough to have anything more than physical with me—fine, fair—*that* was what didn't compute. Everything about him was confusing, and I didn't do confusing anymore.

"Stoner, I trust you at work. Implicitly. Outside of work—" Ben took a deep breath. He stepped close, so I moved back. "It's not…about trust. I'm afraid of you."

"What's that supposed to mean?" I tried not to think of my own fear, the image of him with a sword at my throat, and kept moving backward until my legs hit the rose-covered bed. I fell back onto it, scrambling to sit upright.

He gripped the bedpost, leaning over me. "I tried to deny it, to tell myself I wanted to come back to Texas because of my dream of turning it blue." He shook his head. "But the truth is, I couldn't stop thinking about you when Sarah suggested we move."

He knelt in front of me and reached for my hands, pressing my palms flat against his chest like I was stanching a bleeding wound. "I couldn't stop thinking about you when I got the job with the governor. I pushed for the Green Machine bill because it was the right thing to do, but also because I knew you were involved, and there was a chance I'd get to work with you. Fucked up, right? For a million reasons. Because of Sarah, and— Do you know what it's like to want the *one thing* you're not allowed to have? The *one* person you know you can't be with—to think of her all the time? I invented a hundred new forms of torture, Stoner, a thousand ways of convincing myself wanting you would pass. But it never did. Why do I have perfect control over myself, except when it comes to you? See? The things I'm capable of doing—you terrify me."

I did know what it felt like to want the one person I couldn't have, but as soon as I recognized it, a huge, yawning chasm opened inside me, a well I'd once discovered was bottomless and never wanted to confront again. I pulled my hands from his chest and lunged off the bed, stepping around him. "We said no feelings, Ben."

"I remember," he said roughly, rising to his feet. "Let's say I'm not talking about feelings. Let's say I'm talking about wanting to touch you in the middle of a conference room when both our bosses are watching. Stoner—are you seriously walking away from me again?"

There it was. His words struck a long-buried wound. I spun to face him. "Like you walked away from *me*? Like how I kept calling you, and texting you, and coming to your apartment, and got nothing in return? You *erased* me. You got in your car and you left for California and you didn't say anything to me for five whole years. Do you know how desperate that made me feel? You talk about not wanting to repeat what I put you through. Well, what about what you put *me* through?"

And there it was: my dirty little secret. Ben had every right to shut me out and leave me five years ago, after what I did to him. In fact, I should've expected both the leaving and the icy reception because my father had left our family for Michelle, and I myself had punished him with silence, so there was precedent for both. But the truth was, I still couldn't believe Ben had actually done it to me. This was why apologizing to him hadn't left me feeling like we'd settled our account. There was more to make up for. I'd struck the first blow back then, but he'd hurt me right back.

Ben hurt me. I'd been so caught up in guilt over what I'd done, I'd never allowed myself to sit with it.

Ben's eyes were stormy. "I thought you *wanted* me to leave. I thought I was doing you a favor. I figured you cheating was your way of getting out—your way of ending us because you weren't happy with me anymore."

"No," I cried. "I was *too* happy with you."

He stared, visibly shocked. Then, before I knew what was happening, he was closing the distance between us.

"What are you doing?" I took a step back and tripped over a rocking chair, stumbling backward.

Ben caught me with an arm around my waist. His gaze was too intimate, striking lightning down my body, but I didn't look away. I was mesmerized by his frown, by the way his eyebrows knit together to form a grave expression.

"I'm doing what I should have done five years ago, when you got scared and pushed me away," he said. "I'm coming closer."

"No," I said, feeling desperate. "No feelings."

"Fine. I promise." His voice was hoarse. "Just let me." His eyes dropped to my mouth.

No feelings: he promised. This was just a taste of what it felt like to be close.

The instant I nodded, he cupped my face and kissed me. The kiss was drenched in need, his lips insistent until I opened my mouth for him.

"Ben," I breathed, drawing back and shaking my head. "You asshole. You went away and grew up."

He pressed his forehead to mine. A lopsided smile spread over his face. "One of us had to."

With that, he seized me and walked me backward until my shoulders hit the wall, just like he'd done at the restaurant, picking up where we'd left off. I gasped, but he pressed his lips to mine and swallowed it.

All pretense dropped. Every game, every joke, every cutting word meant to keep him at bay. I slid Ben's tux jacket down his arms, hands flying to his shirt, sliding away the bow tie, unfastening his buttons with surprisingly shaky fingers. Suddenly, I didn't care about Slittery or the bill, about Sarah or anything else. I cared only about getting as much of Ben as close to me as possible.

I was stunned by my hunger for him, stunned at how quickly my body abandoned my control, hands moving of their own volition, mouth humming as he kissed down my throat. Only one thought surfaced: I got to touch him again, kiss him again, after all this time, and it was surreal. But my hunger was bottomless; no matter how much I got, it wasn't enough. This was the problem with me: my natural instincts, if not suppressed, had me wanting more than anyone could ever give.

"Tell me how to keep you," I whispered, smiling at Ben with the lightness of a joke.

He raised his eyebrows, eyes falling to the places where we entwined. I traced the flush of color as it rose over his cheeks. "I think you have me."

Our lips met, lighting sparks inside me. I unzipped his pants, feeling him push, hard and thick, into my hand. His breath hitched for a moment and then he kissed me harder, driven by need, this man who was always in such perfect control.

He slid his hands under the chiffon layers of my dress, the rough pads of his fingers and smooth nails trailing fire up my thighs. I arched, and he pressed into me. The room was cold but for the heat of his palm, cupping me through the thin layer of my panties, and then his fingers, stroking.

I bit Ben's neck and he pulled back to watch me, eyes liquid fire, as he slid the piece of silk aside and circled his thumb over me the way I loved, the way I'd missed, the way I'd tried to repeat by myself but never could. He circled over and over until I was rising off the wall and then he pushed a finger inside me, slowly, then out again, thumb still rubbing. I bit my lip to keep the sound inside. He curled his finger and I bucked, riding the rhythm of his hand.

I'd spent too long waiting. As soon as I thought it, I knew that's what I'd been doing. For five years, but especially since he'd come back to Texas. Waiting and waiting until I could shatter the pretense between us, close the distance, kiss him, feel his arms hard and strong around me. I wouldn't wait any longer.

I tugged at Ben's pants and he slid out of them and kicked them off, lifting me higher against the wall.

"Wait," he said. "I don't have..."

"My purse."

He lunged for my purse on the floor, still gripping me, and found the condom inside it. I was back up against the wall before I could blink.

He rolled it on, then froze. "Lee—"

But this time I swallowed his words and wrapped my legs around him. He gripped my hips and I pressed myself against him, practically begging, until finally he pushed inside me with a catch of his breath. I closed my eyes as he filled me, ground my head against the wall, plaster rough on my shoulders. Ben groaned my name again and goose bumps pricked my skin.

"Bed," I instructed, and he spun away, holding me tight against his chest as he lowered us onto the four-poster bed, the comforter cool against my back.

He held my face in one hand and kissed me; with the other, he gripped my hips and lifted them, sliding into me, filling me so deep and then pulling back, then over again, pushing deeper and deeper.

I closed my eyes and arched to meet him, letting my hips move, letting my body have what it wanted so badly. I'd tried for years not to think about Ben, about how big he was, how good he felt. I'd tried so hard to not use the memory of what he felt like pushing inside me when I touched myself, when I was with other men, but I could never hold out for long. Now that he was inside me again, real and not imagined, and my body was on fire, I realized the only thing I should regret is that I hadn't spent every minute of every day fucking Ben Laderman, who could make nerve endings come alive inside me other men couldn't touch.

Fuck it. I'd never been able to resist the memory of Ben in those unguarded moments, not for five years, and now I wanted everything I'd dreamed about.

I gripped his shoulders and he knew what it meant, our bodies in tune like we'd never left each other. He rolled onto his back and pulled me on top of him, drawing me down with maddening, teasing slowness.

I gasped, arching over him as he pushed into me, inch by inch. He clutched my hips and I kissed him like a wild thing, biting his lip until he sank deeper. I rocked my hips, the pressure building, until I gasped, "Ben, *please*."

The way he was looking at me, so intense, had me clenching

around him as I moved. He gripped my hips, guiding me in a relentless rhythm, rubbing me hard against him. He pulled down the straps of my chiffon dress and his warm mouth found my nipple, sucking, tongue flicking, and then I was over the edge. He caught my moan in his mouth and slowed, but only for a few precious seconds, and then his hands were gripping my hips, pumping me faster.

"I missed you so much." The words tore from his lips.

It was possible I was going to die in this madwoman's attic inside the Governor's Mansion, or we would get caught, but I didn't care. All I cared about was that Ben's hands were sliding up my waist as he said, "Fuck me, Lee," in that ragged voice, and then I was pulsing as waves of pleasure crashed through me, and he didn't slow—no, he was just getting started.

21

A Gentle Knife in the Back

Ben dragged his teeth down my neck, making me shiver, our spent bodies pressed together on top of the bed, limbs tangled.

"Vampire," I accused, and he smiled devilishly. In the lamplight, he could pass for it: his hair was black as midnight, long lashes casting shadows on his cheeks, the midnight blue rings around his irises enough to pull you in.

I tilted my head and Ben pressed his lips to the places he'd marked with his teeth. "My chest hurts," he said against my throat.

I curled my fingers into his hair, deliciously tired. "Why?"

He sat up, pressing the heel of his hand into his chest, and looked down at it. "I think I'm too happy."

"No such thing."

"I think I've wanted this for too long. My body doesn't know how to process the fact that you're here, and I can do this." Ben leaned in and pressed a kiss to my lips, achingly gentle. "And this." He slid down the bed and kissed my hip bone. "And this," he said, breath warm between my legs.

"What are you—" *Oh.* His mouth closed over me, and all the tiredness washed away as my body sparked to life again, his tongue hot and circling.

From downstairs, a crash sounded, followed by raucous laughter, and Ben and I jumped apart.

"*Shit.* I actually forgot there was a party going on," he said.

I sat up, tossing him his shirt. "Cockblocked by Texas politics. Happens to the best of us. Hurry up, get dressed." I'd forgotten about the party, too, and now it hit me: my bosses were *literally* downstairs. I was risking my carefully cultivated veneer of professionalism; potentially my job. *Dangerous move, Stoner.*

Ben pulled his clothes on, adjusting his bow tie rakishly, with a little wink. I stepped into my dress, turned, and he zipped it up my back. But before I could bend for my shoes, he swept me into his arms and tackled me back into the bed.

"Ben *Laderman*," I protested, laughing and shoving his shoulder. He grinned, his finger tracing over my collarbone, over the curve of my shoulder, then down to my wrist, eyes following.

"What are you doing?"

"I promised myself I would memorize you," he said softly.

I laughed, tilting his chin to catch his expression. But when I did, I stilled. Ben was giving me a look I remembered all too well. The too serious one that made the world stop for a moment, made everything pause, hold its breath, waiting for what would come next.

"You're looking at me funny," I said weakly.

"Lee." Ben's voice cracked with nervousness. Under my fingers, I could feel his pulse beating wildly in his throat.

My own heartbeat sped until I felt dizzy. "What?"

"I—"

Outside the door, the floor groaned with footsteps.

Ben and I stared at each other in horror; then he rolled off the bed and pulled me to my feet. I'd just shoved my boobs into my dress when the doorknob rattled and I froze.

Someone was here. Someone had found us. I shot a desperate look at Ben, but it was too late. The door swung open and two people tumbled in, kissing like their mouths were on fire and the only remedy was to tamp the flames with their tongues. The couple stumbled into the side table just like I had, and twisted so I could see their profiles.

I gasped, hands flying to my mouth.

It was *Dakota*. And the governor.

At the noise, they wrenched apart, eyes swinging for the source. The moment Dakota saw me, her face fell. But her horror had nothing on mine.

Dakota Young—my boss—was having an affair with the governor of Texas.

"Oh, thank God," the governor said, wiping his mouth on his sleeve. "It's only you two."

"Lee." There was so much worry packed into that single syllable that I couldn't look Dakota in the eyes.

"Right…" said the governor, eyeing Dakota and catching on that this was actually worse than he'd judged. "Not ideal to run into your head of PR, I guess."

Dakota stepped forward. "I'm so sorry, Lee." She waved a hand between herself and Governor Mane. "This just happened. It took me by surprise. We meant to end it, but things have just been so crazy, with the bill and the Herschel launch—"

"How long?" I asked, finding that my cool, calm and collected voice had activated out of nowhere, like a muscle I'd trained, swinging into action.

She shot a guilty look at the governor. "Maybe…a month or so? Maybe six weeks."

"Six *weeks*?" All this time, I'd been busting my ass trying to get our bill passed, worrying about being a more-than-perfect employee, worrying about letting Dakota down, and she'd been getting busy with Grover Mane and lying about it? I couldn't wrap my mind around it. This was Dakota Young. She didn't do the wrong thing. She was kind and respectful and good. She was the opposite of everyone who'd ever let me down. The opposite of *me*. I'd counted on that.

"Hey, Lee?" Ben shot a worried look at the open door. "Maybe we should talk about this somewhere else."

"Good idea," said the governor, adjusting his cuff links. "Here's a better one—let's all relax and forget this ever happened."

"But you're married," I said to Dakota, ignoring them. "George is *downstairs*, for Christ's sake. Probably brainstorming ways to defend you against Slittery." As much as I tried to push it out of my mind, I couldn't help but remember the moment I'd found my father's emails on his desktop; the sinking feeling in the pit of my stomach when I realized he'd chosen Michelle over me. His love and loyalty had gone to *her*, when it was supposed to go to me, and my mom and Alexis. I hated that I could still feel that sixteen-year-old inside me, confused and in pain, unable to understand why life was unfolding this way.

"I know it's wrong," Dakota said quietly, twisting the ring on her finger. "It's a huge mistake. I never should have started it, or taken risks like this—"

"If anyone finds out, the bill is dead." I laced my fingers together and looked between the governor and Dakota. "You realize that, right?" I was talking to them like they were children, I knew, but my shock had given way to cold anger over what they'd jeopardized. "If anyone so much as catches a hint of this, the media will have a field day. The Green Machine will be toxic. Hell, Lise Motors could be tanked."

Had I, a citizen of Texas seeking the passage of a state bill, technically hooked up with a member of the governor's administration, thus potentially impugning the perception of said bill? Sure, but Ben and I were nobodies. Dakota Young and Grover Mane? The whole country would sit up and pay attention. It was utterly reckless.

The governor gave a rueful laugh. "Christ, you and Ben have been spending too much time together. You sound just like him."

You could have heard a pin drop.

I turned to Ben, my movements jerky, as if part of me was trying to hold myself back, trying to keep my mouth from asking the question. If I never asked, I could stay in the moments before, when we'd stretched out together on the bed, kissing, Ben giving me his too serious look.

But living forever in the good parts was impossible. And I'd never been one to flinch from the truth.

"You knew?" I was amazed at how even my voice was.

I could read the truth in his eyes—but he said it out loud anyway. "I swear, I just found out." His tone was pleading. "Grover said they were ending it."

"You kept it from me." He'd asked me to open up. Trust him. Be honest. And little by little, I had been. He, on the other hand, was lying the entire time. Another way he'd kept *me* at arm's length.

"Grover asked me not to tell anyone—and besides, it's their business. They're adults, Lee. I knew they were jeopardizing the bill, so I told him they had to find a way to stop, at least until it passed."

"He was quite annoyingly insistent about it," the governor

added. "And, in case you're wondering, I will respectfully refrain from asking the two of you what *you* were doing up here in my guest bedroom."

At this point, I couldn't have cared less what the governor was insinuating about Ben and me in front of Dakota. All I cared about was the fact that Dakota and Ben had betrayed me.

They'd acted like we were in this together. Ben had literally said we were a team—and actually, fuck *that*, Dakota and I had been closer than a team, like family. Certainly, my feelings for both of them had far exceeded what I was supposed to feel for coworkers. Yet again, I'd given too much of myself to someone—*two* someones—and they'd let me down, left me behind. It was the exact scenario I'd built my entire life around avoiding. The sinking feeling clutched me once again, that bottomless well opening back up, so quick and so easy it was like I hadn't spent years trying to make it go away. And I was confronted, just like when I was younger, by my sheer capacity for pain.

Well, one thing had changed since then. I could play the hurting game, too. Colder and better than anyone.

I swooped my heels from the floor and padded quickly across the room.

"Lee," Dakota called, at the same time as Ben reached for me, fingers brushing my arm.

"Wait," he begged.

I cut my eyes in his direction. It was the most I would allow. "Do not follow me. Do you understand? I'm done."

I strode down the stairs and out the door of the Governor's Mansion with my head held high and my heels in my hands. Like some fucked-up, tired Cinderella who'd done this one too many times.

22

The Pursuit of Happiness

I shot my head out of the pile of blankets when I heard the front door opening. My sudden movement—a thing unprecedented of late, as evidenced by the sloppy pile of pizza boxes within arm's reach—disturbed Al and Bill, who were curled protectively around my massive blanket-fort. They'd gathered here under the guise of comforting me; but really, they were happy I was miserable. It meant I'd transformed into a prone mountain of a person, nothing more than a lap for kneading, hands for scratching and occasional tears for a delicious, salty snack.

I grabbed the stereo remote and paused Frank Ocean.

"Alexis, good, you're home," I called into the entryway. "I thought of another reason you should never have a personal hero."

"Hey," she said, practically bouncing into the room. She

was grinning way too brightly as she shrugged off her peacoat, slapping her cheeks to warm them.

I eyed her suspiciously. "What?"

She widened her eyes. "What do you mean, what?"

I waved a hand at her. "Your skin is glowing, your cheeks are flushed and your eyes are literally sparkling. You're a goddamn cartoon character. This is not the appropriate energy to bring into this house of mourning. So, what is it? What are you so happy about?"

"Oh, *Lee*." Alexis sank into the couch next to me and somehow found my hands through the blankets. "You'll never guess what happened."

"Ben and Governor Manc got their penises chopped off in a freak ice storm, and now they've committed to life as eunuch monks."

That threw her for a second, but she rebounded, flashing that thousand-watt smile. "Chris called."

Mentally I took out my creaky flagpole and started spinning the red flag up to full mast. "Oh? Did he want to talk about voluntarily chopping off his penis, too, in apologetic sacrifice?"

"*No.* Lee, you have intense Lorena Bobbitt energy right now. It's disturbing."

I made a "well, get on with it" gesture.

"He told me he loves me, and he's so sorry, and he wants to get back together." Her eyes shone.

I laughed. "That's hilarious. He did not."

She frowned. "He's serious."

"What happened to that woman he left you for?"

"He broke up with her when he realized he was still in love with me."

I snorted. "Alexis, please don't tell me you fell for that."

Her face screwed up. "People make mistakes. He said he'd spend the rest of his life making it up to me."

Her tone was earnest, urgent. It sank in: she was serious.

I kicked the blankets off. "Lex, please don't go back to him. He treated you like shit. Worse than shit. He can't just fix everything with a phone call. He'll cheat on you again."

Her eyes filled with tears, which— *Shit.* "No, he won't. I trust him."

"Just because you want people to be different doesn't mean they are," I said, desperate to make her see. "They show you who they really are through their actions."

"He is showing me. He's begging me to come back."

"No—"

"Lee, I miss him." A tear slipped down Alexis's cheek. "It took that disastrous hookup with James at the Governor's Ball to make me realize." *Senator James Janus*, I mentally corrected her. "I *love* Chris. I tried not to, but I can't help it. I don't want to help it. I want to be with him. Be happy for me."

Panic seized me. There was no way. Alexis was making a mistake. She was going back for second helpings of pain. Chris was going to take her heart and tear it to shreds. I couldn't let that happen.

But before I could say anything, a tentative smile wobbled over her face. "Please tell me you're happy for me," she said softly, and leaned in to hug me.

I jumped back. "No. You're being *weak*. You're being a doormat, Alexis. I can't sit here and nod and squeal when I can see plain as day he's going to break you again. You're going to be right back here on my couch in no time."

She froze, her arms still stretched to hold me. "I'm not a doormat."

"Then stop acting like one."

She leaped from the couch, the look on her face flashing from stunned to angry. "Not everyone is as intensely punishing as you are, Lee. Some of us make simple mistakes and move on. Some of us are capable of love and forgiveness."

"Well, I guess when Chris cheats on you again and breaks your heart, you shouldn't come running to me."

Alexis spun and lunged for her coat. "Don't worry. You couldn't pay me a million dollars to run to you."

She stomped out the door and slammed it behind her, making Al and Bill skitter under the couch.

I slammed my back against the cushion. Fucking Alexis. What was she thinking, taking Chris back? How much of an idiot did you have to be—how pathetically lonely—to take a person back who'd acted like that? A person who'd cheated on you so egregiously. Like I'd done to Ben.

Ugh. Something tickled my face. I brought my fingers to my cheeks, only to find them wet. Great. I was crying.

In a matter of days, I'd managed to ruin three of my most important relationships. Dakota hadn't tried calling *once* since the Governor's Ball, so I didn't know if I even had a job anymore. Ben had called and called for days straight, but eventually he'd stopped. Now Alexis was gone, and not just for a little while. For good.

I didn't want to cry. I was tired of feeling so much. More than that—I was tired of being trapped inside this brain. I wanted a break.

I knew what to do. I rolled off the couch and slumped to the kitchen, where I poured myself a splash of whiskey, even though it was only four in the afternoon. It washed wonderfully down my throat, biting the entire way. *That*—that was the only kind of pain I wanted to feel. The kind that helped me float outside my body.

I picked up my phone and scrolled through the texts, passing Mac's and Claire's names. I didn't want to see my friends.

I didn't want to see anyone who knew me or loved me. I didn't even want to see anyone who liked me very much. I wanted numbness.

By the time Kyle came over with four of his friends, I answered the door holding the whiskey bottle.

"Stonerrrrrr," Kyle crooned, catching me in a quick, one-armed hug as he walked in. "Meet Andromeda, Lucius, Katya and Little Timmy. Dudes, this is the chick I told you about. I promise you, she's down for anything."

The four of them streamed in, nodding to me, all kinds of young and Austin weird.

"Alcohol's in the kitchen," I said. I turned to Kyle. "Only four?"

"Hey," Kyle yelled after his friends. "She wants to get *lit.*"

"I want to forget I have a face," I corrected.

One of them turned around and dug in his pocket. "I've got the thing for that." He held out a baggie with small yellow pills. Each one wore a smiley face.

"What are they?"

He shrugged and grinned. "More fun if you don't know."

I held out my hand. "Give it."

"Okay," Kyle yelled, cupping his mouth like a megaphone. "Shit's getting real."

"Call more people," I told him, popping the smiley face. "I want to be surrounded by fuckers I don't know."

"Hey, man." Kyle held his hands up in surrender. "You heard the lady. Nothing that happens after this is my fault."

There was loud music all of a sudden. Like someone had clapped headphones on me and sound jumped to life. I had a feeling it had been playing for a while, and I'd only just noticed, which was funny. My living room was crowded with people.

I'd never seen a single one of them in my life. The other thing was, they glowed. No—each of them carried an aura, a haze of color around their outlines. That was nice. I would have to tell Mac the meditation ladies were right about one thing.

"Hey," said a guy, bumping my shoulder on the couch. He held up a joint. "You want a hit?"

"Why not?" I said, and tried to take it.

He laughed and swooped something out of my hand. "You might want to put your drink down first."

"Oh. Ha." With my newly free hand, I got busy disappearing.

"You're so fun tonight," someone said to me sometime later, when I was in the kitchen. The person had an arm around my shoulder, squeezing me. I realized it was Kyle.

"Want to do tequila shots?" asked a girl I'd learned was Andromeda.

"No, you go ahead," I said, and she shrugged and lined up the shot glasses.

I had a momentary impulse to tell them I'd gotten that bottle of tequila in Mexico City years ago, and the woman who sold it to me out of her family's tasting room had been the smallest, sweetest woman I'd ever met. But they wouldn't care. And neither did I; not anymore. The impulse faded, and I was left with a comfortable, buzzing blankness.

Kyle lifted his shot glass, spilling sticky liquid down my arm. "To Stoner, a ridiculous human being. We could probably light this house on fire, and she wouldn't give a damn. It's amazing."

"To Stoner," Andromeda said. She leaned over my arm. "Can I lick it?"

"Do whatever you want," I said. I felt her tongue slide wet and warm against my skin.

"Hot," Kyle said. "Can I kiss you?"

I tipped the bottle over their shot glasses to refill them and laughed. "Kyle, I honestly don't give a fuck."

Kyle kissed me, and then Andromeda did, and then a third person, and someone laughed in the distance, saying, *That girl's wild.*

In some amount of time there were hands everywhere, mouths up and down my face and my neck. Which was okay; which was good, actually, because I could barely feel my body anymore, and the touching helped me figure out where my boundaries were, the raw and vulnerable places where my skin met air. Good to numb those places; to cover them with other people.

I spun away. I could tell there were more people in my house than there'd ever been before, but the thing was—the funny thing was—they also didn't exist. I could walk through them like gauzy curtains, gently pushing until they parted. It was nice to have company like this. To be surrounded by people, and at the same time alone.

"Hey," said Lucius with the smiley face pills, popping up in front of me. He shook the baggie. "You want another?"

I swayed, and he caught me, and we both laughed. "Probably not," I said.

"Look, that guy's naked." Lucius pointed to the living room, where people were dancing and jumping into each other. Sure enough, alone in the corner, a naked man danced in circles all by himself. His aura was a peaceful butter yellow.

"Hilarious," I said.

"Let's dance." All of a sudden, the music was so loud it shook the walls.

It was all I wanted to do. I grabbed Lucius's hand and pirouetted into the middle of the crowd. For hours, or minutes, or days, there was only my blood pumping, my sweat rolling, as I leaped and jumped with strangers to the thumping music.

"Turn it *up*," I yelled, and they cheered and the world was nothing but a tilting floor and escalating noise, vibrating under my skin.

Then I was in my bedroom, sitting on the floor, surely. Because that was—yes, that was my bed I was leaning back against. I recognized the duvet cover, which I'd ordered proudly from a company in Point Reyes, California, when I got my first real paycheck.

Ha! Imagine thinking that was important. The girl who'd bought this duvet cover was a stranger, and I felt a sense of accomplishment that I'd managed to get so far away from her. This was much nicer, to be on the outside, looking in.

There were people sitting in a circle around me, Kyle one of them. We were playing some sort of game. Someone flipped a quarter and drank, and a few seconds later they were all making faces and laughing.

Then the mood in the room shifted. I could feel it, even without looking at anyone's face. Someone dropped to their knees in front of me.

"Lee?"

I looked up to find Ben Laderman. Surely, a mirage.

I touched his leg. Nope. Solid and real. I knew I was angry at him, but at the moment, it didn't seem very important.

"Guys!" I yelled. "Ben's here. Now it's a party!"

The circle cheered. "Benny boy!" called Kyle, who was friendlier when he was drunk. "Get yourself a beer. We're playing quarters."

Ben squinted at me. I'd never seen his face in such vivid detail. I could account for every freckle, every pore, every cell. *Whew*, he was pretty! Even his pores. Even the dark, slender hairs of his eyebrows, the ones that didn't quite fall in line. The waves on his head looked black from far away, but up close I could see the individual strands of chestnut, like a secret just for me. The way he was holding his mouth—tight and drawn at the corners—made his cheekbones sharp and pronounced, which was a trick I would have to remember for selfies. And his eyes—it was trippy to have them locked on me like this, like I was the only thing that existed.

"You're very handsome." I patted his cheek. "And I'm not just saying that because the smiley face made everyone beautiful. I really mean it. Why are you here?"

Ben looked amused. "You texted me and told me to come over."

"Huh." I held up my hands and wiggled my fingers. "Wily. And full of surprises."

"I don't mean this in an infantilizing way," he said, leaning closer. "But are you okay? Do you want me to kick all these people out of your house?"

I patted his cheek again. "Benjamin, I'm the best I've ever been. These are my new best friends." I gestured at the circle of people. "You remember Kyle. That girl next to him is Andromeda, also known as Mermaid Hair. That's Lucius Smiley Face, the guy next to him's Little Timmy Tattoo Hands, and she's Katya, or Nipple Piercing. What? That's what they told me to call them."

Ben raised a dubious eyebrow.

I pointed to the last guy in the circle. "I'm sorry—I forgot your name."

"Ragnar," he said.

I gave Ben a pointed look. "I rest my case."

"Nice to meet you all," Ben said politely.

"What does the hot man do?" Andromeda gave Ben's arms a once-over. "Construction worker, by the looks of it."

"He works for the governor," I said. "Policy director."

"Oh." Her face blanked. "Too bad."

"Let's get Ben caught up." Little Timmy tossed rolling paper onto an old birthday card I'd gotten from my grandma—where had he found that?—and tapped weed onto it, folding and rolling slickly. Clearly an expert.

"Very nice," Lucius said. "Very generous of you, man."

"No, no—wait." Kyle's face was grave. "Ben works for the government. They drug test and shit." He gave me a proud look. "I learned that when I looked up the law for my new phone app."

"It's just pot," Little Timmy said, unimpressed with Kyle's warning. "It's medicinal."

"Do it, do it," Andromeda chanted. "There's no room for government killjoys in this house."

Ben looked at me.

I shrugged. "You can always leave."

"No." His mouth set in a determined line. "No more leaving. I go where you go. Keep your pot, but toss me a shot glass. I'll at least kick your asses in quarters."

"Oh, *yes*." Lucius clapped him on the back. "Welcome to the party, Guvna."

"I think I'll live to regret this," Ben said, and took his shot.

Much later, when the world returned to me, coming back like a blurry film slowly crystallizing into sharper detail, Ben and I lay side by side on my bedroom floor, looking up at the ceiling. It was eerily quiet.

I looked around the empty room. "Hey. Where is everyone?"

Ben's chest shook as he laughed, the sound floating up. "They left for tacos like an hour ago. You gave every single one of them your phone number. I'm pretty sure you planned a vacation with Andromeda. You don't remember?"

"Oh. Not really."

Ben folded his hands over his stomach. "Man. It's been a long time since I've done anything like this."

"What? Had fun?"

"No. Said fuck it to everything and went wild. It reminds me of grad school. I don't know how I was able to party so much back then and still get good grades. Where did all that energy go?"

"Everyone was wild back then." It hadn't just been me, dragging people along all the time. Back then, everyone was on my level. "It was fun."

"Yeah. But also exhausting."

I yawned. "Very."

Ben's voice was light. Purposefully casual. "Hey, Stoner?"

"Mmm?"

"Do you think maybe you do this kind of thing a little too much? As a Band-Aid, when you're unhappy?"

I considered, then burst out laughing.

"What?" He turned on his side and put his head in his hand, studying me.

I grinned. "This is an intervention. You are intervening me."

He shrugged. "How am I doing?"

I looked at the dark space under my bed, into the farthest corners I couldn't see, feeling his eyes on me. "Yes. I probably do this too much. It's nice to turn the feelings off sometimes."

"I hear yoga is good for that."

I snorted. "Yeah. Tried it. You know, I can still remember the night I realized exactly how good alcohol could make me feel. Like I could leave my own brain and go on vacation."

"That is nice," Ben said. "Personally, I like the gym. That's where I get a break from my brain."

I sighed. "I concede the point. I might be getting a little old for this."

Silence grew between us. It wasn't the uncomfortable silence of one person catching the other at a rather bleak moment in her life. It was a peaceful quiet between two people who'd known each other for a long time, who were lying side by side, arguments cast away. Walls down.

"It's probably the tequila telling me to say this," Ben said, "and I kind of hope you don't remember in the morning. But… I'm lying here, and all I can think about is the night we met."

I looked over at him, but he was staring at the ceiling. A small smile lit his face. "You were so cool. It was like you didn't care what anyone thought. Like you had this secret, and no one could touch you. And there I was, with this massive chip on my shoulder, determined to one-up everyone I met, which in reality just meant I cared a lot what everyone thought. I always wanted to be more like you."

That was a surprise. No one ever wanted to be like me. "Ben, the secret was, I'd given up on people. I didn't care anymore, for the most part. I don't think that method suits you."

"Maybe not. But it was intoxicating to watch." He closed his eyes and laughed. "You probably thought I was such a fool back then. I told you I loved you so fast."

He yawned, the lines around his eyes creasing. "I had all these plans. I'd get the clerkship, become a judge, run for office. Marry you, become a political power couple. Start a family, become the world's best dad. I had it all figured out. And then it crashed and burned."

"It atomic-bomb exploded."

He smiled sleepily. "It never turns out how you expect, does it?"

As I watched, his face relaxed. A minute passed, and then Ben was asleep. He really was a scientific marvel.

He'd left me alone with only his words for company. *It never turns out how you expect.* I exhaled, long and deep. It really didn't.

There was something I needed to do. I sat up, crept through the messy house—a problem for Future Stoner—and found my jacket. Then I slipped out the door.

* * *

I lay on ice-cold dirt, a place where grass normally grew. But it was winter, so there was only chilled, packed mud. At least there were stars. I rolled over and looked at the gravestone. It stared back at me rather judgmentally.

"Hi, Dad."

I brushed dirt off my leg. "I know what you're thinking. And no, I did not break your rule about drinking and driving. So, you can stop with the attitude. I walked here, thank you very much."

I dug in the ground, getting mud under my fingernail. "How? Well, I bought a house just a few blocks away right after you died. It was a very normal knee-jerk purchase because I am a very well-adjusted person. Who just happens to want to pass by this cemetery once a day on her way to work.

"You're dead, by the way. In case the cemetery thing threw you. But I guess you probably knew that. It's still a shock to me. Sometimes I forget when I'm asleep, and then when I wake up, I have to remember all over again. I think it actually hurts as bad as when Alexis told me the first time. But obviously, that's not your fault. Unlike everything else! Which is a joke, by the way. I know you were always fifty-fifty about my sense of humor, but now you're just going to have to suck it up."

I sat up. "Man, do you remember how *angry* I was at you? Obviously, who could forget. Eleven years we didn't talk, which is almost as many years as we did talk. That's sad, Dad. When I think about that sometimes, I get very, very sad."

My voice seemed to die in my throat. "I always read all of your corny Christmas cards. You had a very dad sense of humor, if we're being honest. I did appreciate you signed them by yourself, without Michelle."

I leaned forward and scratched dirt from the words in the tombstone. *Richard Thomas Stone. Beloved Father and Husband.* The last four words covered over so much messiness.

"After you died," I said, "I felt like if I kept being angry at you, it would keep you alive somehow. Like if I kept things normal, kept this thing between us unresolved, it was only logical that one day I'd still get the chance to resolve it with you. And before you say anything—yes, I know that's very narcissistic, thinking what I do has some effect on cosmic forces like life and death. But there it is. That's why I've driven past you a million times, but never visited."

The top of the stone was layered with grime. I tugged my sleeve over my hand and rubbed it away, then sat back down cross-legged.

"There. Good as new."

It was very late, and I had the place to myself. Surrounding my dad were other members of his family, all of them together in the family plot.

He and I sat in silence. He was waiting for me to gather my courage, which was hard. I almost couldn't speak past the lump in my throat, but finally, I got it out. "Dad. I miss you."

There was no response. Not even the wind stirring. I laid my head against the gravestone, cheek pressed to the cold.

"You fucked up. I really was so betrayed by you. But I'm not perfect, either. That's what I came to say. I'm not perfect, and neither were you, and we're only human. So I forgive you. Do you forgive me?"

Again, the night stretched, quiet without interruption.

"I really would give anything for you to talk back," I whispered.

We sat like that for a long time, until the cold night bit at me and I couldn't feel my hands. I rubbed my cheek against the stone and smiled. "All right, Dad. I'm going home. But don't worry. Like I said, I'm just around the corner."

I pressed my fingers to his name. "Forever and a day, okay? That can be ours from now on."

23

For the Best

The problem with catching your boss having an affair with a high-ranking politician is you still have to show up when she calls a meeting. Ben and I sat awkwardly across from each other in the Lise conference room. Just the two of us, waiting on Dakota and Wendy. We were looking at our phones, at the glossy finish on the table, at the white of the walls. Anything but each other.

When I came home from the cemetery last weekend, my house was empty. I'd crawled gratefully into bed and slept for a record fourteen hours, waking up in the late afternoon to a place in dire need of deep cleaning. Most of the details of the night before were hazy, which I assumed was a blessing. But I remembered all the parts with Ben.

I'd done far crazier things at a house party than put aside my differences to play quarters with an ex. But what we'd said that night, after everyone else left—hell, even the fact that I'd texted Ben seven times, all variations on Help me Captain Planet, I'm trapped in a beautiful prison with dancing smiley faces, please rescue me, oh never mind, it's my house, come anyway, and omg Willie Nelson is in my bedroom braiding people's hair you better come I'm not lying, and he'd actually shown up—was enough to make my cheeks burn every time my eyes slipped and I caught a glimpse of him.

The silence was searing. I found myself wishing Dakota would walk through the door. And then, *no*—immediately, I clawed that wish back. She and I hadn't seen each other since the Governor's Ball, and so however awkward things were between Ben and me, they'd be ten times worse with Dakota. Even Wendy, who liked to pretend Lise employees were work robots and things like interpersonal dynamics didn't exist, had noticed things between Dakota and me were strained. She'd stopped by my office to ask me what the deal was.

I'd sworn it was nothing, but she hadn't believed me. I could feel her suspicious eyes trailing every move I made all week. Besides being unnerving, it was a pain. I'd had to take one-hour-long lunch breaks, and not a minute more. Thank God the office was closed next week for the holidays.

"Shit," Ben muttered to his phone. Then he looked up at me in surprise, as if alarmed at himself for breaking the sacrosanct rule of no talking.

I put down my phone. "What is it?"

He tugged at his tie and cleared his throat. "Nothing with the bill or anything."

I sat up straighter and crossed my legs. "Seriously. What is it?"

He gave me a guilty look. "It's Sarah."

I surprised myself with how quickly the thought crossed my mind: *Is Ben back with Sarah now that we didn't work out?* I flinched at the needy undertone of my own internal monologue. I'd told Ben I was done with him, after all.

It wasn't the easy choice, or the one that felt good. If I chose to do what *felt* good, I'd throw my phone at Ben's head, yelling at him for betraying me. I'd storm off, refuse to work with him, or else I'd tell him to get on his hands and knees and grovel. Or I'd climb across the conference table and kiss him until he couldn't think straight, until he promised to never hurt me again. These were just the first things that came to mind; it wasn't like I'd given it much thought.

But, in the days since my house party, which now felt like some last hurrah, some final, bookend chapter—in the days of solitude sitting alone in my house, without Alexis, or my friends, without even a glass of wine—I'd decided I wouldn't keep choosing the thing that felt good and easy. I would try making the *right* choices. I would, literally and figuratively, get my house in order.

So what Ben Laderman did with his romantic life was officially none of my business.

"I told her a while ago that I could do something important for her," he explained quickly. "But it turns out it's the weekend Will's coming in town. It's my only chance to see him. I'm going to have to tell her no."

Curiosity got the best of me. "What is it?"

"She does the Run against Cancer half-marathon every year to raise money for breast cancer research." He paused. "Her mom died of it when she was young. She has to go out of town for work, and I was going to fill in for her so she could still raise money."

Her mom. Immediately, my heart was in my throat. "I'll do it."

Ben blinked. "What?"

"I'll run the marathon in her place."

He frowned at me. "Don't get me wrong, that's really nice, and it sounds like she's desperate enough to say yes, even to you, but… Stoner, you were winded that day running down the stairs at the Governor's Mansion. You had to lie on the ground for minutes after we ran out of the wine festival. I'm not sure you know what you're getting yourself into. Sarah raised a lot of money with pledged donations, but she only gets it if she crosses the finish line. She needs someone to fill in who can…do that."

"I said I'll do it," I said firmly. "Send me the details."

Ben raised his eyebrows. "Okay." He held up his phone as he typed. "Doing it now. Sarah will be grateful, despite… being very angry at us. And working hard to kill our bill."

I nodded curtly. "Well, I kind of owe her, so…"

We both looked down at our phones again. The silence stretched until Ben's voice broke through—a single, urgent plea.

"Lee."

I glanced up at him, but left my fingers fake-typing on my phone, so he'd think I was in the middle of an important work email. Though, with my luck, I'd probably manage to accidentally pull up the Japanese sex-toy website I sometimes liked to lurk in—trying to figure out which parts of what things went in which holes, obviously. My fingers were probably in the middle of an inadvertent thousand-dollar sex-toy shopping spree.

Ben leaned over the conference table, his forearms flexed, face earnest. "Can we please talk about what happened at the Governor's Ball?"

I shrugged. "No need." And glanced down at my phone. Dear God, I *was* on the Japanese sex-toy website. I dropped my phone like it was on fire and it clattered to the table.

"I said all I needed to say," I added quickly, glancing furtively at the glowing screen. A mysterious, three-pronged, peach-colored object vibrated suggestively in the center of it. In plain sight. For all Bens to see. I scrambled for the phone and practically threw it in my lap, crossing my legs to keep the thing secure.

"Well, *I* didn't say all I needed to say." Ben's blue eyes gripped me. They burned with singular intent, demanding my body sit up and pay attention, that it burst into a thousand goose bumps.

My body obeyed.

He took a deep breath. "I never meant—"

I was saved when the door flew open and Dakota strode in on tall heels, Wendy keeping pace behind her. She walked to the head of the conference table and clutched the back of a chair, but didn't sit.

Seeing Dakota again was as weird as I'd expected. I stared at the chair in front of her, unable to bring myself to make eye contact. Had Dakota broken it off with the governor, or were they still going? Would she ever tell her husband, George, or was she planning to take the secret to her grave? If she didn't dump the governor, would she dump me instead?

The pain was like someone had taken a knife to my heart. If there was one thing in my life that was pure and uncomplicated, it was my love for Dakota Young. I'd thought she was infallible. I'd bet so much on it.

I had the weirdest impulse in that moment to run from the conference room to my office and slam the door, like I'd done the night my father came home after I'd found his emails, and I'd disappeared to my room.

Dakota cleared her throat.

I looked up. She flinched when we met eyes, but gathered herself, brushing her hair coolly from her shoulder. "Lee. Ben. Thank you for meeting me at such late notice. I promise I won't keep you long." Her smile looked strained, and though she now trained her eyes on Ben, they kept flicking to me. "I—well, I'm positive I'm not the person you most want to see right now."

Wendy's eyebrows twitched in confusion. That was all—just a twitch—but it was enough of a tell. She didn't know what Dakota was referencing, which meant she didn't *know*.

"But," Dakota continued, "I wanted to update you on a new approach to the Green Machine."

A new approach? My spine straightened, and—tension be damned—I shot a look at Ben. He looked just as confused as I was.

Dakota beckoned Wendy forward. She stepped to Dakota's side, eyes calculating. "Seeing as how that *oil tyrant* Samuel Slittery circumvented civic engagement by going straight to the senators and offering campaign donations, we all know the Green Machine's toast."

My heart sank. Why was Wendy calling the Green Machine's time of death? We still had hope. Before everything had blown up at the Governor's Ball, Ben and I had hobnobbed with tons of people. There'd been sincere interest in the bill. And I'd spent the week reflecting on Ben's words from that night—not any of the feelings stuff, or the betrayal stuff, but before that, when we were watching Slittery suck up to Senator McBuck. *Whether this bill lives or dies is on our shoulders now. I just wish I could figure out some way to get around Slittery.*

Without my friends, Alexis or Ben around, without any booze or pot, without the distraction of the campaign or checking up on Dakota, I'd had time to think. I'd racked my brain. And come up with an idea.

Apparently, Ben and I were on the same wavelength.

"Wait a second," he said, placing his phone delicately on the conference table. "I really think we still have a chance. Slittery,

McBuck, all those old men in the legislature—they represent the past. We need to talk about the future *to* the future. Climate change is a top issue for voters under thirty-five."

"Voters under thirty-five are mythical creatures." Wendy's voice was cutting. "You might as well be talking about lobbying the unicorn vote. Sorry, Ben, but we all know people under thirty-five don't turn out, especially not in state elections. State lawmakers aren't afraid of them."

"But they could be," Ben urged, and for a moment I forgot everything between us and just watched him, admiring his passion. He put his hands flat on the table and leaned in, his eyes bright behind his glasses. "We could launch a big campaign to rally the youth vote. Get them yelling, *marching*, if they'll do it. A sit-in at the capitol."

"It's a good idea," Dakota said, looking at Ben kindly. "Even a noble one. But it won't work."

Ben's face fell. "But—"

"Roy McBuck doesn't care how much noise college students make when he knows they'll be silent come November."

"I've got a way," I said quietly.

Everyone's heads turned. Ben, though he'd just been shot down, looked at me hopefully.

"The governor can persuade Janus and Wayne to give us their votes back. They made commitments to us. It's what their constituents want. They're swayable. Our biggest hurdle is still McBuck. And yes, campaign money is seductive. But nothing—*nothing*—trumps the will of the people. In his heart, McBuck knows that. I bet he felt free to take Slittery's money because he knew at the end of the day, we hadn't won over his district yet. So, let's win it."

"How?" Wendy asked.

I was loath to admit it, but my plan involved a little thing called compromise. The very same thing I'd once told Ben was the death of politics.

I looked at Dakota. "You worked your ass off for decades, and now we're about to roll out one of the most in-demand new motors in automotive history. You and I both know we need a new manufacturing center to meet the demand for the Herschel. Let's put it in McBuck's district. That will create thousands of high-paying jobs."

I glanced at Ben, and was buoyed by the excitement on his face. "Mendax Oil employees don't like working there anyway. We saw it firsthand. Give them an alternative, and even better—a sense of pride and mission—and they'll support us. I really believe it. They'll make their voices heard with Senator McBuck."

Ben nodded eagerly. "She's right. If we can offer a solution to address job loss, I bet you anything they'd side with us."

Wendy looked thoughtful. "It's got promise, actually. We were just about to start the conversation about where to put the new center, and Hudson County was on the list."

Dakota walked out from behind the chair. "I'm sorry, Lee, but no."

"No?" Ben repeated.

I could do nothing but blink. Dakota had never dismissed me like this, in all the years I'd worked for her.

She sighed, and when she spoke, she avoided my eyes. "I'm tired of playing politics. I don't want to gamble anymore. We want to pass this bill, and there's an easy, straightforward solution."

"Which is?" I asked.

Even Wendy leaned in for the answer.

Dakota straightened. "Slittery's not the only one with money to spend on campaign donations. I'll simply give Janus, Wayne and McBuck a bigger check. Boom. Easy. We win."

"You can't do that," I burst out, stopping myself at the last minute from leaping out of my seat. "That's not who we are. We don't buy votes. Paying for the Green Machine bill would be enabling the worst part of politics. It would open us up to attack from our opponents, who will say we just paid to have our way. And they'll be *right*. It's our burden to convince people if we want to change the law."

Dakota shook her head. "It's not pay-to-play. Lise Motors has no government contracts on the line. I've vetted it with Legal."

"Look, you know I'm a pragmatist at heart," Ben said. "Bottom line, I care about winning. But I'm with Lee on this one. Using money like this may not be illegal, but it's dirty. It's not the right approach. Was this the governor's idea?"

"It doesn't matter whose idea it was," Dakota said curtly. "I'm sorry you two feel this way, because I know this was your baby, but it's how it's going to go. We tried it the hard way and we got close—you did a remarkable job—but we couldn't bring it home. I'll bring it home. It's too important to gamble on."

I couldn't believe what I was hearing. First the affair, now this? Who *was* Dakota anymore? Where was my idol, the woman I trusted?

Dakota could probably tell it was time to cut and run, because Ben was sitting there with a stunned expression, and God only knew what my face looked like. Even Wendy looked taken aback.

Turning sharp on her heel, Dakota strode to the door. Just before she left, she paused and looked at me over her shoulder. Her eyes were soft. "I know you don't approve, Lee. And I really wish—" She cleared her throat. "You have to accept that not everything in the world is cut-and-dried, good or bad, right or wrong. Sometimes you have to deal in the gray. I hope you understand my decision one day."

With that, Dakota left, leaving Wendy to scramble after her.

Did she just tell *me* the world was gray? You've got to be kidding me.

It was hard to breathe. In a short matter of time, I'd lost my relationships with Dakota, Ben and Alexis—and now I'd lost my dream. The thing I cared about most in the world. My bill.

I felt tears well in my eyes, hot and stinging, and I sprang from the table, mortified that Ben would see. I did my best to dash out of the room and down the hall while still maintaining an air of professionalism, in case anyone was watching. I just needed to get to my office, and then I could cry alone.

"Lee, wait."

I glanced behind me. Oh, no. Ben was following me. Talking to him was the last thing I could handle right now.

I darted into my office and shut the door, flinging myself into my desk chair. A few seconds later, there was a knock. I could tell it was Ben because, unfortunately, the walls of my office were glass and we were staring at each other through them.

I pretended like I was busy on my computer, all while trying to take deep breaths to quell the urge to scream.

Ben knocked again. This time, Dakota's executive assistant leaned over from her cubicle to peer at us.

Fine. Ben Laderman wanted to talk? I would talk. I shot from my chair, opened the door and beckoned to him, keeping my voice low. "Follow me."

Ben gave me an amused look, but obeyed. I led him through the office, all the way to the pumping room, which sat in the farthest corner of the building. None of my colleagues had given birth recently, so staff had taken to using it for naps. It was windowless and private. Perfect.

Ben stepped inside and I locked the door behind us, swiveling to face him. "Okay. *What?*"

"What do you mean, what?" He gave me an incredulous look. "Our entire campaign just went up in flames. Don't you want to talk about it?"

I leaned against the door and crossed my arms. "You heard Dakota. Her mind's made up. At this point, I think it's better if you and I accepted our fate and moved on to being two professionals with limited contact who happen to live in the same city. Like we originally planned."

Ben's eyes narrowed. "Bullshit. You're still mad at me for not telling you about Dakota and the governor. *Understandably* mad," he added, when I started to protest. "But Jesus Christ, Lee. I found out about their affair a week before you did. I honestly thought they were going to end it, and it would all go away. No harm, no foul."

"How ironic. Given the fact that you've been upset about being cheated on for five whole years."

He lowered his voice, neatly sidestepping my dig. "Dakota's married. That's next-level. If people started gossiping about her having an affair, it could really hurt her. I didn't want to be responsible for putting that secret out in the world. I wanted it to go away."

I threw my hands out. "That's exactly why you should have *told* me. I'm her comms director. It's my job to minimize damage. Which means I need to *know* the damage! Besides, let's be honest here. First, I find out you were considering Slittery's request to negotiate a deal without me. Then I find out you knew about the affair and didn't tell me. You were keeping all sorts of things to yourself. You used to be the most competitive person I've ever met. I *know* that Ben is still inside you, no matter how Zen you pretend to be. Admit it—you liked the advantages because you wanted to win. Ben vs. the world."

"*Yes*, okay?" The words burst out of him. "Yes, I wanted to win. I wanted to pass the bill so bad that maybe I made the wrong decisions. And maybe I *did* want to be the one who got it over the finish line."

I crossed my arms. "So much for being a team. That's what you said, right?"

"Okay, I get it. I fucked up. Old habits die hard. But are my sins really worth cutting ties with me?" Ben took a step toward me, and it became hard to look away from his eyes. "Or are you doing that thing where you push people you care about away when you realize they're capable of hurting you? Remember, with your dad? And then with me, when you thought I was cheating?"

That struck a chord. Anger flashed to life. "People I *care* about? How many times do I have to remind you we agreed to no feelings?"

He studied me, jaw tightening. "So, it's true? You really don't care?"

"I— It was— Look, we made a deal. For this exact reason, so when things inevitably went south, we could walk away without our hearts broken like the last time."

"You know what? I survived heartbreak. I found ways to manage. But without you, I was only ever surface happy."

I shook my head. "Surface happy isn't so bad. Let's go back to the way things were. In fact, why don't you go get Sarah back? At least she could help us with McBuck."

Yes, I twisted the knife. We were crossing into dangerous territory: too intimate, too risky. All my instincts were screaming at me to create a diversion and flee.

"*Stop* it." Ben's eyes were wide. "You're doing the same thing you did when we broke up." Emotion swept his face, and he turned so I couldn't read it. "I'm telling you, I can't take it again. All these months, I've followed you around Texas dressed like a medieval lord and a cowboy and Captain Planet. Anything, just because you asked me to."

He took a deep breath and turned back to me. And I wished he hadn't, so I didn't have to see the hope in his eyes. "I've lain awake and thought about you every night. I've taken every chance to spend any bit of time I could get—with you, your friends, your family. I've been trying to get closer and closer, don't you see? Don't push me away when we finally have a chance."

"Ben—"

"Before you say it—fuck no feelings. Lee, I'm in love with you. You know I am. Every moment over the campaign, I've been falling back in love with you. And it's been so fast and so easy it's obvious I've been in love with you this whole fucking time. I swore to myself we'd be nothing more than colleagues. Then just friends. I told myself I was pathetic for considering this again, because you cheated and broke my heart. And maybe I am pathetic. But you know what? I don't care. The only thing I can't take is you doing the same thing you did to me before. Please don't push me away. I need you to have grown up at least a little."

There it was, Ben's line in the sand. A decision for me to make.

I *wanted* to make the decision that felt good, here in the moment. But he was right about growing up.

"Ben." My voice was gentle. "Of course I love you." I'd been kidding myself for months—not to mention years—pretending I wasn't in love with him. I'd put my heart on ice, but I'd never stopped loving him. Unthawing these last few months, feeling the sheer intensity of joy and desire and longing for him again, had been confusing at first and then wonderful.

His entire body lit: his eyes brightened. His shoulders lifted. He took a deep breath and reached for me—but I put up a hand.

The problem was, recognizing we loved each other didn't solve our problems. I wasn't Daisy David, or any sort of Disney princess—I knew love didn't conquer all. Eventually, I would do something to mess us up—get needy, act twisted—or Ben would change his mind and leave me, and I'd be right back where I started.

"I just wish it was enough," I said.

Ben's face jerked—sharp, like I'd slapped him. I could see him struggling to steady his breathing, to keep his shoulders high. He either wasn't going to look at me, or he couldn't.

So I did us both a favor. I took one last look at him and slipped out the door.

Love had never stopped anyone from hurting anyone else. That was the hard truth, and it did no good pretending otherwise. Starting now, I would do what was pragmatic, what was mature. It would save us both a lot of trouble, in the end.

24

New-Age Radical

'Tis the season to be— Actually, you know what? Fuck Christmas. Yeah, I said it. Stupid, cheerful holiday. It could take its candy canes and mistletoe and shove it.

I glared up from my armchair at Mac and Zoey, who were dressed as elves, singing "Deck the Halls" as they wound lights around the world's saddest little Christmas tree in the corner of my living room. Claire and Simon sat cross-legged on the floor wrapping presents, tubes of paper, an industrial-sized package of tape and somehow only one pair of scissors between them. Annie stood over my fireplace, hanging our traditional friend stockings. I got zero delight—*zero*—out of what used to be my favorite sight of the year: the worn *Stoner* stocking, its underwear-clad-Santa's belly all stretched out from years of being stuffed with stocking presents that were a little too big and bulgy to strictly qualify as stocking presents. Otherwise known as the best kind of stocking presents.

My friends had turned this house into a stupid winter wonderland. Even the cats were in a festive mood. The moment Ted the finance guy sat down on the couch to watch Mac string the lights, Al and Bill had emerged out of their hiding spots and hopped onto his lap. Now they were snuggled into small, downy circles of fur by his side. They'd taken to Ted as instantaneously and inexplicably as Mac had.

I narrowed my eyes in suspicion. What was that bland amortization wizard's secret? From the outside, Ted looked like a fraternity boy ascending semigracefully into middle age. He must have chocolate-flavored skin or keep shiny ribbons in his pockets—*something* to explain both Mac's and the cats' attraction.

My mom buzzed in from the kitchen, holding a ladle. "All right, ladies. Who wants more eggnog? Lee, I mixed another batch without bourbon for you."

"Sssss," I hissed. "Without bourbon it's like drinking sugary egg froth."

"What was that?" Mom chirped. "About my delicious, world-famous eggnog?"

"Nothing," I mumbled, and held out my mug dutifully. I was the one who'd asked for it sans booze, after all. But I didn't have to like it.

It was our annual Wrapping Party. Every year, Mom, Alexis, Claire, Simon, Mac, Annie—and recently Zoey—came to my house the Saturday before Christmas. We wrapped presents, drank our weight in wine and eggnog, ate pizza and watched *It's a Wonderful Life* to get in the Christmas spirit. Then everyone came back the day after Christmas, and we filled each other's stockings and had a big Unwrapping Party. I loved this tradition.

Normally.

This year, I had not invited them over. I had not decorated or purchased food. I had not even put pants on. I was in the middle of a perfectly good sulk, staring at myself in the mirror in the dark while Elliott Smith played at full volume, when out of the blue, my doorbell rang. And there they stood, like some demented carolers' group, grinning at me with all their unwelcome cheer. They carried wrapping paper, grocery bags full of food, and greasy pizza boxes. Zoey had her arms wrapped around a pathetic little Christmas tree, the clear runt of the litter at the tree farm. As soon as she saw me looking, her eyes lit up, and she stroked her hand over it like she was Vanna White presenting a brand-new Cadillac.

It, and they, were expressly unwelcome.

It, and they, did not care.

Claire had shoved in first, obviously, pushing me aside when it was clear I wasn't inclined to move. Simon followed, shrugging apologetically and keeping his gaze carefully above my pants-less bottom half. Annie had breezed by, kissing me on the cheek and assuring me they'd brought every supply, not to worry. Zoey told me the tree's name was Clifford and asked where to put him, and Mac air-kissed both my cheeks and whispered, "It's Ted's *first* Christmas with us!" She tugged him into the house before I could answer, "And maybe his last."

That left Mom, a grinning older man who was presumably her new boyfriend Ethan, and Alexis glowering at her shoes. Oh, boy. Super. Not awkward at all.

Mom hugged me, then turned to Ethan. "E, this is my eldest daughter, Lee. Normally she wears pants, but her boyfriend and her boss both broke up with her."

"They did *not*," I protested. Honestly, the woman made me sound pathetic.

Though, in fairness, I had fallen into a bit of a slump since the Lise office closed for the holidays. And yes, since I also hadn't seen or heard from Ben in over a week. I couldn't stop thinking about the fact that Dakota's checks were probably already on their way to the senators, and the Green Machine bill was a done deal. A dirty, dirty done deal. And Ben was probably at his mom's house for the holidays, way up in North Texas. Or maybe he was with Sarah, after all?

Mentally, I slapped myself. I didn't care.

Ethan, who couldn't see inside my head, smiled and held out his hand. He had a warm smile that made his eyes crinkle at the corners. "That sounds like a reason to avoid pants to me. Hi, Lee. It's great to finally meet you. I've heard so much."

I sized him up. He was handsome, early sixties, same as my mom. Hair half gray, half brown, still plenty of it. Good dresser, and he'd made the effort of putting on a brown sports coat, like he was going somewhere fancy. Boy, would he be disappointed by my chamber of sadness. But still—it was cute.

"My mom deserves love," I said. "And she especially deserves a little action. But I don't need a new father, just so we're clear."

"Lee." Mom was aghast.

Ethan rolled with it. "Message received and appreciated. Not trying to step on any toes."

I nodded. "Good. Glad we got that out of the way." I swept a hand inside. "You two can come in." I turned to Alexis. "You can't. You've been banned."

She tossed her head and stomped past me anyway.

So that's how I found myself hosting a party, even though my plans for the evening had consisted only of more mirror-staring while contemplating where my life went wrong. Caving to an aggressive lobbying effort by my mom, I'd even put on pants. But that didn't mean I had to enjoy myself. My home had been invaded.

"At my last party, a stranger got naked and rubbed that on his balls," I said to Claire, as she picked up the remote to start

It's a Wonderful Life. She dropped the remote like it was on fire and gave me an evil look. I'd washed the thing, obviously. But Claire didn't have to know that.

"Sometimes my cats like to spontaneously vomit," I said to Ted the finance guy. "It's so weird. You can never tell when they're about to start." Both of Ted's hands froze midscratch, and Al and Bill looked up to see what the holdup was. Ted peered at them nervously.

Ha. Spreading holiday gloom. Now I knew how the Grinch felt, and it was pretty good.

"Lee, come help me in the kitchen," my mom called.

Grumbling, I staggered out of the armchair and slumped into the kitchen. Ethan was wearing a little chef's apron he had to have brought with him, because it certainly wasn't mine. He was in the midst of arranging the food into a beautiful spread over my dining table.

"Looks good," I mumbled, stuffing an iced cookie in my mouth. "Like a magazine."

Ethan beamed. "Thank you. I took a class—"

"I went to see Dad," I interrupted, grabbing my sad bourbonless eggnog from the counter.

That stopped everyone in their tracks. Alexis whipped around from the stove. "At the cemetery?"

I rolled my eyes. "No, at the mall."

"Well, *excuse* me. You've never gone to see him before."

Mom walked over and rested her hands on my shoulders. "What did you say to him?"

"Just, you know..." I looked away. "That I forgive him. And I'd be by more often." I didn't mention I was still waiting on his answer to my last question: *Do you forgive me?*

Her eyes shone. "I'm so glad, Lee. I'm proud of you."

I let her hug me for a second, then backed out of her arms.

"It's not a big deal. I just thought you'd want to know." I waved at Ethan. "Seeing as how you're moving on and all."

"God, you're being such an Eeyore." Alexis busied herself with the bread bowl. "Be happy for those of us who found love."

"How's Chris?" I shot back. "Did he not come because he's with his other girlfriend's family?"

I hightailed it out of the kitchen before Alexis's roll nailed me in the forehead.

"So, spill," Mac said, as I walked into the living room. She'd finished with the Christmas tree and had shoved Al and Bill over to sit next to Ted on the couch. Clifford the tree blinked hopefully at me, its little string lights not doing much to hide the way it listed hopelessly to the left. "Why aren't you drinking anymore?"

Everyone stopped what they were doing. Annie even froze midstocking hang.

"I'm just taking a break," I said, clutching my eggnog. *To make sure I can*, I added to myself. "A reset. I figured I could stand to take it down a notch."

Claire raised her eyebrows. *Great.* Here it came. The teasing and skepticism from my friends. But, to my surprise, she said, "Meagan and Molly are planning a few dry months. Maybe I could do it with you."

"Meagan and Molly?"

"They're her new mom friends." Simon tied off a perfect bow on a present. "They're planning a big holiday yoga party for all the students at Mikey's school. It's good stress relief for kids *and* parents, you know."

Zoey's jaw dropped. "Wait. You won the cool moms over? The child yoga instructor? The *calligrapher*?"

"Turns out they were just intimidated by me," Claire said breezily, tearing off a strip of tape. "Which makes sense. They're not sharks or meerkats at all. They're actually kind of the best, apart from you guys. I invited them to hang and found out they get together once a week to drink wine and talk about how to self-actualize while occupying traditional roles like wife and mother. Except during the dry months, obviously—then it's just self-actualization."

"Look at you." Annie nodded approvingly. "Reaching outside your comfort zone."

"Gee. Thanks, Mom."

Mac nodded at Ted. "You know, Stoner, we were *just* thinking about doing a cleanse."

"Oh, yeah," Ted said, taking the risk of scratching behind Al's ears. "We were talking about getting healthy over the holidays, dropping some weight. A new lease on life."

"Less than two months of dating and you're already an old married couple," Claire muttered.

"I want to do what everyone else is doing," Zoey piped in. She shot a glance at Annie. "Though I recognize that can sometimes be my insecurity talking."

"No, let's do it." Annie stepped away from the fireplace. "It couldn't hurt to take a break from booze in the lead-up to the wedding."

All my friends looked at me.

Who *were* these people?

"Let me get this straight," I said. "The same women who call any wedding, bar mitzvah, baptism, child's birthday party or Wednesday afternoon without booze *a sheer waste of our brief mortal lives* are rallying around not drinking? During the holidays?"

Claire shrugged. "We have layers. So sue us. But don't, because I will defeat you."

Annie tugged on my sleeve. "Hey," she said, voice low, "I

know your head's kind of spinning, but will you come with me for a sec? I have something to ask you in private."

Curiosity got the best of me. I set my mug down and scrambled out of the armchair, following Annie into my bedroom.

She bounced onto my bed. "Close the door."

"What's with the mystery?" I shut the door and leaned against it, trying not to think about the fact that Ben and I had lain side by side right where Annie's feet were dangling.

Her face glowed. "It's about the wedding."

"Oh?" *Stoner, we'd like to ask that you not attend, so as not to contaminate the wedding with your negative energy. Your particular extra-strength brand of love-repellent. Your full-fledged marriage-Grinchness.* I steeled myself.

"You've been my best friend since grad school," Annie said. "And I love you. So..." She laughed. "God, it feels like proposing again. Here I go, out with it. Will you be our maid of honor? Zoey's older sister is going to be our matron of honor, just so you know."

Um. What?

"You want *me*?" I was glad I was leaning against the door, otherwise I might have fallen over.

"Yes." Annie grinned. "Of course."

"But...I'm terrible at relationships. Almost everyone I know has either cheated on someone or been cheated on. Most of them both. And...I kind of don't believe in love, remember? That has to be the world's worst résumé for a maid of honor. What if my mere presence inadvertently curses your marriage?"

Annie waved a hand. "Oh, you believe in love. Stop being silly."

"*Excuse* me? Have you not been listening to me for the past five years?"

Annie cocked a brow that said, *Are you kidding, how could*

I escape it? "Yes. I have. And what I've heard is the pain of a very tenderhearted person who *loved* love, who was a terrible romantic, and who got hurt. Deeply. By people she trusted. You developed a defense mechanism, Stoner, which is very understandable. You were doing the best you could with the information at hand. But your shield isn't working for you anymore. Actually, I think it stopped quite a while ago. Right around the time a certain someone came back into your life."

I pushed off the door. "If you're talking about Ben—"

"Of course I'm talking about Ben." Annie's face was gently exasperated—which, for her, was practically outraged. "*Finally*, I'm talking about Ben. We haven't been allowed to talk about him since he left, even though it's obvious he's haunted you for five years. I held my tongue when he came back and you lit up like a Christmas tree." She saw my dubious look. "Okay, not a Clifford-the-Christmas-tree kind of tree. A normal one, not in need of rescue by Zoey. It's obvious you love him, is what I'm trying to say. It's been obvious for a while."

"Joke's on you." I fell into bed next to her. "I fully cop to being in love with Ben. I told him so. But it's not enough to make a relationship work."

"Of course it's not," she said.

I rested my head in my hand. "Okay. *Thank* you. No one else agreed with me. Ben definitely didn't."

"You also need trust and forgiveness."

I waved a hand. "Whatever. He's forgiven, I guess. He made a few mistakes. He was competitive. I can relate to that. But I don't know how *anyone* really trusts anyone else these days. Seems very dicey."

To my surprise, Annie shoved my shoulder, and I fell over. "Hey! What was that for?"

"Not Ben, doofus. *You*. You have to forgive *yourself*. And trust yourself."

"Maybe I should just marry myself while I'm at it," I grumbled.

Annie tapped my nose. "That's the spirit."

I stayed on my back, scoffing at the ceiling. "No offense, but you sound ridiculous. Like you're one second away from trying to sell me mood-altering crystals. And we both know what I do with those."

"Try out this story," she said. "Your dad cheated on your mom and left, and you felt like he betrayed you. Proved you weren't worth sticking around for. Then your first boyfriend did the same thing, then your next important relationship, too."

She was talking about the Four Major Heartbreaks. I'd never told her that's what I called them, or that I even thought of the relationships that way. But apparently, Annie was secretly clairvoyant.

"Over time," she said, "you became convinced you were fundamentally worth leaving, and that when it inevitably happened, you would fall apart. That's a lot of anticipated pain, and your brain is literally hardwired to avoid it. It's natural you'd come up with some crutches to protect yourself. Think about it. Your desire to avoid relationships has never been about other people. It's always been about *you*, at your core, not believing you're worth loving, and not trusting yourself to be okay no matter what happens."

Annie rolled over and snuggled next to me. At first, I was too shell-shocked by her words to respond. But after a minute—and after spitting out a mouthful of her hair that had floated onto my face—I wrapped an arm around her.

"You…might be right. A little bit."

"Zoey could have a change of heart tomorrow and walk away from our engagement. You never know. I have to trust I'm going to take care of myself if that happened. That I'd be okay. You have to, too. That's the only way to really be in control."

We lay in silence. Outside my door, I could hear Mac start singing "O Holy Night," and my mom jumping in to harmonize. They were the only two people I knew who shared the delusion they had the vocal chops to pull off the high notes. I smiled to myself.

"Yes," I said to Annie. "Is my answer to your wedding question. In case you were wondering."

"I wasn't," she said. "You're really quite legible, you know. From the outside looking in."

I dropped my chin to rest on her head. "This is unfair. When did you get so smart? Was it grad school? I didn't get this smart in grad school."

I couldn't see her smile, but I could feel it. "A little bit from grad school, a little bit from almost marrying the wrong person because I was too afraid to deal with my shit." She sighed happily. "What a day for me. I *finally* counseled Lee Stone. My white whale." There was a beat of silence. "That'll be five hundred dollars, by the way."

25

Let the Free Press Die

I wore all black to the Green Machine's funeral. Otherwise known as the "Wrap Meeting on SB 3," according to my Outlook calendar. We were seated in the small conference room in the Texas State Capitol, the same room where I'd met Ben for the first time, after five years apart.

How ironic. Just like that first meeting, today Ben was doing his best to avoid looking at me. He wore one of his sober navy suits and leaned practically all the way out of his chair, body twisted away from the table, tapping his leg. The message couldn't be clearer: *The last place I want to be is in the same room with you.*

Which made sense, given what I'd said to him the last time we spoke. It occurred to me that Ben had tried to get close to me three times now, and three times I'd rejected him. In fairy tales, three was a magic number. Maybe after trying three times, Ben had been released from the curse of loving me.

I couldn't deny how much I ached looking at him. How much the thought of him moving on squeezed my heart. If Annie was right, and the issues keeping us apart were really ones I had with myself, what had I allowed myself to lose? It had been all I could think about the rest of the holidays, especially during the uncharacteristically chill, alcohol-free New Year's Eve I'd spent googling *growing up for dummies* and then, guiltily, *Clark Kent shirtless gifs*.

"All right," said the governor brusquely, typing on his phone. He and Dakota were sitting on opposite ends of the conference table. "Let's make this brief. We're here to close the loop on the bill. Dakota?" He said her name sharply, with zero inflection. Interesting.

"The senators have accepted my donations." Dakota nodded at Wendy. "We've had conversations with each of them, and we'll have their support when the bill hits the floor next week."

"Great," said Governor Mane, setting down his phone. For the first time, he flicked a look at her. "So that's it, right? We won."

She nodded stiffly, then turned to me. "Lee, Ben—do you have any thoughts you want to share?"

This roused me out of my sad-Ben-watching stupor. On the one hand, boy, did I ever have thoughts about the way they'd handled my bill. On the other, what was the point?

I'd been asking myself that question a lot lately. Now that I'd fumbled the ball and Dakota had to step in to save the Green Machine, I could forget my promotion to vice president of public affairs. The thought of returning to my normal communications work filled me with weariness and a little bit of dread. What if I'd outgrown my role?

I looked at Dakota and Wendy, and a thought struck me: What if I'd outgrown *Lise*? Without the goal of passing the

Green Machine pulling me out of bed every morning—okay, *okay*, and the thought of seeing Ben, too—my life felt hollow and purposeless. So, maybe it wasn't worth sticking my nose in Dakota's business yet again. Maybe I should let this bill die alongside my ambition.

"Actually, yes," Ben said, stopping his foot tapping and turning to face us at the table. "I do want to get something off my chest."

Like they'd been taken over by alien intelligence, all five of our phones started buzzing at the same time—over and over, practically hopping off the table.

"What the hell?" Wendy grabbed for her phone.

The door to the conference room burst open, and a young man I recognized as one of the governor's junior aides stood there, red-faced and panting. "Governor, sorry for interrupting, but you have to see this. It's all over the news."

My stomach dropped.

The aide showed us his iPad, which was streaming Fox News 7. "Breaking news out of the state capitol, as details of a jaw-dropping scandal are coming to light," said the anchor, a pretty blonde woman in a power suit. "Fox 7 is the first to report that Texas State Governor Grover Mane is allegedly having an affair with prominent local businesswoman Dakota Young, CEO of electric vehicle company Lise Motors."

Oh my God. It had leaked.

"What? Bullshit!" Wendy spun to Dakota. "This is utter fabrication. We have to call the station *right now* and tell them they're lying on air!"

Dakota's face was leached of color. The governor's was bright red. Neither of them said a word, until the unspoken truth became plain.

"Jesus," Wendy breathed. "All this time?"

Dakota nodded, the movement slight. "We ended it. But… yes. It's true."

Wendy turned to me. "Is this why you and Lee have been so weird? *Lee* knew and I didn't?"

I couldn't speak. The very worst thing that could possibly happen was happening. Instinctively, I turned to Ben, and saw my horror mirrored on his face.

"Not only is the fact that Young is married raising eyebrows," the anchor continued from the iPad, "but she and the governor are well-known to be working on what climate change activists have called a groundbreaking clean energy bill this session. Now critics of the bill are calling its integrity into question."

The screen cut to Samuel Slittery, and the sight was like a punch to the gut. He shook his head sorrowfully. "You know, I always thought there was something fishy about the way Governor Mane relied so much on a woman—uh, this particular woman—for transportation and energy policy. Well, now we know Dakota Young was sleeping her way into a position of power."

"You've *got* to be kidding me," Dakota growled.

Slittery sighed dramatically, and I knew he was loving this with every fiber of his being. "There's just no way SB 3—what people have been calling the Green Machine bill—can pass. The public simply cannot trust the democratic process has operated the way it was supposed to. Frankly, in my opinion, the bill would have been a disaster for Texas anyway. The people of Texas don't want weak electric cars. They want big, brawny, manly trucks like the new Ford Guzzler XXL, an exclusive collaboration coming later this year from Mendax and Ford Motor Company."

"You have got to be *kidding me*!" Wendy shouted at the screen.

I was watching my worst nightmare unfold in real time.

The camera cut to Senator Roy McBuck, who was walking through a parking lot, wearing a cowboy hat. "I'm afraid the Senate is going to have serious questions about the legitimacy of the SB 3 bill. The people of Texas can rest assured my colleagues in the Senate and I have no tolerance for corruption. That's all I'll say at this time."

"That man was willing to sell himself to the highest bidder," Ben said through gritted teeth. "And he has the nerve to talk about corruption."

The video flashed back to the anchor, who gave us a grave look. "There you have it, folks. The first scandal of Governor Mane's administration—and boy, is it a doozy. Will it spell the end of Lise Motors? The end of the governor's once-vaunted political career? Stick with us here at Fox News 7 as the details unfold."

26

Sure, It Looks Bad

The governor was the last to arrive, wearing a tan trench coat and a baseball cap, giant sunglasses shielding his face. He probably thought he looked convincingly incognito, so I didn't have the heart to tell him in reality, he looked like a slightly more masculine version of Carmen Sandiego.

"Good, you're here," Wendy said. "Now we can begin."

"You have a beautiful home," said the governor as he shuffled in. Even in the middle of a crisis, he couldn't turn off the charming politician.

We'd needed a war room, and with reporters dogging Governor Mane's and Dakota's every step, it needed to be off the beaten track—none of our offices and neither of their homes would do. Wendy had volunteered her condo as refuge.

It had been twenty-four hours since news of the affair broke, and by now the national outlets had sunk their teeth into the story, with splashy articles everywhere, from the *Wall Street*

Journal and the *Washington Examiner* to *USA TODAY* and *Politico*. But what really gutted me was the coverage in the *New York Times* and *Washington Post*. How quickly the papers I'd most admired turned on two of their darlings: Dakota, the feted female inventor revolutionizing the auto industry, and Grover Mane, the more-acceptable-than-most governor of Texas, now simply fodder for prurient gossip.

But they weren't the only former friends to betray us. I couldn't get a single reporter at a radio, print or TV outlet to take it easy on Dakota, or even press pause in their coverage until they got all the facts. When I'd reached out, all they'd wanted was a quote. Apparently, none of the relationships I'd spent years building held water when it came to a scandal the entire state of Texas, if not the country, was watching. I'd peeked once at Twitter yesterday—just a glance at Lise's mentions—then shut my entire computer down and considered burning it. God help us.

"Where do we begin?" Dakota asked wearily. She'd arrived this morning in sweatpants, looking wan, her eyes bloodshot. She had to have spent the last twenty-four hours talking through her affair with her husband, George, and maybe even with her children. I had a flashback of confessing I'd cheated to Ben, and felt a wash of sympathy. I knew how painful that conversation was.

Speaking of Ben—he was in the kitchen helping Cody, who was once again cementing his title as world's best husband.

"We begin," Cody announced, walking out of the kitchen in oven mitts, holding a tray of baked goods, "with homemade banana bread and blueberry muffins. Ben has orange-cranberry scones cooling on the counter, so don't fill up too much."

Ben walked out of the kitchen behind Cody, fingers wrapped

around a mug of coffee. Our eyes caught and he looked away quickly.

"Comfort carbs," said Cody sagely, then scooted back to the kitchen.

"It has to be Slittery who leaked it." The governor picked up a muffin and settled into Wendy's couch. "I don't know how he found out, but it had to be him."

"We were about to win," Wendy pointed out. "Makes sense that he pressed the nuclear button."

"I'm going to assassinate him," said the governor, then looked around guiltily, as if he was being recorded. "Politically speaking, of course."

"It doesn't matter who leaked it, at the end of the day." Ben drew his ankle up to rest on top of his knee. "What matters is we're up shit's creek." He was casual today, in jeans and a soft-looking gray sweater. He had to have gotten a haircut in the last twenty-four hours, because his hair was shorter than it had been in the conference room. Maybe he was preparing in case he needed to go on camera. I found myself transfixed.

It looked good, and made him seem a little younger, closer to the Ben I'd met in grad school. His was my favorite face, I realized. For one brief moment, I let myself remember the way he'd looked at me when we stretched out in bed at the Governor's Mansion, right before we'd heard the footsteps.

Ben's eyes flicked to me, catching my staring, and I blinked away in shame. *Come on, self. Cool, calm and collected. Step up in this moment of trial and tribulation.*

"Ben's right," I said, injecting confidence into my voice. "We need to focus on damage control. Lise's stock is tanking, and there's already rumors the Tea Party might try to run someone new when the governor's term is up."

"What else do we know?" Wendy asked.

I blew out a breath. "I don't have the polling back yet on

public opinion. But I think it's safe to say, given the headlines and the tenor of social content, that we are deeply unpopular right now. The main headline—" I winced "—is that Dakota slept with the governor to get a bill favorable to her company passed. Quid pro quo, so to speak."

"As if I wasn't a perfectly eligible bachelor in my own right," the governor grumbled.

"Not the point," Wendy said icily.

"I've been weighing a few different plans," I said. "We obviously need to put out a more fulsome statement than the one we've been giving about it being a private, personal matter with nothing to do with the Green Machine bill. I think if we confront this head-on, and don't try to hide from the discomfort, we could start a bigger conversation about the gendered response to this news. I mean, 99 percent of the chatter has been about Dakota and what an evil, cunning seductress she is. People are calling for her to step down from Lise, as if her work performance has anything to do with her personal life."

"We have investors calling us with the same request," Wendy said, with a pained glance at Dakota.

"Beyond a few rumors about running another candidate—rumors that will probably blow over soon, let's be honest—where's the outrage for the governor?"

"Now, wait a sec," Governor Mane said, holding out his hands. "I don't think the answer is to stoke more anger, just at a different person."

Ben and I rolled our eyes at the same time.

"That's not what she means," Ben said. "Lee's saying we should call the media and the public on their shit. Let's try to save this, obviously. But if we're going to go down, let's go down swinging."

There. Ben got it. As I shot him a grateful look, it hit me: Annie was right. Weirdly, though Ben *had* hurt me multiple times in the past, I continued to trust him. It was me I didn't trust. *Me* I was worried was too messy, not right, worthy or strong enough. My problems were between me and me.

"I have to apologize," Dakota cut in. She spoke softly, staring at her hands like they held a scrying bowl with a vision of the future. "I'm the adulterer. I'll say it was my fault and step down. It's the only chance of saving the bill."

"Sorry, Dakota, but the bill's fucked," Wendy said. "At this point we need to be worried about saving the company."

"And that's a huge, giant *no*." I rose from my seat. "You are not falling on your sword over this. That's not fair. The governor is equally to blame."

The look on the governor's face told me he did not like *that* point, but I didn't care.

"We can find a way to fight back," I said, feeling purpose surge in me. The old fighting spirit, the drive to protect my mentor. "You didn't hurt anyone. You and the governor didn't start your relationship until after we were all working on the bill, so you didn't pervert the democratic process…until, you know, the end there with the campaign donations. But for the most part, things have been on the up-and-up."

I paced around the living room, letting my thoughts lead me, speaking them as they came. "The entire time we've been working on the campaign, you were also working day and night on the Herschel motor. Which was poised to blow the socks off everyone and make our investors tons of money, might I add. Those turncoat bastards."

I threw my hands up. "No *wonder* you needed a little stress relief. Honestly. And you know what? We all make mistakes. Hell, take Ben and me."

Ben's eyes widened as he realized what I was going to say; he shook his head furtively. But here's the thing: What if I wasn't ashamed of myself? What if when I made a mistake, I understood where I'd been coming from, why I'd made the decisions I'd made, and had a little empathy? What if I tried radical forgiveness for everyone, including myself? I could practically feel Annie resting on my shoulder like a little angel, whispering in my ear.

"The truth is," I said, "we hooked up, too."

"Oh, Jesus Christ." Wendy put her head in her hands. "I give up."

"Was it unprofessional? Probably. Did we cross ethical lines? Maybe a smidge. But did we jeopardize the democratic process? No, of course not! So, we're basically the same," I said to Dakota. "Only you're a little more famous and married than me."

The governor burst out laughing. "Oh, Benny boy. When I told you I appreciated your over-and-above dedication to the job, I had no idea how right I was."

Ben flushed bright red. "Tell me if you want me to report myself. Or if you want my resignation."

Governor Mane slapped his knee, then waved a hand at himself. "That would be the height of hypocrisy, no?"

Wendy tried to fight it, but she couldn't. Against her will, a smile cracked her face. Then Dakota started laughing. "Oh, wow," she wheezed. "We are a *mess*."

"Maybe we are, on the romantic side," I said. "But we're still damn good at our jobs, and when it comes to whether or not we should keep them, that's the fact that matters." I squared my shoulders and turned to Dakota. "I'm sorry I got so angry at you. I was holding you to an unfair standard. The truth is, it's kind of better that you make mistakes. That means you're a little more like me. Which means my dream of being like you one day is maybe attainable."

Dakota's bloodshot eyes softened, and her shoulders lifted like a weight had been removed. "I appreciate that, Lee. So much. Though I fear no one is quite like you, in a good way." Her smile dimmed. "But I have to insist on falling on this sword. It's what a good leader does. I can't let down Lise, and everyone who works there and counts on me. I can't let my personal mess undermine the progress we were making. So, I'm going to hold a press conference to own up, apologize and offer to step down." She winced at me. "And I'm going to need you to plan it."

"I *strongly* disagree with that plan."

"As do I," Ben added, standing dramatically so he and I looked like the knights of the round table.

"Me, too," Wendy said, rolling her eyes at us from her seat on the couch.

The governor was damningly quiet.

"I recognize your objections, and thank you," Dakota said. "But I am the boss, so unfortunately, my say goes."

Wendy, Ben and I looked at each other. What more could we do?

"All right," I sighed. "I will plan your terrible press conference."

"Good." Dakota stood and adjusted her sweats. "With that settled, I have a broken heart waiting for me at home. Wish me luck."

I followed Ben out of Wendy's house and down to the street. "Hey!" I called. "Wait up."

Ben was power walking, and he didn't slow.

"Hey!" I raised my voice to his back. "Trisha Smith from CBS 12 here—do you have a comment about the governor's affair?"

Ben jerked like he'd been electrocuted, then whipped around. "Stoner, that is *not* funny," he hissed.

Maybe not, but he'd stopped, so…

I jogged to meet him. "Walk you to your car?"

Ben rubbed a hand across his mouth. "Doesn't seem like I have a choice in the matter. So, what's the ask? You want help planning the presser? Whatever it is, make it fast. I'm in a hurry."

"Yeesh," I said, as I scrambled to keep pace with him. "So brooding."

He turned to me. "Yeah, well, my life has officially hit rock bottom. Things already sucked, what with the affair breaking and the bill dying and the constant media requests. And with you..." He shot a glance at me, cleared his throat and decided to move on. "On top of that, I just watched my boss let the woman he had a relationship with take all the blame. And he didn't say a word. So now I have to find a new boss."

My eyebrows shot up. "You're going to quit? What happened to 'Grover Mane is the best way to get good bills passed until we can turn Texas blue'?"

Ben's pace quickened, his long legs taking impossible strides. "There are some things you don't do, and Grover just did one of them. Turns out he's not a man I can respectfully disagree with, because he's no longer a man I can respect. I'll find another way to turn Texas blue."

Whoa. Ben's eyes were steely. He was in full-blown mock-trial, take-no-prisoners mode. Desire surged through me, lighting my body on fire. Yes, I was a simple creature. I would not apologize.

"I didn't come out here to talk about the press conference, or anything related to work. Except maybe to say thanks for having my back in there." I took a beat. "As usual."

He nodded curtly. "You were making good points. No need to thank me."

"Well..." *Christ*, this was hard. We finally arrived at Ben's Prius, and he stopped awkwardly, his hand on the driver's door.

This was one of those times I could really use the comforting weight of my flask in my pocket, but, since I'd temporarily broken up with alcohol, I'd have to charge forward solo.

"Look," I burst out. "I'm trying. I'm absolutely stumbling through it, but I'm trying to make the right, mature choices, not the easy ones."

"Good…for you?"

"The last time we talked, I was feeling a lot of anger at you, and shock over Dakota's plan for the bill. Honestly, I felt hopeless and like things were spinning out of control. I thought it didn't matter how we felt about each other, because in the end, it wouldn't stop us from hurting each other. Judging by history," I added.

Ben looked uncomfortably at his feet. "Why are you telling me this? And before you answer, please consider it's not a whole lot of fun being trapped on the Lee Stone emotional roller coaster. I'd really prefer to get off, if given the choice."

Oh, *that* hurt. But maybe Ben didn't understand what I was saying.

"I talked to Annie," I said, forging on. "She made me realize something I think my mom was trying to tell me a while ago. It's not that I think what you and I have isn't enough. On some level, I'm convinced *I'm* not enough. Deep down, I don't trust I'm worth sticking around for. And I don't trust myself to be okay if things go wrong between us. That's why, when you wanted to give us a chance, it felt like a safer choice to just not start at all. I know that's kind of pathetic, but I'm working on it."

There. Now he had the raw, unvarnished truth.

Ben finally looked me in the eyes. "I'm glad you're thinking through this, Stoner." A ghost of a smile passed over his lips. "Glad you're figuring your shit out."

There was something in his voice—some sadness, some

note of resignation—that had my pulse fluttering, my brain saying, *No, wait.*

"Don't you see?" I wanted to touch Ben, but something told me not to, so I pressed my fingers into my thighs so hard it would surely leave a bruise. "I took all my sadness and made it into a sword to protect myself, and now the sword's stuck in my back. It's me with the problems, not us."

Ben's blue eyes tracked down the street before he turned them back on me. I recognized a stall tactic when I saw one, and my throat clenched up.

"I'm glad for you," he said gently. "But while you've been going around hurting yourself and learning better, you've been hurting me, too. And you don't get unlimited passes to do that, no matter how I feel about you."

The truth of what he was saying hit me: I was figuring out my shit, and good for me, but Ben was the man I was learning on. He had been five years ago, and he was again now. The man I'd used as a punching bag, getting out my growing pains, making the mistakes that would turn me into a better human on the other side. That wasn't fair to him. He deserved someone who was already whole.

"Okay," I whispered, the sound soft against the breaking of my heart, a near-debilitating pain I would keep inside, so as not to burden Ben. "That makes sense." I blinked quickly. "It really does."

"Are you okay?" He searched uncertainly down the street. "I don't see your car. Do you want me to drive you to it?"

I shook my head. "The reporters figured out my license plate. Apparently, only one person in Austin drives a Lise Model XX with the license plate COMBOSS. In retrospect, probably not my best idea. So I scootered here. I'll be fine."

"Ah." Ben looked down at his hands. "Well, I'll see you at the presser, I guess."

"You won't resign before then?"

"Either way. I'll be there."

With that, he sank into his car, shut the door and drove away. I watched his car get smaller down the long road, until he hit a turn and disappeared.

My hands were shaking, but I pressed them firmly together. Dakota was handing herself over to the wolves, and Ben was tired of waiting for me, but you know what? Fair. Their choices. It hurt like holy hell, but it was out of my control. And it wouldn't stop me. I would continue to get my house in order. I would continue to learn to love and trust myself. I would honor my commitments, right my wrongs, and I would never, *ever* give up.

27

Some Guys

"This is Trisha Smith with CBS 12, and we're live at the Austin City Run against Cancer half-marathon, in hour eight of one woman's harrowing journey to the finish line. Marathon organizers tell me she's already set a record for the longest time it's ever taken a runner to finish in the race's thirty-six-year history, and they've actually delayed shutting down to see whether or not she can make it. As more and more viewers tune in via cable and livestream, it's safe to say the saga has officially gripped the city of Austin.

"As you can see, the woman in question has actually given up running at this point, and is now on her hands and knees, crawling—well, I'll say it—rather pathetically toward the finish line. This is presumably why Austinites on Twitter have dubbed her the Sad Crawler. In fact, #SadCrawler has just made its own record as the most-mentioned hashtag among Travis County Twitter users in the last year.

"Oh, here she comes now, around the bend. Let's see if we can get a comment. Ma'am, CBS 12 here. Do you have something to say to the thousands of people watching you right now?"

"Arrgggghhhh," I growled into the microphone, dragging my legs forward. They felt like tubs of liquid that had accidentally gotten attached to my body, and now I was responsible for lugging them around when I'd really rather leave them behind.

I managed to pull my head up, and there it was, like a gleaming mirage. The beautiful, beautiful finish line. It was nothing more than a white chalk line drawn across the street, but I felt in that moment like maybe I would kiss it, marry it, *worship* it—start a cult devoted to The Great Finish Line in the Distance—if only I was allowed to reach it.

It could have been the dehydration talking. Or maybe the naive, simple girl who'd started this race hours ago—a girl I could barely remember, though I *could* recall the way she'd snickered at the other runners at the starting line, those overserious fools with their nipple guards and ridiculous head-mounted hydration systems—maybe that girl had died. Obviously from flying too close to the sun, a tragic victim of hubris. And now I was stuck in purgatory, reduced to a simple collection of gelatinous muscles with one sentient thought: *Finish.*

The microphone, with its colorful CBS logo, shoved back in my face. Trisha Smith, wearing one hundred pounds of makeup—boy, would we be a contrast on-screen—frowned at me with theatrical concern. "Ma'am, could you tell us your name?"

"Stone-er," I grunted, crawling forward, now as much to get away from her as to make it to the end. Unfortunately, she was more than able to keep up with my pace.

"Hmm. Let's stick to Sad Crawler, then. What's going through your head right now?"

"Must—finish—race." Sweat poured down my face into my eyelashes, making it hard to see. I blinked and focused on moving my bright red hands forward, one in front of the other.

The lady would not give up. "What's filling you with this unquenchable drive to finish? What is it that's keeping you from quitting, even though it's obvious to anyone watching that you're far from a natural athlete, that maybe you haven't stepped foot in a gym in years?"

"Two years," I confessed into the mic, lurching forward.

"Do you hear that, Austin? Two whole years since this woman has exercised. Let that be a lesson to us all. What's keeping you going?"

"Sarah—only—gets—money—if—I—finish," I rasped, training my eyes on the beautiful white line, letting my vision tunnel. "Her—mom—died—and I—committed—thought—crimes—against—her."

Trisha lunged away from me to address the camera directly. "The story of Sad Crawler takes a fascinating twist as the woman in question appears to confess to criminal acts. More details to come."

Just a few more feet, just a few more feet, then all this could end. But suddenly, every muscle in my body stopped working. They simply gave up, waved the white flag.

I slumped to the street and laid my cheek against the asphalt. Mmm. That was nice. So much cooler than my skin. Comfortable, like a pillow, go figure. I closed my eyes. Maybe a short nap.

Noise swelled around me, and I cracked an eyelid. Behind Trisha and the line of other runners, all of them with their fancy *I Made It* stickers pressed to their shirts, was a crowd of observers. Their eyes were glued to me, cheering. I'd forgotten about them in the agony of pushing my body forward; stopped seeing them when my vision narrowed, blocking everything else out. But there were many people now, and they were all shouting encouragements at me.

I opened both eyes.

"Stoner," came a voice that was familiar and close. No. It couldn't be. Now I was definitely hallucinating.

But I pushed myself up to my elbows, wobbling a little, just to make sure. And I was right. It was Ben. Standing on the side of the street next to a handsome, slightly younger doppelgänger I recognized as his brother, Will. They were both staring at me with the kind of concerned look you gave a kid who'd climbed to the top of the monkey bars and was threatening to jump off.

"What are you doing here?" I croaked.

"Are you kidding? We saw you on TV at the airport and rushed over." Ben studied me. "Are you hurt? What's happening?"

"I'm a doctor now, Lee," Will said. "Or, well, I'm in med school. But I can help you if you need it." He radiated so much Ben-like goodness I felt myself blinking back tears.

"You raised a good one," I choked to Ben. Then I gulped a breath, pushing the air past my dry, sore throat. "And you were right. About the marathon. I didn't know what I was getting myself into."

"The *half*-marathon," Will corrected. "It's only thirteen miles. Most people can walk that in under five hours, so…"

"Do you want us to pick you up and carry you out?" Ben asked. "Just tell me, and we'll do it."

"Louie," Trisha called to her cameraman, scampering to where Ben and Will stood. "Please tell me you're getting the double love interests."

A chant started from the crowd. I squinted. It sounded like

they were saying— Yes, that was it. *Fin-ish, fin-ish, fin-ish.* I'd always loved chants. Their words stoked a fire in me.

I looked at Ben and remembered what I'd promised myself: I would never, *ever* give up. I would right my wrongs. I would trust myself to be what I needed.

I shook my head. "No. I'm going to do it. I'm going to finish."

Will shrugged doubtfully. "O-kay."

"Good for you, Stoner." Ben knelt on the side of the road and clapped his hands together like a coach. "You can do it."

I could do it. I would even finish upright, on my own two legs. I staggered to my feet, and my knees immediately buckled. Okay, scratch that. I would finish on my hands and knees. But I would finish.

Every muscle shaking, every breath a struggle, I pushed myself forward, crawling with one arm in front of the other.

"You're almost there!" Ben called. The chanting from the crowd swelled.

I gritted my teeth. One, two, three lurches—and then my hand was on the finish line. I dragged my body over it and collapsed in sweet relief, twisting my face to kiss the chalk as I'd promised.

I'd *done* it. I'd come through for myself. And paid back a little of my debt to Sarah for being unconsciously in love with her boyfriend and cheating in my mind.

The crowd was going crazy. Ben, Will, Trisha and her cameraman rushed over.

"There you have it," Trisha gushed. "Sad Crawler has done it, a triumph of the human spirit. Twitter is ablaze with celebration, with one user reporting she hasn't cried this hard since her wedding day."

"Ben," I called, closing my eyes. "Can you please pick me up and take me home now?"

★★★

As we turned onto my street and Ben grabbed his phone to answer a call, Will leaned over from the passenger seat and eyed me, sprawled across the back.

"You know," he said, in a lowered voice. "You broke my brother's heart. Like, tore it out and ripped it into tiny pieces. I've never seen him like that before."

"Yeah," I sighed. "I know. Sorry about that."

Will tucked his hair, which was as dark as Ben's, behind his ears. "I was planning on punishing you with a few choice words." His eyes tracked over my prone body. "But I think karma might be one step ahead of me."

"Oh, Will," I said weakly. "You have no idea."

Ben dropped his call as we pulled into my driveway. "Hey," he said. "Were you expecting Lex?"

I sat up, despite my body's protests. Sure enough, Alexis's silver Jetta was sitting in my driveway. "That's weird. We're not really talking at the moment, so I have no idea why she's here."

"Is this Alexis, your sister?" Will's eyes gleamed. "I remember *her*."

"You're out of luck," I said. "She's dating the world's biggest tool. Ben, sorry to say, but I'm going to need some help getting upright."

A few awkward minutes later, after Ben had given up trying to get me to walk and had simply picked me up, fireman-style, and carried me to my front door, Will fumbled with my keys and we were inside.

"Alexis?" I called. "You in here?"

Ben laid me gently on the couch and stood. "Sarah texted. She said thank you, and she's no longer jealous of you at all. And she swears she had nothing to do with Slittery leaking the affair to the press."

"Well, small victories still count," I muttered. But something inside me warmed at the idea that Sarah might hate me 10 percent less.

Ben surveyed the living room with his hands on his hips. "Last time I was here, there was a naked man in that corner, using the drapes as a cape."

"I finally figured out who he is," I said. "It's that guy who walks around Second Street with a parrot on his shoulder."

"We partied with the *Second Street Pirate*?"

"You guys are weird," Will said. "Make Austin *less* weird, in my opinion."

"Lee." Alexis streaked out of the hallway, mascara running in black tracks down her face.

All my muscles screamed as I sat up too quickly. "What's wrong?"

Alexis buried her face in her hands. "It's Chris. He's cheating *again*."

To my utter astonishment, Chris popped out of the hallway behind her. "Lexy, you're overreacting. The texts were just a joke. We didn't mean them."

"What the hell is happening?" Ben demanded.

"And why are you in my house?" I added.

Poor Will froze like a deer in headlights, blinking at all of us.

"We came over because I left my blow-dryer here and I needed to pick it up." Alexis raised shaky hands to wipe her face. "It was supposed to be a quick stop, but Chris had to use the bathroom—"

"Gross," I interjected. "And probably illegal, without my consent."

"When he was in there, he got a text. I wouldn't have looked, normally, but you got in my head, Lee! So I peeked."

"Invading my privacy," Chris said hotly.

"Shut up," Ben and I said at the same time.

"I found his text messages with a girl named Kim. She was telling him all the things she was going to do to him as soon as he ditched his girlfriend and came over."

"Oh, that's not good," Will murmured.

Disbelief acted like an opiate for my sore muscles, letting me sit up straighter on the couch. "Are you kidding me, Chris? *Again?* You didn't learn your lesson the first time?"

My poor sister, with her trusting, forgiving heart, her steadfast belief in love. I'd been wrong—those were good qualities, and they didn't deserve to be squashed. They *certainly* didn't deserve to be exploited.

Chris looked at me and blanched. He backed away, putting a hand up. "You stay away from me."

Alexis wiped her nose. "I can't believe what a fool you made of me. I defended you. Gave you chance after chance. I *loved* you. But you were lying to me this whole time. This is so humiliating."

"I'm sorry," Chris tried. "I get lonely sometimes, you know? Maybe I look for comfort in the wrong places."

"How can you be *lonely*?" Alexis cried. "You have me, and we do everything you want to do all the time. Stop making excuses."

"Well, maybe I have needs you can't satisfy," he shot back, striding for the door. "Have you ever thought of that?"

Alexis and Will both gasped.

Chris gripped the doorknob. "You know what? It's not a maybe. I *do* have needs you can't satisfy. You should really learn to be more adventurous in bed, Lex. You're like a timid little mouse. It can get really bor—"

I lunged, but got only as far as the next cushion before flopping. "Goddammit, my arms are too weak to hit him!"

"Don't worry," Ben said calmly. In one smooth motion, he

took an impossibly long step toward Chris, pulled back and punched him clean in the face. "I got it."

"Ahh!" Chris shrieked, clutching his nose. *"I just healed this!"*

"Get out of here before I get handsy, too," Alexis called, with uncharacteristic swagger.

"You'll want to keep that nose elevated," Will advised, sounding very much like a doctor. "And get some ice on it. It'll help with the swelling."

Chris gave him an incredulous look, then scrambled out the door, slamming it behind him.

"Well." Will turned to Ben. "That was quite macho of you. And here I thought you were just one of those legal types who liked to kill them with words."

Alexis flung herself at Ben and wrapped her arms around him.

"Really?" I asked. "So when I punch Chris, it's all *no, Stoner, you're out of control.* But when Ben punches him, suddenly he's your hero?"

Alexis ignored me. "Thank you," she said to Ben. "I promise, that's the last time anyone will have to punch Chris."

Ben patted her on the back, then released her. Alexis turned to me and sighed. "If I tell you that you were right, how long until you let me live it down?"

I shook my head. "I wasn't right. Especially when I told you to avoid relationships and have meaningless sex for the rest of your life."

Will coughed and thumped his chest.

"Chris just happens to be an anomaly who made me look right," I concluded.

"What in the world is *up* with you?" Alexis stepped closer to scrutinize me, and her eyes widened. "Oh, God. You're in running clothes. Lee, who did this to you?"

I pointed at Ben. "And you, Brawler. I thought you said violence wasn't the answer and everyone deserves forgiveness."

He shrugged. "They do. Except for some guys. Some guys just deserve to be punched."

28

Out of the Pan and Into the Fire

Despite how hard I'd dragged my heels, how thoroughly I'd researched the physics of stalling time and how piously I'd prayed to St. Joseph, the patron saint of continued employment, the worst day in the world had nevertheless arrived. I was basically a supervillain now, because Dakota had forced me to use my considerable talents for evil.

The presser was set up spectacularly on the steps leading up to the Lise office. I'd arranged the podium at the top of the stairs, in front of the sweeping glass doors, which had *Lise Motors* splashed across them—basically, framing up the perfect shot. I had the tech equipment, and it worked flawlessly. I'd invited all the local reporters and reporters from the Austin bureaus of big nationals, so everyone was accounted for. It was a clear, unusually sunny January day, so I'd even done well with the weather.

And I'd run Dakota through her talking points a million

times, until she could say them with her eyes closed. The problem was, I hated her talking points. I hated that we were doing this presser. I hated all the reporters in the crowd for so quickly accepting my invitation to our public shaming, when I had to cajole and woo them to cover our success.

But, despite my feelings, the hour was nigh. Even from our waiting place behind the glass doors, I could hear the anchors instructing camerapeople on where to stand, jockeying for positions closest to the bottom of the stairs. We'd decided the governor shouldn't attend, obviously, or he'd face a barrage of questions. But near the back of the crowd, I spotted Ben, and the nervous storm inside me calmed.

His presence reminded me it would be okay. We were in this together. Though Ben did look on the outside how I felt on the inside, underneath my professional mask: miserable. I stepped on my tiptoes to see what he was wearing. It was his puffy North Face jacket, not a suit.

Had he already quit? I wished I could talk to him, but except for when he'd rushed to rescue me from the race, there'd been no communication between us. Likely he was enjoying the peace and quiet now that he'd disembarked from the Lee Stone emotional roller coaster.

"All right, Lee. Are you ready?" Dakota smoothed her dark hair over her forehead and jiggled her shoulders, her classic press warm-up ritual. She looked fantastic, of course, in a black business suit with such sharp lines at the shoulders I felt certain Wendy had picked it out for her.

I rested my hands on those sharp shoulders. "Just say the word, and I will spirit you out of here into some car they'd never suspect—a Hummer or something. And I'll tell the press the announcement's canceled."

Dakota shook her head. "You sound like my husband.

George doesn't want me to do this, either. But I can't see another way." She tugged my sleeve. "Come on. It's showtime."

I took a deep breath, opened the glass doors and strode with Dakota to the top of the stairs. Immediately, cameras lifted and started flashing.

I squeezed Dakota's hand and left her standing just to the left of the podium. Then I walked up to it and adjusted the microphone. There was a buzz of collective anticipation from the press.

I was supposed to give the opening remarks. They were brief: introduce Dakota, emphasize her accomplishments and remind everyone why we were here today. My hands shook, but I gripped the sides of the podium until they stilled.

"Good afternoon," I said, approving the way my voice came out, deep and sure. "My name is Lee Stone, director of communications for Lise Motors."

Suddenly, a woman holding a tape recorder gasped. "Oh my *God*. It's Sad Crawler. From the marathon."

The noise level in the crowd notched higher. Reporters abandoned me to frantically search their phones, presumably to google images of the woman from the race and compare.

Okay. This was embarrassing. I hadn't really expected the marathon to come up, and it was throwing me a little. Time to wrest control back.

"I'm here to introduce Dakota Young," I said. "Lise Motors CEO and *Car and Driver*'s Woman of the Year."

"She's not Sad Crawler," a man in a baseball cap shouted. "She's Princess Fountain Oops!"

"Ooooooh," the crowd breathed, the name clearly striking a chord.

Excuse me. Princess Fountain—what?

I lowered my mouth to the microphone. "Reporter, please explain."

The man held up his phone, as if I could see what was playing from this distance. "It's a video going around the internet," he said. "Two women at Disney World dressed as Belle and Mrs. Potts from *Beauty and the Beast.* They're running, and then some kid tackles them into a fountain right in front of Cinderella's castle. Someone set it to a dubstep track. It's hilarious. And it's you! You look exactly like Belle. The whole internet's calling you Princess Fountain Oops, don't you know?"

Apparently, my decision to avoid checking Twitter so I couldn't see what they were saying about Dakota had been a grave miscalculation.

"My God, she's Sad Crawler *and* Fountain Oops," someone else yelled. "What are the odds?"

What were the odds, indeed? *Oh*, this was not good. I'd gone viral—not once, but twice—just as I'd warned Mac all those months ago, when we were fleeing across the Magic Kingdom. A warning she'd scoffed at, might I add. But not even my epic *I told you so* was going to take the edge off this humiliation. This was a serious blow to my credibility. My two worlds were meeting, and it was as bad as I'd feared.

I looked through the reporters and found Ben's face. Strangely, he was grinning, as if we both weren't watching my career dissolve before our eyes. He gave me a thumbs-up, then mouthed, *You got this.*

Okay. Right. I could bounce back. I could lean into this because a little notoriety never hurt anyone. I squared my shoulders.

"You are correct," I said to the crowd. "I am both Sad Crawler and Princess Fountain Oops. However, today I am here in my professional capacity to talk to you about a very serious matter involving Austin's political and business communities."

To my great relief, the reporters quieted.

I glanced at Dakota. She nodded encouragingly. Ever supportive. Ever kind.

I knew what I was supposed to say. I was supposed to talk a little more about her career, then describe the accusations against her. Then I was supposed to hand over the mic and let her implode everything she'd worked her whole life to build. Over the fact that she was a cheater. To be honest, this was the kind of severe public humiliation I used to fantasize about punishing my father with when I was younger. When I felt the most hurt, I would imagine something just like this, where he had to own up to his crimes in front of a million judging eyes. Since that fantasy was obviously impossible, I'd punished him the only way I knew how, by taking myself away. And look where that kind of thinking had gotten me in the end.

No—this was wrong. My instincts were telling me not to say what I'd prepared. My heart was urging me to say something else entirely, something Dakota wouldn't like, something she'd probably fire me for.

But Dakota was announcing her resignation in mere minutes. So—right. There was that.

I looked once more at Ben and decided: I would trust myself.

I cleared my throat, and the reporters leaned in. "Dakota Young is the most brilliant person I've ever met. Not woman. Not woman under forty. Person. Period. She invented the world's best electric vehicle, and then she raised the bar with the Herschel motor. Which we were *supposed* to unveil at a press conference a few weeks from now, except we're having this one instead. Dakota is a tireless champion for the environment, for animals' rights, for her employees and especially for other women. She has been a champion of mine since the day I met her."

The reporters were getting comfortable listening to me list Dakota's virtues. I would change that soon enough.

"Yet for years, you have ignored her. Oh, you paid attention when we pointed out your sexism in shining a light on Elon Musk instead of her. But otherwise, you don't care. You didn't want to hear about the threat of climate change or the Green Machine bill Dakota and the governor were working on together. The bill that, if passed, would save our sorry, gas-guzzling asses for a few more years. Oh, no. Too boring."

A murmuring started in the crowd. I could feel Dakota step closer out of alarm. But I gripped the podium and leaned closer over the mic.

"But now you catch wind that this accomplished woman has made one mistake—not with her business, mind you, or in the actual course of trying to lobby for the bill, but in her personal life. And you are like sharks circling in chummed water. Did you question the source of the leak? Did you happen to wonder if there was a reason Samuel Slittery—CEO of a company that would do anything to see the Green Machine killed—was offering himself up as your star interviewee? No. You were so hungry to run your headlines about Dakota the succubus, seducing the governor, that you ignored the bigger picture. What sexist bloodlust."

"Lee," Dakota hissed. But I ignored her. I had already jumped over the edge of this cliff, and now there was nothing left to do but get where I was going.

"You ignore the fact that you've created an impossible environment for women in power. If you honestly assessed yourselves, I think you'd find you are part of the problem. You let men get off scot-free. You let them make mistake after mistake, and you excuse it by saying, *Oh, yes, he's a flawed person, but it's the work that matters.* Where's the takedown of Grover Mane? Where are the questions about his fitness to lead? Dakota was planning on offering her head on a platter to save her company today because that's what you demand of women for one misstep. But I say no."

I looked through the shocked faces to find Ben's again. He didn't look horrified, or even surprised, like I'd expected. Instead, he looked thoughtful, his eyes cast far away, like he was imagining something. I didn't know how to read the expression, so I decided to keep going.

"Dakota made a mistake. Yes, she stepped outside her marriage. So what? Even if you think that's not right, men have been juggling debauchery and day jobs for years. Think of nearly every politician you know. Hell, think of all those politicians in the movies. *Eyes Wide Shut*, for example. Everyone thought it was totally believable that all those men in Venetian masks could go to orgies by night and be powerful politicians by day. Why shouldn't a woman have that same luxury?"

Okay. The reporters were frowning in confusion. Maybe I had gone a little sideways. "To be clear, I'm not saying anyone *should* be in an *Eyes Wide Shut* sex club situation. I'm just saying no one questioned those men's time management skills."

Yikes. *Wrap it up, Stoner.*

"Who among us is perfect?" I demanded. "Serious question. Who among us hasn't made a mistake? You know some of mine already. I ran from children at Disney World because they scare me, and landed in a fountain. I signed up for a half-marathon I had no business running. But there's so much more. Once, I accidentally hit a pigeon with my car and it exploded in a puff of feathers. I tried to go out and put it back together, and when I couldn't, I gave it a funeral that was really subpar. I once babysat my friend's four-year-old and accidentally packed my medically prescribed marijuana in his lunch bag. Don't worry. I got it back in time. And you know what else? I've cheated, too. Five years ago, I cheated on the man I loved because I wanted to leave him before he left me. How silly is that?"

Crickets. The reporters were looking up at me like I'd just told them—well, all the things I'd told them. In desperation, I combed the crowd until I spotted the reporter who'd shown me the Princess Fountain Oops video. "You, sir—come on. Haven't you ever made a mistake?"

The man's neck twisted as he eyed the TV cameras. But then he seemed to decide something, and his chest swelled. "I cheated on my first wife," he called. "It wasn't a good relationship, but now I'm in a loving second marriage."

"See?" I said. "Good for you!"

"One-way streets confuse me," someone else shouted. "I can never drive down them the right way. I clipped a side mirror on the way here."

"Okay," I said, "whoever's mirror's broken knows who to find."

"I fantasize about the governor when making love to my husband," a woman yelled. "I completely understand why Dakota did it."

"Gross, but I'm sure he'll be happy to hear it. The larger point remains. Would you want to be written off just because of your one mistake? No. Think about that the next time you call for Dakota's head."

There. I was done. One last glance at Ben as a treat. His hand was covering his mouth, but I could tell he was laughing, because he was shaking and his face was red and his eyes were sparkling. Well, okay. Not the performance review I was hoping for, but then again, that was really up to Dakota to decide.

I stepped away from the mic and faced her. Shit. She looked pissed.

"Dakota, I'm sorry. I just couldn't let you—"

"Thank you," she said crisply. "For teeing me up."

I blinked, and it hit me: she *was* pissed, but it wasn't at me.

In stunned silence, I watched her step behind the podium, twist the mic down to her level and turn her blazing eyes on the reporters. "Hello. After that, I don't really think I need to introduce myself. So, let's get straight to the point."

She raised an eyebrow. "As my colleague Ms. Stone just reminded me—rather colorfully—my personal relationships have nothing to do with my company or my work. So I am here today to offer two apologies only. The first is to my husband, George, and our two children. The second is to the staff at Lise and in the governor's office, for whom I've made life difficult."

When she straightened her spine, the sharp lines of her suit settled like armor over her shoulders. "To the rest of you, I do not apologize. As an engineer, I'm a big fan of logic, and the logic here is as follows. I owe you nothing when it comes to my personal life, and so I have nothing to be sorry for. Instead, I will offer you a few promises."

The reporters crowded close to the bottom of the stairs. She had them in the palm of her hand. She was so good. I loved her.

"I promise," Dakota said, her voice echoing through the space, "that I will continue to drag this country, kicking and screaming, into a greener future. I promise I will continue to create the best damn electric vehicles in the world, bar none, to give us a shot at rolling back what we've done to our planet. And if any of my critics or my competitors or even my investors want to try to use my personal mistake to wrest away the company I've built or the bill I support, then I promise a fight. To them, I offer these immortal Texas words—*Come. And. Take. It.*"

She turned to face me, still wearing her warrior face, then remembered her talking points and spun back to the microphone. "Oh. Thank you. There will be no questions at this time."

29

Favorable Numbers

The instant I stepped into the state capitol the next day, I regretted it. Once, I'd walked these halls lamenting the way all the important people buzzed past me. Talking fast into their phones, not giving me a second glance, all my email requests for meetings to talk about climate change secure in their deleted folders. Today, those same people stopped and turned as I walked by, their eyes and whispers tracking me down the long terrazzo floors. No doubt about it: this way was worse.

I finally made it past the central rotunda, which one staffer clearly forgot was a whispering gallery, since I heard, "Can you *believe* the spectacle she pulled?" loud as a bullhorn. When I spun around, a woman jumped like an electrocuted cat on the other side of the room. I left her with her small heart attack and continued to the governor's office.

The junior aide I remembered from the day the affair broke

popped out of the double doors, his eyes glowing. "Ms. Stone! You're here!"

The warm reception threw me. "Uh, I guess I am."

"Will you sign this for me?" The aide thrust a pen and a copy of the *Austin American-Statesman* into my hands. "You're famous."

I looked down at the headline. "Sex Club Spokeswoman Takes Political and Media Worlds to Task for Alleged Sexism." Well. I supposed Sex Club Spokeswoman was an upgrade from Sad Crawler and Princess Fountain Oops. It was at least a little bit professional. I uncapped the pen and slashed my signature across the large picture of me standing at the podium. They'd caught me midblink, and the caption below read, *Eyes Wide Shut: Passionate Lise Motors employee argues women should have the right to participate in politics by day, orgies by night.*

Well played, media. This would explain why my phone had been ringing off the hook.

"Thank you," the aide gushed. "I believe in everything you said, by the way. I thought it was great."

I blinked at him. "You do? How did you even see it, if most of the coverage is like this?" I waved at the newspaper.

"A bunch of the left-leaning stations played your whole speech," he said. "And a ton of reporters uploaded it to their personal social accounts." He waved the *Statesman.* "It's just the old guard that doesn't like you." He winked. "Which honestly makes the rest of us like you more."

Had I just fallen in love with a junior staffer? I shook myself. *No, Stoner, focus.*

"Well, I appreciate that more than I can say." I nodded toward the office. "But I'm actually here to see Ben Laderman. Is he in today?"

The aide's face turned grave. "You didn't hear? Ben resigned. He flew out of here afterward, saying he had to get on the road to do something important. The governor's even more pissed at him than he is at you and Dakota."

Ben had warned me. He'd told me this was exactly what he was going to do. The problem was, by the time the press conference ended and I'd searched for him in the mayhem, ignoring the shouted questions from reporters, he was already gone. I'd called and texted, but so far, he hadn't answered. I'd never even been to the house he'd moved into after splitting with Sarah, so I couldn't sit on his front stoop until he appeared. His office had been my last resort, and now my hope of seeing him was swept away like dust in the wind.

A road trip? Where in the world was Ben Laderman, and what was he up to?

The aide tapped me. "But, Ms. Stone, Anita wants to speak to you. She saw you through the window and said to bring you in."

"The governor's pollster?"

Grover Mane cared so much about keeping his finger on the pulse of public opinion that he'd hired a pollster in a permanent position on his staff. Anita Jones was a legend, too—she had an incredible track record of capturing the way the winds were shifting ahead of everyone else. I'd always wanted to talk to her, but this was curious indeed.

"Yep." The aide opened the office door and beckoned. "Come on."

Inside the governor's office—which was really a hub of smaller offices, united by a big, open reception area—the mood was jovial. People waved and smiled as the aide led me to a door with a plaque that read Anita Jones, Director of Research. I squelched the urge to hunt through the offices until I found the one that said Ben Laderman, Director of Policy. If they hadn't already chiseled his name off, that is.

"Ah," said a voice, so deep and gravelly it could only belong to a smoker. "If it isn't the Sex Club Spokeswoman, in the flesh."

Anita Jones sat behind her desk. She was maybe in her sixties, with close-cut white hair and steely eyes. "Sit," she said, and pointed to the single chair in front of her desk. She turned her gaze to the aide. "You. Leave."

He scampered away and I took my seat, looking around at her walls. She had copies of awards and magazine stories hung everywhere, with titles like, "Texas Pollster Pro on Ten-Year Streak Predicting District Races" and "Betting against Her Peers, Anita Jones Comes Out on Top Yet Again."

Okay. So the woman was impressive.

"The whole office loves you, much to Grover's chagrin." Anita pulled a pack of Marlboros out of her desk drawer. "You enjoying the fame?"

"Not really." I squinted at the cigarettes. "Are you actually going to light one of those in here? Isn't it illegal?"

"Eh." Anita waved a hand at the door. "The stakes are low. These fuckers need me. Shut that, then crack the window. Or are you too precious to handle a little cigarette smoke?"

I *was* too precious, but I was also a little intimidated. So I got up, shut the door and pushed the window up as far as it would go.

Anita lit her cigarette and took a drag. "Mmm. Just like the good old days. Now sit down again. Ben said you'd be by, so I got everything ready for you."

What was she talking about? I cleared my throat. "You talked to Ben?"

"Course." Anita cracked open a folder to reveal a printed page, filled with rows and rows of numbers. "He rang me up right after your little press conference. Called in a favor." She gave me a level stare. "Though, between us gals, there's no favor that man could ask for that I wouldn't oblige. No favor at all, if you catch my drift."

I gulped. "I feel like this is that locker room talk I keep hearing about."

She waved a hand. "After working in Texas politics for thirty years, I've got a laundry list of grievances to repay. And if I choose to sexually objectify a delicious gubernatorial staffer every once in a while, the male body politic should count itself lucky that's all I'm doing. You feel me?"

"Your energy is intense," I said, swatting away cigarette smoke. "But I do feel you."

"Good. After your speech yesterday, I had a feeling we'd get along. So, here it is." She jabbed a finger at the piece of paper in her folder. "Put short, you did it."

I blinked. "Did what?"

She eyed me. "You saved the bill. Yesterday at nine a.m., nobody in Texas outside a small circle of politically connected people had even heard about the bill. No offense," she added. "I know it was your job to publicize it."

"We chose a targeted approach," I said defensively.

"Well, in that case, you failed, because as of noon today, Dakota's trending, you're trending, *Eyes Wide Shut* is trending and the Green Machine bill is trending. Everyone's talking about it."

I drew a shaky breath. "And? What are they saying?"

"The bill's favorables are through the roof. My team polled thousands of people—" She cocked a brow. "What? We work fast to match the news cycle. We polled thousands—made sure to get an even bipartisan split—and combined that data with analytics from Twitter, Facebook, Instagram and TikTok."

This was almost dizzying. "TikTok?"

"Don't discount TikTok. The bill's most popular there. It's the younger demographic. They care about climate."

I didn't want to hope, only to be disappointed. "What exactly are you saying?"

Anita harrumphed and blew a ring of smoke. "I'm saying that thanks to your speeches yesterday—Dakota's, yes, but especially your wild roller coaster—the Green Machine bill is enormously popular. I just sent copies of this opinion research to every rep and senator in the Texas legislature, like Ben asked. You've got 'em on the hook. Janus and Wayne are in the Unity room—that's the old Alamo room—as we speak, meeting with the governor."

Oh my God. My bill. My *baby*. The Green Machine was still alive. Somehow, we'd saved it. My heart soared.

"What about McBuck?" I asked, seizing on the last missing ingredient.

Anita kicked her legs up on the desk. "He might be your last holdout. You'll probably have to find a way to work him before the vote tomorrow."

"Thank you *so* much." I leaped out of my chair. I had to call Dakota and Wendy immediately, figure out how to push the bill over the finish line. They were going to *faint* when they heard.

"Hold your horses." Anita stubbed out her cigarette. "Don't you want to hear the other results?"

"What other results?"

"Ben had me run your numbers, too. Honestly, woman, you are a mystery wrapped in a puzzle."

I gripped the back of the chair. "Why would he ask you to do that?"

"I am not inside that man's brain." She grinned. "Though I would like to be inside his—"

I waved her on. "Just—what did you find?"

Anita shuffled to a second sheet of paper. "Congratulations, darling. You're as popular as the bill, maybe even more so.

Analysis shows you tugged on the public's heartstrings when you ran that marathon so poorly, you came across as winningly relatable when you tumbled in that fountain, and you captured hearts and stoked indignation when you stood up for your boss to the people in power at your presser."

She skimmed her finger down the page. "These results are from across the state and across demographics, but needless to say, you are particularly beloved among the freaks and weirdos here in Austin. People under thirty-five, *especially* women under thirty-five, adore you. And I can't tell you how many sex positivity accounts have rallied for you on Twitter, because the number was too high for my brain to fully process."

"I haven't checked Twitter in forever," I breathed. My knees were Jell-O. Thank God I was holding on to this chair.

Anita gave me a stern look. "In my experience, these are the numbers of a successful candidate. I want you to take that and chew on it."

"I will…chew on it." I stared blankly at her desk. People *liked* me? They thought of me as a leader?

"Well?" Anita made a shooing gesture. "Go on. Scat. And take care of your McBuck problem before you keel over. I can see the keeling coming in your eyes."

In a daze, I thanked her, stumbled out the door and managed to high-five several staffers on my way out of the governor's office.

The Green Machine was popular, and so was I. No wonder everyone I'd passed in the capitol had stared and whispered. They weren't pitying me; they were jealous. Winning public approval was the Holy Grail. Now, what would I do with this information?

As soon as the fog of surprise cleared my head, I realized I already knew the answer. I knew what to do to bring the Green Machine home.

I clattered down the steps of the capitol, wincing only a little at my still-sore muscles, and dialed a number.

"Hello, Senator Roy McBuck's office," a woman chirped. "This is Kathy speaking."

"Hello, Kathy, this is Lee Stone from Lise Motors."

There was a clanging sound, like Kathy had dropped the phone, then some scrambling. Her voice returned, taking on an awed tint. "The Sex Club Spokeswoman?"

"Yes, that Lee Stone. Could you please put me through to the senator? I have a proposition I think he'll want to hear."

"A…proposition? I, uh, read about the *Eyes Wide Shut* thing and I don't feel comfortable—"

I blew out a breath. "Not *that* kind of proposition, Kathy. You know what, just connect me."

30

With Humility and Diffidence

Texas Monthly once called Texas Legislature Online "good for transparency, sure, but also the most boring channel on the internet, a perfect cure for your insomnia." You'd never know it, though, judging by the way the entire Lise Motors office—all one hundred–plus people—were glued to the giant projector streaming the eighty-seventh Texas legislative session against the wall of our building.

It was D-Day. In moments, the Green Machine bill would pass into the annals of history, or it would die on the Senate floor. The House had already passed the bill, which we'd counted on. The Green Machine's newfound popularity, especially among Democratic-leaning voters, meant that even the representatives Samuel Slittery claimed had been waffling snapped right back in line with their voters' opinions.

All that was left was to win the Senate. And today was the day of the floor vote. We'd stopped business as usual here at Lise in order to watch, turning it into a party, with green balloons, vegan tacos and cupcakes. There was a wall of champagne bottles, which Dakota swore we were opening no matter which way the votes fell—we would use the bubbles to celebrate, or we'd use them to wallow. I looked at the champagne longingly. Stupid alcohol-free self-improvement project.

On one side of me, Dakota squeezed my hand. On the other side, Wendy bit her nails, then caught me looking and yanked her hand away. "Tell me again what McBuck said."

"He said he was intrigued by my proposition to open the manufacturing center in Hudson County."

"Intrigued? That's it?"

I felt like biting my own nails. "He said he needed more time to think, and I'd know his answer when he voted."

"Sadist," Wendy hissed. "People who enjoy power that much should never be given any."

"I think he's going to vote yes," Dakota said optimistically.

"Shhhh, it's starting." I straightened as the lieutenant governor stepped to the lectern on-screen and dropped his head to the mic.

"Senate Bill 3," he announced, "was assigned to the Natural Resources and Economic Development Committee. It has now been cleared by that committee, read and debated on the floor. It is time for the floor to vote."

"I think I might pass out," Dakota whispered. "Wake me when it's over, but only if we win."

"Colleagues," the lieutenant governor intoned. "When I call your name, please respond yea or no. Senator Rodriguez."

Rodriguez leaned over her microphone. "Yea."

"Yes!" I pumped my fist, and the entire Lise office cheered along with me. Okay, so it wasn't a surprise. Rodriguez had been a sure thing. But still, one step closer.

"Senator Abington."

Abington had a hard time finding his mic. Maybe on account of being so old his eyelids drooped over his eyes. "No," he coughed.

"Boo," my colleagues called at the screen. I steeled myself. That was okay. That was expected. Abington was a dinosaur, and we just needed two-thirds to win.

I felt a sudden pang of loneliness, despite being surrounded by Dakota, Wendy and all the people I worked with. The one person I'd imagined sharing this moment with, the person who most deserved to be here, was gone. It had been two days, and I'd heard nothing. Except for the strange Easter egg he'd left with Anita and the polling results—which I was grateful for, don't get me wrong—he'd dropped off the face of the planet. I'd even sucked it up and logged on to my Facebook account, which was a dumpster fire of notifications, just to send him a message. And still, nothing. For the millionth time, I wondered what the important thing was he'd left to do. In the back of my head, a tiny voice whispered that I might need to come to grips with the fact that, just like five years ago, Ben had chosen the high road, and it had led him far away from me.

The votes continued, a mix of yeas and nos, though I was grateful to see the votes generally trending in the yea direction. Finally, it came down to the three people we'd always known it would: Senators Janus, Wayne and McBuck. Those inscrutable bastards. Win or lose, I would at least be happy to stop seeing their faces in my dreams every night. The next time the thought *I wonder what Roy McBuck truly wants and needs, and how I can give it to him* crossed my mind, I hoped it would be in hell. Which I would assume I'd arrive at after truly earning it here in my stint on earth.

"Senator Janus," the lieutenant governor prompted.

Janus leaned forward and flashed a Willie Nelson–style peace sign. "Yea."

Excellent. Also, what a tool.

"Good, good, good," Wendy muttered, her eyes flickering over the screen, counting votes.

"Senator Wayne?".

The old man cleared his throat. "An emphatic yea."

Thank you, Ely Gunther, you wonderful human.

"Okay, well, we don't really need the editorializing, as you know, Senator, but your vote is recorded."

"Jesus Christ," Wendy said, abandoning all pretense and simply chewing her nails. "Only one more. Please, please."

"And Senator McBuck?"

Dakota squeezed my hand so hard I lost circulation. But I didn't care. I would gladly trade my hand for a yes. "Come on, McBuck," I whispered. "You old lug, do the right thing."

McBuck whispered into the microphone.

"Senator, what was that? Please repeat yourself."

"Yea," he announced, in front of God and Texas.

"Ahhhhh," Dakota screamed, leaping out of her chair. *"We won!"*

The office exploded into mayhem, employees everywhere, jumping and shouting.

Wendy pulled me out of my chair and threw her arms around me in our first-ever hug. Potentially her first hug of all time, judging by the viselike way she squeezed me. I was so busy being shell-shocked I almost missed the lieutenant governor's next words.

"Thank you, Senator McBuck. SB 3 has achieved the necessary votes and is now enrolled. It will be sent to the governor's desk to sign."

With those words, it was official. We'd just made history. Texas was a world leader in responding to the climate crisis. We'd done the thing no one thought we could do. I felt almost overwhelmed by the weight of it.

But my colleagues left me no time to wrestle with my feelings. They crowded around, popping champagne bottles, spraying fizzy liquid all over my clothes. I resisted the urge to lick myself.

Dakota raised my hand in the air like I was a champion boxer at the end of a winning fight. "Lee Stone did it! She wrote the bill and campaigned it and swooped in to save it when it was on its deathbed. Lee Stone just changed the world!"

"Three cheers for Lee!" Dakota's assistant called, and everyone raised their champagne glasses.

"You're Lee Stone?" A deliveryman pushed through the staff, holding an enormous bouquet of yellow roses. "Sign here, please."

I signed and accepted the roses, tearing open the card. But it was only the governor.

Dear Lee,

The florist tells me yellow is the color to say you're sorry. Well, I'm sorry for doing my level best to muck up your bill. Congratulations on getting it passed anyway. (Yes, I had a different card prepped in case we lost—glad I didn't have to use it.) I hope we can still be friends.

Yours,
Grover

My heart dropped. Everyone was acting like the Green Machine was fully mine, like I'd gotten it over the finish line all by myself. But every step of the way—from editing the bill language to developing the strategy to the day-to-day hustle up and down the state of Texas—Ben had been by my side. This was his win, too, and the fact that he wasn't here and that no one was saying his name made it feel like he'd never existed. Like these last few months had been a fever dream, and he'd actually never left California to move back to Texas in the first place. Like if I drove across state lines, I'd find him right back in Palo Alto, wondering why the hell his frenzied ex-girlfriend was pounding on his door.

I felt nearly sick with anxiety and longing, all tangled together. I thrust my roses at Dakota. "Will you hold these? They're from the governor."

Wendy swooped in. "Um, why don't I hold them? Just so no one gets any ideas."

I broke away from the party and power walked back to my office, shutting the door and leaning against it. I dialed and brought the phone to my ear. Hoping against hope.

And after a few rings, it went to voice mail, like all the times before. Before I could stop them, tears crept into the corners of my eyes as his familiar recorded voice said, *You've reached Ben Laderman. Leave me a message.*

"Hi, Ben," I said at the beep. "It's me again. The bill just passed. McBuck said yea. Which means we did it. Captain Planet, the Renaissance fair, the rodeo, Willie Nelson, seducing Alice—all of it was worth it."

I wiped my eyes. "I'm going to confess that it feels really weird to pass the bill without you. I don't even know which one of us won in the end. I offered to put the Herschel factory in McBuck's district, but you commissioned the polling and made sure it went out to everyone. I wouldn't have thought to do that, and it changed everything. So, I'm not sure if you're my assistant now, or if I'm yours."

I laughed a little desperately. "Unless you just want to take the L and become my assistant. My submissive. If you're into that sort of thing, which some people are, you know." I cleared my throat. "But, remembering you and your entire personality and how much you like to win, I realize now that's probably not going to happen.

"So. How about this? You have to actually send some sign you're alive to claim the win. You can call me, text me, show up on my doorstep. All perfectly acceptable options. You could even send a carrier pigeon. Skywriting. Just some clue to where you are and what you're up to and whether you're ever planning on talking to me again. Which I really hope you are. Because when I think about having to lose you all over—when I think about not getting you in my life—well, I'd rather lose anything else. This is what I should have said five years ago, but I'm saying it now. Ben, I love you. Please come back. I've been walking around with a Ben-shaped hole in my heart, and it's basically the size of my entire heart. I tried to fill it with anything and everything I could think of, but nothing worked. I didn't feel right until the day I saw you again. So I won't go anywhere. I'll wait for you—"

"You have exceeded your time limit with this voice mail," a robotic voice interrupted. "Thank you. Goodbye."

The line dropped. I stared at the phone—then flew to my texts and typed a hurried message: Please delete that voice mail immediately. To my surprise, three little dots appeared on the screen—Ben was typing. I waited with bated breath. And then they disappeared. I waited some more. Nothing.

Well. I guess you could say that was one kind of sign.

31

Policy Change and Chill

T. S. Eliot was wrong: April wasn't the cruelest month. It was January. Gray, dreary and impossibly long—almost supernaturally long, if you thought about it. Which I was, at length, stretched out on my deck, staring at the sky. Maybe there was a scientific explanation—maybe every year, during the month of January, Earth experienced a flux in the space-time continuum that threw each second into excruciating slow motion, something humans experienced as an impossibly long stretch of cosmic horror. Maybe that was why the three days that had passed since I'd last seen Ben—even the one day since he'd left my text on "read"—felt like a lifetime.

It could also be because my phone hadn't stopped ringing since the vote went through. It turned out work on the Green Machine was far from over once Governor Mane signed the bill into law. There was this tricky thing called implementation, where the government had to actually figure out how to do what it had promised. And there were *lots* of hurdles when it came to changing corporate taxes to pay for the electric vehicle infrastructure. I had plenty of ideas to address both issues, so I'd become a popular person.

Ironic, to be flooded with calls when all I wanted was a single phone call from the one person who wasn't dialing. Or was that more of an Alanis Morissette irony—the not-really-ironic kind? Who even knew if words had meaning anymore. As a communications professional, I found myself alarmingly beyond caring. The only thing I cared about was knowing where in the world Ben was.

In lieu of my normal stress-relief activities, such as drinking wine, I'd caved and started practicing yoga. Or "yoga," as I liked to think of it. It turned out child's pose and cow pose were really quite relaxing, and I could hold both for an entire hour-long session without breaking a sweat, which I assumed was the point of yoga. Truly, I had found a form of exercise uniquely suited to me. My favorite position by far was Savasana, or corpse pose. Not only was lying flat on my back on my deck with my arms and legs splayed an ideal workout, but it also allowed me to listen to Frank Ocean at full volume and cry, otherwise known as emotional reflection time. Thanks to my newfound maturity, I knew that even though the worst might have happened—Ben might have disappeared again—the important thing was, I was going to survive. Annie had told me the only way to be in control of my heart was to trust myself to be okay no matter what, and here I was, doing exactly that. Getting through it.

I felt footsteps depress the wooden planks of the deck. A presence towered over me, blocking the weak January sun. I cracked an eye, saw my-once-again-roomie Alexis peering and paused Frank's crooning.

"What's up, Lex? I love you, but I'm exercising."

She grinned. "I can see that. And I love *you*, so I'm going to tell you to wipe your eyes and sit up real quick."

I sat up. "What? Why?"

She squeezed me in a tight hug. "I'm going out for the night," she whispered. "Call me later." Then she pulled back, winked and disappeared through the sliding glass door into my house.

What the hell? I stood and wiped my eyes. And when I blinked again, Ben was standing in the open back door, gripping the glass, body tense with anticipation, eyes pinning me.

He wasn't a mirage because the sight of him did something to my body only flesh-and-blood Ben could do. He was painfully beautiful, frozen in the door frame. That thick black hair curling over his forehead, his square jaw clenched, blue eyes serious. A sense of gravity filled my chest, my body knowing something a step before my mind. I'd only felt it once before—the night I first met Ben, when we finally made it back to his apartment and he'd shut the door, and then it was just the two of us, nothing to hide behind, no jokes or competitions or other people. It had hit me, in that moment, that I was standing on the precipice of something important, something that would shape my life, and I'd slid with my back to the wall all the way to his apartment floor. Now the same feeling rooted me in place on my deck.

"Hi, Lee." His voice was careful. I wanted to crack through his shield and get to the heart of him.

"What are you doing here?" I was proud of my steady voice.

Ben's Adam's apple moved as he swallowed, like he was nervous, but his eyes remained locked on me. "I came to ask you something."

"You missed the vote yesterday."

He searched my face, still standing straight and rigid. "The bill was yours to see over the finish line. It always was. I knew you'd win."

"You didn't call." I folded my arms over my stomach, feeling suddenly naked and exposed. "Or text, or come see me. Nothing." I kicked my toe against the deck. "You disappeared again, without telling me what was so important you had to hit the road."

At this, Ben stepped through the door and onto the deck. Tension flared inside me—by coming closer, he was tugging some invisible string between us, and now my body was tense, at attention, fighting the pull of him. I dug my fingers into my arms to hold myself in place.

He stopped in front of me. "I was planning."

When, exactly, had my body switched allegiances? He was a magnet, and it was becoming physically impossible not to reach for him.

"I was putting the pieces together," he said slowly. "Talking to people. I didn't want to speak with you or get your hopes up until I knew my plan was solid."

I obeyed my aching body and stepped closer. "What are you talking about?"

He reached out and took my hand, cradling it between his. "I'm talking about this." He dropped to one knee.

"Ben—*what?*" My heart was beating a dizzying staccato—it was going to burst from my chest and float into the gray January sky.

He gazed up at me. "Lee, we've both grown up and changed. But the one thing that never has is how deeply I love you. I am going to love you forever. I know that in my heart—there's no use pretending it would stop, even if we went our separate ways." He put a hand over his heart. "You have me, always."

I could hardly breathe.

Ben took a deep breath to steady himself and looked up at me through his lashes. "I fell in love with you when I was twenty-four and there has never been another path. I need you to know that I'm going to love you wherever you go, whatever you do, no matter how many years or miles pass between us. Nothing is ever going to change that."

Ben was talking about the kind of love I'd convinced myself didn't exist: relentless, sturdy, impossible to tarnish or quell. The kind my secret, tender heart had wanted so badly it had been less painful to write it off than try for it and fail. Here he was, kneeling in front of me, giving me what I hadn't even been able to say I needed.

He squeezed my hand. "But the thing is, I more than love you, Lee. I believe in you." His nervousness radiated in the way his shoulders tensed. "So I'm here to tell you my wildest dream, and to ask you to say yes to it."

Ben dropped my hand and slowly unzipped his jacket, glancing up at me for a second, before he unhooked the zipper and pulled the jacket off, revealing the hard, defined muscles of his arms flexing beneath his T-shirt. His white, short-sleeved T-shirt. His *campaign* T-shirt.

Stoner for State Senate was splashed in bright blue letters across the front.

I took a step back in shock.

Ben leaned forward and took my hand again, steadying me. He spoke quickly. "The state senator for District 14 isn't seeking reelection—that's right here in Travis County. I know you know that, but what you don't know is that a tech mogul has just decided to run for the seat. His name is Hayes Adams. Forty-five, millionaire. Believes in big business. Opposes corporate taxes, says they stifle innovation. Doesn't think climate change is a pressing threat. So far, he's running unopposed on the Democratic ticket, which we both know is the only ticket that matters in Austin."

Ben's eyes held mine. "I want you to run against him."

"What?" I tried to pull back, but Ben stood, holding on to my hands. *This* was what he'd been planning? It was crazy.

"Lee, you're insanely good at public policy. You're even better at figuring out how to connect with people. I've watched you every day, for months now, talk to every kind of person in the state of Texas, and you always know what to say or do that matters to them. You have a master's in environmental policy *and* you have the intangibles—the things that can't be taught."

"Ben, I—"

"You're the most passionate person I've ever met." The look on his face was so earnest, so hopeful. He cracked a small smile. "Maybe a little too passionate, if we're being honest. You're brave, and you'll throw yourself into the fire for a cause or a person you care about. You're an incredible candidate. Are you kidding? Can you imagine if every politician sitting in the capitol was like *you* instead of like Janus and Wayne and McBuck?"

I shook my head. "I don't know what to say."

His eyes grew more intense. "I don't just want a State Senate run, either. I'll put my cards on the table. I want you to spend four years in the Texas leg, and then I want to run you for a US Senate seat."

I yanked my hand back. "The *US Senate*? Ben, I'm too young! And I'm a Democrat in Texas. And a woman. A woman who drinks and smokes pot and has sex like an actual human being."

"Exactly," he said. "Like all the rest of the politicians, but better. That's the point you made at the press conference, right?"

"People aren't ready for that."

"Stoner, women are running for office all over the country. Plenty of them younger than you, with less policy experience. And they're winning. People are hungry for change."

His eyes were hungry as they cast over my face.

"But no one knows who I..." The words died even before I got to the end of the sentence. That was patently untrue—people *did* know me now, according to the opinion research. "They think of me as a joke. I'll mess up at some point, Ben. I'm the *queen* of messing up." There it was, my underlying weakness: at the end of the day, no matter how hard I worked at my professional mask, I would always be Stoner. Better to make it clear to Ben now.

"Maybe you will mess up," he said gently. "And maybe they'll like you for it. You saw Anita's numbers. People connect with you, Stoner. Face it."

People *did* seem to like me a little. And there were plenty of people sitting in the legislature that shouldn't be there, either because they were actively awful, stuck in their ways or had simply stopped trying.

"It was always my dream," I said softly, letting Ben's earnestness sneak under my skin, cause a little tendril of hope.

Ben grinned. "I know. You told me that five years ago, and I never forgot it."

I paced, unable to stop the wheels from turning. "But what would my platform be?"

"Climate, obviously. Putting people over corporations. Racial and gender equity across every field—jobs, health care, criminal justice, education. Equity with *teeth*, not just platitudes—with budgets backing you up. Economic justice, so single moms and other people living on minimum wage don't have to struggle so hard. All the things you believe in that the people in the capitol don't think are possible, or even important."

Slowly, a fire stoked inside me. I had a lot of platform ideas, to be honest. I'd started working on them in college, and even though I hadn't gotten to use them in the campaign with Andy Elliot, I'd held on to them. Worked on them as a hobby, tweaking, expanding. Through grad school and all the years since. It was why I'd wanted to be Lise Motor's vice president of public affairs so badly: one step closer to the dream. But Ben was proposing I go straight for it.

He ran a hand through his hair, making it stand on end. The man's muscles were still so tensed, his body rigid as a board, like he was on edge, holding something inside. "I left so I could go on the road and take meetings, socialize the idea of your candidacy with Texas movers and shakers."

I was pretty sure my jaw had dropped. Ben hadn't run from me; he'd left *for* me.

"Not to promise them you were running or anything," he added hurriedly, "just to gauge their opinion. The ACLU, Texas Democratic Women and the Organizing Project loved the idea. They want to talk policy with you. All the climate groups and the democratic socialists are behind you. The sex workers' union."

I waved a hand. "That one's a given."

"Honestly, everyone left of left of center," he added.

I stopped pacing and spun to him. "But I would need money. Donors. And who wants to fund the Sex Club Spokeswoman?"

"Funny you should ask," he said cautiously. "Because I just had my last meeting a day ago, and it was with a funder who said they'd be in big if you said yes."

"Who?" I pressed, unable, for the life of me, to imagine. *Penthouse*? *High Times* magazine?

"Dakota Young," Ben said.

I actually felt like the world was slipping underneath my feet. *"Dakota?"*

Ben nodded. "I told her I was going to pitch the idea to you, and we'd need backing. She said it was the best idea she'd ever heard, and you were born to be a leader."

Dakota—my idol, my mentor—believed in me. My heart was

doubling in size, or it was melting, I couldn't tell—something was happening inside my chest.

"She said she'd support you with the maximum amount of money she's allowed, and she'd stump for you, write op-eds for you, be in commercials for you. Anything you need."

Somehow, knowing that Dakota thought I could do this made it real. I swallowed past the lump in my throat, but my voice still came out low and throaty. "I'd need a staff. I'd need someone to run the campaign with me."

At this, Ben dropped back onto one knee, hands clenching at his sides—as if this was what he'd really been waiting for. "Choose me."

I tugged at his jacket, trying to pull him up, but he didn't budge. "Ben, don't be silly. You wanted to run for office yourself. Ben Laderman vs. the world."

He shook his head. "I realized I like being behind the scenes. Especially if you're out in front. Let me be your campaign manager."

My hands relaxed against the collar of his jacket. "You're serious?"

Ben's eyes were bluer and brighter than I'd ever seen them. "My dream of politics and my dream of you have always been intertwined. I go where you go. I believe in what you believe in. I believe in *you*. Nothing could make more sense." He closed his hands around my wrists. "Stoner, I see you trying. And I love you so much. Let me be your assistant. Turn Texas blue with me."

Ben was giving me something even better than love: he was giving me commitment. I didn't even question how he'd known that's what I needed, because at this point, I was beginning to realize that by opening myself up to him, I'd finally let him understand me, the way he'd always longed to. And this was the result.

I dropped to my knees so we were level, and pressed my hands to the sides of his face. "I should've known you'd come back, Ben Laderman. You always do."

"No more leaving," he said.

"No more leaving," I promised.

He took a deep breath, steeling himself. "Is that a yes?"

"It's a yes," I said, and every ounce of tension and rigidness melted out of Ben's body. His shoulders sank, and he covered his face with his hand. I felt the weight of something like destiny or history or rightness settle over me. Who knew? Maybe it was even a brush of approval from my father, like a kiss across my forehead, from wherever he was.

I pulled Ben's hand away and cupped his face, sweeping my thumb across his cheek. "I want you to be more than my campaign manager."

"Name it." His voice was hoarse.

"Be my boyfriend."

Looking at Ben's face was like looking at the sun. His smile was impossibly wide. "I'll be more than that, Stoner."

"Don't get ahead of yourself," I said, and he rolled his eyes, seized my face and kissed me.

I put my heart into the kiss. All the impossible hope I'd carried for years; all my love and admiration for the man in my arms, the good and patient and kind person he'd grown into. The feelings twisted up my insides, and I twisted my hands through his hair, drawing him closer, and closer—I would spend my life inventing new ways to get close to Ben Laderman.

He kissed me hungrily, as if he could make up for lost time through the sheer power of his mouth crashing over mine, his hands running the length of my body. He leaned back onto his elbows and I moved with him, sitting in his lap, bending over to capture his mouth.

I could feel him pressing, big and hard, under the denim of his jeans, and rotated my hips against him, sliding my hands under the world's sexiest Stoner for State Senate T-shirt to feel his flat, muscled stomach.

"It scares me," I whispered. "The way you make me feel. The possibility of losing you."

"I know," he said breathlessly, pulling my shirt over my head. "But you'll get over it. And you won't."

I tugged at his shirt and he pulled it off by the neck, exposing his broad, tan shoulders, his abs, the trail of dark hair down his stomach.

"I'm not very good at love." I pressed my hands against his chest, pushing him flat against the deck, and bit his neck, tasting the salt on his skin. He was so warm, like he'd been flushed, heart beating overly fast.

He closed his eyes. "You're better than you think."

"I'll try very hard," I said softly.

Ben opened his eyes, then leaned up and caught my mouth with his, wrapping his arm around my waist. In one fluid movement, he picked me up and rose to his feet. "Come with me," he said gruffly, and strode toward the sliding door.

I wrapped my arms around his neck, feeling the delicious heat of his bare chest against mine. "Ben Laderman. Now that I'm your boss, shouldn't I be the one ordering you around?"

He lifted me higher, walking quickly through the living room and into my bedroom. "I'm pretty sure you've been doing that for months, Stoner."

"Yes," I said. "But now it's official. You're my submissive."

He stopped abruptly in front of my bed and, before I could

say anything, tossed me on it. I bounced once against the mattress, and he gripped my ankles and tugged me toward him.

"Lee." Ben's eyes darkened as he stared down at me. "Take your leggings off."

The change in tone surprised me. Curious, I leaned forward and pulled them off, leg by leg, feeling the bite of cool air against my legs.

He bent over the bed toward me and tugged at my panties. "Now these."

I took a deep breath, hooked my thumbs under the seam and slid the panties down, without dropping Ben's eyes. I was lying in bed naked and light-headed. It had been too long since I'd touched him. My body was starved.

The look on his face was so serious I got a chill. "Don't move," he said, and slid a hand over my knee and up my thigh, tantalizingly slow. The small calluses on his fingers from lifting weights gave me goose bumps. I lifted my hips out of instinct, seeking more contact, and his eyes hardened. "Don't. Move."

Oh. Suddenly I did not mind Ben was ignoring everything I'd said about being his boss. I stilled completely, heart racing, as Ben's hand continued up my thigh, until he found me between my legs. His fingers moved idly, sliding over me, circling the center. He leaned closer, until I could feel his breath on my chest each time he exhaled, and his eyes remained serious, the blue rings around his irises dark. His face filled my vision as his fingers stroked me, the pressure so light I thought I would scream, except the look in his eyes kept me from moving. And then he pushed his fingers inside me.

I shuddered, body tensing, as he brought me to the edge. I closed my eyes—I couldn't help it. I was going to explode.

"I want you to come, Stoner," Ben said, his fingers working inside me. And I did, my body lifting off the bed.

"Please," I begged, reaching a hand below his waist, where I could feel him, rock-hard against the front of his jeans.

Ben unclasped his belt and tossed it aside, then took off his pants, climbing over me on the bed, his body a delicious pressure.

"See how good it can feel taking orders?" he whispered, smiling wickedly. "Now you know why I've grown to like it."

An electric charge raced through me, making my nipples harden, making me wetter.

"This time I came prepared." He held up a condom, then ripped the packaging. "Come here," he said, and flipped onto his back, lifting me onto his lap, knowing what I craved. My hair had fallen out of my yoga bun and spilled over my shoulders. I sank down slowly, inch by inch, hands gripping Ben's hard biceps, eyes squeezed closed as he filled me. The instant I could feel all of him my hips rocked, and he reached down and rubbed me. I was lost to it—I ground against him, forgoing breathing so I could kiss him, bite his bottom lip, steal his air for myself.

He sat up, fingers tangling in my hair, kissing me possessively as I pushed into him. His hands slid to my waist, rocking me up and down his hard length, his mouth at my throat. "I'm going to come again," I said desperately, lips pressed into his thick dark hair, and in response he sucked my neck harder, bringing blood to the surface, pumping deeper into me, until my body went taut and then shattered. Ben kept his grip on my waist, kept moving me over him, a relentless, delicious pleasure, and then I was coming again. He kept going, stealing orgasms from me, my body no longer mine but his to coax and command. Finally, he took a deep breath, and I felt him tense and shudder.

His arms circled my waist and he pressed his forehead against mine. "Love you," he whispered, his voice catching. I kissed him and we sank down into the bed.

"Anything else, boss?" He played with a piece of my hair and twisted it between his fingers. His eyes were tender. "Lee. Stoner. Senator."

I looked at him sternly. "It's Ms. Stone to you."

Ben laughed and kissed the corner of my mouth, his lips trailing to my jaw, and then down to my neck.

"This is where you belong," I told him. "Right here. Never leave."

This was what the opposite of heartbreak must feel like. I thought about each of my Four Major Heartbreaks and smiled tenderly, no longer feeling any sting. Just tiny, baby, idiot Lee, doing the best she could.

Ben hummed against my skin.

I closed my eyes and remembered the day I'd discovered Ben was coming home, in the middle of Disney World, dressed like a fairy-tale princess. I still owed Daisy David a long-overdue thank-you note, come to think of it. She'd dragged me into the land of true love, and although I'd been resistant, look where I was now. What would I even say, after all that had happened? Maybe something like this: *Daisy, Daisy, Daisy. Hat's off, you minx. You sure called my bluff. Happy endings? Maybe they do exist, as long as they're bespoke. A woman with love and power at the same time? Maybe not so stupid, after all. (Apologies for that wedding toast.) Was this your plan all along, Daisy? Could you read me—did you know, underneath, I was secretly a believer?*

If so, what a long con. I can almost admire it.

Ben's lips moved across my collarbone and down my chest, skimming over my stomach. He grabbed my hips and pulled me to the edge of the bed, ignoring my squeal, falling to his knees on the floor. He kissed me once, gently, on each hip bone, then gave me a wolfish smile. “The last time I did this, we got interrupted. But not today.”

And he set his warm mouth between my legs, dragging his tongue across me. And though I was deliciously sore, my body sparked immediately to life.

Oh. Yes, dreams really could come true.

EPILOGUE

One Year Later

The stadium floors shook with the thunderous noise of thousands gathered for the Texas Democratic Convention. They filled the floor, the crowd standing room only all the way to the stage, and pressed into every ascending row, all the way to the rafters. The cheers were deafening. Banners waved from Progress Texas, Texas Democratic Women, Rising Tide. Signs were lifted, some with Adams for District 14, more reading Stone 2024. The power of the Texas progressive movement, what newspapers were calling a fast-rising sea change, was on full display from where I stood, peeking out from behind the curtain onstage.

Beside me, Ben adjusted his headpiece and barked an order through his microphone. All around us, staffers ran by at breakneck speeds.

"All right," he said, twisting the mic from his mouth and turning to me. "Consensus is, Adams was a bore. The street team says anticipation's mounting for you on the floor. And you'll like this—the governor and lieutenant governor showed up."

I pulled the curtain back. "Did someone tell them they got the wrong convention?"

Ben shrugged, a smile twitching the corners of his mouth. "They're personal fans, from what I hear."

I shook my head. "Ben Laderman. I thought they *hated* you after you quit."

"Nope." Ben opened his binder and consulted it, playing coy. "We made up. They like our platform, turns out. Which is a great talking point for us. Progressive but capable of reaching across the aisle."

An idea lit. "We should leak it and send a reporter over—"

"Already done," he said, shutting the binder. "Grover's going to be so annoyed."

For a moment, Ben and I let the craziness swirl around us and stood in our own quiet bubble, grinning at each other. We were a good team.

Then a voice called, loud and booming, over the speaker system. "Last but not least, please welcome to the stage Lee Stone, candidate for state senator of District 14."

My turn. A thrill raced through me, lifting the hairs on my arms.

"That's the signal." Ben gripped my shoulders. "You're going to knock 'em dead, okay?"

Adrenaline washed through my veins. "I know."

I spun, took a deep breath and straightened my shoulders. Then I burst out from behind the curtains, waving to the crowd before me, squinting against the bright lights and flashes from cameras. One foot in front of the other across the stage, that's all it took.

I found my place behind the podium—and gripped it tight, to keep myself steady.

The crowd hushed. I drew myself up and let my voice fill the stadium. "Governor, Lieutenant Governor, esteemed members of the Texas Democratic Party. I am so pleased to be here tonight to introduce myself, and tell you about my vision for the future of the great state of Texas."

The crowd exploded into cheers. I watched them, letting it soak in. All those eager, shining faces. Young and old, male and female, shaking signs with my name on them—okay, fine, mostly young and female, but pry that out of my cold, dead hands. In the very front row, jumping and screaming like they were at a rock concert, were Claire, Mac, Annie, Zoey, my mother and Alexis. Simon stood behind them with Mikey on his shoulders, and Ethan stood behind my mother, hand resting on her arm, warmth and pride suffusing his face. Behind all of them, shirtless Ted waved an American flag. I squinted and saw his chest was painted with giant blue letters: *Stone 2024*. Well, well, well. Once again: Who knew the finance guy had it in him? I would tell Mac I approved.

As I took in the crowd—as I felt the weight of their eyes and their ambitions and their hopes—I sensed the strands of my life weaving together, forming a beautiful braid.

"But first," I called out, "let me tell you a little bit about who I am."

I trusted myself.

Movement behind the curtain caught my eye, and I turned ever so slightly to catch a glimpse of Ben, grinning like a maniac in the wings, waving away a staffer in order to focus on me. This time, I knew how to read the look on his face. He was proud, and in love. He was radiating 100 percent pageant mom energy.

I was in love, too. With Ben, and with my life.

I took a deep breath, and the crowd breathed with me. The cheering quieted. When I spoke again, my voice rang out far and wide, echoing into the heights of the stadium.

"My name is Lee Stone. But you, my friends, can call me Stoner."

I was exactly where I belonged.

★ ★ ★ ★ ★

ACKNOWLEDGMENTS

Is there any greater joy than telling the wonderful people in your life how much you appreciate them? In my humble opinion, there is not, which is why acknowledgments are my favorite thing, apart from wine. Writing acknowledgments while drinking wine? Please indulge me while I savor this.

We'll start with Cat Clyne because she's the reason this book exists. Nothing I say can sufficiently capture the magnitude of my appreciation for my amazing editor, who understood this book and its heroine from day one—but I'm going to try. Cat, thank you for seeing potential in me, fighting for me, having such a great vision for this story, making it so much stronger with your feedback, brightening my life with your marginal notes and funny email threads, being willing to jump into a quick (or long!) Zoom brainstorming session, being tireless and patient and kind, and so much more. You are a dream editor, and I am so lucky that I get to create books with you.

I cannot thank the Graydon House team enough, including

Susan Swinwood, Randy Chan, Gina Macedo, Lia Ferrone, Pamela Osti, Lindsey Reeder, and Gigi Lau. I am so grateful for your support, enthusiasm, creativity, talent, and all the grace and kindness you gave me on this journey to publication. Gina, your incisive editing talents strengthened this book, and your input was like a ray of sunshine. Lia and Pam, thank you from the bottom of my heart for lending your promotional genius to Fool Me Once. Lia, thank you for putting up with my many emails with such kindness—you are a joy to work with. Gigi, thank you for the gorgeous cover that makes me smile every time I look at it. I'm so honored to work with all of you.

Melissa Edwards, agent extraordinaire: thank you for loving this story as much as I do and for being its first champion. You helped shape this book—a few key scenes wouldn't even exist without you—so this is yours, too. You are an incredible human being, in addition to being an incredible agent, and truthfully, I would take a bullet for you. Thank you for lifting me up when I needed it (I needed it a lot this year), for always steering me in the right direction, for being someone I trust implicitly and for having impeccable taste, especially in clients.

To Maria Dong and Samantha Rajaram, having such brilliant writers as early readers for this manuscript might have been the highlight of my entire pandemic year. Your support and enthusiasm brought me so much joy—how can I ever thank you enough?

Lyssa Smith, my shining star, you are the world's greatest CP and such a trusted friend. Thank you for your amazing feedback on this book, for cheering me on and for being human sunshine. I'm so glad I have early access to all of your swoony books.

Ann Fraistat, thank you so much for reading this book early and giving me such helpful feedback, as you always do. I'm so glad Pitch Wars brought us together, and I can't wait to have your beautiful books on my shelf so very soon.

While I truly hope you never read any part of this book besides the acknowledgments (otherwise, I might spontaneously combust), I have to give huge thanks to Stephanie Akhter, James Cadogan, Amy Solomon, Sebastian Johnson, Julie James, Stephanie Getman, Rhiannon Collette, David Hebert and Jen Sizemore for being the most supportive colleagues a person could hope for. I was so lucky to work with each of you, and I'll never forget it.

Kate Boswell, every book is for you first, and then the rest of the world. Thanks for being my creative soul mate.

Thanks very much to Aly Hatfield and Colin Brooks for reading and supporting all of my books (and listening to me talk ad nauseam about them).

Russell Graves, you are a constant inspiration. I hope to one day be as cool as you (unless you move to Florida—then the balance has shifted).

Ryan, Amanda, Celeste, and Ezra, you fill my heart with joy. Taylor and Catherine, I adore you and am so glad you're my family. Dad, you're excited to read every one of my books, even when I tell you that you probably won't like them. Do you know what that means to me? You've always shown up for me; you've always made me feel loved and safe. Mom, I'm so happy you loved this one (sorry about the thrillers). Thanks for being my best friend since day one. Mallory, I read every word of this book out loud to you before anyone else saw it; if there's anything good about it, it's all thanks to you. I will always be your big sister, here to read you bedtime stories.

Alex, you teased me about cracking myself up while writing this book, and I knew what you meant: in a hard year, you were happy to see me happy. No one makes me happier than you.

Lastly, thank you so much to the book community: readers, reviewers, bookstagrammers, booktubers, bloggers, my fellow debut writers, the established writers who have been so kind and welcoming. I love being part of this community, and appreciate you all so much.